THE
SECRETS
WE KEEP

USA TODAY BESTSELLING AUTHOR
LILY WILDHART

To everyone who feels lost.
Like they're in a deep, dark, endless pit that they can't climb out of.
There is a light at the end of the tunnel.
Every day is a win, even the bad ones.
'One day' will come soon.
You'll see.
Just hold on a little longer.

ONE

QUINN

This song is my jam! I haven't felt this free in well… ever. Raising my hands above my head, I shake my hips to the beat, tipping my head back and letting my hair cascade behind me as my body sways.

This is what I've been searching for.

This, right here, makes the years of fear, the years of being made to feel small, the long months of running, almost worth it.

My life should have been like this from the beginning, but I am finally free and I am going to live exactly how I want to.

Hands clasp my waist and I jolt back to reality, the warm glow of tequila in my system fading enough for me to pull out of whoever's grasp it is. I turn and see an obviously wasted guy, who I give a tight smile to before pointing off the dance floor.

I probably should head to the bathroom. I might be free but that doesn't mean that I can relax. Being a woman in a city, with zero people I know, still makes my entire existence a risk, but it's totally worth it to be free from *him*.

Making my way through the throng of bodies, my buzz continues to recede as I push past the people, but I lost count of the shots I've taken so my head is definitely still fuzzy. I push open the first door I come to and the thud of the bass from the club slips away as the door closes, my footsteps clumsy as I walk into the wall before I realize I'm not in the bathroom.

Way to go, Quinn.

Voices draw my attention as I step further into the weird little hall that seems to open to some sort of storage room and, despite knowing this is a stupid idea, the tequila in my system fuels my bad decisions tonight. This definitely isn't the first one I've made in the last hour and I mean, what's the worst that could happen?

Stumbling down the little hall thing, I clasp a hand over my mouth as I try to stay quiet. When I reach the end of the hall I pause and think twice. The voices don't exactly sound welcoming.

Maybe tequila really isn't making the best decisions tonight.

For a moment, I consider turning back and finding the

bathroom as my bladder screams at me, but my interest is piqued. Like that damn cat, my curiosity is going to get me in trouble. I can just feel it.

Deciding to not get dead, having escaped that particular fate one too many times already in my life, I move to turn back toward the club when I stumble and fall to the ground.

Shit.

There's no way that was quiet. Is there?

I'm trying not to groan as I shift onto my knees before climbing back to my feet, holding my breath and waiting to hear the voices again. They're still talking in low tones, but by some sort of saving grace, I don't think they heard me.

Now fully standing, I realize I kinda fell out of the hall and I can see them.

Three men, all in black suits, standing in front of another guy who is crying on his knees before them.

Somehow, no one has noticed I'm here and I scramble to my feet. I need to get out of here. The voice of the man in the middle calls my attention and I take a step back when I see the gun in his hand.

Holy shit. What is this?

Stupid Quinn. You came here to escape violence, of course your stupid ass literally fell into this shit.

I blink and it's like time stands still.

My ears ring and I flinch as the bang blasts through the

room, then I freeze. I shouldn't be here.

I absolutely shouldn't be here.

The man on his knees in the middle of the room slumps forward as blood drips onto the concrete floor from the hole in his skull.

Why is there so much blood?

My stomach churns as all the tequila in my system starts to rebel. A whimper escapes my lips and every atom of my body screams at me to run.

"Who are you?" the man holding the gun asks as he turns to face me, gun raised in my direction. His voice shouldn't sound smooth as honey. His dark eyes shouldn't feel like they're boring into my soul.

I will my mouth to speak as the three of them walk closer to me, but all I can focus on is the gun in my face.

After being on the run for so long, I thought I'd finally found a corner of the world where I could be safe.

I guess I was wrong.

TWO

QUINN
EIGHT MONTHS AGO

The knock at the door has me pausing the show I'm not really watching, putting down my half-eaten bowl of cereal, and looking at the time on my crappy burner phone. Who in the hell is knocking at my door this late?

I mean, it's not *late* late, but my nearing-thirty ass is definitely considering this to be past the time that it's okay to be knocking at my door. I'm in my pjs for God's sake, this is not a social hour on a Wednesday.

The knocking sounds again and I sigh as I pull my tired ass up off the couch and glance through the peephole.

I see the flowers before anything else.

My heart sinks and the lump in my throat is making it difficult to swallow, but I open the door anyway.

"Good evening, miss. Delivery for you."

I try not to grimace as he hands me the flowers before sauntering off down the grungy hall like he didn't just ruin my life.

Not that it's his fault, he is just the messenger after all.

Once I've closed the door, I check the four locks and the deadbolt on the door to my shitty apartment for the millionth time and berate myself for my paranoia. And yet, I'm not paranoid. The blood red roses in my hands prove it.

He found me.

Again.

My shoulders slump as I try to breathe like my world isn't crumbling around me yet again, and lean against the locked door. I've been running for nearly two years, and each time I think I've managed to escape the clutches of my psychopathic, gaslighting, abusive asshole of an ex— who refuses to believe he's my ex—he shows me that I'm not outside of his reach.

I once thought dating a cop would mean I was safe. Especially a detective. Trent Boseman wasn't some rookie who didn't know the world, he was a man of experience, a man who saw the darkness and protected us all from it.

Little did I know that that shiny façade was just that. A façade. Trent lived in the darkness, wore those shadows like a second skin, and reveled in them.

The map of broken bones and bruises from the five

years we were together are proof of that. Even if he did manage to make everyone believe I was just clumsy. That I was crazy. That he was the perfect guy for putting up with my constant failures in life and loving me anyway.

An icy shiver runs down my spine at the thought of how many people I tried to reach out to for help in that last year of trying to escape who just thought I was 'having an episode'. That was one of his favorite lines.

I grind my teeth together and clench my fists as I try to push down the anger and disgust at my own weakness. I should've left a long time ago, but just like the cliché goes, I thought it was a mistake. That first time, I'd pushed him too far.

It was *my* fault.

My entire life, it's always been my fault, so it wasn't surprising to me that this was my fault too. I deserved what happened to me. Actions have consequences, and that was mine. We're all only human after all, and I'd been conditioned to this point by my parents. Perfection was something I would never achieve. I was worthless, useless, and stupid more often than not. It made sense that it was my fault.

He was a detective. An upstanding citizen in our small town. It couldn't possibly be *his* fault that he broke my wrist and bruised my neck, choking me in a fit of rage.

Obviously, I should have let it go. I should have just

accepted the excessive drinking and the fucking around because he worked hard and he was getting out his frustrations.

Until he realized I wouldn't leave... then he worked them out on me.

A tear slips down my face as my anger wins.

Of course he found me. It doesn't matter that I changed my name, stopped speaking to every person from my past that reached out when the news hit that I'd left him, changed my appearance.

None of it mattered.

He had *power.*

And I am desperate to take it back.

Glancing around the apartment at my meager belongings, I let out a sigh. At least it won't take me long to pack up. The apartment was furnished and I only keep the absolute bare minimum.

At least I managed to be here for three months before the roses turned up this time. I'm getting better at hiding.

Or he isn't looking as hard.

Either way, it feels like a small win and I'm going to cling to it with every fiber of my being.

With shaking hands, I place the roses on the counter and pull the card from the holder thing.

Tawny is written on the envelope, the name I'm using at the moment, and I swear I can see the smug smile on his stupid-ass face as I read the name. I pull the card from the envelope, taking a deep breath and willing my hands to stop shaking.

My beloved darling,
Hide and seek is getting old, don't you think?
You can't run forever, just come home and we can work it
out.
12.03
Always yours,
T

I retch when I finish reading as my entire body rebels at the thought of going back. It took too long and too much willpower to leave. Even if life is hard now, nothing is harder than the way I was living before.

Running to the bathroom, I almost don't make it before my cereal shows itself again as I clutch the porcelain bowl, my stomach twisting as my eyes stream. When the sickness turns to dry heaving and I finally manage to catch my breath, I drop onto my ass and sit against the wall, the cold from the tile seeping into my skin.

I guess it's time to run again and just hope that he doesn't find me, because I know if he does… this time he'll kill me.

After two buses and three trains, all in different directions, I finally pull into the station at Belleview. I can catch a cab from here into the city, but I knew that the town this stop was in is tiny so it more than likely has no surveillance. Even if Trent found my ticket, despite me paying in cash, he wouldn't know where I got off.

Two years of running has taught me plenty, including to not trust people who are supposed to be in authority, like the police—if Trent wasn't enough of a lesson in this, I've seen way too much stuff be let go in small towns when people should have ended up in jail. It's also taught me to carry pepper spray at all times, to sleep so lightly that a fly buzzing will wake me, and to be in a constant state of hypervigilance. On top of that, it's taught me surveillance, introduced me to people who make passable fake IDs, and how to make money without leaving a trace.

At first I struggled. A *lot*. I got by for the first few months on savings I'd slowly withdrawn over six months while making my plan for my great escape. I had no idea what I was doing, staying in a flea-infested motel that didn't require ID for me to check in. Except the walls were paper thin and the bed... I shudder at the memory.

But after Trent found me the first time, I realized that I

needed to get smarter if I was going to really disappear. If I wanted to actually be free. It's amazing what information you can find online and, thankfully, the library in sleepyville, Andolt, where I was that first time, allowed computer use for free.

A lot has changed since then. The only person I'm in contact with semi-regularly is Tommy—the guy who creates my new IDs. Which is the other reason I picked this station. My new ID should be waiting for me in a locker as per his instruction.

I already ditched my last burner but I know he'll have put one in my packet. To be fair, if it wasn't for Tommy, I'd probably be dead already. He taught me everything the internet didn't. He also has contacts freaking everywhere.

I jump off the train, backpack slung over my shoulder, and pull the hood of my sweatshirt up over my head and zip up my leather jacket. This might be the west coast, but it's still cold at the ass crack of dawn, even in the Golden State.

My boots are silent as I make my way off the platform and over to the lockers. I have no idea how Tommy's network operates, or how he always has a place for me to go, but I learned early on to not ask too many questions when it comes to him.

Wish You'd Stayed by The Haunt plays quietly through the one headphone I have in my ear from the old school iPod shuffle I have tucked into my pocket. I slide the padlock code dials to the digits Tommy gave me before I ditched my last phone and let out a huff when it doesn't pop open. Tugging at it again, I try my hardest not to stomp my foot like a toddler. The lock is stiff, but after a few grunts and internal tantrums, it pops open and I find the brown envelope inside, waiting for me like always.

Resisting the urge to open it straight away—because impatience has been my downfall more than once and Tommy loves to tease me about it—I tuck it in my bag, which I sling back over my shoulder and start walking.

It doesn't take long to flag down a cab, which is surprising, considering where I am.

"Where to, miss?" the driver asks as I slide into the back of the car.

"Nearest diner on the outskirts of the city," I respond, trying my best to give him a smile, but I'm tired and it's been too long since I had caffeine.

Running like this is exhausting, but it's better than the alternative. I've spent my entire life living on everyone else's terms, being a punching bag for the men in my life— both mentally and physically—and I refuse to ever live that way again.

The taxi weaves through the dark, quiet night, the only light from the occasional street lamp, the sound of the driver's music softly filtering through the speakers. Just once I'd like to sit back and relax, but I've learned the hard way that relaxing in the first two months of a new place isn't possible.

Thirty minutes pass and I start to see the high-rise buildings all lit up in the distance, and the nervous energy that's had my chest in a firm grip starts to abate a little. Just a few minutes later, I see the neon glow of an open sign as my driver pulls into the lot of a diner that looks to have all of three people in it... and I'm fairly certain two of them work there. "This okay, miss?"

"It's great, thank you." I pay the guy in cash before jumping from the cab, tapping the glass when I'm clear. I suck in a lungful of the harsh, cold air, rubbing my hands together before heading inside.

Once the door closes behind me, I scope out the diner. It's not very big but the dining space is V-shaped with bar seating lining what I'm assuming is the kitchen area.

"Sit where you like, Doll," the server behind the bar says to me with a small smile. I offer her a smile back and head to the far right, where I can see the entire diner, outside, and still have a wall at my back.

My ass is barely on the broken vinyl seat when she arrives at the table, coffee pot in hand. "What can I get you?"

"Coffee is fine, thanks," I respond, trying to stay as nice and unassuming as I can. I want to be forgettable, but being here at the ass crack of dawn with almost no one else around makes that a little more challenging. Though, typically, I've found that people here at this time of day are usually the ones who want to be forgotten—the staff included.

She pours me a cup, and once she leaves, I pour in enough sugar to wake the dead before taking a sip. It's awful, but it's caffeine, so I'm going to drink it anyway. Once she disappears behind the counter, and I've checked the street outside again for anyone watching, I pull the envelope from my bag.

Here we go again.

This is my second week of sleeping about two hours a night, in stints of twenty minutes, and it's showing in the way my hands shake as I try to focus on writing down the order from the group of rowdy teens sitting in the corner booth.

"Hey, lady! Did you even get that?" The typical jock type glares at me like I'm stupid, which I get. I'm not exactly running on all cylinders right now.

"Yes, sorry, bacon cheese melt with extra fries and a chocolate shake. Is there anything else?" I ask with a smile, trying to be the typical, perky server that I've seen in the movies. What's ridiculous to me is that, at twenty-

six, this is my first time actually in a diner. When I walked in here a week ago, having seen the help wanted sign, and not wanting to blow through my savings, despite staying at the cheapest motel I could find, it hit me how sheltered my life has been.

The jock slams his fist on the table and I jump. Startled, I drop my order pad and pen, and my shaking spreads from my hands to my entire body.

Deep breaths, Quinn. He is not Trent. We're safe here.

"Sorry," I stammer as I scramble to grab my things from the floor.

"Is there a problem here?" An older gentleman who has been sitting in my section at the bar daily since I arrived here asks as he moves to stand beside me.

The teens instantly go quiet and it makes me wonder about the man. He's been nice enough, and tips far too generously, but I'm not in a position to complain or refuse it. But these teens almost look afraid.

"No, sir," the jock's friend—yet another jock type— says as he shakes his head. "Brad was just getting a little hangry, sir."

"Well, Brad," the man says, staring at the guy I was taking the order from. "I suggest you get your anger in check and save it for the field. From what I hear, you could use the extra passion in the game."

The jock's cheeks turn red, seeming almost purple

against his white-blond hair. He grinds his jaw together before spitting out, "Yes, sir."

The man softly pats my shoulder. "Well, then let's get you some food, shall we, and not terrorize the wait staff?"

The six kids in the booth all nod and I reel off the order I've taken, confirming it before scooting behind the counter. My hands are still shaking as I hand the piece of paper through the window to the cook. He smiles softly at me and nods, letting me know he's got it.

He was the one who hired me. I don't think he owns the place, but he definitely runs it. He's usually pretty stern, but I catch a glimpse of my reflection in the mirror above the window and notice just how pale I've gotten and how dark the circles under my eyes look in comparison. How the harsh black of the wig I'm wearing makes it all look worse. And it makes sense why he's being so nice.

I look dead.

And, honestly, I kind of feel it.

I thought getting away from Trent would be great. That I'd be free. That life would be better.

Instead, I spend all day worrying he's going to find me, and my sleepless nights replaying the nightmare that has been my entire life.

It's needless to say that life is not what I thought it would be once I left.

Glancing over at my section, I notice the teens are back

to laughing about God only knows what, the infraction forgotten for them, but the older gentleman who stepped in is watching me from his perch at the counter. Taking a deep breath, I place a hand on my stomach, trying to calm the twisting going on inside, and grab the coffee pot, heading back toward him with a smile plastered on my face. "More coffee?"

"Sure," he responds with a smile so warm that it makes the sides of his honey-colored eyes crinkle. "You look like you could do with one yourself. And a burger too. A good night's sleep wouldn't hurt either."

I wave him off with a scoff, despite the churning that remains in my stomach from the kid's outburst. "Don't be silly, I'm fine." I pour his coffee before darting back to put the jug on the heater and make a beeline for the staff bathroom. I barely make it to the stall before the retching begins and I see the meager contents of my stomach again. Tears stream down my face as my whole body shakes, my knees screaming at me from the cold floor against my bare skin—it's been the same ever since my 'fall' down the stairs—and I try not to whimper or make too much noise as my body violently betrays me.

I was supposed to be stronger than this.

Hell, I used to be stronger than this.

Fucking Trent.

Once my stomach stops rolling, I stand up, brush down

my uniform, and flush before heading over to the sink. The flickering yellow light doesn't help the pallor of my skin, but I wash my face and redo my ponytail in an attempt to look half human. It's only when I see some of the faded bruises on my cheekbone that I let out a string of curses because I don't have my makeup here with me.

Just freaking great.

There isn't anything I can do about it, so I pull some of my hair from my ponytail to frame my face a little to try and hide it. Taking a few deep breaths, I mentally pull up my big girl panties and head back outside.

The rest of the afternoon passes in a blur of customers, but the guy from earlier stays my entire shift, which I'd worry about if I wasn't so busy. By the time Donna, who's taking my tables for the evening, shows up for shift change, my feet are screaming, so is my back, and I'm fairly certain I might actually sleep tonight just from pure exhaustion.

"For you," the guy at the counter says as I grab my bag. He slides his check across to me along with his payment. "The name is Tommy, by the way. I'll see you tomorrow."

I give him a quick smile, trying not to be frustrated as I take his payment for the day, despite trying to clock out, and wave at him as he leaves. Except when I look at what he slid over to me, I realize how much money is there and spot handwriting on the check.

For you. I know what it is to try and hide. If you need help, please just ask.

I blink at the scribble, tears filling my eyes. Five hundred dollars for a twenty-dollar check. I shouldn't take his money… but I need every dime I can get. Gratitude and guilt swirl inside of me as I ring out his bill and pocket the outrageous tip, keeping his note in my pocket.

The kindness of strangers isn't something I'm used to, and I'm not about to trust a man I just met, but that small, hopeful part of me wants to cling to the act of human decency.

I make my way back to the hotel, half asleep yet more alert than I have any right being. When I reach my room, I freeze. On the floor in front of the door is a bouquet of white roses. My hands shake as I check my surroundings before crouching down and swiping them from the ground. I pull the note from them and a scream catches in my chest.

You can run, little mouse, but you can't hide.
I'll always find you.
08.08
Come home before this gets out of hand and I have to remind you who is in charge.
Love you.
T

Fuck.
He found me.

THREE

The keys in the envelope led me to an apartment building and, to my surprise, this is one of the nicest places Tommy has set me up in. I've never questioned why he's been so willing to help me, or why he's refused to take money from me, but I've been squirreling away every penny so that one day I can eventually repay his kindness.

I stare up at the building before looking back at the sheet of paper from the envelope.

Yep, this is definitely the right building. I cross the street and head toward the well-lit lobby. The door opens and an elderly gentleman greets me with a smile. "Morning, miss. Can I help you?"

His smile reaches his warm eyes and something about him reminds me of Tommy.

"I'm moving in today," I tell him, trying to seem light

and friendly so as not to make him feel uncomfortable—typical Quinn move, I wear the mask almost too easily—rather than cynical and jaded, which is exactly how I feel when people are nice to me these days.

"Oh, well then please, come in out of the cold. What is your name?" He steps back, widening the door for me.

"Quinn. Quinn Summers," I say, giving him the name of my new identity, mentally slapping Tommy for using my actual first name, as I step into the warm building. He nods like a bulb has gone off in his mind.

"Ah, yes. We weren't expecting you until later, but please come in, Miss Summers."

Holy shit this place is nice. The marble floors, the low lighting, even the decor screams money.

I groan in my mind—I'm never going to earn enough to really pay Tommy back, not if he keeps setting me up in places like this. Though hopefully, I won't have to move again.

It's wishful thinking. I know that much for a fact. Trent has always found me, but that naïve part of me remains hopeful that he'll give up one day.

"The elevators are on the far side of the lobby. If you have guests, please check them in with the front desk and we can allow them up for you. If someone isn't on the list, they won't get into the elevator bank as a key is required to get to your floor."

I smile at the man while trying not to curl up and die inside. Tommy is going to hear it about putting me up here. While I appreciate how secure it is, I don't even want to consider the cost. I swear I can feel my account balance wailing into the abyss about it all.

"Thank you…" I trail off, realizing I don't know his name.

"Eric, Miss Summers. If you need anything at all, please just call down using the phone in the apartment."

"Thank you, Eric."

Checking my keys, he shows me the one for the elevator and demonstrates how to use it to get to my floor. It can also be used to get to the basement-level gym. It doesn't, however, give me access to other floors, which does put me at ease a little.

Once he's given me the rest of his welcome spiel, I head up to the tenth floor, two from the top, and the elevator pings as I reach the long hall. There are only four doors up here but, if anything, that just means less people to potentially see me.

My scalp itches under the wig on my head and the thought of the relief from shedding it once I'm in the new apartment lights a fire under my ass. I head down the hall to the furthest door on the left, apartment 1003, and use the key to open it.

Switching on the light, I pause at the threshold as that

bolt of icy fear runs through me. Eric might have said that no one could get up here, but that doesn't stop the terror. My chest tightens and I chastise myself for my trauma response, even though it's entirely valid. While Trent has never turned up in person, he has always found me. Sometimes he gives me a day, sometimes a few months… but he's always known the date I moved somewhere. He always made sure to include it in his little psycho love notes so I know he's watching.

Taking a deep breath, I wait until my heart rate goes back to something semi-normal, trying to give myself some mental grace. Once it no longer feels like the organ in my chest is going to rip through my flesh and fly across the room, I step inside, closing the door, checking out the three locks and deadbolt already installed.

Tommy definitely knew what he was doing putting me here. If only it actually made me *feel* safer.

I walk through the modest space, taking in the modern kitchen, the cozy living area, the small dining room, two bedrooms both with full bath and shower en-suites, and shake my head.

This is *way* too much.

I pull my burner from my bag before I drop it on the bed and dial Tommy. His number is always programmed in, but I can say it back and forth in my sleep or half dead if I need to. The line rings a few times before he answers, his voice thick with sleep. "What's wrong, Quinn girl?"

"Tommy, don't you give me your Quinn girl shit. This apartment—"

He groans, cutting off the start of my tirade, and I hear the squeak of his bed frame as he moves around. "Is exactly what you need. We talked about this. The small-town hovel thing wasn't working. He keeps finding you. You agreed to try it my way. And this? This is my way."

I groan and scrub a hand down my face. "I know I agreed to try your way, but I can't pay you back for this, Tommy. It's too much."

"I never said you needed to pay me back, Q," he grumbles, and I hear the spark of a lighter and he sucks in a breath, inhaling the smoke into his lungs, despite how much I've moaned at him about it. "Don't start, we all have our vices."

A smile plays on my lips, because he knows me well enough to know I was definitely going to say something.

"Don't change the subject," I start, sighing before dropping onto the bed that feels like a fucking safe haven in a storm. "The west coast isn't cheap. How am I going to stay here?"

"I have friends over there. Which is why I've been trying to get you over there this entire time. Stubborn-ass woman. Didn't you check your pack?" He tuts and I roll my eyes. Being chastised by him is almost like being told off by my dad… ya know, if my dad was worth a shit.

"You know I checked my pack. I didn't see anything about friends or money." My snark is overwhelming, and he barks out a laugh.

"God, I forget how much of a brat you are sometimes." His voice is warm as the hiss of a coffee machine sounds in the background. "I have friends, they're helping. That's all you need to know. The apartment is secure. It's not even in your new name, it's under a business, so it has zero ties to you. The building is frequented by types who don't want people knowing their whereabouts, so the staff are compensated to keep their mouths shut and afraid enough not to betray that."

My eyes widen at his words and I start to question just how much I want his "friends'" help.

"Tommy—" I start, but again, he cuts me off.

"Relax, Quinn, you're safe there. Probably safer than you've ever been other than when you were under my roof. Take a breath, enjoy the California sun. You start your job on Friday, so you've got three days to get situated. Go get some clothes. I know you're still dragging around that dusty-ass backpack with like three T-shirts and a pair of jeans—yes, I included a credit card, it's under one of my aliases so you don't need to panic, and just fucking use it without arguing. You'll need something a little more… well, appropriate, I suppose, for the job, but just try to relax. I have eyes and ears all over the city, so we'll know if he comes snooping."

I groan and pinch the bridge of my nose. That was… a lot. "I need to see a hairdresser, these wigs are killing me, but please don't make me go shopping or use the credit card. The guilt is already crippling."

"Stubborn-ass woman. Use the fucking card! You need it to fit in there. If you don't fit in, you get found. So blend in, Jesus fucking Christ, Quinn. I've never known a woman so terrorized by spending my money before." I let out a cackle, because I've heard all about the women in his life and I already know I am nothing like any of them. "Please?"

I shake my head but know I'm going to cave. He never says please, and if his way means doing this and evading Trent, I don't really have a choice but to give it a try. I'd be stupid to go against his advice, and stupid is something I'm not.

"Fine, fine. But first, I'm going to sleep. You're tapped into the cameras here, right?"

"Course I am, kid, you think I'm an amateur?" He snorts at me like I gravely insulted him, and I smile as I fling myself backward to lie on the bed. "Now get some sleep. We both know you haven't had any in a few days. Then eat and sort your shit out, you hear?"

"Ugh. Yes, Tommy," I whine playfully and I swear

I can hear him roll his eyes at me. "But first... first I'm trying out that tub."

He barks out a laugh at me again, making me smile wider, and for the first time in a few days, I actually start to relax. "You do that, Quinn girl, and I'll let my friends know you made it to town. You know where I am if you need me, but I hope you don't."

"Me too," I say with a wistful sigh as I stand. "Thank you, Tommy."

He makes a weird grunting noise that he always does when I try to thank him and disconnects the call. I walk the apartment once more, opening all the doors to make sure there's definitely no one but me in here, and double check the locks as I finish the sweep.

Maybe, just maybe, this time will be different. Maybe this time Trent won't find me.

The small part of my hopeful heart that still thinks this will all work out clings to that like it's the only thing keeping me going... and it might just be.

My naturally red tresses are now highlighted so much that I'm basically a blonde and I have to admit, as much as I hate using Tommy's money, it's really nice not wearing a wig. Plus, having my own long locks framing my face, I feel freer than I have in a while.

Like I'm not hiding quite so much.

Maybe that's why Tommy kept my legal name here. I can still be Quinn, just a slightly different version of the Quinn I left behind when I ran from Trent. The Quinn I was always meant to be, the one I almost was before I met him.

I make the walk across the city back toward the apartment building. I could grab an Uber, but the sun is shining and the warm air feels amazing against my skin. Spring on the west coast just hits different, apparently. The sights and sounds are a little overwhelming, but that's mostly my own fault for having stayed in small towns for so long.

There's just… so many freaking people.

I take a deep breath and remind myself it's a good thing. It's easy to get lost in a crowd of this many people and Tommy knows what he's doing.

We're doing it his way.

Shaking off the skin-prickling wave of paranoia, I tell myself I can do this. Tonight is my first shift at HellScape—a rock bar that Tommy set me up with a job at. Not so sure about the name, but I checked it out online and it looks pretty nice. Way more upscale than I'd have thought for a rock club, but since my little ball of sunshine self is a total emo girl at heart, we're not complaining.

It doesn't take too long to get back to the apartment building where Sam, the daytime doorman, greets me with a warm smile. He looks much younger than Eric, but he seems nice enough and Tommy swore that everyone here goes through extensive checks, so there's no way Trent can get to them...

God, I hope he doesn't find me.

I let out a breath as the elevator dings before the doors open, and I startle as I find myself face-to-face with a blond guy who looks like a freaking Adonis.

"Sorry, sweetness. Didn't mean to scare you." He places a hand against the door of the elevator and motions for me to get out. I give him a tight smile and a quick thank you as I scurry away.

Really need to work on those people skills, Quinn.

My hand shakes as I attempt three times to put my key in the door, but it's not until I hear the elevator doors close and I'm alone again that I manage to calm enough to actually get into my apartment. Slamming the door shut, I lean back on it and berate myself for being so jumpy and letting fear override everything I've learned the last few years.

If Trent had been out there, I'd have been screwed, my hands shaking so much I couldn't even get in my door. My heart was racing so much that I couldn't even say thank you properly to who I assume is my neighbor—who now very likely thinks I'm a neurotic head case. I mean, not that that's a totally out-of-line assumption, but dammit.

Groaning, I push myself off the door and drop my bags on the counter. I need a shower to wash this whole thing off and freshen up before my shift. I'm going in early to meet the bar manager and learn the basics, but I've done enough bartending the last few years that I'm pretty sure it's not going to take me long to get into the swing of things.

I twist my hair up on my head and turn the shower on, letting the water heat while I empty the bags onto the bed and grab a fluffy towel from the closet.

Got to love Tommy for furnishing this place for me.

Padding back into the steam-filled bathroom, I suck in a lungful of warm, humid air and hold it, counting back from ten before releasing it to try and center myself.

It's safe here, Quinn. Just go with it.

After my mini pep talk, I undress and move under the hot water, letting out a soft moan as the strong stream pelts against my skin in the most beautiful way. I might still not be totally comfortable with the upgrades Tommy put in place for this new living arrangement, but I can't be sad or mad about this shower.

This might just be my new favorite place in the world.

I stand under the hot water until it starts to cool, disappointment spiking through my stomach because it means I need to go back to real life. It doesn't take me long to go through the motions of freshening up, especially since I don't need to wash my hair, and I shut off the water, wrapping the towel around myself, trying to hype myself up for the first night of work.

Anxiety always tries to get the best of me on my first day at a new job, mostly because Trent found me once on day one. I didn't sleep for three days after that, wondering *how* he found me. My brain trips over every tiny thing that *could* go wrong, runs through every scenario of just how bad the night could go, and every single time I nearly tap out.

Hell, a few times, especially at the beginning, it did win, and I did tap out.

Thankfully, I've managed to best it the last year or so, but after the moment on the elevator, I'm more rattled than I'd like.

Telling myself that it's just first-day nerves and that no one is going to punish me for being human and making mistakes, I pull my new black, ripped skinny jeans from the bed, a tank, and a long-sleeved crop hoodie—the back and arms are just mesh—and set them aside. Perfect for the vibe I caught online. Pulling the clip from my hair, it cascades down my back and I decide to leave it down and a little wavy, but make a mental note to grab a hair tie, just in case I get too hot later.

Glancing at the time on my phone, I roll my shoulders

and stretch out my neck. One hour until I need to meet the bar manager. Definitely enough time to get ready and shove some food down my throat. My stomach twists at the thought and I frown.

Or maybe just some coffee. That'll totally work.

I dry off, run my fingers through my hair, paint on my brows, stick on some false lashes, and finish my face before I get dressed. I glance at myself in the mirror and hope I'll do. The casual smoky eye with a nude lip looks good with my casual-but-not outfit. I slide on my all-black Chucks and nod.

I'll do.

Grabbing my phone, I open the Uber app and put in a request for a car to take me to HellScape while I make myself a coffee, sweet and black like my heart, which I pour into a tumbler I grabbed today for the ride.

Deep breath, Quinn. You got this.

My phone pings, telling me my car is here, so I pocket my keys, my phone, grab a hair tie, and head out, making sure about twelve times that all of the locks are in place before I head down.

"Have a good evening, Miss Summers," Eric calls out as I dash through the lobby, and I shoot him a smile and wave. Guess shift change happened while I was upstairs.

I scope out the cars waiting at the sidewalk, noting the plate number that lines up with the one in my app. I screenshot my app notes and send it to Tommy—ya know, just in case—before I jump in the blue car.

"Quinn?" the driver asks and I nod. "Great," is all he responds as I close the door before he pulls away. I pay an outrageous amount of attention to where we're going, following his drive on my maps app to make sure we're going where we're supposed to be. My paranoia might be a little out of control, but you try running for two-plus years and not being a little crazy. That's without everything that happened before I left Trent. All things considered, I think I'm pretty stable and functional.

Once my panic is sated, I lean my head back, trying not to think about how the hell I ended up in this position. I don't mean the running… that's a given considering Trent. What I mean is ending up with a man like Trent after how I grew up.

Living with violence from a young age, I swore I'd never end up in the same position my mom was in. I told myself if a man ever showed me that side of him, I'd be gone. But it turns out that the manipulation makes it harder than I ever imagined. I let out a huff of a laugh. I didn't even realize it was that bad until I saw the pity reflected back at me from a nurse in the ER. It was my fifth broken bone from a 'fall', and while Trent had most people, even me, convinced that it was my own fault—albeit they thought I'd fallen while clumsy, whereas I believed I deserved his anger—she seemed to see through the bullshit. I hadn't seen her around before, so maybe she was new to town. Maybe she didn't know Trent, didn't know enough to believe his lies. But the pity on her face… it broke me. It made me realize I'd become my mom, and horror filled my heart as ice ran through my veins. Shame coiled inside of me like an angry snake.

I'd become everything I swore I'd never be.

It was that day I knew I had to leave.

It took another year before I managed to pull it off, to get the money together and come up with a plan… I've been running ever since.

"We're here," my driver announces, pulling me from my memories, and I berate myself for being so at ease in this car. Apparently, the lull of a big city and Tommy having my details is making me a little sloppy. Which is hilarious, considering my reaction at the elevator earlier.

Maybe I really am a head case.

"Thank you," I respond, tipping him via the app before climbing from the car. Once he pulls away, I stare up at the unassuming building. It looks like any other industrial building. Tall, big rectangular windows up high, rimmed in black, and a black metal double door sitting beneath the HELLSCAPE sign.

I blow out a breath and gather my wits before moving to the door and pressing the intercom button at the side.

"Hello?" A woman's voice filters through the grainy speaker.

"Hey, it's Quinn. I'm supposed to start here tonight." My words are barely out of my mouth when there's a buzz and the door pops open just enough for me to realize whoever is inside is letting me in.

I grab the door handle and shake my head.

Here we go again, I guess.

FOUR

"Quinn?" The voice calls out as I exit the pitch-black hall that I just fumbled my way down, cursing myself out in my head for not thinking about using the flashlight on my phone to light the way.

"That's me," I say with way more pep than I feel. I look up, my eyes adjusting to the lit space, and find a dark-haired, somewhat stern-looking woman assessing me. I'd say looking at me, but she is thoroughly assessing me. Her gaze crawls over my body from head to toe and I freeze under her stare. She kind of reminds me of Pam from *True Blood*, right down to the skin-tight outfit she has on.

"Let's dial back the pep, it's not needed here."

I nod, sucking in a breath, telling myself that I've gotten over my people pleasing ways—thanks for those, Dad— and that I know I don't have to be perpetual sunshine all the goddamn time. "Got it."

"I'm Harper. Don't you dare call me Harp, I will cut you," she says with a toothy grin and it instantly puts me at ease, despite her snarky words.

"No Harp or I bleed, understood," I say back to her as I half laugh.

"Good, now that's out of the way, Hunter told me to play nice with the new girl, so I'll give you enough rope that you can hang yourself. If you fuck up, then it's on you."

I bark out a laugh and shake my head. I like this chick, even if she is brutal. "This is you playing nice? God forbid being on your bad side."

Her smile widens and her black-lined eyes sparkle. "You're getting the picture. At least you're quick. You worked a bar before?"

I nod and run through my experience, watching as she looks more bored by the second.

"Well that'll help, but this place is a little... different. To start with, you'll just tend the front bar. It's tamer out here. But you're going to need different clothes. Didn't anyone give you the rundown of this place?"

I blink at her and shake my head. "I just saw online it's a rock bar."

She chortles, her laugh as husky as her voice. "Oh, cutie, you have no idea. We are a rock bar... but this is a sex club. The basement and back bar will be off-limits to you until I know you're not going to royally fuck up."

I blink at her, trying to work out if she's joking or not.

"Stop looking at me like I just blew your mind and get your ass back here so I can show you how our registers work," she snaps and I jump into action, scurrying across the room to follow her behind the bar. I try to take in the space as I haul ass and realize she's not joking. There's nothing obvious on display, but taking in what she's said, with the booths that have privacy curtains, the oversized birdcages that hang from the ceiling, and the sign above a door that says, 'Toy Chest'… yeah, it's enough for me to realize she's not fucking around.

"So, the front bar is a typical club, anyone can come here to party, but the back and the basement? Those are members only. They have their own separate entrances, but some like to come through here. If you notice people with masks or red bands on their wrist, they are members. Be extra nice, but not *too* nice, you understand? We do not fuck the members."

Her tone is so harsh. Mixed with her raspy voice, it just kind of works, but once she's done scolding me on appropriate fuckery decorum, we jump into general bar function—what's on offer, what isn't, and other such bullshit.

Aside from the stuff out back, it's a normal club.

"You got all that?" she asks, glancing up at the clock.

"Yeah, it's pretty standard stuff."

She glances me up and down again and sighs. "Fine. Now we need to sort out what you're wearing. Lose the tank."

"Excuse you?" I blink at her like she didn't just tell me to get half naked.

She rolls her eyes at me like I'm a tantruming child and sighs again "You're overdressed, Pep. You're going to feel out of place if you're wearing all that once the others get here. So take off the tank. I'm assuming you have a pretty bra on?"

"Well, yeah," I stammer, as she struts away from me.

"Good, I've got a harness that should fit you just right."

A harness?

What the fuck has Tommy gotten me into now? I never thought I was a prude, but apparently I'm learning some new things about myself tonight.

Harper returns with a leather and metal contraption dangling from her finger. "This is one of mine. If you fuck it up, I'll fuck you up, understood?"

I nod at her and reach out to take it from her, but she pulls it back. "Take off your goddamn tank. You're going to need help doing this up. Why the fuck did Meyer hire you? You're going to be eaten alive in an hour. And that's just with Jessica, let alone the others. Jesus fucking Christ."

My ego takes one hit after the other, but I shrug out of the hoodie and take off my tank, fighting every instinct to cover my stomach with my arms as she takes in the artwork that covers a good chunk of my skin. Thankfully, it hides my scars, which is exactly why I have the ink. She finally grins at me again. "Much better. Now you'll fit in. Turn around."

I am going to yell at Tommy so bad later. I typically have zero issues showing my body, but I wasn't prepared for this, and being caught off guard has my inner meltdown switch hovering dangerously close to the 'on' position.

Regardless, I do what she says, the people pleaser part of myself I despise so much taking charge, and she helps me get into the leather straps and snaps the buckles into place on my back and at the back of my throat. I catch a glimpse of myself in the mirror behind the bar and my eyes widen. It's a choker that descends into a pentagram over my chest, loops around my tits, and there's a band of leather that wraps just under my bust.

It's beautiful in its own way and, while it's not something I'd typically pick for myself, it could be much worse.

"Better," she says as I hear voices coming toward us. "The others are here, so get yourself ready, Pep. It's time to sink or swim."

I'm four hours into my first shift and I've broken three glasses and slipped twice. Oh yeah, I'm making a great impression already and well on my way to figuratively hanging myself with that rope. What I *have* learned, however, is that there is definitely a pecking order here and I am on the lowest rung of the ladder.

The people working the basement and back rooms definitely have that air of 'we're better than you.'

Harper has been watching me like a hawk all night and I already made an enemy of one of the other five bar staff working the main floor with absolutely no idea how. But Jessica—my apparent new enemy—has made it her mission tonight to slam into me every chance she gets.

I guess Harper was right about her.

So far I've worn two of the drinks she 'accidentally' spilled and her stiletto heels have bruised my feet so much that I'm fairly certain I've broken my toe because of her.

But it's fine, it's totally fine.

Mikey seems nice enough, but he is flamboyant as hell and makes my people-pleaser pep look like a walking thunderstorm. Tori has been the nicest to me, helping me out when I've been obviously drowning in cocktail orders, and seems to be just generally nice. The others have just gotten on with their night and left me to it.

I have to admit that my fascination with the dancers in the cages has been more than a little distracting, but I guess this is one of the differences between working in a small town bar and working in a hotspot nightclub in the middle of the city.

Thankfully, I've been too busy all night to even think about the sheer amount of people in here, or Trent, or well... any of the things that haunt me.

"Take your break," Harper tells me, nodding to a door behind the bar, which I learned earlier leads to the break room. I open my mouth to object but change my mind and nod. My feet will absolutely thank me for getting off of them for ten minutes, so will my very aching knee that I've been ignoring for the last hour since I reluctantly took some pain meds.

I push the door open and it's like I step into a bubble once the door closes. My ears ring in the silence and it takes a few seconds for me to even out. Murmurs finally reach me as my hearing comes back properly and when I turn into the break room, the conversation stops entirely as I find myself being stared at by people I haven't met yet.

Awesome.

I beeline for the coffee machine and pour myself a cup, adding enough sugar to send someone into a diabetic coma, all while ignoring the stares I can feel piercing my back. Someone sidles up beside me and bumps my hip. "Ignore those bitches. Everyone here has a stick up their ass tonight."

I turn and face the newcomer, a crazy-pretty girl who looks way younger than me, with long black hair cascading down her back. I try to ignore the fact that she's wearing leather chaps, a leather bra and panties with a choker, and not much else. Try and fail.

She grins at me, putting her hands on her hips and radiating a full I-don't-give-a-fuck vibe. "I'm Yen. I work in the basement. It's kinky fuckery down there and it's freaking awesome." She winks at me and I can't help but laugh.

"Sounds like fun," I respond, before taking a sip of my coffee. She motions over to the sofa and I sit with her, sighing as I take my weight off my feet. "I'm Quinn."

"Oh, I know who you are, sweet cheeks. The bosses have been talking about the new girl. Why do you think Jessica has such a thing against you? She was the favorite and now there's a new shiny toy around."

I blink at her like she just spoke to me in Japanese. "I haven't even met the boss."

"Bosses," Yen states, tucking her shiny black hair behind her ear. She's so freaking dainty it's unreal. I swear if I breathe too hard she'll fly away. "And just because you haven't met them, doesn't mean they don't know who you are. Plus, ya know, they're watching."

"I'm sorry?" I must sound like an absolute idiot, but I have no idea what she's talking about.

"The mirrored wall above the dance floor out there? That's their offices. You can't see them, but they can see you."

"Not creepy at all," I say as a shudder runs down my spine. Finishing my coffee, I put the cup down, my stomach grumbling at the lack of food, but by now, my body should be used to it.

She laughs, a musical little giggle, and shakes her head. "I can tell you haven't met them. The last thing you'd call them is creepy."

I quirk a brow at her but she just shrugs. "Anyway, Harper mentioned to me that you needed some outfit inspiration for work?"

"Of course she did," I groan, burying my face in my hands. "I'm sure I'll be fine."

"Oh I'm sure you would, but I *live* for shopping, so let's go. Tomorrow. Hand me your phone." I'm not sure what it is about her that makes me so willingly give her my phone, but I do and she taps in her number before hitting dial. "I've put my number in and called mine so I have yours. I am *not* a morning person, so if we say like, one? We can grab lunch, shop, and all those things."

"Sure?" I respond, not really knowing how I ended up

agreeing.

"Great," she says as she jumps to her feet. "Best get back to it, I have appointments to keep. See you tomorrow!"

She bounces out of the room and I feel like I just survived hurricane Yen. I also notice everyone else has already cleared out of the room, so I rinse out my mug, pop it on the rack, and take a deep breath.

I can do this. Lord knows I've survived far worse than a shift at a club with some mean girls.

It's four in the morning as I walk through the door into my apartment, and every inch of my body hurts. Turns out that even with all my experience in bartending, I was not prepared for a night at HellScape.

Once I make sure the apartment is empty, because I'm still paranoid as hell, and make sure that the front door is fully locked, I zombie myself straight to the bed and faceplant onto it. I *need* to shower, I'm beyond gross, but all I want to do is die for a few hours on this cloud of a bed. Sleep hasn't exactly been my friend the last few years, hell, even before that, but since I ran, nightmares have plagued me every time I've closed my eyes.

I'm just hoping that tonight I'm so tired that they stay away.

Reluctantly, I push myself up, groaning as I do, and head to the bathroom. I wait until the room is full of steam while I discard my now-gross bra and jeans—Harper took the harness back before I could leave—and climb beneath the hot spray.

I don't think I'll ever get used to just how good this shower is.

A ping from my phone has me groaning and climbing from the paradise of the hot spray, wrapping my hair in a towel before doing the same to my body and padding back out to the bedroom to find it.

Tommy:

Good night?

Me:

Good night? TOMMY, YOU SENT ME TO WORK IN A SEX CLUB

Tommy:

Got to get my amusement in some way, Q girl. Anyway, I knew you'd stay up front, I made sure of it.

I let out a sigh, shaking my head as I pinch the bridge of my nose. This man might be my guardian angel, but sometimes I just want to shake him.

Me:

Well I'm glad you got your kicks. She made me walk around in a bra and a harness all night. Also, it's full of mean girls.

Tommy:

I can fix that.

Me:

Don't you dare. These are battles I can fight myself. Any new searches on me? Movement with Trent?

My stomach coils with panic, like a snake waiting to strike, as I wait for his message. My leg bounces as I force myself to stay seated on the edge of the bed rather than pacing like my entire body is screaming at me to.

Tommy:

Nothing, Q girl. I told you, you're safe here. There's no way to trace you. Now get some sleep.

Me:

I've thought I was safe before… but thanks, Tommy, you're a lifesaver. Literally. You get some sleep too, old man.

I smile, hearing his scoff in my head, which helps me relax a little.

He said I'm safe. No searches. No movement.

So maybe let's try to relax a little more, huh, Quinn?

I dry off my hair and climb into some pj pants and a tank, rechecking the locks and shutting off all the lights as I make my way back to my room, before climbing under the duvet.

Letting out a sigh, I set up the rain sounds on my phone and take a deep breath before doing my Yoga Nidra routine to try and relax the muscles in my body so I can actually sleep. Trent has taken so much from me for over seven years now.

Tonight, I'm going to try and reclaim this one thing.

My goddamn sleep.

The front door slams and I wince, my heart rate instantly picking up like it's trying to break out of my chest. It's been four weeks since Trent had a bad day. I was hoping the good run would last longer, but he doesn't slam doors when he's in a good mood.

I stay perfectly still, a smile pasted on my face as I stir the soup I have on the stove. It's his favorite. Creamy chicken noodle. Today was a much colder day, so I made the soup and baked a fresh loaf in the hopes that his good mood would continue.

Now I just have to hope it saves me from his ire.

Except I've learned that hope is lost here.

"Quinn!" he bellows through the house, and my hands shake despite my death grip on the wooden spoon.

"In here," I call out, trying to keep my voice from shaking as hard as my hands. "Is everything okay?" I ask when he storms into the kitchen. He stands in the doorway, his mood filling the space, stealing the oxygen from my lungs until I can practically taste his anger.

My entire body feels pressed on by the weight of his mood and all I want to do is run. So far away. But I can't. Not yet. I don't have enough saved.

Just a little longer.

"What are you doing?" he asks, his jaw clenched as he closes and opens his fists at his sides.

"I made your favorite," I stammer, hating the way my fear turns up the corner of his lip. I move to turn the stove off, hoping it cools quickly enough that it can't be used against me.

Again.

Putting the spoon down on the counter, I turn to face him, keeping my head bowed, hoping that if I don't provoke him, he'll just go out drinking with his friends, maybe get a hooker and let off steam that way.

It's usually a good fifty-fifty chance of which way it's going to go. Except lately it's been more 90/10 and my body aches because of it.

"Oh, did you now? And why would you feel the need to do that? What did you do wrong to need to make up for it?"

He takes a step toward me and I hate that my instant reaction is to take a step backward because it widens the smile on his face.

"I... I haven't done anything. It was cold and I thought you'd like soup." I clasp my hands together in front of me, trying desperately to stop them shaking. He gets off on my fear, and if I get too afraid...

Well, consent isn't exactly something that bothers Trent anymore.

Not with me anyway.

"I think you're lying to me, Quinn. Why would you lie? You know that just makes me angry. Why would you want me to be angry with you, Quinn?" He pauses, tilting his head, watching me like a wolf watches its prey. "I think you like it when I'm mad. Is that what it is, Quinn?"

An icy shudder runs through my entire body. I know disagreeing will make it worse, but so will my silence.

"N-n-no." I manage to get out the word, but it's little more than a whisper. "I don't like it when you're mad."

"Lying to me again, Quinn? Tut, tut, tut. That just won't do, will it?" I flinch at the sound of his belt unbuckling, my knees going weak to the point that I'm amazed I'm still

standing. *"I think we need to teach you a lesson."*

"Please," I beg softly. *"Please don't."*

His laugh booms across the space as a tear slips down my cheek. I don't bother to wipe it away. There's no point.

He takes a step toward me and I move backward again, hating myself a little more as shame curls up inside of me. "Do not run from me, Quinn. Not unless you really want to make this fun."

A sob rips through my chest but I hold it back in my throat, knowing that it won't help.

Nothing ever helps.

He darts across the room and wraps a hand around my ponytail so quickly that I barely have time to register the movement. "I really wish you wouldn't make me do this to you."

"You don't have to," I whimper as he yanks my head back, exposing my throat to him. I keep my hands clasped in front of me because I know fighting back is a waste of my energy.

"Oh, but Quinn, you asked for it. Who am I to deny you the lessons of life?" His warm breath on my skin rolls my stomach and I think I might be sick.

The first blow to my cheek startles me. It's only when I taste blood that I come back to reality, pain radiating through the side of my face, blood trickling down my chin from my split lip. The second hit to my stomach steals my breath as I double over, clutching my stomach, unsure whether to pray for air, or hope that I lose consciousness.

It wouldn't be the first time.

Breath rushes back into my lungs as I fall to the floor and his foot connects with my back. I curl into a ball, knowing that kick won't be the last.

All I can do is pray he gets bored before I break.

I take myself to that dark place inside of me, that place that doesn't feel pain and disassociates from what's happening. At least, in here, my mind is safe. He can break my body, but he can't take my mind. Not anymore.

He pulls me from that thought as he drags me toward the stairs by my hair. I grip his hand on my ponytail, the pain from his wrenching enough to send more tears down my cheeks as I try to find my footing.

I stumble as he drags me up the stairs, my ankle rolling before I crash onto the hardwood.

"So clumsy, Quinn." Trent's disappointed tone makes my heart sink. Just another thing I'll be punished for.

"Please, Trent."

"See, I knew you wanted this," he grunts as he pulls me over the top stair and drags my body along the carpet toward our bedroom, the bare skin of my legs stinging from the movement. The door bounces off the wall from the force he opens it with and the last sliver of hope I clung to disappears as he pulls upward until I'm standing. "Don't

tell me you don't like this," he says before he kisses my still-bleeding lip.

Disgust roils through me and it takes everything I can not to fight against him. Fighting won't get me anything other than nearly dead.

"Good girl. I knew you liked it," he says softly before tearing at the buttons of my dress. I try to slow him down in the hope that if he's calmer, it won't be so bad.

Because rape is rape, but maybe he won't make me bleed if he's calmer.

"Do not test me, Quinn!" he shouts and I start to cry again as I still. "Your tears won't save you either. You know how much I like them."

I whine softly as he tears my clothes from my body before hitting my other cheek. He punches my stomach again, stealing my breath once more before lifting me and throwing me onto the bed.

I go back to that dark place in my mind.

He can't get me there.

FIVE

MEYER

Standing in the quiet room above the writhing masses is a different sort of power. Knowing I can see them, but they have no idea I'm here. Except, tonight, I'm not watching them.

I'm watching *her*.

The girl Tommy sent to us for protection. I don't know her entire story, mostly because he didn't know it all, and the check I ran on her when he gave us her actual name didn't have much information beyond a picture of her from her driver's license, which is a fairly old picture, and her hospital records, which were extensive.

They alone were enough to boil my blood and get me to agree to help her.

Except, from the moment she walked into the club and went toe to toe with Harper, I've been enraptured by her, unable to focus on anything else.

Her picture did her little justice.

Admittedly, she's aged and experienced a lot more of the world since that picture was taken, but the woman before me, the pain that radiates from her eyes… she stole my soul the minute I saw her.

It's an outrageous way to feel, considering I haven't so much as spoken to her, but when I see something I want, I do everything in my power to make it mine. I claim it.

Nothing escapes me once I have it in my sights.

She looks like a tiger disguised as a kitten, and there's a twisted part of me that can't wait to feel her claws.

My lips twist up at just the thought of it.

A knock pulls me from my thoughts and I glance over my shoulder to see Hunter entering our office. He and Rory are two of the only people in this world I trust, followed by Tommy, Harper, and Denton. I learned long ago to keep my circle small, and it hasn't done me wrong.

"I see you discovered our new hire." I can hear the smile in his voice and drag my gaze from her to pay him attention. "She's a skittish little thing. I ran into her at the apartment earlier today. I thought she was going to pass out right in front of me."

"Can't say I'm surprised. You're a hideous sight to an unsuspecting female," I tease as I sit at my desk. He rolls his eyes, running a hand through his long blond hair as he drops onto the couch opposite the desk.

"I can't help that women fall at my feet, Meyer. It's just this Cali boy charm of mine." His grin is wide as he leans forward. "These green eyes capture them and my washboard abs reel them in until they're helpless to resist me."

"Modest too," I say with a laugh. "Can't forget that."

His eyes light up with mirth, "Definitely can't forget that."

"Rory on his way?" I ask him. Rory, my enforcer, was out collecting on a debt for me the last I heard. They don't tend to go wrong for him, the sheer size of him, along with his reputation, tends to make grown men piss their pants in front of him, but there's always a risk.

"Yeah, he called in a few minutes ago. He got what he was looking for and delivered a message about late payments," Hunter confirms as he stands, moving to the bar in the back corner of the room where he pours three glasses of whiskey. Bringing one to me and keeping one for himself, he retakes his seat and I find myself turning again to watch her.

"She's definitely got something about her," he murmurs, and I nod. There's definitely no denying that.

Moments later, a blood-spattered Rory walks through the door with no announcement. He spots the whiskey and moves to the bar, throwing back the drink before pouring another. Once he sinks that one and pours yet another, he moves to stand by the mirrored window I've been staring out of.

"That her?" he asks, tilting his head toward her, and I nod. "Do we get to keep her?"

I smirk to myself. I should have known that my call for her wouldn't be mine alone. Thankfully, I have no issues sharing with my brothers.

"I second that request," Hunter chimes in, and my smile widens.

"I don't see why not," I say, hope bubbling in my chest like it hasn't in a lifetime. "We just need to go slowly, so as not to spook her. According to Tommy, she's got some issues."

"Issues can be dealt with," Rory grumbles, his fists clenching. I happen to agree with him, we know she's running, and from whom, but, apparently, she doesn't want him dead.

Yet.

I'm sure we can persuade her. Would make her life much easier. Slaying your own demons has a way of offering freedom that is unattainable any other way.

"Speaking of issues…" I start and Rory grunts, cutting me off before dropping onto the chair beside the sofa.

"It's handled. I already dropped the cash in the vault."

I nod, leaving it at that. I don't need to check his work.

Neither of them have ever let me down, not once in our entire lives.

"So, the girl… do we need to watch her?" Rory asks, blunt as ever.

"Tommy said he's keeping tabs on her ex, but I'd feel better with one of ours on her, just in case."

Rory nods as Hunter moves around the desk and leans up against the wall, I assume to watch Quinn more closely.

"You don't think she'll notice? She's hyper vigilant. I trailed her here on my bike. You should've seen how she was just about getting in her Uber."

Rory snorts a laugh. "I'm more skilled than that. You should know better."

"You're also a great fucking hulk," Hunter counters. "You're kind of hard to miss."

"I guess we'll find out."

I quirk a brow at him. "You want to stay on her?"

"For now. Until I can decide on someone else I trust enough. Not like I need to follow her into the apartment building. Sam and Eric will keep us updated on her movements or visitors there."

I mull over his words and nod. "It shouldn't interfere with business, so fine. But find someone else quickly, just in case you're needed elsewhere."

"I could speak to Denton. He won't follow her himself but he might have someone," Hunter says then shakes his head. "Nope, I can ask Yen. Quinn will never suspect her."

"You think she's up to the job?" I ask, skeptical as hell. The girl has worked this club for six years and has done plenty of other jobs for us since we saved her from a trafficking ring, but loyalties can change if the circumstances are right.

"Yeah, and a friend is way less intimidating to keep tabs on her than some skulking bodyguard."

"I still think we need more than Yen," Rory objects as he shifts in the chair, which just barely contains his mass.

"Speak to Yen," I tell Hunter before turning to Rory. "You follow her tonight and tomorrow, make sure there's no immediate threat. Yen won't be able to be with her all the time, so it makes sense to have a tail on her too. Easier to protect her that way. But Yen can feed us information if we need it."

They both nod at me before I turn my attention back to the woman in question. She might a little skittish and not like the way I do things, but I have a feeling that, soon, that kitten is going to be putty in our hands.

SIX

QUINN

After nightmares haunted my dreams and I woke up screaming, sweating so much I needed another shower, I gave up the hope of decent rest. I've spoken to enough therapists to know that, until I resolve the issues with Trent, my dreams are going to be plagued, but dealing with Trent isn't something I'm willing to do anytime soon.

It's taken me too long to reclaim certain parts of myself to even consider facing him yet. Facing him might help me sleep, but never seeing him again helps me live.

I pick living. Because I merely existed when I was with him and I refuse to go back to that.

But this is how I find myself, coffee in hand, standing in the third bus station of the morning, go-bag in hand. Multiple running options are necessary in a city this size. I have another bag ready for the train station, and one tucked away in the apartment if I have to leave an alternate way, but I spent an hour planning escape routes before I put the bags together and started getting lockers across the city.

Sliding the bag into the locker before me and locking it, I remove the key, tagging it with the key chain I grabbed earlier before pocketing it. It clinks against the others in my pocket already, but I feel more secure knowing they're there.

I'll keep all the keys on me, like always, and change out the key chains for colored tabs so I know which is which, but to everyone else, they just look like random keys.

Scoping out my surroundings again, making sure there's no one following me, I finish my coffee and drop the cup in the trash before heading to the bagel truck across the street. My stomach twists at the thought of food but I've barely eaten since I got here, and I can feel myself flagging. I know better than to let myself get to this point, so I browse the menu while I wait in line.

"Morning!" The bright and sparkly girl asks as I reach the front of the line, "What can I get you?" I order an egg, bacon, and cheese bagel with avocado and pico along with another black coffee and tap my card once she rings it up. "Coming right up."

Smiling back at her, I take a step back and continue to take in my surroundings. Some might call me overly paranoid but that's what has kept me safe up until now.

Tommy might think his way is best, that Trent won't find me here, but Trent always finds me.

The girl waves me down, handing me my coffee and bagel wrapped in foil and wishing me a good day before she turns to the next person in line. I grab a handful of sugar packets and put them into my coffee, taking a sip to ensure it's sweet enough before unwrapping my food.

I practically inhale the food after taking the first bite and groaning as the flavors hit my tongue. It's like my hunger gremlin woke the second I tried to eat, and I was starved. Even the stares from the people around me aren't enough to make me feel ashamed for the voracious devouring of the bagel heaven I've found.

After making a note of the truck, because I am *absolutely* coming back here, I finish my coffee and drop a twenty in the tip jar before pulling up the maps app on my phone and rechecking the route to the train station. It's not too far from here. I tried to make my morning as efficient as possible, but that doesn't always work when planning escape routes. Like how I avoided the local police station this morning because there's no doubt in my mind they have security cameras, and the last thing I want is my face on their tapes. Plus, just seeing the police and their uniform makes me feel less safe than being in the roughest neighborhood.

The upside of all of this is discovering more of the city.

Like this bagel truck. There are little nuggets dotted all over and it's those small things that help me feel more at home. It's the small things that Trent can't take from me.

God, I hope he doesn't find me.

I can't even really imagine it, him not finding me, me actually being able to call a place home. It feels unattainable, even though it's my deepest, darkest hope.

As I wander, I make the decision to search out a self-defense class. The city is bigger, which makes it easier to hide in, but it also means that there's a lot more people willing to do terrible shit and I'm sick of being a victim.

Mentally, I add it to my to-do list, proud of myself for thinking of it. I probably should have taken one before now, but Tommy taught me the basics. He gave me my trusty knife, which I keep in my pocket, and up to now, I haven't needed to use it.

I'm going to hope that remains the same, but a girl should always be prepared.

After a thirty minute walk across the city to the train station, I do the drop-off with my last go-bag before letting out a deep breath.

Contingency one in place.

Now I pray that I don't ever need to use them, but I won't exactly be getting my hopes up.

My phone pings and I pull it from my pocket, groaning a little at the text.

Yen:

Morning cutie. Meet me at HellScape at one, and we'll grab food before we shop!

I'd almost forgotten about our planned outing. I have not had enough sleep to deal with a girls' shopping trip, and I'm not sure enough coffee exists in the world for me to get through it on barely three hours sleep either. That's before I start to think about my poor feet. I had intended to take a long, steaming hot bath and curl up on the sofa to start the new murder drama I saw advertised while I was scrolling through TikTok as I tried to fall asleep last night.

Checking the time, I groan harder. It's already twelve, which means I have an hour to get my shit together and head over to HellScape. I'm working again tonight and I'm going to need to attempt a nap after this shopping trip if I have any hope of surviving another night.

I debate whether to go and change before the shopping trip. My ripped jeans, boots, tank, and jacket aren't exactly high class, but they're comfy as fuck and exactly what I needed.

My stomach growls—despite the bagel I ate half an hour ago, which apparently awoke the hunger gremlin who is an angry little demon—and helps convince me that this shopping trip with her isn't such a bad idea after all.

Even if I could Uber back to the bagel truck, get food, and still get to HellScape with time to spare.

Dammit, Yen. I really want another bagel.

I promise myself I'll take a trip out tomorrow to get another. Spotting a coffee shop a few doors down, I duck in, the noise of the place almost overwhelming since it's way smaller inside than I thought, and order myself a Red Eye.

More caffeine is necessary to survive this day.

Once I have my coffee, I pull up my app and order an Uber to work. I'm going to get there early, but screw it.

I've never been late in my life, I'm not about to start now.

Once the car arrives, I send the screenshot and location to Tommy, like always, then try to relax a little as I sip on the coffee in my hand.

Shopping is just not my thing, nor are 'girls' days' or whatever the hell they're called. I mean, sure I was kind of that girl in college, but I was masking so freaking hard just trying to fit in, trying to be the girl who wasn't riddled with trauma from a shitty childhood and pretending that I was normal.

It lasted two years—one advantage of being the people pleaser I am. I had so many credits before I got to college, and took so many online credits, that it didn't take me long to complete my degree— then I met Trent and my bachelor's in Marketing and Business Administration became no more than a piece of paper that I'll likely never use.

We pull up at HellScape, and I notice a motorcycle parked at the bottom of the stairs down the side alley—stairs that lead up to what I'm assuming are the offices on the second floor where the bosses work—that I don't remember seeing last night.

I wonder if it's Yen's.

Checking my phone, I realize there's only five minutes to spare before I'm supposed to meet Yen, so I lean up against the door to HellScape, fairly certain no one is inside if Yen isn't here yet, and proceed to get as comfortable as I can while I wait.

Not that I relax even a little, glancing at every car that passes, checking to see if Trent is inside of it.

God, I'm exhausted.

"Hai, cutie!" Yen calls out as she sashays toward me with a wave. Her long black hair is up in a slick ponytail that swishes behind her as she walks, and I double take at her outfit.

"Yen, you look like you're walking on stilts to go shopping!"

She laughs that twinkly laugh of hers, waving me off like *I'm* the ridiculous one here when she's literally stilt walking across the parking lot. "Oh, you're hilarious. I'm short. I've worn heels like this my entire life. I swear I can't even wear flats now, they make my legs ache. Anyway, I look fabulous and that is what is important."

I laugh, shocked at her outlook, but maybe she isn't riddled with issues like I am.

"You ready to eat and shop?" she asks before pulling her keys from her back pocket. "Just gotta grab something from inside and then we're good to go."

"Sure," I respond, moving so she can unlock the door. I follow her down the darkened hall, the sound of her heels on the concrete echoing as we move, making it feel far more eerie than it did yesterday.

She heads up to the bar, up the stairs to the offices, and hover in the doorway as she steps inside the small windowless room. It's sparse in here, just a few sofas, a kitchenette-style area, and a giant freaking safe. She heads straight to the safe, taps in a number, and it beeps before the door makes a whooshing noise as it opens.

My jaw drops when she removes a stack of bills before shutting it again.

"Yen…" I start, not really knowing what to say.

"It's fine. Meyer told me to kit you out, and it's for work so it's on his dime." She shrugs, like I'm supposed to know who the hell Meyer is and just be okay with the giant stack of money in her hand. "Stop looking like we're about to be arrested. Boss man can see us in here. Wave to the camera," she says with a giggle, waving to the corner. I notice the dome on the ceiling, a red light blinking lazily, and realize she's right.

"Still doesn't feel right," I mutter as she breezes past me. Closing the door, I hurry to follow her in case there's someone else around. Just the thought of getting caught taking money from a safe makes me want to vomit, but she had the code and there was a camera.

That's what I repeat in my head as I follow her down the stairs and back outside into the bright, warm day.

"Okay, let's do this. But first, food. I am *starving.* Any requests?" My stomach grumbles at her question, making her laugh.

I shake my head. "I'll eat pretty much anything," I tell her, and she pulls her phone from her pocket.

"Right, you're new here. I know just where to go." She taps away on her phone before looking back up at me. "Our ride will be here in a few."

Her phone rings in her hand and she looks at me apologetically. "Sorry, I need to take this."

She answers the call and takes a few steps away while I try my best not to listen. I stand like an awkward bystander, waiting for the car, desperately trying not to look as out of place as I feel.

Friends have been something of a foreign concept my entire life. When I was younger, I was isolated because my dad was a stellar human being and keeping me isolated meant no one would find out about his bullshit. Not that anyone would have believed me if I told them that he beat me and my mom while being so high I'm not sure he knew what was real and what wasn't.

Hell, no one believed me as an adult, so I have zero doubts anyone would've believed me as a child.

Then there was college. The few 'friends' I made there were fair-weather at best. There for the fun, but it wasn't exactly deep.

Tommy is probably the only friend I've ever really had... and I love him, but he's not exactly the get-drinks-and-dinner kind of friend.

So all of this just feels... weird.

"Sorry about that," Yen says as the Uber pulls up to the sidewalk. "Let's go!"

I get in the car, my heart racing because I don't know where I'm going and I can't send a screenshot to Tommy. Every part of me is screaming that this is a bad idea.

Taking a deep breath, I try to calm myself while Yen chats away to the driver. It takes a minute before I realize I can just send my location to Tommy, which I do, and that helps calm me a little. My phone pings and I let out a breath.

Tommy:

You don't need to keep doing that, Q girl. Meyer, the friend of mine who's helping you out, won't let anything happen to you in his city. Now relax and try to have some fun.

I frown at the screen.

One. Relaxing isn't what I do…

And two… Meyer.

Pretty sure that's the name Yen used at the club…

So Tommy's friend is also my boss. Good to know.

The car pulls to a stop, pulling me from the rabbit hole that threatened to suck me in and Yen grins at me. "Prepare yourself for the best burrito of your life."

My stomach growls in response to her words. I've had a ton of burritos and tacos in my life, because yes, I'm that girl, but she also looks so excited at the prospect of food that I almost believe her.

"We'll see," I say with a hint of skepticism and a smile so she, hopefully, knows that I'm mostly teasing.

She bounces from the car undeterred and I thank the driver as I slide out after her. I follow her down a side alley, wondering where the hell she's taking me as the sounds of the city retreat a little in the enclosed space. She pauses in front of a nondescript door that doesn't have any signage and I wonder why she's stopped.

"Welcome to my favorite Mexican place in the entire

city."

I glance around again, trying to work out what the hell she's talking about, feeling awkward as fuck. "Er, Yen... there isn't a restaurant here."

She rolls her eyes at me and bangs on the door beside us. "Don't be so willing to believe just what you can see. You'll get much further here if you learn to see the bigger picture."

I have no idea what she means but the door beside us is yanked open and a flood of noise spills into the small space. "Yen!" The burly middle-aged man says with such warmth that I know instantly, despite having almost never experienced it myself, that Yen is family with this person. Blood or found, doesn't matter.

Family is family.

She hugs the man tightly and I try not to fidget on the spot while they talk in Spanish. Languages were never really my thing so, while I know it's Spanish... I have absolutely zero idea what the hell they're saying.

"Come in, come in," the man says to me, waving me in after Yen. We walk through a small hall that opens to a busy kitchen, which we're quickly ushered through until we reach a giant restaurant space.

Why we didn't come in the front door, I'll never know, but I'm not about to ask that question right now. The man seats us and continues to talk to Yen as I pick up the menu to have a look.

It's also in Spanish.

Awesome.

"Flip it over," Yen says to me in between talking to the guy, and my cheeks heat when I flip it and see the menu in English. Yeah, I don't feel stupid at all.

I never thought I was unworldly, but California is teaching me a lot it would seem.

Half of the menu might as well still be in another language for as much as I recognize the dishes. Yep, definitely realizing how sheltered I've been between my parents and Trent.

"Is there anything you don't like? Anything too spicy?" Yen asks, drawing my attention from the menu.

"No," I say, shaking my head. "I've never tried anything wild or crazy, but I eat most things. Spice isn't a problem."

"Good," she exclaims before rattling off what I assume is our order to the guy.

I guess I didn't need the menu after all.

He nods at her before turning and heading back toward the kitchen, giving me Yen's full attention. Which, with her super-bouncy ways, feels really intense.

"So, new girl," she starts just as someone approaches our table, leaves two glasses of water, and disappears again. "Tell me something about you. I'm intrigued… especially since the bosses seem so protective of you already."

I squirm uncomfortably in my chair. This, right here, is exactly why I keep my distance from people. They want to know things, but there's so little I can say.

"I have no idea why they're protective. My uncle got me the job. He said he was friends with the boss and I'm new in town so he wanted to help." The lie tastes like ash on my tongue, but it's not like I can tell her the truth. Especially when I don't know *why* the bosses would be protective. I know Tommy's friends are helping him with my situation, but they don't know me. They have no reason to be personally invested in my safety.

It's weird.

But I don't say any of that out loud.

She looks at me skeptically and I try not to fidget under her stare. "Where are you from? I can't place the accent."

"Back east," I tell her. "But I've bounced around a lot so my accent isn't really set I guess." At least that's not a lie. Not entirely. I might have been lying the last few years everywhere I've gone, but it's never gotten easier. It never feels good. "What about you? Are you from around here?"

She barks out a laugh and shakes her head. "No, I was trafficked here as a teenager."

It's said so casually that at first I think she's joking, but then she takes a sip of her drink and continues blowing my mind. "I'm originally from a small village outside of Ho Chi Minh City, but I went on a trip with school when I was twelve and I was taken. A whole group of us were. I won't give you all the details, but I ended up in the States, where life was basically hell for a few years, but then I was saved. I've been at HellScape for six years and the rest is history. My story isn't that interesting."

"I beg to differ," I choke out, absolutely floored. "That's one hell of a story."

"Yes," she says, her lips tilting up at the edges. "But mine isn't a mystery."

I take a sip of my own drink, trying to think of how to change the subject, but Yen interrupts my panic spiral. "It's fine, it took me a while to tell my story too, and you hardly know me. But just watch, we're going to be besties. I can feel it."

I laugh when she winks at me. Then plates and plates of steaming hot food are brought to the table and I don't know where to look, overwhelmed by the sheer amount of choices. "I like to have a little bit of everything and I figured this way you get to try different stuff."

"Thanks," I respond, half question, half statement.

"Well, dig in. Santos will get offended if you don't at least try the food," she giggles the last sentence and I grab my fork. I put some rice, chicken, and veggies in my mouth and groan as the flavors burst on my tongue. "Good, right?"

"Um-hmm," I groan as I nod. "I'm going to end up in

a food coma, I already know it."

"See, I knew we'd be besties."

I laugh at her but take another mouthful, slipping into food heaven. I might be dreading the next part of this trip, but maybe if I eat enough, I just won't care.

"Are we done yet?" I whine like a petulant child and Yen laughs at me.

"I've never met a girl who hates shopping like you do. It's weird as fuck."

I shrug at her because I know that, thanks to my trauma, I'm definitely a little weird. "I'm *quirky*."

She grins at me again and puts the leather bikini back on the rack. "You're definitely something." Her gaze runs over me for what feels like the hundredth time, like she's still trying to figure me out, which I get. Curiosity is a bitch, and I'm a puzzle, but we've been shopping for *four hours.*

Four.

Hiding the scars that mar my skin hasn't been the easiest, but I've just argued about showing those areas of my body that aren't covered with ink. What I've learned from this, is that Yen is creative as hell at finding a way to make it look as if I'm showing skin without showing skin and somehow still making it look sexy. It's definitely been a learning experience, but I am exhausted.

We start work in a few hours and I desperately want to go home and soak in my tub for a bit.

Hence the whining.

"I suppose you have enough to get you started at least," she says with a sigh. I scoff at her use of 'at least'. I have more bags than I've ever had while shopping currently clasped in my fingers.

"This is an obscene amount of shopping. This will last me years," I deadpan, and she scoffs.

"At HellScape, you need variety. Trust me, we'll be shopping again before the end of the month."

"The hell we will," I grumble. "The food I'll happily let you shovel down my throat, but this is almost akin to torture."

"Oh, babe, this is nothing like torture." She winks at me and I want to curl up and die.

"Sorry, I didn't—"

She waves me off, interrupting me. "It's fine. I know it's just a phrase, I'm just giving you shit. Now grab your bags. We should probably get going because I need a nap before work."

"Now *that* I can get on board with."

We head out of the store and she gives me the lowdown on the other people in the club, but I tend to keep to myself, so I note who she says to avoid and ignore most of the rest. As we reach the exit, her phone starts to ring.

"Hey, B, what's up?" she says cheerfully as she slows to a stop. I pause with her, my stomach sinking as her face drops. "Shit. What happened?"

She pauses again, her face displaying every emotion. "Fuck, okay, on the way. Just... don't do anything until I get there, 'kay? Love you. I'll be a few minutes. Don't move."

She hangs up and turns to me. "I have to go. I'm so sorry."

Without another word, she flags down a cab and is gone in a heartbeat. I have no idea what just happened, but it doesn't exactly fill me with joy.

I chew on the inside of my cheek, wondering if I should've offered to help, but really, I know there isn't much I could've done. First, because I don't know what happened, and second, my skills are fairly limited.

Rather than hang out in the open, despite feeling calmer than I have in a while—apparently, Yen has that effect on me and I'm not sure if it's a good thing or not—I grab my phone and order myself an Uber. I don't tend to trust a hailed cab on my own. I've seen too many stories on the news that make me shudder.

It doesn't take long to arrive and I hop in the back. Taking a screenshot, I pull up my thread with Tommy and pause as I see his message from before. He said I don't need to send him the screenshot...

On the one hand, that's absolutely terrifying, but on the other... the idea of not having to be so on guard all the goddamn time...? It's still terrifying, but in an entirely different way.

I close the thread, not sending the message, a slight tremor in my hand as I put my phone away. The thought of trusting people again is such an out-there concept because, before I came here, I honestly thought I'd be running from Trent for the rest of my life.

Hell, I might still end up doing exactly that, but Tommy was right. There's something about being in a big city that feels like I could get lost without trying too hard, and I know he would have done everything in his power to help me disappear here.

So maybe, just maybe, I need to start trusting him the way I keep saying I do and honor my promises to him to try and actually live my life.

Yep, even the thought is absolutely terrifying. But I swore to Tommy when I agreed to try his way that I'd trust him. Part of that is actually listening to him.

Baby steps.

Not sending the text is a baby step. I can still be on guard while trusting him and trying to not be so... neurotic.

The Uber pulls up in front of my building and Eric is

there, opening my door for me. I grab my bags and scoot out of the car. "Thank you," I say to the driver and Eric. He closes the car door before rushing ahead of me to open the door to the building.

"Of course, Miss Summers. We're here to help you in any way we can." He smiles warmly at me, so I thank him again and head to the elevator. Once I make it back into my apartment, the bags discarded by the locked door, I practically run to the bathtub.

I add oils and bubbles to the running hot water, taking in a deep breath of the infused steam.

Heaven.

Discarding my clothes and tying my hair in a messy bun on top of my head, avoiding the many mirrors in here, I turn off the faucet and slip into the hot water. I let out a sigh as I sink into the bubbles. This tub really is my new happy place. It's so deep that the water covers my shoulders as I lie back and close my eyes, enjoying the heat drenching my muscles as I float slightly.

The old aches in my body from the bones that didn't heal quite right, and the ache in my back from one too many 'falls' down the stairs start to abate, making me feel lighter. I try not to think about the scars that cover my body, both physically and mentally, but sometimes the memories haunt me even at my calmest moments.

My fingers run across the scars on my ribs, up to the

one on my sternum. I don't have to see the scars to know the pattern of them across my skin. Sometimes Trent would hurt me in places no one would see… especially at the beginning. But other times, he got too carried away, or he just stopped caring. Whatever it was, the raised ridges on my skin tell a story all of their own, one I'd rather not share with other people—which might explain why I haven't had sex for two years.

I mean, it might be the whole, running-for-my-life thing, but there have been times when it could've happened. I *wanted* it to happen… for Trent's hands to not be the last ones on me, but I've always stopped myself.

Not because Trent took my body at his will, but because I didn't want to have to explain the markings.

If anything, I wanted to fall into bed with someone else to take that slice of power back… but I still haven't.

The mind is a weird place… Well, mine is anyway.

Trent has taken so much from me—including this bath apparently—but maybe if I am as safe here as Tommy says, I can start to reclaim some of those pieces.

My phone starts to ring and I lean over the edge of the tub, pulling it from my jeans.

An unknown number.

My heart sinks as my stomach twists.

Please don't let it be him.

My hands shake as I try to swipe across the screen and

hit the loudspeaker option. "Hello?"

"Pep. You need to come in early. Get your ass here."

I let out a deep breath as relief floods me. "Sure thing, Harper. Everything okay?"

"Just get here."

The line disconnects and I frown at the phone. This might be the weirdest job I've ever had, but I'm not about to keep the scary dominatrix waiting, so I lift my ass from the tub, mourning what was supposed to be a relaxing soak, and grab a towel.

Night two.

Ready or not, here I come.

SEVEN

Voices reach me before I even get to the end of the hall at the front area of HellScape. Ever since Harper hung up, I've been wondering if this is about me and Yen being in the office earlier and her taking that money. To say my stomach is in knots is an understatement.

"New girl, finally," Jess snarks as I enter the space, and Yen rolls her eyes before strutting over to me.

"Ignore mean girl number one. She's got her panties in a bunch because her stylist fucked up her hair." Yen's voice carries across the room, and my eyes go wide as sniggers start from the group of people standing by the bar as Jess sneers at us.

"Any idea what this is about?" I ask Yen quietly, but she shakes her head.

"Not a clue, but I'm sure we're about to find out." She

points to the staircase and I see a man emerge from the door at the top. His eyes are the first thing I notice. They're like pools of amber, warm and inviting, despite the cold and intimidating air that radiates from him as he looks down at us like a king surveying his kingdom. He runs a hand through his dark hair before making his way down the stairs. "Lord have mercy, he shouldn't look that good."

I take a minute to look over the man who I assume is our boss.

Meyer.

Gray suit pants hug his thick thighs like a second skin with a tucked-in white button-down that stretches across his obviously lean body, the sleeves rolled up showcasing the colorful ink that decorates his skin.

Yen is right. Lord have mercy, because goddamn. He might come across as cold and intimidating but he also screams sin and all the things you know you shouldn't want yet still crave.

Dangerous. That's what he is.

It's only when he reaches the bottom of the stairs that I realize just how tall he is, at least a head taller than anyone else here. Even standing at five seven, I'd have to tip my head back to hold his stare.

He moves to stand in front of us all and Harper moves to his side. She doesn't look quite as terrifying standing next to him but together they look like they could burn the world and walk away laughing.

I wonder if they're together. They definitely seem… familiar. Comfortable.

"One of our locations was compromised this morning," he starts, and I want to vomit. Does he mean this one? The safe?

Oh, God.

"Thankfully no one was hurt, but that doesn't mean that we didn't take a hit. I need you all to be on high alert for the foreseeable future. You know the usual faces but there might be new players, so just be aware. Snakes come in all shapes and sizes. Rory will be managing security here until we get to the bottom of it, so you'll see extra guys around. Just act normal. Our clients don't need to know anything is wrong. Am I making myself clear?"

The panic starts to recede when I realize he's obviously not talking about the money Yen took, but my heart is still at full hummingbird pace in my chest. Murmurs of agreement sound around the room as people nod, but I stay quiet because he might as well be talking Japanese for all the sense it's making to me.

As if he hears my thoughts, he catches my eye and I swear he smirks. It's gone in a blink, so I half think I dreamt it up, but I'm sure I saw it. "New girl, Harper and Yen will bring you up to speed."

His gaze stays set on me and it takes every ounce of

will I have to hold his stare. He smirks again before looking away and talking to Harper while everyone else disperses. Why we couldn't have been told that later, and why we had to come in early, makes no sense to me, but then someone walks in with a dozen pizza boxes and cheers go up.

At least they're feeding us, I guess.

"So that," Yen starts, taking my hand and pulling me toward the bar where the pizza boxes are laid out, "was Meyer. Sex on legs, dripping with bad boy vibes, but completely untouchable."

I stare at the pizza, knowing if I eat anything else I'm probably going to be so sick tomorrow, but also, that cheese looks *so good.*

Fuck it.

I take a slice of gooey pepperoni pizza, my mouth watering at the cheese pull, and take a bite as I mull over her words. "What do you mean untouchable?"

"I mean, in all the time I've known him, he hasn't touched one of the girls in here. And trust me, some of them have tried. Really, *really* tried. At first I thought he was into dick, ya know—I get it, being dickmatized is a thing—but nope. He's just… untouchable."

"Huh…" is all that falls from my lips. There isn't much to say to that, though her oh-so-casual use of dickmatized tickles me. "So, what can you tell me about what Mister Cryptic was explaining? Why didn't they call the police?"

She snorts a laugh at my question. I mean, I wouldn't call the police, they're as useful as taste buds in an asshole, but still. This is their business.

"Oh, right, yeah, that. It's nothing to really worry about. There are some... not-so-above-board dealings that the guys dabble in, so police are a big no around here. Apparently, one of their other locations was hit because of that and we just need to be watchful in case anyone tries anything here. You're front of house though, so you should be good. It's the back room and basement where the trouble will land if it does." She says it all so casually, like it's nothing at all, but I can't help but feel uneasy.

Not above board could mean police, and police could mean Trent.

Oh, God, do not have a meltdown, Quinn. Nothing's happened yet. You're okay.

"Are you okay?" Yen asks as my breathing gets heavier.

"I—" I try to speak but the world goes a little fuzzy.

Fuck my actual life right now.

"She okay?" I hear a male voice.

"I don't think so," Yen replies, and the next thing I know, I'm being lifted into the air and bundled against someone's chest. We're moving away from the crowd and then all of the noise fades away as everything goes dark.

"You're safe in here, Angel. Let us know if you need anything." I'm placed down on something soft, which I think is a sofa, then I hear a door clicking shut and I'm alone again. At least in here, in the darkness, it feels safer, and I manage to regulate my breathing to where I almost feel normal, despite being highly embarrassed.

As if I just had a mild anxiety attack at work.

On day two.

I can never come back here.

The anxiety over my anxiety attack starts to push me back toward the edge, so I lie back down on the sofa and take a few deep breaths, walking through my practices of three things I can touch, three things I can hear, and so on, until my heart rate comes back to normal.

Once I'm more evened out, I curse my parents and Trent again. I *might* have been normal if they hadn't all messed me up so damn bad.

And now I have to walk out there after everyone watching me get carried in here. I don't even know who carried me.

Fuck my life.

A knock on the door interrupts my spiral and light spills into the room just before I hear Yen's voice. "You okay, Q?"

I smile at the shortening of my name. "Other than the body-scorching embarrassment you mean? Yeah, I'm fine. Just had a moment. Sorry."

"You don't need to apologize," she says as the door

closes. Her heels click on the hard floor and moments later a dim lamp illuminates the room. "You want to talk about it?"

I chew on my lip and shake my head. "Not really. I just… baggage, ya know?"

"Oh, I know," she responds with a dry laugh. "And you have nothing to be embarrassed about either. If you think you're the first person to have a panic attack here, you're sorely mistaken. Though, you might be the first to be rescued in quite that fashion." She wags her brows at me, and I bury my face in my hands.

"Not helping," I say with a laugh. "Who was my savior anyway?"

"Oh, just Hunter." Her eyes sparkle with joy as she says his name, but it means absolutely nothing to me considering I didn't even see the guy. "Jessica looked like she was going to spit freaking needles and I loved every second of it. I despise her entitled ass."

I just blink at her, because I *so* needed more reasons for the mean girls here to hate me, but also, do I really want to be friends with people like that anyway? "Who is Hunter?"

She opens her mouth to respond but before she gets a word out, Harper is yelling loud enough for us to hear her in here. Yen jumps to her feet and scurries from the room and I follow suit, not wanting to be in any more trouble. "Party's over, doors open in thirty. Get your shit together and get to work!"

After an insane weekend at work and being invited out with some of the girls—including Yen, who basically bullied me into agreeing—I finally have a day off. I've lain in bed for the last hour since waking, straight up refusing to move.

I have a dozen things I need to get done today, laundry included, but I just. Don't. Want. To.

Instead, I'm lying in my cocoon of comforter, enjoying the quiet. Despite the fact that it's probably lunch time, the city seems quiet, the peace of it only destroyed by the growling of my stomach.

When it gurgles again, I let out a sigh and resign myself to the fact that I am, in fact, human and my body has needs beyond staying in bed all day.

That said, Mondays could definitely be worse. So I put my laundry in, tidy up what I can, grab a quick shower, and ready myself to face the day.

I need food and I want to walk around the city again to make sure I know my escape routes if I need them. You'd be amazed what you forget when you're in panic mode.

After puttering around before changing the laundry and checking my phone, which is delightfully free of notifications, I pocket it, grab my purse and keys, then head out. I slip my headphones in while I wait for the elevator, swaying my hips a little as *I think I'm in love* by Taylor Acorn plays. The elevator dings as the doors open and I find myself face-to-face with the blond god from the other day.

"Morning," he says to me with a playful smile on his face.

"Uhm, hi. Morning," I stutter.

"Can I—?" He points behind me and I realize I am fully in the way of him getting out.

"God, sorry," I say as I step to the side, my face on fire as embarrassment floods me.

He grins wider. "Don't be, I can't think of a better way to start my day than being accosted by a beautiful woman."

He winks before stepping out of the car and I literally run inside, jamming my finger on the close door button, hearing him laugh as the doors finally shut.

Sweet baby Jesus. You'd think after everything with Trent that men would scare me, that I'd want to batten down the hatch and never look at them again.

But I'd happily lie down for that guy, in that freaking hallway, and screw his brains out.

Apparently, not getting any for two years is finally starting to get to me.

Probably should do something about that.

Probably won't.

I'm awesome like that.

Waving to Eric as I leave the building, a bounce in my step despite the embarrassment I can still feel under my skin from my latest elevator encounter with the man I now realize has to be my neighbor, I'm actually almost looking forward to today.

Yes, I'm doing recon work and double checking my escape routes, should I need them. But a little, fragile piece of me dares to feel hopeful that I won't.

That this time, in this huge city, I might actually be free.

Wishful thinking, maybe, but I tuck that little piece of me behind some steel-reinforced brick walls to keep it safe while desperately clinging to it despite knowing that it's foolish to feel this way after not even being here a month.

The amount of time between moving into a new place and the day the flowers show up is never consistent, definitely part of Trent's game to keep me on my toes and conditioned to be in a constant state of panic. Though it's never longer than six months.

Never long enough for me to get truly comfortable.

So why do I feel this way already?

No freaking clue. I wish I knew so I could evaluate it, work out what it is about this time that has me letting my guard down a little already, despite knowing how foolish that is. That I knew so I could protect myself against it. Alas, all I have are my walls and that growing puzzle piece of hope.

I practically skip across town, bouncing between subways and Ubers as I make my way to the bagel truck I discovered last weekend, doing a happy dance when I get there and it's not insanely busy. On the one hand, that's a freaking crime, this place is so good it should have a line that wraps the block, but on the other, yay me because I don't have to wait to eat.

The bright and shiny girl from the weekend is working again and greets me with her megawatt smile. "Morning! Egg, bacon, and cheese bagel with avocado, pico, and a black coffee?"

She blows my mind as she reels off my order from the other day. The fact that she not only recognizes me despite the hundreds of customers they might get, but that she remembered my order. I've done her job and that shit is like... genius level. Even if it is mildly terrifying to the part of me that wants to hide from everyone and everything, there's something almost kindred about her that makes it not scary.

"Yeah, that'd be great, thanks." I check her name tag. Martina. "Thanks, Martina."

"Pssh, that's my mama. Everyone calls me Tina." She winks at me before turning to start my order. Moments later, she's handing me my coffee and I pile in the sugar while I wait for the bagel. An itch on the back of my neck makes me stop still. Less of an itch, more like a prickle of awareness.

Someone is watching me.

I try to act normal, pretend like my hands aren't shaking as I stir my coffee, put the lid on the cup, and take a sip as I look up and glance around me, trying to take in every single face. My paranoia is sky high after all my years running, but I've learned to trust my instincts.

The downside of a busy city is there are a lot of people. It's easy for me to hide here, but that means it's easy for him to hide too.

Keeping my back to the truck, I try to be as subtle as I can as I scan my surroundings again. The prickle is still there, that full-body awareness that someone is watching me has my body practically vibrating and all of the happiness that was coursing through my veins has been replaced with ice.

I can't even taste my coffee as I sip it while I try to pretend to be casual.

In the distance, I see a guy at the end of the block by the traffic lights, just leaning against the wall, looking in this direction. I don't recognize him and, despite the distance, it's impossible not to notice his size and his tattoos. Even from here he looks like he could snap me in two.

Shit.

He looks up and it feels like I catch his gaze. Rooted to the spot, in full freeze mode, my heart feels like it's going to break through my ribs.

Please don't be watching me. Please. Please. Please.

"Here you go," Tina calls out, and I squeak as I jump at the sound of her voice, cursing as some of my hot coffee spills on my hand. "Oh, God, I'm so sorry! I didn't mean to make you jump." She rushes from the side of the truck, paper towel in hand, apologizing as she takes my coffee while I mop up the burning liquid from my skin.

"It's fine," I tell her as I try to calm my racing heart. "It wasn't you. I was just a million miles away." My voice shakes as I speak, and I try to find the guy again, but he's gone.

Maybe he wasn't watching me.

Maybe it was a coincidence.

But I don't believe in coincidences.

Not anymore.

"Here, have it on the house. I am so, so sorry." I shake my head as she continues to apologize profusely.

"Honestly, it wasn't you. I swear. I'm just a space case today. I'm paying for my breakfast." I force a laugh to try and reassure her that I'm okay and that I'm not about to demand she gets fired or something.

"Are you sure?" she asks, panic still filling her wide

eyes. I recognize that look, that reaction, and my heart fills with sorrow. It's enough to distract me, to calm my heart, so I can focus on her and reassure her that I'm not going to flip out.

"I swear. And look, I'm not even hurt," I say, showing her my hand. "I'm fine, we're fine. No harm, no foul." Placing my hands on her shoulders, I make her still, just to make sure she can see that I'm serious. "It's okay."

She lets out a deep, rattly breath, and nods. "Okay."

Nodding, I let go of her, knowing that, while touch *can* help, unwanted touch can do just as much harm. I take my coffee and bagel from her, keeping a warm smile on my face to try and show her that I'm no threat to her. "Okay."

"Sorry, I just really need this job." Her smile is a little wonky and she pulls in on herself, like she's trying to make herself small, all that bright, sparkly personality that I've seen the few times I've been here running for the hills.

"And I'm not going to do anything to jeopardize that. Promise. Are you okay?" My question is tentative, because I know how easy it is to hide, and like clockwork, I watch her bright and sparkly mask slide back on.

"I'm fine, silly. You're the one who spilled hot coffee." She waves me off and moves to go back to the truck, but I sidestep so I'm still in front of her.

I let my own mask slip off and I know the moment she sees my pain, as if it's a reflection, because she sucks in a breath and pauses. "If you're not okay, I'm going to be here pretty often and I know it's easier to talk to a stranger sometimes."

She nods but doesn't say another word, so I let her pull herself back together, slide on my own 'outside' mask, and move aside so she can go back in the truck. Once she's in the window she makes a grabby hand movement at me. "Pass me back your bagel, that one's going to be stone cold by now."

"Charge me twice," I say, keeping hold of my bagel until she agrees. I make sure to tap my card, ensuring the extra charge is on there before handing her the bagel in my hand.

I might have a lot of things to worry about, and the guy who might or might not have been watching me is definitely high on that list, but knowing that I helped her today, even a little, makes me feel lighter. I can't help but wonder if that's why Tommy helps me as much as he does. Because I sure as hell can't help myself, but her? Her I might be able to help.

And there is something magical in that.

I stare at Yen in horror as we stand with the four other girls from HellScape outside of the bar they all thought would be a great place to go after the dinner and cocktails we just had—which, admittedly, was the most fun I've had in forever, and the only reason why I agreed to keep the night going, despite it being a Wednesday—and regret all of my decisions.

"Karaoke?" The word comes out of my mouth like I just swore or something, because seriously. Karaoke?

I do not sing in public. That special little show is reserved for my shower and my shower only.

"Oh, come on!" Yen pleads. "Karaoke is hilarious, plus no one said you have to sing."

"Swear on everything you hold dear that you will not, under any circumstance, force me on that stage." My face is deadpan and I'm holding her to this because no freaking way.

"Fine, spoilsport. We only have one rule. No one records anything on girls' night."

The others, who are apparently the girls Yen is closest to at HellScape, who also all work downstairs, nod feverently.

"What happens on girls' night, stays on girls' night," Belle, the beautifully petite girl who looks like she could be the Disney princess she's named for, says solemnly. "Plus, we don't need clients having evidence that we're anything but who they want us to be."

"Got it," I say with a nod of my head.

I allow them to practically drag me into the karaoke bar. The very drunk guy on stage singing *Proud Mary* is enough to make me rethink my decision, but Tara, the redhead of the group, grins as we reach the bar and asks, "Tequila?"

Belle, Amelia, and Sofie all woo so very loudly, and I glance at Yen, who looks about as happy about the woo-girl thing as I feel. The downside to partying with early twenty-somethings. Though, I guess even at twenty five, Yen isn't feeling the woo either.

I am *so* not a woo girl. I am too old to be a woo girl. Hell, I'm the oldest one in our group tonight, but I nod anyway, maybe with enough tequila I could be a woo girl. I also haven't drank enough, well outside of a few times at college maybe, to get to woo-girl relaxation. I also don't intend on getting to woo-girl levels tonight, because lack of control isn't something I do.

The bartender is in front of her in seconds, that charisma-filled smile of his front and center as she orders the shots, and he winks as she tells him to get one for himself too.

Oh, how nice it must be to be so normal, so casual, and so free.

I'm only a tiny bit jealous, but I also know that it's likely these girls have *something* too, because well, I mean, look at Yen. You'd never know she was trafficked, tortured, and God only knows what else just by looking at her and watching her interact with people.

Wearing a mask is easy. I know that as well as anyone.

I can't help but think that the rest of these girls are just... well, normal.

At least, I hope they are.

Anddddddd I'm spiraling.

I take the shot the second it's offered to me and slam it back. I really need to get out of my head a little. Yen slides me her shot, pulling a face, so I take hers and drink that too.

"Slammers are so not my jam," she says to me quietly. "But you try telling her no."

I cover my mouth to hide the laugh. "I get it, but I can't take all your shots. I won't walk out of here and I don't drink much."

"Pssh..." She makes noises at me like I just spoke to her in Swahili. "We don't blaspheme like that here, Quinn. Alcohol is our friend, especially on girls' night."

I roll my eyes at her dramatics. "Then why am I drinking your tequila?"

"Because," she draws out the word for effect and I laugh again. "I started drinking whiskey cocktails earlier and I am not foolish enough to mix the two."

"See, now that makes sense. I need water."

The karaoke pauses and a round of boos and applause

sounds across the room from the many, many drunk-off-their-ass humans in here. Yen orders herself a drink and grabs me a bottle of water before we head over to a booth that is somehow available in here.

Noting my surprise, Yen leans in as a woman stumbles onto the platform stage and the opening bars of LeAnn Rimes' rendition of Blue starts playing, and I groan so freaking hard.

"Meyer owns this place too, hence the booth."

I pull back and blink at her. "Just how much of this city does our boss own?" Maybe I should ask Tommy about who, exactly, his friend is.

Yen just shrugs at me and smirks, while the others do another shot and follow it with another woo. I disguise my eye rolling by taking a sip of my water and glancing around the room. This is definitely nothing like HellScape, but now that I know Meyer owns this place too, I can see some things in here that seem similar. Like the amount of security, the somewhat-scowley face of who I assume is the bar manager—he's nothing like Harper, but he carries himself the same way she does—and the somewhat-high-end furnishings, considering this is a karaoke bar.

It has that, *je ne sais quoi* about the place.

Yes, I heard that on TV. Yes, I know what it means, but I'm still laughing at myself for using it, even just in my head.

"Let's sing!" Tara squeals as the *Blue*-style torture ends and Belle claps her hands together before the four of them take another shot. I side eye Yen, who just shrugs at me.

"You guys go sing, I'll watch the booth," I tell Tara, just firm enough that they boo at me but don't complain. The five of them shimmy out of the booth and head toward the stage, the sound of people talking humming in the air. I adjust where I'm sitting, so my back is to the wall and I can take in the entire place.

Some habits never die.

I groan as *Girls Just Want To Have Fun* starts playing, then laugh as the five of them pile on stage looking like the weirdest version of the Spice Girls I've ever seen in my life. Sofie is rocking that Baby Spice look, while Yen is definitely Emo Spice—a new member I just decided existed. I press my lips together, trying not to laugh too much as the screeching begins.

One of them can hold a tune, I can make that much out, but the others… yeah, they easily drown out whoever the singer of the group is. They're laughing, dancing, and having fun, and I realize this is the first time I've done something like this and not felt like a spare part.

The only reason I'm on the outside is because I'm keeping myself there. The thought is a little startling. I think I'm so conditioned to keep to myself, to not trust anyone, to have to keep secrets, that I just automatically isolate myself.

Cursing myself inside my head, I take a swig from my water bottle and mentally stab Trent in the eye. He took this from me too. He might not have made me this, but he definitely reinforced it and took it to this extreme.

Fuck him.

And my parents.

I'm supposed to be safe in this city and I'm tired of not living. Of just surviving. And even though the fear of Trent finding me is still so freaking visceral, I realize that he always finds me, but I never cherish the time I have *before* that.

I just live in fear… and I'm done. I still need to be safe, more cautious than most, but I have my escape routes. I have Tommy and, according to him, I have his network of friends here keeping me hidden.

Flagging down the passing server, I order skittle bombs for the table as part of my just-now-adopted 'fuck it' attitude. I'm going to start living, dammit.

I deserve that.

And I'm starting right the hell now.

The girls finish destroying Cindy Lauper's masterpiece and head back to the table just as the shots arrive. Yen quirks a brow at me, but I push a shot at her and quirk mine right the hell back. "To girls' night," I say, lifting the shot.

The girls repeat the words as a half-laugh-half-shout,

with Yen joining in but obviously skeptical before tipping the shot back.

"What in the name of all that's fruity was that?" she asks and I laugh.

"Skittle bomb. Cointreau, an orange liqueur, and red bull."

"Well, shit, let's get some more!"

I grin as she flags down the server working the booth area and orders another round of shots. I ask for another bottle of water too because I am not twenty-one anymore and the hangovers are *real*. They just hit different now that I'm closing in on thirty and I don't have a three day window to recover.

Probably should've eaten more earlier too but, well, as Tara would say… YOLO.

God, it sounds ridiculous even in my head.

The shots arrive at the table, and while they're skittle bombs, sure, there are four shots for each of us.

Good lord, Imma pass away. One of them has a freaking sparkler in it!

But I embrace my new-found mentality, even if just for the night. Tonight is the night I start living.

So I drink with the others, I even give a woo a go, and firmly cement that I am, indeed, *not* a woo girl, but it's hilarious anyway. I join their next karaoke round, we dance until my feet feel like they're going to fall off, and I just… I try to have fun. It's a weird concept, but it feels so good that I embrace the joy of girls' night.

"Bathroom. Need the bathroom!" I yell at Yen. Apparently, the karaoke is over and the DJ has started playing, so now I can hardly hear myself think, let alone speak to anyone.

"Want me to come?" she asks and I shake my head, smiling.

"You're good. I'll be back. Grab me more water?"

She cackles at me but nods. "Sure thing, grandma."

I flip her the bird and walk away from the booth toward the bar, since the glowing pink bathroom sign is on the far side of it. Pushing through the crowd of people, I realize I feel looser, freer than I ever remember feeling.

This is good.

Tonight I really am reclaiming my life. Starting fresh.

Could be the booze talking, but I am here for the positivity of it all.

"Sorry!" I call out after walking into some dude, which I only realize I've done as I notice the front of my top is a little wet. I look up and my jaw drops. "You!"

Elevator guy smirks down at me, his bright green eyes crinkled at the edges as he says, "Me."

I feel my brain short-circuit as I try to speak, noticing his shoulder-length blond waves are pulled back, showing off that cut-from-marble freaking jaw line. The way his leather jacket hangs from his broad shoulders and his black T-shirt stretches across his obviously ripped chest definitely aren't making my brain work any faster.

"Let me get you another drink!" I say when I finally get my wits about me, a hand on his arm as I lean in to make sure he can hear me, hoping he didn't notice my moment of being struck stupid by just how hot he is.

Again.

"Oh, absolutely not. I'm not going to let the prettiest woman in the bar buy me a drink, but, if you'll let me, I'll buy you one."

I can't tell if it's the alcohol in my system or just the way he puts me at ease and makes the voices in my head quiet, but I find myself agreeing.

"What's your poison, Angel?"

I press my lips together, trying not to laugh at the cheesy nickname, but something in me likes that he's a stranger, that he doesn't know my name. Definitely isn't just how freaking hot he is scrambling my brain.

No siree.

Couldn't be.

Ha that rhymed.

Oh I might've had too many shots already, yet I still find stupidity falling from my lips. "A Matador. Tequila, pineapple juice, and lime."

"Your wish," he says, winking at me, the 'is my

command' a silent implication that makes me laugh as he places his hand on my lower back and leads me closer to the bar. He tucks me inside his arm, shielding me from the amount of people in here—which still blows my mind cause it's a freaking Wednesday—and once our drinks are ready, he pushes the glass toward me.

"So what's your name, Angel?" he asks as I take a sip, enjoying the fruity burst on my tongue.

I coyly look up at him through my lashes. "Does it matter?"

His laugh makes his shoulders shake and butterflies take flight in my stomach. "Not if you don't want it to."

This might be completely reckless. Entirely stupid. I mean, who trusts a stranger these days? But he lives in my building, and he's hot, and well… he can't be some sort of psycho serial killer, right? I can't have *that* much bad luck.

I finish my drink as we sway to the music, my back pressed against his chest, his hand on the waistband of my jeans, his thumb stroking the bare skin of my stomach, and hell, it's been way too long since someone touched me right because I swear I can feel every single stroke in every fiber of my being.

"Want to head back to my place?" he murmurs in my ear, pressing his lips against the sensitive skin just below it, making me suck in a breath and gasp.

This could be such a bad idea, but living. Not surviving.

I can't seem to make my lips work, so I nod and it seems that's all he needs. He takes my glass from my hand and puts it on the bar before intertwining his fingers with mine and leading me from the bar. I pull my phone out and send Yen a quick message so she knows I'm not dead.

Me:

Heading home. All good. See you tomorrow.

Yen:

Oh I saw. Have fun ;)

I laugh when I read the message and slide my phone back in my pocket. The cold air as we exit the bar is like a slap in the face, but he shrugs off his jacket and slips it over my shoulders. "Let me grab a cab."

His warm, spicy scent envelops me and, somehow, something about it just makes me feel safe. Calm. Like the voices in my head are quiet.

Since the day I left Trent, I've trusted my gut, my instincts, my intuition, and nothing about him screams, run far and fast, so I decide right then that I'm in this.

He takes my hand again and we move to the edge of the sidewalk where he hails down a car almost instantly. It's a black sedan and doesn't look like a typical cab, but what do I know?

Opening the door, he guides me in, climbing in behind me, and it's only then that I see Jessica from HellScape in the entry line, staring at us like I just kicked her puppy.

I shrug it off because well, she hates me anyway, for nothing more than existing, but I'm not letting her steal this from me.

He gives the driver the address before turning his attention back to me. Cupping my cheek with his hand, he moves in slowly, giving me time to stop him if I want to. But tonight isn't a night for no.

It's about reclaiming things that were taken from me… and this? Yeah, I deserve to reclaim this.

Even if my hands are shaking.

He studies me closely, like he's waiting for me to bolt, so I close my eyes and lean in, pressing my hands against his chest as his lips touch mine.

He starts soft, tentative, like he's still giving me time to back out, but the feel of him against me sets my soul on fire.

I want him.

I *need* him.

I clasp his T-shirt in my fingers and he stops being so gentle. His hands move from my cheeks to my ass and he lifts me so I'm straddling his lap, his jacket falling to the wayside as he does.

If there wasn't so much alcohol in my system, I might

feel embarrassed for the poor cabbie. But then again, maybe not. Because holy God, this *man.* His fingers grip my skin as his tongue battles with mine and the groan that escapes him when I grind down on him makes me come alive.

One of his hands moves from my ass to my hair, gripping it tightly, and for a second I think I shouldn't like how hard his touch is, shouldn't enjoy the tight hold he has on me, but I push it away.

I get to like and enjoy whatever the fuck I want. Trent doesn't belong to this moment.

This is mine.

EIGHT

Music plays in the background as I grind against him again as he kisses and licks up the column of my throat, pulling on my hair to tilt my head back, exposing me to him before he nips at my earlobe, sending a shudder through my entire body.

Who knew that would feel that good?

"Such a pretty little angel," he murmurs. "Tastes so sweet."

I push back against him again, whimpering a little at the hard length of him against me.

He releases my hair and grips my chin, making me look into his piercing green eyes. "Soon, Angel. I won't make you wait."

"We're here," the driver calls out, and I feel my cheeks heat.

Right.

The driver.

Oops.

Hot Guy still grips my chin, amusement playing out in the tipping of the corners of his lips at my obvious embarrassment.

"Thanks, O'Connor," Hot Guy says, and I blink at him. *He knows the cabbie?*

I don't get another second to think about it because the door opens and I realize Eric is standing there.

Oh, God. Throw me in a hole and let this embarrassment end.

"Stop."

Hot Guy says just one word and silences the voices again, the embers inside of me bursting back into a flame.

He lifts me from his lap and slides out of the car, holding out a hand to me, which I take as I climb out. I step onto the sidewalk and he dips back into the car, grabbing his jacket, which he places back on my shoulders before taking my hand.

"Eric," is all Hot Guy says with a nod before he leads me inside, straight to the elevator. Once those doors close, it's like my skin feels unbearable, like the distance between us shouldn't be there. I shift from one foot to the other when I hear a quiet, "Fuck this."

He hits a button on the panel and the car halts, a buzzer

goes off once, then there's nothing but silence.

A heartbeat later, he has me pressed against the wall, cocooned by him, and another whimper escapes me.

Who even am I right now?

His lips conquer mine again and I melt at his touch. "Tell me, right now, if you want to stop this."

The words break through my haze and I blink at him. "I don't want you to stop."

"Thank fuck," is all he says before kissing me again, taking both my wrists and putting them above my head, pinning them with just one hand. "Tell me if you want me to stop. At any time."

His words are like a balm to my soul. Not that I didn't already feel safe with him, which is insane because he's a complete stranger, but because he's giving me something I've never had.

Some control.

"Don't stop," I pant, my chest heaving under the intensity of his stare. He uses his other hand to trail down my cheek, throat, across my chest and down my ribs, until he reaches the exposed skin at my stomach again.

"So soft," he murmurs before running his lips down a similar path to the one his fingers took. But he stops at the crook of my neck this time, scraping his teeth against my skin, eliciting a shudder from me as thrill runs through my body.

I try to rock against him but the hold he has on my arms makes it difficult and I feel his grin against my skin as his fingers move from my stomach to the waistband of my jeans. He undoes the button in one quick movement and pushes his hand beneath the material.

My back arches as he brushes his fingers against me. "So wet for me already, Angel."

His eyes light up, like I'm a shiny toy he's about to enjoy playing with, and I am so here for it. He gently brushes his fingers against me again and I rock, trying to encourage more. Anything. Just more.

"So impatient."

"Says the man who stopped the elevator," I sass back, eyes wide after the words fall from my lips. Where the hell did *that* come from? But the panic recedes when he laughs.

"Touché. I don't like to wait, but I think I'm going to have some fun with you."

My muscles tighten as his finger pushes the fabric of my panties aside, rubbing up along my slit and getting me wetter by the second.

My hips search out more, following his touch every time he teases me and pulls slightly away.

"Just so we're clear. We're not going anywhere until I get two orgasms out of you. One on my tongue and the other on my cock."

The heat on my cheeks is instant at his words. Who

talks like that? I mean, clearly he does and my pussy is all for it judging by the gush of heat I know for a fact he felt on his finger. God damn. Who knew dirty talk was so hot?

"That's a good girl." I watch, in rapt attention, as he slides his finger out of me and brings it to his mouth, sucking and licking every inch of it.

"Like I said, I'm going to have fun with you."

Dropping to his knees, he pulls down my jeans as he goes and I have to fight the urge to cover myself up. His eyes snap to mine, mirth dancing across his features.

"Do you really think you can hide from me?" I mean, we're in a tin can stopped between the fourth and fifth floor with mirrors on three of the four sides, so I'm guessing no, I cannot hide from him. My mouth is dry, my libido doing cartwheels and begging me to just go with the fucking flow as I drop my hand and try my best to relax.

God, I hope there are no cameras in here.

"That's a good girl," he repeats, his voice like melted caramel. In any other moment, him calling me a good girl would have my inner feminist protesting, but I just push that bitch back down and bask in the warmth of his praise.

Slowly, my thighs part, my hands finding the metal bar that runs around the elevator so I can hold on for dear life as his mouth places a barely-there kiss on my stomach.

"Coming is the name of the game and screaming is how it's played, you understand?" Fuck, how can he be so playful in a moment like this? That spot where he just kissed me is on fire, burning a hole straight through to my pussy and melting everything inside.

"What-what if someone…" I'm worried someone will call in an emergency for the stopped elevator, but I can't get my words out. The last thing I need in my life right now are the doors to this elevator opening and getting an audience of five hot firemen watching me get off on a stranger's mouth.

Oh shit. Now, I'm fantasizing about being watched while I orgasm. Who am I right now?

"I don't know what you're thinking, Angel, but it's making you wetter by the second. By all means, don't stop." Pushing a finger inside my pussy, he keeps his eyes on me, my mouth falling open as he curls the digit in what feels like a hook and pulls me closer to his mouth.

A second finger joins the first just as the tip of his tongue flicks my clit. My muscles go rigid, my hands clutching the bar on either side of me like it'll save me from making a sound. It won't and I have a feeling his goal is to drag those screams from me. He wants this whole building to know he made some unsuspecting, innocent girl come in the elevator with a few dirty words and a magic tongue.

I mean, there are worse ways of dying from embarrassment, right?

Tapping my outer thigh, he sucks in his bottom lip and

rakes his teeth over it like he's fighting his own battles, like taking his time is physically hurting him.

Ha!

"I see your patience is losing the battle."

Why am I sassing this guy back? The longer we banter, the longer he's going to draw this out and the closer the reality of a door full of emergency workers seeing me half naked.

"I love the thrill of a challenge." His last word is made more potent by the thrust of his two fingers inside me, down to the knuckle. I gasp, my breath catching in my throat as I see a couple of stars dancing behind my lids.

All that is forgotten as he flicks my clit twice before sucking it into his mouth and taking a long pull.

Oh, dear God, please don't make me scream, please don't make me scream, please don't—

I didn't know I could feel like this. That this is what ecstasy is supposed to feel like. Holy mother of freaking everything, I'm barely staying upright and I get the feeling he's only just getting started.

He lifts my leg up and over his shoulder, buries his face in my pussy, his mouth French-kissing my clit while he fucks me in time with his fingers. With every plunge and every nip of his teeth, I gulp in air, fighting the urge to pull away from him and wanting to push his head closer into me at the same time.

The overwhelming feeling is real and a sliver of panic writhes through me, but I push that the hell away. *This moment is mine, dammit.*

I bring myself back to the guy on his knees in front of me, pleasure rippling through my body as his mouth works over my clit. One hand abandons the steel bar and lands on the back of his head, fingers curling and nails digging into his scalp as I grind my pussy all over his face.

Who even am I right now? Old me would never *grind* anything, let alone my pussy on some poor stranger's mouth. Okay, not poor. This is totally on him and new me loves it.

The burn on my ass cheek brings me back to the moment and I realize he just… spanked me?

A suck in a breath and he looks up at me. Apparently, he felt me tighten up.

"You okay?" he asks, and it takes me a second to nod.

I am okay. I just wasn't expecting it, and it's not like he knows my past…

It didn't hurt, it was just a shock, and I actually… kinda… well, I liked it. Like, it made everything focus. Everything quiet.

"I'm good."

"Good, because I'm not even close to done yet, Angel."

I don't have time to respond because he's back to his wicked ways, pulling an orgasm out of me with scissoring fingers and magic lips that know how to trap my clit just so his tongue can flick it back and forth.

Oh, God, that feels good.

So good.

Sooooooo good!

"That's it, Angel. All over my tongue." His words are like a trap door opening. They release every pent-up feeling I've held back for... forever. My body tenses just long enough for my inner walls to squeeze his fingers and my muscles to spasm with a full-body orgasm running through my entire bloodstream. My head drops back against the wall of the elevator as his mouth does the opposite of relenting.

This guy does not give up, he just keeps sucking and flicking and biting and holy shit, this orgasm is like a Shakespeare monologue. It just keeps on going.

This is what an orgasm is supposed to be like? Well fuck me stupid, Sir.

It's only when my knees are reduced to jelly that I realize he's holding me up and pushing me against the wall, his jeans pushed down and his cock standing proudly.

When did he stand up?

Did I pass out from an orgasm?

"You coming on my mouth is the hottest thing I've ever seen, tasted, or felt."

I don't have time to feel embarrassed because he's

suddenly kissing me, his wet lips tasting of… me. He's kissing me with the same mouth he just had on my pussy and wow, I taste so… lusty.

"You like that, Angel? I can feel you trembling in my arms. You like tasting your cum on my lips, don't you?" His mouth is back on mine and his tongue sweeps across my lips before thrusting inside my mouth and taking my breath away.

As I get lost in his expert kiss, there's a wetness at my stomach that gets my attention, but he won't let me look. He's got one hand holding my chin, fingers digging against my jaw, while he controls every movement we make. As he licks and sucks on my lips, his hips are pushing into my stomach, grinding his very hard cock against my skin and… oh my God, I think that wet spot is his precum. He's so turned on by giving me pleasure that he's painting himself on my skin.

Why is that so fucking hot?

Reaching back with his free hand, he puts just enough distance between us to look me in the eye as the tell-tale sound of foil tearing greets my ears. Still watching only me, he does his voodoo magic down there and, before I know it, his words make me instantly gush with desire all over again.

"I'm about to fuck you into next week and although your screams earlier were like music to my ears, I think we can do better."

I screamed earlier? How did I not notice that?

My head nods like my body knows better than to listen to my brain. The words "Yes, sir," tug at the very tip of my tongue but I veto that idea in a heartbeat. I am a strong independent wom—

Oh, hell. Who am I kidding? I will happily give up my feminist card if I can feel that again.

My eyes pop open, my mouth slack with the sudden pleasure coursing through my entire system. I am full, my pussy stretched to the limits of what it could possibly take, but it doesn't hurt. It's complete and utter bliss that I didn't even know existed.

It's not fair that I lived without this in my life for so long, but I think if Hot Elevator Guy is up for it, I'm going to start enjoying this much, much more often.

"Fuck! You're so tight, Angel. I'm going to need a second."

The words are strained and I tip my head back against the mirror behind me. "I'm going to need an eternity…" His chuckle makes the heat return to my cheeks, a nervous smile dancing on my lips. "I said that out loud, didn't I?"

"You sure did and now I feel like it's the challenge of a lifetime, ruining you for all other men." He winks at me, and it's on the tip of my tongue to tell him I'm already ruined, but this time I keep my mouth firmly shut.

His words are still circling in my mind when he pulls out and slams back inside me, taking me out of my head and into this moment. The movement is hard and unforgiving in the best kind of way. My back hits the wall as my thighs squeeze his hips. I'm reaching for something, anything, to grab as he slowly fucks me, in and out, long pulls and quick plunges to the hilt.

Every time our bodies come together, a gasp escapes from between my lips as his balls slap against my skin. We're all sweat and moans bouncing against the metal of the elevator. The strong scent of sex fills my nose every time I inhale, trying to breathe through the insane amount of pleasure from his cock fucking me right over the cliffs of reality.

Wrapping my arms around his neck, I transform into some wanton, sex-crazed woman seeking out her pleasure, satisfying her needs in a way I've never felt the confidence to do before. Something about him, the way he looks at me, the way he so obviously wants me, is enjoying me, rids me of any doubt that might have crept in. I grind my pelvis against him with every thrust, my clit rubbing against the happy trail of coarse hair that leads to this man's exceptionally talented dick.

Hugging his head to my chest, he plunges inside me as he takes my nipple, T-shirt and bra along with it, into his mouth and sucks hard enough to make me cry out in the small space. My pussy walls contract, his dick seeming somehow even bigger, swelling and pulsing inside me as my entire body rubs against his, my mouth opening and closing as I try, almost in vain, to get air inside my lungs.

We both sound like animals, grunting and groaning with every thrust and suck and bite.

"Oh my God, oh my God…"

"That's it, Angel, come all over my dick and do it fucking now!"

I gasp, once, twice. Oh, God, I can barely breathe. What is this guy doing to me?

"On my dick, now!" My entire body gives up the fight at his demanding words.

We freeze, his dick buried so deep I can feel him everywhere, my muscles so contracted I'm afraid I'll squeeze the life right out of him.

"That's it, yes!" I rub my clit as my body shakes and my mind goes blissfully blank.

Hot Elevator Guy roars his orgasm into the elevator and I'm not sure who's louder, him or me, but one thing is fucking clear, the entire building knows why the elevator is out of use. But in this moment, I can't find it in me to care.

He pulls out of me, straightening himself out while I try to make my legs work again, and restarts the elevator. We finish the ride up in a comfortable-yet-weird—for me at least—silence. He doesn't take his eyes off me the rest of the journey and once we reach our floor, he walks me to my door.

"We should do that again, Angel," he says as he leans against the wall by my door as I fumble trying to put my key in the lock.

Looking up at him, I bite my lip and nod, heat filling my cheeks. "Won't hear me saying no."

The smirk he gives me in response is priceless and I almost want to roll my eyes at him. "I'll see you soon," he says as I open my door. "Just don't keep me waiting too long."

"Uh-huh," I murmur as I enter the apartment. "Soon."

Pushing the door closed, I lean back against it and let out a deep sigh. Contentment and a hint of embarrassment floating out of me on the breath.

"I'm going to hold you to that," I hear through the door, followed by footsteps that get quieter as he leaves.

Tonight was entirely unexpected, but totally freeing. I feel… lighter, in a way I hadn't entirely realized I was weighed down with before.

Maybe more time with Hot Elevator Guy is exactly what I need.

The moment my eyes open, I smile, and I can't remember the last time that happened. Am I hung over? Yes, yes I am, *but* I feel so freaking empowered by reclaiming a part of myself last night that my hangover somehow doesn't feel so bad.

I should probably feel *something* about the fact that I didn't get Hot Guy's name, or the fact that I'll probably run into him again… but I mean, I saw him. He's probably had more one night stands than I've had hot dinners.

Stretching out, I feel the remnants of last night in my muscles and get that zip of joy again. Not only did I reclaim that part of myself, but it was actually *good.* I've heard horror stories about dealing with straight guys. How they don't get you off, it's all about them, and people having to finish themselves afterward. I'm so glad that isn't what happened because I might have just given up all together and taken a vow of celibacy.

No, he definitely knew what he was doing and a part of me wants to do it again, but that isn't how hookups work.

At least, I don't think so.

Never really done the whole hookup, dating thing outside of Trent. God knows I wasn't that person in college. That required more of a mask than I was willing to wear.

Oh man, I'm out here at twenty-eight, single, and realizing I have no idea how this game works.

I grab the pillow on the other side of the bed and smush

it against my face, groaning into it.

It's fine, bigger fish and all that.

Fairly certain I have bigger things to overcome on this journey than working out the rules of dating. Shaking my head at my dramatics, I move to get out of bed and groan.

Yup, there's my nearly-thirty body rejecting all the dancing I did last night. I can't tell what hurts more, my head, my knee or my back. Oh wait, nope, could be my shoulders.

This would all be fine if I could spend a day recovering, but I have to work tonight and I get the feeling a hangover isn't something Harper will accept as an excuse for me moving slower than normal. Taking a deep breath, I force myself to stand up, weeping on the inside about the pain that radiates through my body, and hobble through to the kitchen.

I grab my phone from the counter where I left it last night.

Three percent battery.

Stellar choices made there last night, Quinn.

I don't think I've slept with my phone more than a few inches from my hand the entire time I've been running, just in case. After flicking through the notifications, I go back into my room and plug it in to charge before deciding I need a bath.

A soak in a steaming tub of bubbles has to help.

Right?

I turn on the taps and pour in *way* too much bubble bath with a huge smile on my face as the vanilla scent fills the air before grabbing my bluetooth speaker and hooking it up to my phone. Tara told me about a podcast last night called *Murder and Makeup*, and while something so violent probably shouldn't pique my interest, I'm intrigued.

It's not that I like being around violence, hell, these days I actively avoid it, but learning the reasons why people do what they do interests me immensely, so I scroll through the app she showed me right back to episode one, doing a little happy dance that there's literally hundreds of episodes.

How to keep my brain busy when I start to spin out.

Perfection.

Once the bath is nice and full, I shut off the taps and pad into the kitchen to grab a bottle of water, which I meant to do earlier before I got distracted by my phone. I desperately need coffee and food too, so as soon as my muscles are looser, I'm all over that.

I get undressed and decide to rinse last night off of me in the shower before I jump in the tub, the beating of the water pressure feels like heaven as I scrub down. Scratching at my scalp is enough to make me moan as I wash my hair.

Apparently, getting back in touch with my body last

night really has woken up a few things.

I run through my daily to-do list, including finally looking for a self-defense class and finding somewhere to buy some more bedding, because I absolutely need to strip my sheets before I get into bed tonight.

Once my day is in order in my head and I'm finally clean, I exit the shower and practically skip across the bathroom to the tub. "Alexa, play podcast."

"Starting podcast on Spotify," rings through the speaker and I grin. I could totally get used to this upgraded life Tommy has put in place for me. I try not to let that voice in my head tell me how much harder it's going to be to give this up if Trent finds me, because I'm finally having a good few days and Trent has stolen enough of those from me.

I sink into the hot water of the bath, breathing in deeply as the vanilla fills my senses while the podcast starts to play.

This. This right here is what I've been missing the last two years. And while I don't regret not listening to Tommy in the first place and trying things my way—because I desperately needed that control back then—I'm definitely glad I finally agreed to give his way a go.

I lie there and soak, enjoying two episodes of the podcast, learning about true crime across the country, which is as chilling as it is terrifying, before my text ping sounds through the speaker. Ignoring the first, determined to turn into a prune before I climb out of what is now lukewarm water, I let out a sigh when it pings another three times.

Apparently, someone wants my attention, and if that someone is Tommy... well, then I'm going to really regret ignoring the first ping.

Grabbing my towel from the ground, I stand and wrap it around myself before climbing from the tub and walking maybe just a bit faster than needed when another ping goes off.

God, I love Tommy, but please don't be him. Don't be bad news. Please.

My hand shakes as I grab my phone and relief fills me when I see it's just a group chat blowing up my phone. I guess normal people have those... I never have. A part of me feels sad about that, but well, I have one now. It's a small and probably stupid thing to feel warm and fuzzy about, but between being included and it *not* being news about Trent, I feel like I could walk on air.

Yen:

Bitches, I am DYING. Brunch and mimosas to start the day?

Belle:

Dying? I feel fine, but I'm never going to say no to brunch.

Tara:

I'm in, just tell me when and where. I'll go drag Sofie out of bed.

Yen:

Of course you're not dying, you young asshole. I'm OLD.

Tara:

You're not old, just wise ;)

Yen:

Fuck off.

Amelia:

I think I'm still drunk, but I'm in for food.

Belle:

Yeah, you're right, Yen. Definitely saw some grays last night. Might need a touch up.

Belle changed Yen's nickname to Grandma.

Grandma:

ASSHOLES. All of you. Don't know why we're friends.

Tara:

Calm down, getting angry can't be good for your heart.

The messages just keep going and I literally laugh out loud at the snark but obvious love between them.

Me:

I definitely need food, might skip the mimosas. What's the plan?

Dropping my phone back on the bed, I start to make myself feel human again. Once my hair is dry and straight, I pull on a comfy pair of jeans, a tank, and an oversized sweater that falls off one shoulder in an attempt to look half decent, but still be comfy.

Yen:

Olivia's Bistro. Thirty mins. See you bitches there.

I pull up my Uber app to check how long it's going to take and see it's going to take twenty five minutes to get there, so I order the car right away then run around like a loon to put my Chucks on, grab my keys, and practically run out the front door.

Straight into Hot Guy.

Why does the universe hate me?

"Oh, hey," I say with a smile before turning to lock my door.

"Running out?" he asks with a casual smile as he leans against the opposite wall.

I nod as I pocket my keys, trying to casually scurry the hell away toward the elevator. I push the button and the door opens. I send up a thought of thanks and step inside as I answer him, "Yeah, busy day. I'll see you around?"

I hit the button for the ground floor and turn to find him still down the hall, watching me, amusement all over that insanely beautiful face of his.

He nods as he stands up straight, jamming his hands into his pockets. The doors start to close, but I don't miss his words.

"Oh you can count on it, Angel."

Brunch was great. I even went shopping after with Yen to get a few things for the apartment to make it feel more like home. After that, I spent a few hours putting everything in its place and my body was back to aching before I could even think about work.

Where I've been for the past five hours.

It's one in the morning and I still have two hours to go, at least. I haven't eaten since brunch and I am so freaking ready for my bed. I've officially turned into that whiny bitch that everyone hates, but so far, I've managed to keep my commentary in my head.

I plod into the break room, grunting as I drop onto the sofa and I swear my feet actually throb the second that I'm off of them. It's empty in here because I'm so late taking my break, but I'm kind of thankful for that because I really just need some quiet. I can't deal with the mean girl shit tonight and, while that has dialed back to Jessica and Heidi at this point, I just don't have the energy for it.

The creak of the door opening makes my heart sink a little as my body tenses in case I need to run, but I glance over just to make sure whoever it is isn't a threat. When I see Belle, my body relaxes and I tip my head back, closing my eyes.

"You still feeling it?" she asks as the sound of the refrigerator door opening hisses through the small space.

I groan at her and she laughs.

"No. I mean… well, yes, but also, working when hungover is such a bad idea. I'm too old for this shit."

Her laugh twinkles through the room and the sofa dips as she sits beside me, so I open my eyes and actually pay attention. "You're only as old as you feel. Trust me. Some of the clientele in the back room… now *they* are old."

She wrinkles up her face, her nose twitching as she does, and I can't help but laugh. "You play with the oldies?"

"Oh, hell no," she says, eyes wide. "Meyer lets us pick kinks and stuff before we're allocated a section. Plenty of the guys and girls here like the older guy thing, so I leave that to them."

My curiosity is officially piqued. I'd have thought clients rule supreme with choice of partner, like you see in the movies, but apparently, I was wrong. She must see my shock because she giggles at me.

"I'm not a whore, Quinn. I get to pick who I play with and what I do if I want to. Most of the time, it's more about showing than doing, anyway. The basement is different, but the back room… it's pretty tame, and the guys are so strict about the client list that it's more like a taboo party."

"Oh I didn't think you were a whore—" I start and she laughs again, cutting me off.

"I know you didn't, silly. It's fine. You haven't been back there, you don't see it. To be fair, the rules in place about people up front going out back or downstairs are pretty strict too, so I can't even sneak you in. We'd probably both get fired. But all our medical is taken care of, the other benefits are insane, especially for club work, ya know? Who wouldn't want to have fun and reap the benefits? I'm young, I'm beautiful, and if I can make a fuck ton of money off of that now, while also having better insurance coverage and general benefits than my sister who is a hotshot lawyer, damn straight I'm going to do it."

She has a fair point. A decent benefit package is almost impossible to find these days, especially with good medical. I don't even know if I have the same stuff, but all things considered, I don't really care because Trent would likely find me if I had medical coverage or used a hospital or something.

"Hell yeah you should," I say to her before glancing at the clock. "Ughhhhh. I have to go back out. Next time let's go drinking on, like, a Tuesday, so I have a day off before work. I'm nearly thirty and way more of a grandma than Yen."

She giggles at me again and nods. "Deal. No more Wednesday sessions. Did you see Sofie's YumYum videos from last night?"

I pause once I stand, eyes wide. "She put videos of us on social media?"

My heart races a mile a minute. I can't be on social media. He'll find me.

Shit.

Panic floods my body and I lose all sense. I practically run from the break room and head to the basement to find Yen. Rules be damned.

"You can't go down there," Harper snaps as I reach the

door.

"You don't understand. I need… Yen. I have to speak to Yen. Fuck."

I pull at my hair and the room starts to go fuzzy.

This can't be happening.

I need to leave.

"You can't go down there."

"Then I have to go. He'll find me," I utter and her eyes go wide. She glances up at the windows to the bosses' offices but I don't care. I know they helped me get situated, but if my face is on the internet, Trent will know where I am.

He'll find me.

And at this point, I think if he actually gets his hands on me… well, I don't think I'll survive the encounter. His rage was never controllable, but after being gone for this long, making him work to find me… embarrassing him the way he'll say I did…

Yeah, I won't survive the punishment that follows that.

"Quinn, what's going on?" Harper asks, but I shake my head.

"I can't. I need to go. I'm sorry. I won't be back."

Panic flashes in her eyes as I turn and she grabs my arm, but I pull it free.

I need to go.

Right the fuck now.

NINE

HUNTER

The strut in my step as I walk up the back stairs into HellScape has me feeling like a fucking school boy with a crush, but I don't give a fuck. I swear I can taste her on my tongue. Her vanilla scent is stuck in my nose and she's all I've been able to think about since I left her at the door of her apartment last night.

I push open the door to Meyer's office, really fucking glad that this room is sound proofed, and grin at him when I find him leaning back in his chair, watching her like a little stalker again. Turns out I'm not the only voyeur in the group when it comes to Quinn. I flop down onto the sofa, grin still plastered on my face.

"You look too fucking cheerful. I assume you managed to get her to go home with you last night?" Meyer's question is little more than a grumble as he turns away from me to watch her. He isn't usually one to share stories or ask questions, so I know it's rubbing him that I claimed her first. Not because he's pissy that I had her, just that I was there first and he's… well, territorial would be an understatement for Meyer.

"A gentleman doesn't kiss and tell."

"And you're no fucking gentleman."

I laugh at his quip. It's not like he's wrong, but we have rules for a reason and this time, I don't want to share—which is weird as fuck, but for now, I want to keep last night as mine.

"Maybe not normally," I tell him as he spins back to face me in his chair. "But I think, for now, I'm going to keep this one to myself."

He quirks a brow at me as he leans forward on his desk. "Understood. Any issues I need to know about with security?"

"Not as far as I know," I tell him, shaking my head. "I'm going to pull Yen up here shortly and get some information from her, since she'll likely know more first-hand than we do right now. But I'm going to try and get some more firsthand details myself tonight."

He rolls his eyes at me and I swear if they could turn green they would. But we agreed to share, and that is what we'll do. He'll get his time with her, just like Rory will, and I have a feeling they're going to have just as much fun getting to know her as I did.

As I intend to keep doing.

Who would've thought me moving my life to that building for a few weeks to keep her secure while everything settled down—as per Tommy's request—would end up being a good thing? I take back every moment of complaining I did before now.

"Any signs of her ex?"

He nods and I sit up. Not the answer I expected.

"I set up a trace to know when her name and face is being searched for so that we can block anything that pops up, normal stuff, except I'm monitoring it myself rather than letting Lew handle it."

"You got time for that?"

"I'm making time. He's been searching but obviously he hasn't found her yet, and I've been keeping tabs of my own—his phone is tapped, and Henry and Jon are there now surveilling him—so we have eyes on him at all times."

"I'm not surprised he's still looking for her, but this cat and mouse thing he has going on with her is fucked up." I mean, we've done some fucked-up shit in our time, but only to people who deserved it. Well, mostly.

"Nobody likes to lose their favorite toy," is all he says in response before turning back to face her. He's already in full protective mode, which is weird in itself. Meyer wouldn't usually oversee these things himself, that's why we have people. I don't think he's even so much as spoken to her, and yet…

Well, I've known him our entire lives, I know when he's just fixated, but this seems different.

There is just something about Quinn that is… mesmerizing. It's like she captivated us without even trying.

A knock at the door pulls me from my musings and Meyer switches into 'boss mode' before calling out, "Come in."

The door opens and the tiny demon spawn that is Yen struts into the room like the soul-sucking little gremlin she can be, that wicked grin of hers on her face. "You summoned me, Boss man?"

I press my lips together to hide my smile as she stares down Meyer. Balls of freaking steel this girl. Not that we don't adore her like a little sister, especially after everything she's done for us, but that doesn't mean she doesn't know exactly how to push Meyer's buttons—just like a little sister would.

"You know I hate it when you call me that," he grumbles at her while I lean back and mentally eat some popcorn, because watching these two go back and forth is some of the best entertainment I get.

"Yeah, but you know how much I love calling you it." He rolls his eyes at her and she winks at me, making me shake my head. Most people wouldn't dream of even speaking to Meyer, let alone speaking back, but Yen... she's a special case. I'm almost positive that every time she pisses him off he just sees her in that room, dirty, in chains, but still trying to protect the other girls from the men with guns storming the place.

God knows it's not something I'm ever likely to forget.

"Updates?" he asks her and she lets out a sigh, flipping her hair over her shoulder. Sometimes I think we forget how young she still is...

Until moments like this one anyway.

"She had a good night, we drank, we laughed, we sang. She didn't exactly spill her life story to me, but I think she's starting to trust me, to feel safe here. Last night is a testament to that, because from what you guys said, she doesn't usually drink much, and well, she was having a great time. Wasn't she, Boss man?" She turns to me and winks and I bark out a laugh.

The sass on this girl...

How it hasn't gotten her killed is beyond me, but I wouldn't change a thing about her. While I'm starting to feel a little gross about having her spy on Quinn, the other side of me wants to make sure she's protected at all times, so I can deal with feeling a little gross.

"Okay, good. Just keep doing what you're doing. We have more eyes on her now, but they're at a distance."

"Oh, I know. I've seen them. And if I've seen them, you better believe *she's* seen them. She's jumpier than a cat on a hot tin roof when she's sober. She's exactly how I was… after. Every little noise is as loud as a gunshot. Like I said, she's starting to relax, and she's starting to trust, but have no doubt, if she gets spooked, she's going to run so fast none of us are going to see it coming."

The door flies open and Harper barges in the room, bringing Meyer and I to our feet. Harper isn't one for dramatics and my heart starts to race, prepping for whatever the fuck is about to go down. The last time she barged in here like this, we were about to be raided.

"What's wrong?" I ask her as she pants, eyes wide, her gaze bouncing between Meyer and me.

"The girl. Quinn. She ran."

I grab my phone and dial Rory while Meyer loses his shit. "What do you mean she ran?"

"I don't know, she was fine, then came back from her break trying to go downstairs to find this one," she rambles, pointing at Yen. "Then she just said she had to go and wouldn't be back."

"Who was with her in the break room?"

"Belle." Harper responds and Meyer just looks at Yen, who nods.

"Already on it."

She hauls ass from the room, running on the stilts she

calls shoes, and Rory finally answers. "Do you have eyes on Quinn?"

"She's supposed to be with you assholes, so no, I don't. What happened?"

"She's running."

"Fuck, I'm on my way." The line drops and I turn to Meyer.

"I'll head to the apartment. She might go back there before she leaves. I can try to stop her."

"I need to call Tommy," Meyer says, already dialing our old friend as I run from the room down to my GSXR.

I'll reach the apartment before she does, I just need to hope that's where the fuck she went. After this, I'm going to install a fucking tracker chip in her. Because she doesn't get to run from us.

Not now.

Not ever.

#

QUINN

Today has been a good day. The sun is shining, the snow-capped mountains in the distance are visible in the light of spring, and well, today is my last day in this town. The sunshine feels like an omen, like the universe is finally on my side. I feel like my entire life has been leading to this point.

The moment I finally get to be free.

The struggles I've faced, the things I've survived, I just need to make it through this last day. The urge to leave now is like an itch under my skin, but I have a plan, and that means tomorrow. Trent is working a double tomorrow, so I can leave with plenty of time to get ahead without him knowing I've gone.

So for today, I just need to act normal, enjoy the spring day, and hope that I survive one last day so I can get away from here.

I can't find it in myself to be even a little sad. This town holds nothing but bad memories. From the screaming matches my parents used to have, the way my father would wield his anger like a sword that would mete out his own version of justice upon anyone that came his way, to me somehow falling for a man that is almost a carbon copy of him.

Not that you can tell from the outside, of course. My father, at least, never tried to hide that he was a monster, a drunk, the worst kind of human. No, he didn't care that people knew what he was, because in this small town, especially in the place I grew up, no one cared about the monsters. Trent though… he's supposed to be one of the good guys. He was supposed to be the hero in my story. The slightly older guy, the sophisticated, mature man who would help me work past my trauma. He knew my past and swore to protect me, to never hurt me. To keep me safe.

Somehow, I think that makes it worse.

The lies and manipulations to get me to a place where I couldn't see the monster that lived inside of him until he'd already woven enough of a story to ensure no one would believe me if I said anything. Part of that happened before me. Everyone sees him as this upstanding guy, the one who saves the day. They believe the story he's built of his life.

But behind closed doors… that's where the real Trent

lives.

I don't know how his work buddies don't see it. They've seen him drunk and I know how he runs his mouth when he's had a few too many, but they seem to just laugh it off. Like the nice guy couldn't possibly be that way. That it's just the liquor talking.

The drunken ramblings that are nothing more than just that.

I'd like to think they'd be horrified if they knew the truth, but a big part of me knows that even if they were presented with cold hard facts—like my dead body—he'd probably still be able to convince them that it wasn't him. Or at least that it wasn't his way.

Oh, the charm of a monster. The pretty words that are so easy to believe when they belong to a face like his. I can't even blame them. I fell for it and I was actively trying to find shelter from the other monsters in my life.

Out of the frying pan and into the fire.

I finish planting the bulbs that Trent demanded be done today in his fit of rage last night. It's taken me all day because my wrist is now very much sprained after his latest outburst. He apologized this morning, just like he always does, and I accepted it, just like I always do, because what else can I do? Tell him I don't forgive him? Yeah, all that's going to do is land me back in the hospital and I need to be able to move and function tomorrow.

I mean, my wrists and ribs are already wrapped up tight, I did that this morning after he left. The sheer amount of medical knowledge I've picked up the last few years... well, it's just kind of sad really.

But no more.

Not after today.

Tomorrow, I get to be free.

The front door slams, jolting me from my thoughts as terror holds me captive. He shouldn't be home yet. It's barely past lunch time.

"Quinn!" he roars. The sounds of him clattering through the house make me wince but I still can't make my body move. More doors slam and I finally manage to scramble to my feet, trying to brush the dirt from my clothes so as not to enrage him further.

"Where the fuck are you?" His shouting makes my pulse race. The downside of living on the outskirts of town, our neighbors are several miles out. No one can hear a thing. I used to think it was nice being away from all of the people in town... then I learned that this was just part of how he gets away with what he does.

"Why are you out here?" I jolt as the back door bounces off the wall from the force he pushed it with. I open my mouth to speak but nothing comes out. It wouldn't help me anyway. "Are you fucking mute now or just stupid?"

He stares down at me and I feel about two inches tall

because I still can't speak, and even if I could, he'd twist whatever I said anyway.

"I don't even fucking care. Where is dinner?"

He turns and storms back into the house and the thoughts rush through my head that he has to be on something because it's barely past lunch and he shouldn't be home yet, but then I realize this is just an excuse. A reason for him to turn his anger on me. To justify it to himself.

My entire body screams at me to run. Fast and far away. But he has the car keys. He has everything.

He has the power.

He roars my name again and I dart inside, against every single instinct I have.

I just have to survive today.

I'm so busy rushing inside to find him that I don't see the fist swinging my way. It's not until I'm on the ground, my face throbbing, that I realize what even happened. My cheek throbs, the screaming agony almost feels like it's broken.

"Why do you make me like this?" he asks, almost remorseful. But when I don't answer, because my whole face hurts, his anger explodes again. "WHY DO YOU MAKE ME LIKE THIS?"

I curl up on the ground to try and shield myself from the blows that rain down on me, trying to go to that place inside myself. Time passes so slowly, yet so fast, and I lose track of everything but the pain. When he's finished, I stay where I am while he goes upstairs to shower. Mentally, I try to take stock of the pain. I don't think anything's broken. At least I hope not. I can't run if things are broken.

It takes longer than I want to admit for me to be able to move and I bite down on my lip to stop the cry from falling from my mouth as I stand. Tears slip down my cheeks at every step. My pain meds are upstairs. If I can just get to them, I'll be okay.

Each movement up the stairs is agony and I get dizzy a few times from the pain.

This is the worst he's been in a while. I don't remember the last time I hurt this bad all over.

I reach the top step and a wave of dizziness washes over me again. I lose my hold on the railing as everything goes dark.

The beeping of machines is the next thing I hear and my eyes sting against the harsh light as I try to open them.

No, no, no.

The beeping gets faster as panic grips me. I can't be in a hospital. I was supposed to escape.

But I feel the cast on my wrist and the matching one on my leg and I know I'm not going anywhere.

I'm trapped.

Again.

"Oh, good. You're awake." Looking up, I see a nurse standing in the doorway of my room. I recognize her from school, she was a few years ahead of me—the downside of a small town. Everyone knows everyone.

"You gave us all quite a scare. That was some fall you took. You're going to be in here for a few days while we monitor your head, and then it'll be recovery at home. I'll let Trent know you're awake, he's been worried sick since he found you."

Yeah, I bet he has.

I open my mouth to speak but it's so dry I can barely move my tongue and my throat feels scratched up to hell.

"Let me get you some water," she says before disappearing and a tear of despair runs down my cheek.

Months.

It's going to be months until I'm healed, and that's only if he doesn't break me again. I saved for an entire year and now… it was for nothing.

I'm never going to be free of him. Not until I die.

I don't really remember how I got back to the apartment, I just know that I can't run in what I'm wearing. My brain is going haywire. This isn't how this happens. You'd think I'd be used to running by now, that I wouldn't panic, but

Trent hasn't found me yet.

He will though.

My face is online and there's no way he won't find it. I've been so freaking careful up to now and I was just really starting to like this new life.

Though three weeks isn't really enough for me to have gotten used to it, so at least giving it up shouldn't be too hard.

But then why does this feel so much harder than every time before?

It might be because I'd decided to reclaim parts of myself, because I actually started to make friends, because I realized just how much I've been missing... but even with all of that I can't stay.

If Trent finds me... no matter how much he wants his possession back, I know him. I know his anger and that will win out. It always does. He'll want to teach me a lesson and this time, well, he'll probably kill me. Likely by accident, but he'll still do it and not even blink.

Not until he realizes he has to clean up his mess anyway. Though he'd probably just blame me, say I attacked him or something. Fuck knows. He's a detective... I'm pretty sure he knows how to get away with murder.

I rip off my clothes and pull on a pair of jeans, a black tank, and a hoodie before dialing Tommy. He needs to know I'm compromised.

It only rings once before I hear his soothing voice down the line. "Calm, Q girl. I know what you're going to say, but you're safe. I've already dealt with it."

My knees about give out and I slide down the wall to the floor, a sob stuck in my chest. "How?" I ask, barely able to form the word.

"I have an alert set up for your face. The minute the videos were posted, my program ran and wiped it from the internet automatically. So they just need deleting at the source and you're good. Even if Trent had an alert set up, he wouldn't have gotten to the videos in time before the program erased them."

"Are you sure?"

Tears slip down my face and I can't quite work out if it's fear or relief. "I'm sure, Quinn. You know I wouldn't tell you you're safe unless I was one hundred percent sure. You're safe. Take a breath. Do you need me to come to you?"

I take a few deep breaths, tipping my head back to lean against the wall. "I can't keep doing this, Tommy."

My voice breaks as tears start falling even faster down my face. I haven't felt this broken since... well, ever.

"I've already told you, Quinn. You tell me you want him gone, my friends and I will make it happen." He's so cut and dry about it, but it makes my stomach twist. Trent has done unspeakable things to me, but I don't think I can say yes. Even now, when I'm terrified, sick to my stomach, and just so, *so* tired. I don't know that I could live with myself. Some people would think that's all I'd want. Him gone from this world. And maybe it's selfish to not say yes, because what if he's hurting someone else with me gone, but I just... I can't.

"You don't have to say anything now, Q girl, but know that the option is always on the table for you."

"Thank you, Tommy," I croak. "I don't know..." I trail off and he gives me a minute, because Tommy is the best and he always knows what I need. "I don't think I'd have survived this long without you. Thank you."

"You never have to thank me, Q girl. We all deserve a chance at happiness and freedom. Now take a deep breath. You're safe, he hasn't found you, and you're still free."

"I was ready to run. I ran out of work. Told them I wouldn't be back. Fuck, Tommy, I still can't stop my hands from shaking. I was on my way out the door when I called you."

"Oh, I have no doubt, but you'd probably be less safe on the run than you are where I have you now. So just promise me, next time you get the urge to run or you get scared, you either call me first or you get ahold of Meyer."

"Okay," I whisper, my throat still so thick I can barely speak.

"Promise me, Quinn."

He's so firm that I find myself promising. He's kept me safe until now and I have no reason to doubt him.

"And maybe, just maybe, open up to the girls you're obviously making friends with so they don't post your face online again."

I hiccup a laugh that's half a cry. "That feels a little too like getting comfortable, Tommy."

"You're safe," he repeats, like he's hoping it'll sink in soon. "You can get comfortable here and maybe, just maybe, letting people in will help keep you safe. Like it did with me."

I nod, despite the fact he can't see me. "I'll try."

"That's all I ask. I'll call Meyer and let him know you won't be back to work tonight, to call off the search that is undoubtedly happening since you ran. Just take a minute and collect yourself tonight, then tomorrow, we start again, okay?"

"Okay," I agree, letting out a shaky breath. "I can do that."

At least, I hope I can.

"Call me if you need anything, okay?"

"I will."

He ends the call and I stay sitting down, just taking a few minutes to breathe until there's a knock at my door. My heart races despite Tommy's reassurances. Even if Trent had seen the videos, he wouldn't be able to get here that quickly.

I don't think.

The knock sounds again, so I climb to my feet, tentatively walking to the door and checking the peephole. I let out a deep breath when I see Hot Guy, but I really don't relish the thought of seeing him right now.

Except he knocks again and I watch as he runs a hand through his blond hair. I take another deep breath, wipe the tears from my face, and open the door a little, just enough to look through, keeping it on the chain. "Hey."

"Oh, hey, sorry. Are you okay?" Concern crinkles his eyes at the edges as he frowns, taking in the God-awful sight of me.

"Fine, just a long night. Did you need something?"

He scratches at the back of his neck and hops from one foot to the other. "I was going to see if you wanted to grab some food."

"At two in the morning?" I ask, laughing.

"I mean, yes?"

"Bye, Hot Guy."

"What did you call me?" he asks with a chuckle.

"You heard," I respond as I shut the door.

"What about tomorrow?" he shouts through the door and I shake my head.

"Ask me tomorrow," I shout back, watching him through the peephole, seeing the smile spread across his face.

"I'm going to do that, Angel." He turns and heads down the hall, out of sight, and I laugh again.

That was weird, but definitely the distraction I needed right now.

I gather myself and glance around the apartment, relief flooding my veins that I don't have to leave yet. This is supposed to be a new start and I vowed to myself to make the most of it. That's exactly what I intend to do, but first, I guess Tommy is right.

I need to speak to the girls, at the very least Yen, and explain some things so this doesn't happen again. And maybe, just maybe, it'll help me start to move past what Trent did to me. It might just mean that I can actually start fresh.

At least, here's hoping.

After a crappy night's sleep, riddled with nightmares of Trent finding me, of waking to him standing above me, I quit attempting to rest at about nine in the morning and decided to head out. I need something to distract me from the monstrous reel playing on repeat in my head.

I make my way across town to the bagel truck, checking in on Tina while grabbing my new favorite breakfast. Once

I know she's okay and I've eaten, I pull up the group chat before I can change my mind.

Me:

So, lunch?

Yen:

I'm in. You okay? You disappeared last night.

Me:

I'm good, will explain.

Belle:

Count me in, I'm starving.

Sofia:

You're always starving, but yeah I'm down.

Tara:

Like I'm ever going to say no to food.

Amelia:

What she said.

Yen:

Dim Sum?

Me:

Hell yes. Love Dim Sum.

Tara:

Bonsai?

Yen:

Of course. I'll let them know we'll be there at two. That way I can head to the gym beforehand.

Me:

Send me a location?

Yen:

I'll swing by and grab you on the way.

Me:

Sounds good!

Amelia:

Meet you guys there! Going to go back to sleep!

I smile at my phone despite the churning in my stomach. At least I have a few hours to try and prepare myself for the conversation I'm about to have, but at the same time, I also have a few hours to stress out about it.

So much fun.

Taking a slow walk back toward the subway station, I stay alert, my senses still in hyperdrive after last night. Tommy told me I was safe, and he's never been wrong, but Trent... well he's always been ten steps ahead of me. Tommy might have completely changed up how we did things this time, but that doesn't mean Trent didn't see that coming. That he didn't have the same alerts set up that Tommy did.

I take a deep breath, trying not to panic.

Tommy said I was safe, and I have to believe him. He's watching Trent closer than usual, he said as much when he moved me here. Just an extra level of precaution since we were doing it his way.

Stepping onto the subway, I push out a breath, trying to rid myself of all the stress and panic. I'm not being followed, he doesn't know where I am, and once I let the girls in on a few things, they won't put my face on the internet again.

I hope.

By the time I make it back to the apartment, I've gotten in my daily steps already because I walked about four different diversion routes just in case. Apparently, I haven't quite gotten a handle on my paranoia just yet, which, considering my freakout was only last night, is understandable. I'm trying to give myself some grace about being more alert than normal, despite still chastising myself—both for being sloppy the other night and for how I'm acting now—but I still can't find it in me to regret the other night.

Even the questionable choice of going home with someone I don't know. If anything, that bit was more empowering than it was reckless... but that doesn't mean it wasn't still reckless. Trying to work out the line of what is going to keep me safe but also allow me to actually live is going to be a tightrope I walk for a while I think.

I grab a shower, look up Bonsai online, and decide that my jeans and hoodie won't work. So, true to nature, I blow out my hair, leave it straight and pull my jeans back on with a band T-shirt I picked up the other day and slide on a pair of Docs with a leather jacket.

Chic but casual.

I put a tiny amount of mascara on my lashes and decide I'm done. Checking my phone, I notice a message from Yen that she'd sent fifteen minutes ago telling me she'll be here in twenty, so I run around grabbing my phone, purse, and keys before hauling ass out of the apartment and down to the lobby.

Panting, I suck in a breath.

Jeez, I really need to start working out again. Which reminds me, again, that I need to look into a self-defense class. I swear, one day I'll have my ducks in a row, but apparently, today my ducks are squirrels and they're rioting.

As I step out of the door that Eric opens for me, a car pulls up to the sidewalk and I see Yen sitting inside. She waves and I walk quickly to the car, sliding inside and pulling on my seatbelt as we move into traffic.

"So… last night?" she asks the second I'm settled, and I blow out a breath.

"Quick version? I'm hiding from someone and Sofie put my face online when she uploaded videos from the other night. The person I'm running from has the means to find me if I'm not super careful and I panicked. My guardian angel reassured me that he'd had the videos taken down, that I just needed to get her to delete them, and that the person searching for me didn't get a chance to see them. He's friends with Meyer and that's how I ended up here, kind of living in their version of witsec I guess. Long version… well, that I'll explain to everyone at lunch so I don't have to keep reliving it out loud."

She watches me closely for a beat then nods. "Understood. No more putting Quinn online. Do you need help? You can move to my place for a few weeks if you need to lay low."

A warm fuzzy feeling I'm not used to fills my chest and I shake my head. "Thank you. I appreciate it, but no. Apparently, my building is safer than Fort Knox when it comes to finding me, so I'm going to stay there."

"You want me to come stay with you for a bit? Extra bodies and all that?"

I open my mouth to tell her no, but close it again. That isn't the worst idea and I'm fairly certain I can trust Yen. She works for Meyer, who obviously trusts her, and Tommy trusts *him* with my life, and with his own, so I have to believe that she's worth the trust I already feel toward her.

"You don't have to answer me now. Let's do lunch, think on it, and we'll talk later. I'm not exactly attached to my place, so I don't mind ditching it for a few weeks if it will make you feel better."

"Thanks, Yen." She smiles at me and squeezes my hand, holding it in silence the rest of the drive, offering me a comfort I haven't allowed myself outside of Tommy for longer than I care to remember.

We arrive at Bonsai and I let out a whistle. It looked fancy online, but in person... it's a whole other experience. "I guess you west coast guys really like to show up right, huh?"

She lets out a laugh as we climb from the car. "Thanks, O'Connor," she calls out as she closes the door, and for a second, something tickles at the back of my brain, but she links arms with me and pulls me into Bonsai, pushing the wisp of a thought from my mind. "This place was created for influencers. They hate 'our type' in here, but they also know I work for Meyer, so they wouldn't dream of refusing me entry."

"So, what exactly does Meyer do? Beyond owning a few clubs, having issues with people who are storming some of them, and being able to invoke enough fear to stop people being rude to you?" My curiosity is beyond piqued and, while that definitely got the cat killed, I can't stop myself from wondering. Especially with her having told me that he saved her... and that he's helping to save me too.

"A lot of people are scared of Meyer. It's not that he's a bad guy, far from it, but he's willing to do bad things to prove a point. He has fingers in a lot of pies, most of them aren't exactly legal, but he's that guy that won't sacrifice you to save the world. He'd burn the world to save you, ya know?"

"No, I have no idea what you're talking about," I say with a laugh, and she giggles back.

"I guess I'm saying I can't really tell you what he does, but what I *can* say is that if you're under his protection like you say, nothing and no one will touch you without severe repercussions."

I nod, feeling a little better, but while she might know Meyer, I know Trent. Consequences aren't really something he worries about because of who he is. I guess he and Meyer might just have that in common. "Got it."

She walks straight past the girl at the maître d' stand and heads to the back of the restaurant where the girls are already sitting, but my attention is pulled from the girls to the decor. This place is *insane.* There is a freaking cherry blossom tree in the middle of the restaurant, stretching up to the ceiling and spanning so wide at the top, it literally blows my mind. The trunk is rooted in a garden of sorts, surrounded by a legit pond in the middle of the room. Koi swim around in the clear water, topped with water lilies and other plants I don't recognize.

"Yeah, they took the whole Asian theme to the extreme, but it's pretty," Yen murmurs to me as we move through the space, obviously noticing my awe at the decor. "It could be seen as offensive if I really wanted to get my panties in a wad, but the food is good and the chef is a friend—"

"Of course he is," I joke, because Yen seems to have friends everywhere.

"What can I say? I'm a people person." She giggles at herself and I laugh, shaking my head. "But yeah, he's a friend, and like I said, the food is really good. Despite some of the staff being jerks, it's still a good place to eat. Plus, we have a table reserved here, like twenty-four-seven thanks to Meyer, so we can always get a seat."

We reach the table and she beelines straight for Sofie, holding out her hand. "Phone."

I blink in horror, watching this play out, totally not how I expected it to go. Except Sofie hands over her phone without question and Yen taps away on her screen before looking over at me and nodding. "All gone."

"Huh?" Sofie asks.

"Videos of Quinn. And if anyone else has any, delete them right the fuck now," Yen demands as she moves to one of the empty seats and motions for me to sit beside her.

"Does someone want to explain?" Tara asks as she pulls her phone from her pocket.

I take a deep breath and start to explain the absolute chaos that is my life. I tell them some about Trent, who he is, what he does, skirting around the more horrific stuff, but tell them enough so they know he's a bad guy. After explaining about the videos being online, the fact that I nearly had to run for my life, again, and a brief explanation of the last few years of my life, there is a mix of horror, pity and understanding reflected back at me from them.

"That explains why my account was restricted," Sofie mumbles, and Yen shoots a glare at her.

"Seriously?"

"I'm not complaining, I was just confused is all. I'm sorry I put you in danger, Quinn. I just, well, I didn't know. I always upload to my socials, it's part of, well, life." She shrugs, and while a part of me wants to bite back that that isn't everyone's life, I hold my tongue. She's young, she obviously hasn't lived a damaged life, and I can't hold that against her.

"I'm really sorry you lived through that," Belle says, smiling sadly at me, and for a second, I think I see some of my own pain in her eyes. God, I hope not. "We'll do whatever we can to help, and no more videos."

"Thank you," I respond as the others all agree with her.

Yen clears her throat, drawing the attention from me, and I swear I could kiss her for it. She waves down the server who has been purposefully avoiding our table. "Now, enough of the downer stuff, let's eat!"

ELEVEN

FIVE MONTHS LATER

To say these last few months have been a rollercoaster might just be the understatement of my life. I've finally managed to settle myself, despite some of the insanity that's happened at work—including a group of guys storming the place with guns. Yeah, not going to lie, totally nearly ran then, but Tommy talked me down and Yen reassured me that Meyer wouldn't allow it to happen again.

I've barely seen the illustrious Meyer since that day he spoke to us all when I first started at HellScape, and the other two Yen told me about... well, I haven't seen them at all.

But life has finally settled into a routine. Tommy has been tracking Trent and he seems to think he's given up searching for me, and I've been able to actually, well, *live*.

Yen and the girls have been my saving grace here. They keep me busy when the world gets too much or the fear starts to creep in. Hell, Yen even moved in after the whole internet scare thing. She swears she's leaving any day now but I've almost gotten used to having her around. After I got over the whole her being in more danger by being close to me thing—which she pointed out was ridiculous, considering her history and the fact that my building is likely more secure than a military base since it turns out Meyer owns the building—we just kind of accidentally became actual friends.

It's a strange thing to think about, the fact that I have actual friends now. It's not something I've ever had before Trent, or allowed myself to have since I started running.

Somehow, it doesn't even really feel like I'm running anymore. Yet that little voice in the back of my mind likes to chirp up that Trent would always let me fall into a false sense of security before he told me he knew where I was. And he always knew when I moved too.

I'm just trying to convince myself that this time is different. That he won't find me. That I let Tommy do this move his way and that's why it's different.

Because it *has* to be different.

The only thing I've been slightly sad about is that Hot Guy seems to have disappeared off the face of the earth once Yen moved in. He never claimed that rain check after my night of panic and his two a.m. check in, but I'm trying not to focus on the random guy who let me experience what was the best sex of my life.

Not that the bar was exactly high, but still.

I haven't let myself get close enough to anyone else since that to fall into fuckery again, and a part of me almost doesn't want to ruin that experience.

Though, it's not exactly like I've had to beat the guys off with a stick. If I'm not at work, I'm with the girls, and any guy who has made a move… well, they seem to disappear mid conversation. It's weird, but well, I guess that's city life.

I'm adapting. It's taken a minute and I'm positive Harper still hates me, though she did fire Jessica on like, my fourth week after she basically assaulted me at work, so maybe hate is too strong of a word, but still… the other girls who were kind of assholes with Jessica have backed off since she left. Like the head mean girl was gone and they lost their *oomph*.

Definitely not complaining.

About anything, really. Other than the fact that fall isn't really fall here. I miss the array of colors that come with fall back home, but I can deal with missing the colors of a season changing when, for the first time in forever, I'm actually experiencing life.

"Please tell me there is coffee." Yen stumbles into the

kitchen where I'm scrolling through the news, sipping on a mug of the dark wonder she's in search of. "Thank you, sweet baby Jesus, for gracing us with the dark bean of life."

I giggle as she pours herself a mug and drops onto the chair beside me at the kitchen table. "Big night?"

She groans and drops her head onto her arms on the table. "Tara started everyone on Jäger. I really need to stop trying to keep up with the pretty, young things."

I roll my eyes at her dramatics. "Yen, you *are* one of the pretty, young things. Tara is what, three years younger than you?"

"Don't you start with me. You can't keep up either."

"Yeah, but I'm nearly thirty and I stopped trying to keep up with them like two months ago when I realized I'm too old for that shit."

"You're not that much older than me. How come you get to play the old, decrepit card?"

"Because I'm older than you and that's how it will always be." I stick my tongue out at her and she groans again.

"You're such a brat. Please tell me there's food."

"No, I need to do a grocery run. We have like, a stick of cheese and maybe a frozen burrito. We hardly eat here so it almost seems pointless buying that much."

She takes a sip of her coffee, letting out a happy squeak as she does. "Truth. I guess we could go get bagels and check in on Tina. Make sure she's okay."

I've been going back to see Tina and eat at the truck at least twice a week since I got here. Last week she had a black eye and I wanted to commit murder—because obviously I can stand up for people who aren't me, duh— but she begged me not to do anything and swore that she'd be okay. I hated walking away and doing nothing, and I didn't bother reporting it because experience tells me that's pointless, but I also know too well how you can't help someone if they don't want to be helped.

"Yeah, that sounds good to me." I take another sip of my coffee, very much enjoying the fancy-pants coffee machine Yen brought with her and the fancy-ass coffee beans she has delivered for it. I still don't know where she gets the money for everything, especially considering her past. I know that she does extra work for Meyer, but she hasn't divulged and, well, I'm hardly one to pry. Especially since it's probably illegal from what she's said of Meyer's other businesses and I kind of just don't want to know. "I'm going to jump in the shower then we can head out."

"Sounds good. I also need to shower to wash last night off me."

I laugh at her and shake my head. "I don't even want to know."

She winks at me, laughing softly. "You know you do. Your poor, dried up vajay needs some form of fulfillment, and if that means living vicariously through me…"

I plug my fingers in my ears as I stand. "La, la, la, I can't hear youuuuuu."

I hear her cackle despite my fingers in my ears and remove them as I dash into my room. Today is going to be a good day. I can just feel it.

"Shit!" I spin as Harper curses loud enough that I hear her over the music in here. Tonight is insanely busy. It's a Thursday, which is usually our quietest night, but it's the start of the new semester at the college nearby and apparently, that's causing chaos tonight.

"Everything okay?" I ask after sorting my order and I notice her looking down at her phone. She taps furiously on the screen and, for a second, I don't think she heard me because she doesn't acknowledge me, so I move down the bar and take my next order.

Twelve freaking skittle bombs. Joyous.

Once they're poured and I take payment, side-eyeing the kid with the babyface who tries to hit on me, I walk back near Harper to grab a mouthful of water from the bottle I keep at the far end of the bar.

"Can you close up tonight?" Harper asks, and I look over my shoulder, thinking she's got to be speaking to anyone but me, except there's no one else there. "Quinn!"

I jump a little at her shout but shake it off. "I mean, I've never done it here before, but sure. It can't be that different than what I'm used to."

"Just close out the registers and make sure everything is wiped down and restocked for tomorrow. The others will help, then I just need you to set the alarms and lock up. Bobby will stay with you till everything's closed up."

I nod, taking it all in. Bobby is a gentle giant that works security during my shift. Well, I say a gentle giant... he's gentle with us. I've seen him literally lift a grown man from his feet and throw him, so maybe not so gentle, but he's always been kind to me. "Yeah, okay. I can do that. I just need the alarm details."

"I'll text them to you. Delete it once you're done for fuck sake, so I maybe don't lose my job."

"Understood," I say with a nod. I'm still not convinced Harper doesn't hate me, but she's this brash and blunt with everyone from what I've seen, so maybe it's just Harper being Harper.

My phone buzzes in my pocket and I grab it, letting her know I got the info.

"I've got to leave, if anything goes wrong, grab Yen from downstairs or Ellie from the back. They're running those areas tonight. If all else fails, grab Bobby or try for Meyer, Hunter, or Rory. I think they're still upstairs." She hands me a set of keys and I pocket them along with my phone.

"Got it." I'm really hoping that nothing goes wrong because well, I really don't want to be the one in charge if shit hits the fan. Call me a coward, but Harper's wrath isn't something I cherish the thought of.

The rest of the night runs pretty smoothly, other than a few of the staff getting their nose bent out of shape that I'm the one with the keys. I don't get it either, since I'm definitely still the new girl here, but I wasn't about to tell Harper no. Not that I say that when people get weird with me. I just suck it up and keep working, telling them it's probably because I'm one of the oldest working here.

The crowd just gets more insane, to the point security starts throwing people out, and once closing time hits, I am *wiped*. I end up working harder during closing, like I somehow have to prove myself to the others as to why Harper gave me the keys instead of them. Which is ridiculous, it's probably just because I was the closest person to her when she needed to go.

Doesn't mean I don't still try to overly prove myself, because well, hello, perfectionism and thank you, trauma for the gifts that just keep giving.

"You good doing the last bits? I have a date with Luca," Yen asks as she checks her reflection in her handheld mirror.

"Date," I scoff, jokingly. "Y'all don't date."

She grins at me and winks. "No, we fuck, which is much better. Who needs a date when you can get fucked so good that all thoughts disappear? Magical dick like that is as rare as a unicorn, my friend."

I bark out a laugh, mostly at Yen, but a little at the flush creeping up Bobby's neck. You'd think working here he'd be used to it.

"Yeah, go. Bobby will watch my back while I lock up and I'll order an Uber to get home."

She chews on her lip like she's second guessing herself. "You sure?"

"Go ride on wonder dick. I'll be fine."

Laughing, she gives me a one-armed hug before pulling on her jacket. "Okay, don't wait up. I'll see you in the morning."

"I'd say don't do anything I wouldn't—"

"But I'm not a nun," she deadpans and I laugh again.

"Something like that."

"Laters, sweet cheeks." She finger waves as she heads down the hall out of HellScape, leaving me with Bobby.

"I'm nearly done," I reassure him, and he nods, moving toward the main door. I do a last check for stock, make sure I've closed out all of the registers, and grab my stuff. Letting out a deep breath, I pull my phone from my pocket and glance over the alarm instructions again, because the last thing I want is to set it off and cause bigger problems.

One last glance around and it occurs to me that I should probably check the offices upstairs to make sure everyone is gone but somehow, that feels remotely terrifying.

Time to pull up your big girl pants, Quinn.

Letting out a deep breath, I make my way up the stairs at the back of the room toward the offices.

"Hello?" I call out down the hall, no sound but my voice echoing off the walls comes back, so I suck it up and knock on each of the doors.

The last one at the end of the hall makes me hesitate. It's Meyer's office. That much I know just from the layout. I don't know why he makes me so nervous, I've met him all of once, but maybe it's that I know just how much I likely owe him via Tommy. Or it could be all the things I've heard from Yen, which admittedly isn't much, but a man that strikes fear into the hearts of people throughout the city, who has the ability to hide me, and all of the other things about him, are probably cause enough for my racing heart.

"Come in," sounds through the door and I chastise myself for a minute before twisting the handle and opening it. Meyer looks up at me, those amber eyes of his holding me captive for a second.

Looking at him, it's easy to see how someone could mistake him for just a businessman. The suit, the hair, the sharp jawline. He screams power and money. But it's also easy to see the darkness behind his almost-glowing eyes—well, to me anyway. Like finds like.

His sleeves are rolled up his forearms, showing off the ink that paints them, and I find myself mesmerized by the art. It's beautiful and totally not something I would've thought he'd have.

Not that I've thought about him much, but still.

"What can I do for you, Quinn?" His voice washes over me like a hand stroking down my spine, and I'm struck stupid for a second as my brain stutters.

"Hi, erm, sorry." I trip over my words, trying to remember why I knocked on his door. "I'm just locking up for Harper and I wanted to make sure the building was empty so I could set the alarm."

"Of course, I hadn't realized the time. Give me a moment and I'll be out of your hair."

I blink in shock. Did he just basically apologize for still being here? "Okay, no problem."

He closes the files on his desk and shuts down his computer before standing and grabbing his jacket. "Are you settling in okay?"

"I, erm, yes. Thank you. For everything. I know that Tommy said you've helped a lot with everything for me. I probably should have said something already—"

"Quinn," he interrupts with a smile on his face as he

stares down at me. "Take a breath. It's fine. You do not have to thank me."

"Sorry." I say, looking down at my feet. "But still, thank you."

"You're welcome," he says, laughing softly as he locks the door to his office. We're heading down the hall, me just a step in front of him, when he pauses. "I'll head out the back way. It's a fire door, so it'll automatically lock."

"Okay, have a good night."

"You too, Quinn." He squeezes my arm and I swear it's like being struck by lightning. He walks away like he didn't notice a thing and the fire door closes with a loud bang, bringing me out of my stupor.

Well, shit.

What the hell was that?

I shake it off and head back down to Bobby. "Looks like we're all clear. You ready to go?"

"I've been ready to go home for hours," he jokes.

After setting the alarm, I wait a moment for the exit chimes to begin then haul ass after Bobby outside. Locking the door and checking it twice, I finally pocket the keys and feel a bit lighter. Who would've thought that locking up a nightclub would be the responsibility that felt too big?

"You want me to wait with you while you get your Uber?" Bobby asks, and while a small part of me wants to say yes, I've done a lot of work these last few months on trying to live my life rather than being fearful at every step. I've been taking a mix of self-defense lessons, I carry pepper spray, hell, I even started therapy to try and help me start processing through all of the things. But living the way I have for as long as I have, it's going to take time to get out of certain habits.

"It's fine, you get home. I know you're as tired as I am."

He smiles but still looks a little unsure, so I order my Uber and show him it's only three minutes away. "See? I'll be fine."

"Okay, Quinn. Have a good night. See you tomorrow." He walks over to his car and waves as he drives away.

I check my phone again and my car has been changed. It's now seven minutes away.

Awesome.

Still, it's only seven minutes. I contemplate walking home, but that's a long ass walk after a night of being on my feet. Plus, then I'm outside alone for way longer than seven minutes. And there are cameras here.

I'm fine.

I'm *totally* fine.

The sound of a trash can spilling over in the distance spooks me and I let out a squeal before heading back to the door and hiding in the alcove of it. I can see thanks to the street lights, but I'm fairly certain no one can see me here in the darkness.

I can't help but feel a little stupid. It was probably just a cat or something. Being afraid of everything is exhausting. Tommy keeps telling me he can 'fix' the Trent situation so I don't have to be afraid anymore, but well… I still can't say yes. Even after everything he's done to me, I don't know that I could live with that stain on my soul.

Headlights flash down the road and relief floods me. I check my app, but realize that it's not my Uber.

Who the hell else is going to be out here at this time of night?

The car slows as it drives by the club and, as it passes beneath a street lamp, my breath catches in my chest.

He found me.

TWELVE

RORY

Watching her as she hauls ass across the lot at the sound of trash cans being knocked over is almost cute and I feel the corners of my lips tilt up. It used to be so infrequent that I'd smile, but since she arrived, since I've been tracking her, I've smiled more than I think I have my whole life. Like when she almost caught me when she was at the bagel truck. I smiled because she's obviously smart as hell. Not that I'm going to admit the smiling to anyone. Or smile unless I'm alone.

Absolutely not.

People would just make fun of me if they saw me smile. I don't smile.

The tracker I've installed on her phone flashes on my screen so, even if I couldn't see her, I'd know she was there.

Failing that, there's the tracker I slipped into her bag, the one I put in the sole of her favorite shoes, the one in her watch, and let's not forget the one in her jacket.

The second I get a chance, one is going under her skin. That one couldn't be left behind. But despite Hunter and me insisting, Meyer made us hold off.

The last few months have been tense. Business has gotten hot in way too many areas, so watching her this way is all I've been able to do. But at least I get this. Hunter has been a pissy little bitch about the fact that he's been away sorting out supply line issues the last few months.

The downside of being a diplomatic people person, I guess.

Bully for him.

The upside of being the guy who does the wet work means I'm never far from home. Also means that, despite Meyer putting other people on Quinn duty, I'm always watching her too.

Even if not directly, I have the trackers. So if anything happens to her… well, I'll be the first through the door and whoever is trying to hurt her will regret what little life they have left. I'm more of an ask-questions-later-if-they're-still-alive kind of guy.

A car approaches, slowing as it passes HellScape, and I make a note of the plate. I don't recognize the person behind the wheel, but that doesn't mean anything. It's dark and I'm far enough away that I probably wouldn't recognize Meyer and I've known *that* asshole my entire life.

It pulls away and her Uber arrives a minute later. She steps out of the shadows, tears running down her face, and everything else fades away.

Who or what the fuck made her cry?

She runs to the car, darting inside so quickly I barely process it through my rage as the car starts pulling away.

I rush to my car and take off after her. Seeing her cry does not sit well with me, but until I know what happened, I won't sound the alarm.

Except... if it was that car...

Nope, I need to check the cameras at the front of the club first. Or speak to her. Though, explaining *how* I saw her crying might just be an overstep when she's never even met me before.

Semantics.

I catch up to her car but stay far enough behind that if she's spooked she won't see me. It's not hard to realize that she's hyper aware of her surroundings most of the time, even when I know as little about her as I do.

I know about the shitty ex, the fact that she's been on the run, and that she's hiding. Her medical file we managed to get was enough to make my blood boil, so I stopped reading after barely more than a cursory glance.

Beyond that, I don't know much about her.

Except that she loves breakfast at the bagel truck on the other side of town and that when she thinks no one is watching she'll sing and dance while she walks down the street. I know that every time she sees a puppy, she's completely besotted and I can see it on her face that if she thought she could have the life where she could have a dog, she'd have an entire pack.

And the part of me I didn't realize existed before, wants to give her that.

Except Tommy said she doesn't want the ex dead. Personally, *that* I don't understand, but I've always had a higher-than-normal bloodlust. It's what makes me so good at what I do.

We reach her building and I watch her run past Eric into the building, tears still streaming down her face. The second she's in the elevator, I abandon the car and walk straight to the welcome desk.

"Did she say anything?" I ask, more than a little brash, but Eric is used to me by now. At least, he should be.

"Not a word, sir. Would you like me to check in on her?"

"Give her twenty minutes, then yes. Let me know immediately. Do *not* let her leave. Lock the doors if you need to. Do you understand?"

He looks at me with wide eyes, gulping, but he nods.

"Yes, sir. Of course."

Asking him to hold someone hostage is kind of outside the scope of his actual job, but he signed up for whatever it takes. Every person that works in this building did. We rarely ask it of them, beyond keeping their mouths shut tighter than a nun's legs, and they're paid well.

Plus, they don't have to deal with me if they stick to their end of their deal.

However, if they open their mouths, I get to have the best kind of day with them as my entertainment.

Rules are rules. Without them, we're little more than animals…

And I'm a bigger, faster, meaner animal than most.

I nod at him before turning and leaving, going back to my car. The only thing I can think of is that car, so I need to check the cameras.

And I probably need to call Meyer.

Fuck.

It's been two days since I followed her back to her apartment. She's called in sick to the club both days, much to Harper's annoyance, but Harper needs to dislodge the stick up her ass. She's been in love with Meyer for way too long and the longer nothing happens, the firmer the stick gets.

Thankfully, I haven't been there much. I've been bouncing between the apartment building she's holed up in and the strip club that was held up a few months ago. Meyer seems to think me being here more often will make the Demons think twice about trying to fuck with our shit again. Personally, I think the scummy bikers don't care if I'm here or not if there's pussy, drugs, and guns here. They're organized enough, but they just try to take what they want rather than cultivate it, even if it fucks with their numbers.

The joys of dealing with a stupid fucking MC on the outskirts of our territory.

Me being here has at least made Elise feel a little better—running this place has her more stressed lately than I've ever seen her—even if Bruno's nose keeps getting bent out of shape. Though if he makes one more comment, I'll break his nose and show him what it really means to get it bent out of shape.

"Oh hey, hottie," is purred into my ear as hands run over my shoulder and down my chest. Once upon a time, I'd have used the girls in here as much as they enjoy being used by me in the hopes of having their position elevated, but since Quinn arrived, their touch makes my skin crawl.

"Unless you want to lose your hands, I suggest that you remove them from me."

The girl squeaks and her hands disappear before she practically runs across the bar.

My thoughts go back to Quinn, hiding away. We heard from Tommy, she's convinced the car that passed the club was her ex and the images on the camera weren't clear enough to disprove her theory so, until we know for certain, we're letting her hide out.

The only person that's seen her is Yen, who has been keeping us updated on how she's doing. Which is terrible and I want to just take this guy's head from his body and free her from the grip he still has on her.

Except Meyer told me to be patient and abide by her wishes, which is proving harder than I'd have ever imagined. All I want to do is fix this, in the most brutal way possible, so that she doesn't have to be afraid or hide or run anymore.

But I can't. So instead, I made Tommy send me everything he had from the deep dive he did on the ex.

Trent fucking Barker.

Detective. All around do-gooder and absolute fucking tyrant.

Even a psychopath like me can see he's the worst kind of monster… and I include myself in that grouping. I might be prone to violence without an inkling of remorse, but I have lines. Women and kids are the line. Unless the women are really fucking deserving, but it's still harder. I actually feel something then.

Which isn't exactly a common occurrence.

Me and feelings… we're distant cousins on the best of days.

"You need anything, Boss?"

Being called boss still wigs me out, despite being Meyer's left hand for… however long it's been since he rose up and took his place. I smile at the bloody memory.

"Rory?"

Elise's voice pulls me from my daydreaming and back to the dingy strip club. "Whiskey."

She nods and sashays over to the bar, leaving me in my darkened corner as I look out over the club. It's one of our better earners, and is mostly above board with our income stream, which is exactly why we keep the dirty shit here sometimes. Like the barman who doubles as a dealer and the guns stored in the secure room in the basement.

Everything has layers and this place is no different, but I'm starting to hate it here.

Hunter had his time with Quinn, Meyer gets to stalk and watch her whenever she's at work, but, despite us already deciding that she's going to be ours, I've had no time with her beyond following her.

And that doesn't count.

My phone buzzes in my pocket and I sigh as I pull it out and tap on the screen.

Meyer:

It wasn't him. Tommy said he's been in Summerville the entire time, which confirms what our guys said. Have they been dealt with for dropping the ball?

I scrub a hand down my face before typing back. The guys I had watching Trent lost track of him for eighteen hours. Plenty of time for him to fly here, find her, and get home. My rage was at boiling point, but they're still on him so I haven't dealt with them yet.

Me:

Not yet, when Jean and Luca get here to take over and they're home, I'll handle it. For now, they're terrified and on their best behavior.

Meyer:

As long as it's handled, I don't care. Tommy is going to call her, so she should be back tomorrow. I'm going to need you here tomorrow. Dario wants a meeting.

Fucking Dario DeMato. The leader of the Demons and all round scum. We've been attempting a tentative peace with the Demons for years, but after their attack a few weeks ago, that peace is over.

I've seen to that.

I've never had so much fun with explosives and small, planned attacks as I have the last few weeks. I guess he's tired of losing people and money.

Me:

I'll be there, just tell me when.

Meyer:

You swinging by here tonight? Got some things to discuss about the basement.

Me:

I'll head over now.

I pocket my phone just as Elise arrives back with my whiskey. I chug back the double and slam the glass down on the table. "Tell Bruno to be on alert. I'm heading out for the night."

She pouts at me, fluttering her lashes, and I roll my eyes.

Fucking women.

"You really leaving us defenseless?"

I quirk a brow at her as I stand, towering over her small frame. "Elise, you have more firepower here now than some small countries. Defenseless isn't something I'd call you."

She pouts again and goes to put a hand on my chest but thinks better of it before making contact. "Fine."

"Know your place, Elise. I won't tell you again."

Her eyes go wide as she stares up at me, but she nods and takes a step back. Thank fuck for that. I'm so over dealing with her bullshit.

Climbing into my car, I check the trackers on Quinn. She's still at home and, lucky for me, her apartment is on the way to HellScape. I smile to myself at the thought.

Guess I'll check in on her on the way. Seems only right… and definitely not just me wanting to try and catch a glimpse of her.

I might be a monster, but I'm going to be *her* monster, whether she likes it or not.

THIRTEEN

QUINN

Day three of hiding from the world. Of calling Tommy every few hours for an update. Of persuading Yen that I'm too sick and contagious for her to come home. I hate what Trent has been able to do to me yet again.

Tommy has been telling me he doesn't think it's him the last two days, but I don't know if I can believe that. I saw him with my own eyes. But I also know my paranoia has made me see him before when he wasn't really there. My therapist says it's a trauma response, that until I face him or deal with the trauma I have from him, it's likely I'll continue to see him.

But until I know, without a shadow of a doubt, that he hasn't found me, I'm hiding in this fortress of an apartment building.

Usually, I'd be gone already, but there were no flowers

and no note. It's the only thing that has me questioning if it was or wasn't him.

He always sends flowers.

I'm clinging to that right now as I hole up in my bedroom, only leaving to scavenge for snacks. Eating hasn't exactly been on the forefront of my mind the last few days, but the gurgling of my stomach wins occasionally.

My phone rings, making me jump, and I almost throw it in the air in shock. I've kept the apartment silent since I started hiding, just in case someone was outside, so I could hear them.

"Hello?" I say as I answer Tommy's call.

"It wasn't him, Q girl. My people confirmed. He's been in Summerville this entire time. He's working a case and stayed at the station for about forty-eight hours. There's camera footage of him there at the time you thought you saw him."

"It really wasn't him?" My voice is so small and I flash back to the Quinn of many years ago, who believed Trent loved me. That I made him mad. That it really was all my fault.

I'm not her anymore, but if I keep running like this, I don't know that I'll ever not have a part of her with me.

I just don't know how to face him and come out the other side alive and whole. Because even if I survive the encounter physically, I know it's going to break me in other ways. Facing him, what he did to me, knowing he won't take any responsibility for anything he did… it almost seems pointless.

But I don't see another way around not living in fear anymore and I'm tired.

So freaking tired.

I don't know if I *can* run anymore. Nearly three years doesn't sound that long, but the constant moving, looking over my shoulder, having zero connections… I don't *want* to live like that anymore.

For a moment, I consider taking Tommy up on his offer to deal with Trent, but he speaks and pulls me from my thoughts. "It really wasn't him. You're safe, Quinn."

"Am I though?" I whisper. "Will I ever really be safe with him out there, chasing me like I'm his favorite kind of prey?"

"Quinn…" He trails off and I can hear the pity in his voice and it tears through me. "What do you want to do? We can stop hiding you, we can deal with him, or I can come with you to face him once and for all if that's what you want. You tell me what you want to do, sweet girl, and I'll make it happen. And I won't judge whichever option you pick."

My heart swells because Tommy is the only person in my life who has never let me down. He's made me feel safe the entire time I've been with him, and if he wasn't old enough to be my dad, maybe I'd just actually hide *with* him.

I smile at the errant thought. Just no.

"I don't know," I tell him and I can almost see the sad smile I know will be on his face. God knows I've seen it plenty. "But I'm going to make a choice, because I can't keep doing this."

"Okay, Q girl. You just let me know and you know I'm here for you. Always."

"Thank you, Tommy. For everything."

"You don't need to thank me, Quinn. Ever." He ends the call and I go down a rabbit hole in my head. His words remind me of what Meyer said to me the other night and it makes me question societal standards. Because Trent is considered the best type of human. He's a detective, a pillar of his community, and people look up to him while Meyer is supposedly a criminal. With everything Tommy does, I guess *he* is too, yet they've done more good than Trent has ever done. At least from what I can tell.

It's a little mind-blowing to think of it, and yes I'm aware this is me distracting myself from thinking about what to do about Trent, but while I know I have to make a decision now, I still don't feel ready.

What I should probably do though, is shower, eat, speak to Yen, and actually try to go into work tonight. It's a Sunday, so it should be a quiet night, but still… I should make the effort after calling in sick for two days.

Though I feel awkward as hell because Meyer probably knows why I've been hiding since I was talking to Tommy, and I don't know if he'll have told Harper the truth or not.

Yep, so gross to think about.

It's almost enough to make me want to continue hiding, but I've survived far worse than a few awkward moments, so I shake off the gross and start pulling myself together.

After what feels like a life-changing shower and a slice of toast that barely put a dent in the pit of hunger that has emerged since my shower, I feel almost human again. The fear that Tommy might've been wrong still swirls in the pit of my stomach, but he said there was camera footage of Trent when I thought I saw him.

Though if it wasn't Trent, it does make me wonder who the hell it was.

That's not a problem for me though. If it wasn't Trent, whoever it was, was likely looking at the club itself, or just slowing to check their phone or something.

At least that's what I'm going to tell myself anyway.

I grab my phone and drop Yen a text asking if she wants to grab food since I'm 'feeling better'. I'll tell her the truth when I see her, but I knew if she'd known the truth all along, she'd have wanted to be here with me, and I couldn't put her in danger like that if Trent did know where I was.

My phone pings and I laugh when I see her response.

Yen:

Thank fuck that is over. Yes, let me come back, shower, change and then food. We need to catch up. You missed a ton at work this week. I have ALL THE TEA.

Me:

Well then hurry up. I need the tea as much as I need food.

Yen:

On my way!

Now that I know we're heading out, I open the curtains and check the weather before getting dressed. Putting on a cozy sweater with jeans and my Chucks, I pull a beanie over my head to hide my very messy locks and just as I finish, Yen walks through the door.

"You don't look like you were sick." She quirks a brow at me as the door closes behind her, cocking her hip to one side with her hand on it.

"Go get ready, then we'll talk. I'm starving."

She rolls her eyes at me, then sighs exaggeratedly. "Fineeeeeee. Give me ten, I just need to change. I'll shower before work."

I try not to fidget while I wait for her to get ready, but

fail epically. By the time she shows her face again, I'm pacing the kitchen. She looks at me like I've lost my mind, but well, I'm pretty sure I lost it long ago… if I even had it.

"You ready?"

Nodding, I grab my keys, phone, and purse, making sure I have everything I might need. I feel as jumpy as a puppy on the Fourth of July. Telling myself I just need food, we head down to the lobby where we wait for the Uber she's ordered us. Once we're in the car and moving, she looks at me, arms folded, and I gulp.

She has this no-nonsense look on her face and nervousness floods me, regardless of how silly that is, as I squirm in my chair under her gaze. "Now, spill it."

We're finishing locking up HellScape—Harper said I owed her—and Yen is still giving me shit about pretending to be sick. "I could have helped you. You really need to learn to trust people. I get that it's hard, because well, trauma, but I'm not him. Hell, I moved in after you told me about him, and I know you said you did it so I didn't get hurt, but damn, I can shoot. Really fucking well. If he'd have broken in, I could've solved all your problems."

I bark out a laugh and shake my head. "Everybody is so quick to just kill him and end my problem."

"I don't get why you're not that quick to make that decision, all things considered. The men that hurt me? Yeah, I had exactly zero issues making the decision to make them hurt as much as they hurt me and the other girls."

I shrug because I don't really have answers. "I don't know what to tell you."

"I bet if it wasn't you he hurt… if he was your bestie's douchey boyfriend who did all this stuff, you wouldn't hesitate to protect her."

"Never really had a bestie," I say, shrugging again. "So I can't really say. But probably not."

"It's because it's for you. You're not putting yourself first, even though you ran. You're still protecting him. It's not quite the same as how you protected him before by not telling people what he was doing, but it's still protecting him."

I open my mouth to dismiss her, but close it again.

Is that what I'm doing?

I'm aware that I'm terrible at putting myself first, recognizing my own wants and needs, that's a trauma that I don't have Trent to thank for, but it doesn't make it any less prevalent. Also, being aware of it doesn't make it any easier to change.

Thank you, brain, for intellectualizing most of my emotions.

"I guess. I just… murder or whatever, seems a little extreme. I don't want his blood on my hands, I'm not sure my soul can wear a stain like that."

"After what you said he did to you? And I know you didn't even really touch the surface… I'd say murder is almost too good for him, but it frees you, so win-win."

"I didn't realize you were so bloodthirsty," I joke, and she grins at me as she finishes checking out the last register.

"Oh, I usually leave that to Rory, but I'm not averse to bloodshed when needed."

"Rory?" I ask, and she looks at me like I've lost my mind.

"Meyer's left hand? Have you really not met Rory? You've been here for like, six months."

"Definitely don't think so. Other than that day I had an anxiety attack, I haven't seen Hunter either—though, I didn't actually see him that day because, well, panic. And I've only seen Meyer all of twice. I just didn't think they were here much."

"I guess they've been busier than usual," she says nonchalantly, but something about her shock seems off to me, like she's squirmy, but I don't call her on it. I don't need to know the bosses, and I know she works closely with them, that she's known them a really long time, but that doesn't mean I need to know them.

To be honest, as captivating as Meyer is, I don't think

that I could have men like that in my life again. Sure, they seem to wield their power for good from what I've seen, but Yen has implied some of the stuff they do and I know the violence that comes with that.

I don't want violence or violent men in my life ever again.

It's all I've ever known and I'm so far over it, I might as well fall off the edge of a cliff with it. This corner of my world is meant to be safe and, for now, it is. I don't want to go back to that life.

"You ready to go?" Bobby asks as he exits the hall to the main exit of HellScape.

I look over at Yen, who nods, grabbing her stuff. "Yup, we're done." I glance back at Yen and ask, "Did you clear the offices?"

"Yeah, Meyer left a few hours ago, we're the last ones here."

I grab my stuff from behind the bar, double checking that I have Harper's keys. "Awesome. Then yeah, let's go. I miss my bed."

"Luca is going to give us a ride home," Yen says, tapping away on her phone as we're walking toward the exit. I somehow haven't met Luca yet, but she seems happy, so who am I to question anything?

"You sure? If you're staying at his place again, I can just get an Uber."

She stops dead and stares at me. "Like I'm letting you go home alone again so soon. Shut the fuck up."

I just blink at her in shock and then laugh. "Yeah, I guess that's fair."

Bobby waits for us at the exit, and once we're locked up, he stays with us until Luca pulls up. "See you ladies tomorrow."

"Night, Bobby!" I call out to him and he lifts a hand to wave goodbye as Yen opens the car door. I open the back door and slide onto the seat, trying not to feel awkward at the major PDA happening in the front of the car.

Playing with my phone to pass the time till they separate, I try not to pay them any attention until Yen giggles in the front seat.

"Luca, this is Quinn. Quinn, Luca."

I glance up and smile at the blond guy in the driver's seat. "Hi."

He just nods in response, his gaze sweeping me quickly before turning back to Yen. "To your apartment, then mine?"

"Yes, please," she responds and he takes her hand, kissing the inside of her wrist, before placing it on his thigh and pulling away from the curb.

A part of me feels a little jealous. I've never had that. That soft, slightly-possessive-but-in-a-good-way alpha energy guy. Luca radiates all of those things as he moves through traffic, one hand on top of Yen's, the other on the wheel.

I stop watching them, feeling like a total creeper, and stare out of the window, watching the city lights pass us by. It's not long until we pull up in front of the building and I'm saying goodbye to them both, thanking Luca, then feeling really happy that I'm out of the car.

Not that I want to be ungrateful, but being a third wheel isn't my idea of a good time. I head inside the lobby as Eric opens the door for me and beeline for the elevator, paying zero attention to my surroundings. Apparently, being on hyper alert these last few days has made me sloppy, because I walk right into someone and nearly fall flat on my ass.

"I am so sorry," I say as I look up and find Hot Elevator Guy staring down at me, his hand on my arm keeping me on my feet.

"We've got to stop meeting like this," he says with a grin, and I feel heat climb across my chest and up my throat.

"You're back." I cringe the moment the words fall from my lips, because stalker much?

"Yeah, business took me out of town for a few months." He removes his hand from me when he realizes I'm not going to fall and a part of me misses his touch. Though that could just be because we're about to ride the elevator where he blew my mind and I haven't had sex since that night.

Could definitely be that.

"But I'm back now."

The elevator dings and the doors open. He waves me in then follows behind me and I don't know if it's just me, but I feel like I'm going to come out of my skin being in here with him again.

I don't understand where the reaction comes from, so I clasp my hands together and lean against the wall. He doesn't say anything, just watches me the entire ride up with a smile on his face. When we reach our floor, he lets me out first and stays a step behind me until I reach my door. I unlock it and head in, only turning back to say goodbye when I find him standing in my doorway instead.

"Don't think I've forgotten about that rain check, Angel."

I blink at him, stunned stupid for a minute.

He smiles and steps back into the hall. "Not right now, but soon, we're going out. I'll see you around. I'll wait here till you lock up."

I just nod, speechless, and close the door, engaging all the locks and leaning on it when I'm done.

"Just make sure to say yes, next time, Angel," I hear through the door and my heart races.

Totally not how I saw my night ending.

FOURTEEN

It's been two weeks since I thought I saw Trent and I'm slowly starting to relax again. Tommy has been checking in and has told me that people are watching him, so if he makes a move, we'll know before he does it.

Obviously, that doesn't mean he doesn't know where I am, it just means he's not coming after me right now. But I'm taking the small wins and trying to get on with living my life. Though, moving past it isn't easy, even with therapy, which is exactly where I'm leaving now.

Tommy insisted on me moving my kind of, sometimes, online therapy to seeing a professional in person a few times a week. Said he was worried about me and that this was the next step. I didn't disagree with him, so we found a therapist and he ran every single check available to make sure she was someone we could trust. I've been coming here for the last two weeks and it's been tough. I've been coming four times a week, but we just agreed to drop down to twice a week now that she's got an idea of my backstory.

Well, really, she wanted me to keep coming four times a week but the thought of the bill, which Tommy insisted on covering, makes my eyes water, so I insisted we drop it down.

Continually revisiting everything that's happened throughout my life is definitely helping in some aspects. Though I've always been aware of *why* I act the way I do for the most part, being told that it isn't my fault, and that it's a trauma response... and somehow, it's a relief. Validating almost. The fact that there's a small part of me that believes I didn't—and still don't—deserve better than how my parents treated me, than how Trent treated me. The same part that probably doesn't want Trent dead because well, he wasn't always awful and maybe I did bring out that side of him. The same, small, damaged part that maybe still has some sort of attachment to him.

Working through that realization is where I'm at currently, and I never thought I'd have homework from therapy, but seeing my therapist so often is definitely hurtling me toward a door I don't know if I'm ready to open yet. But baby steps. Giant, leaping baby steps.

Yeah, I'm a contradiction, I know.

The Uber home doesn't take long and I find Yen

watching some reality show about meeting the love of your life in a pod where you can't see them but you can still hear each other, and roll my eyes.

"Don't you judge me," she calls out without even turning to look at me. "I can hear your judgment from all the way over here. This is mindless escape in the best form and I love it. I mean, really, who goes on TV to find the love of their life? Can you imagine?"

"Not really," I call back as I open the door to the fridge and sigh.

We really need to start adulting properly and actually go grocery shopping rather than living on chips and dip and takeout.

"But then, I guess meeting in person hasn't exactly gone that well for me either, so who am I to throw shade at how they parade their lives out for everyone to see? I just can't imagine having my love life on a show for the world to see." A shudder runs down my spine as I stand up and close the fridge. "Absolutely not."

"Same, but it is fascinating. You judge, but I guarantee if you sat and watched even one episode with me, you'd be hooked my friend. *Hooked.*"

I laugh at her while grabbing a bag of chips from the cupboard and drop onto the sofa next to her. "I don't know about that."

"Uh-huh. You'll see. How was therapy? Or are we

still not talking about it?" she asks as she reaches over and takes a handful of chips from the bag. I side-eye her, because these Lays are my favorite, but shrug it off.

"It was okay. Still just talking while she nods and listens, making noises here and there as she jots down notes. She thinks I should join a gym, start building healthier habits into my lifestyle. I told her about the self-defense class and she said it's a start, but it's just once a week and she's thinking like four to five times a week."

"Four to five times a week? Does this bitch go to the gym that often?" Yen scoffs, and I can't help but laugh softly at her.

"Probably not, but she's probably not quite as broken as I am."

"We're all a little broken," Yen responds with a shrug. "It's how you put yourself back together that counts."

I stay quiet and find myself getting lost in her stupid show just like she warned I would and mentally berate myself for getting sucked in.

"We should probably eat something more substantial than chips before work," Yen says as the episode ends and she checks her phone. "We've got like, four hours. That's plenty of time to get ready and grab food. You down?"

My stomach rumbles so loud that I want to die. Probably should've eaten this morning, but I spaced on that thinking about my day. "I'm gonna say yes."

She cackles at me as she turns off the TV. "Okay, get your ass in gear and remember we agreed to go out tomorrow. No take backs."

I groan because I totally forgot. Going out this often, while fun, is exhausting. I missed this life in my early twenties because, well, Trent. But I'm thinking it might be time for Yen to go back to her own apartment and time for me to slow down with the nights out. But that's a conversation for another day.

"Fine, fineeeeee. You better feed me real good though."

She winks at me and laughs again. "When have I ever let you down?"

"We should go to Light Up!" Tara exclaims, and Amelia, Belle, and Sofie agree wholeheartedly. Yen looks torn, and I have no idea what Light Up is, so I have no vote.

"We probably shouldn't," Yen says, but it's not that convincing and she's not exactly fighting that hard. I can't help but wonder what's going through her head.

The servers clear the final plates from our table at Bonsai, leaving just the array of cocktails that we are working our way through.

"What is Light Up?" I ask, and four alcohol-fueled voices jolt back at me with excited babble. I just about make out that it's a new club that just opened up and that it's *the* place to be, apparently.

I really am too old for this.

"Anddddd," Belle tags on. "Luca manages the place so he can get us on the list to jump the line!" I glance at Yen, who looks like she wants to crawl under the table. Maybe I should've asked more about Luca, but she said it wasn't serious and she was just having fun…

"Okay, well, I'm good with wherever."

"Four votes outweigh you, Yen," Tara exclaims, sticking her tongue out at my friend, who sighs, before hailing down the server.

"Tequila shots, doubles, all round, please." The server nods and rushes away while I sit and contemplate what is going on with Yen. She's been fine all night up to now. "Fine, I'll speak to Luca to get us on this list."

"Yassss!" Sofie squeals as Belle claps her hands together and Amelia chugs down the cocktail in front of her.

"Yes, yes, we can go," Yen caves and I side-eye her, silently trying to ask her what's up, but she shrugs and drinks the cocktail in front of her in one go.

I guess I'll try and ask later.

"Sounds good to me," I tell the table, taking a cocktail for myself and chugging it back because, while I don't want to be *drunk* drunk, I also need a few drinks to make me feel like a 'normal' person rather than the anxious, stressy mess I've been the last few years. It might have been a few weeks since the scare of thinking Trent had found me, and I've mostly moved past it, but I constantly walk the line of drinking enough to loosen up while not drinking so much that I do something stupid if Trent *does* show up.

Ah, the joys of being me.

But I'm certain that, knowing what she does, Yen wouldn't take me somewhere I could get into trouble. I trust her, she's earned that much the last few months. She didn't have to move in with me, or baby me the last few weeks. She doesn't have to check in with me when she's away for a night or two, but she does.

I guess that's what having a friend is like.

I refocus and realize they've all been talking about Light Up and I missed all of it, but the tequila shots are brought to the table and I take mine with the salt shaker and the slice of lime, taking part in the woo before doing the shot.

More shots follow, and I start to decline after three, but somehow still end up doing two more before we pile into an Uber to head to the club. The world is a little fuzzy, but not enough for me to worry. Yet, I have this glow I haven't felt in a while.

The glow of forgetting, of letting go.

Of being free.

And for a change, I lean into it. What could it hurt to let go for one night?

While I'm sure that is probably the tequila talking, I've been saying for months that I want to live and not just survive. This feels like part of it. Having a normal night out, like a normal twenty-something, and maybe not staying so rigid the entire time because of potential consequences. I mean, last time I let loose a little, I met Hot Elevator Guy...

Definitely not a bad outcome. Besides, what's the worst that could happen?

The drive takes longer than it should because of traffic in the city, and Yen is glued to her phone most of the drive, so I lean into the party feel with the others. When we get to Light Up, one of the doormen comes to the car and opens the door for us. When I see Luca, I realize Yen must have told him which car we'd be in.

Look at us getting VIP treatment.

We practically fall out of the car laughing at Belle's latest story of her with a client—all I'm saying is whips, handcuffs, and a kink for food and farting—before being ushered inside the club. The tequila haze blocks out the things I'd usually take in, and we're escorted to the VIP section and given a booth.

A booth that already has an ice trough on it with bottles of champagne, vodka, whiskey, and tequila, along with glasses lined up on shelves on the wall.

Well, shit. This place really is a whole different experience.

Sofie grabs six shot glasses and pours out tequila, handing a shot to each of us. "To being young and beautiful!"

I'll drink to that. I lift my glass and do the whole thing before throwing back my shot. That irritating sensible voice in my head questions again if this is a good idea. Sometimes I feel like I have a split personality because I want to be here and I want to have fun, but also... the voice.

I push it down with a second shot of tequila that Sofie hands to me, when *Oh My God* by Usher and Will.I.Am starts playing and I'm thrown back to being eighteen.

"Holy shit, I love this song!" Tara squeals and jumps to her feet. She takes my hand and pulls me from the booth, the others following behind us to the dance floor.

I let my body fall into the rhythm of the song, letting the music wash over me, the tequila making me feel at ease in my body and my brain for the first time in a while, and just dance without a care in the world.

This song is my jam! I haven't felt this free in well... ever. Raising my hands above my head, I shake my hips to the beat, tipping my head back and letting my hair cascade backward as my body sways.

This is what I've been searching for.

This, right here, makes the years of fear, the years of being made small, the long months of running, almost worth it.

My life should have been like this from the beginning, but I am finally free and I am going to live my life exactly how I want to.

FIFTEEN

Hands clasp my waist and I jolt back to reality, the warm glow of tequila in my system fading enough for me to pull out of whoever's grasp it is. I turn and see an obviously wasted guy, who I give a tight smile to before pointing off the dance floor.

I probably should head to the bathroom. I might be free but that doesn't mean that I can relax. Being a woman in a city, with zero people I know, still makes my entire existence a risk, but it's totally worth it to be free from *him*.

Making my way through the throng of bodies, my buzz continues to recede as I push past the people, but I lost count of the shots I've taken so my head is definitely still fuzzy. I push open the first door I come to and the thud of the bass from the club slips away as the door closes, my footsteps clumsy as I walk into the wall before I realize

I'm not in the bathroom.

Way to go, Quinn.

Voices draw my attention as I step further into the weird little hall that seems to open to some sort of storage room and, despite knowing this is a stupid idea, the tequila in my system fuels my bad decisions tonight. This definitely isn't the first one I've made in the last hour and I mean, what's the worst that could happen?

Stumbling down the little hall thing, I clasp a hand over my mouth as I try to stay quiet. When I reach the end of the hall I pause and think twice. The voices don't exactly sound welcoming.

Maybe tequila really isn't making the best decisions tonight.

For a moment, I consider turning back and finding the bathroom as my bladder screams at me, but my interest is piqued. Like that damn cat, my curiosity is going to get me in trouble. I can just feel it.

Deciding to not get dead, having escaped that particular fate one too many times already in my life, I move to turn back toward the club when I stumble and fall to the ground.

Shit.

There's no way that was quiet. Is there?

I'm trying not to groan as I shift onto my knees before climbing back to my feet, holding my breath and waiting to hear the voices again. They're still talking in low tones, but by some sort of saving grace, I don't think they heard me.

Now fully standing, I realize I kinda fell out of the hall and I can see them.

Three men, all in black suits, standing in front of another guy who is crying on his knees before them.

Somehow, no one has noticed I'm here and I scramble to my feet. I need to get out of here. The voice of the man in the middle calls my attention and I take a step back when I see the gun in his hand.

Holy shit. What is this?

Stupid Quinn. You came here to escape violence, of course your stupid ass literally fell into this shit.

I blink and it's like time stands still.

My ears ring and I flinch as the bang blasts through the room, then I freeze. I shouldn't be here.

I absolutely shouldn't be here.

The man on his knees in the middle of the room slumps forward as blood drips onto the concrete floor from the hole in his skull.

Why is there so much blood?

My stomach churns as all the tequila in my system starts to rebel. A whimper escapes my lips and every atom of my body screams at me to run.

"Who are you?" the man holding the gun asks as he turns to face me, gun raised in my direction. His voice shouldn't sound smooth as honey. His dark eyes shouldn't feel like they're boring into my soul.

I will my mouth to speak as the three of them walk closer to me, but all I can focus on is the gun in my face.

After being on the run for so long, I thought I'd finally found a corner of the world where I could be safe.

I guess I was wrong.

"Quinn?" I startle as my name falls from his lips, but my body still won't move.

"What the fuck is she doing here?" the one in the middle, that I realize is Meyer, asks.

"Fuck if I know. Yen should know better," the blond one says, and I blink again, not believing my eyes.

Elevator Guy?

"What do we do?" the third one asks. He looks terrifying. From his huge stature to his buzz cut hair, to the ink painted all over his body. The only thing that doesn't scream *run away*, are his eyes—bright blue, like the sky—that give me a false sense of safety for a second. But I'm not safe.

They have guns.

They just killed someone.

I just saw them kill someone.

Holy shit, they're going to kill me too, aren't they?

Silent tears stream down my cheeks as Hot Elevator Guy steps toward me and crouches in front of me. "You don't need to cry, Angel. You're safe here."

A laugh bubbles up in my chest and spills from my lips. Safe is the last thing I feel right now.

"Let's take her back to the house. We obviously need to talk and things are going to change now." Meyer glances at the two of them as he speaks before locking eyes with me and I feel everything and nothing all at once. Hot and cold. Terrified and safe. The urge to run and the desire to stay.

I never said I wasn't fucked up.

Regardless, it's easy enough to say the tequila haze has faded from my system. I feel stone-cold sober and I almost wish I wasn't.

"Change?" I ask, stuttering my way through the word. I clench my fists to stop my hands from shaking as I make an attempt to stand.

"Hunter, help her up," Meyer says. The short-haired one stays silent at Meyer's side while Hunter, who I know as Hot Elevator Guy, offers me a hand. When I don't take it, he lifts me in his arms and holds me for a moment.

"Can you stand?" he murmurs and I nod, not trusting my mouth to not say something stupid. He holds me for a moment more before lowering me to my feet.

A strong urge to slap him runs through me, but I resist. I just saw them kill a guy, probably not the best idea to start hitting one of them, but how fucking *dare he* sleep with me, pretending he didn't know who I was, when he very obviously did.

It occurs to me then, as betrayal runs through me like a sharp blade, that Yen knew who he was. She saw me with him that first night at the bar. She didn't tell me who he was, and she had chances.

She lied to me.

She lied to me and I let her in my apartment, told her things about me that I've never told anyone. My already fractured-beyond-repair heart cracks a little more, because of course she wasn't really my friend.

I trusted her…

I think I'm going to be sick. I really can't trust anyone. Why wouldn't she tell me who he was? I knew she was involved in illegal shit, and I never judged, so why wouldn't she trust me? I can't believe she betrayed me like this.

My dad's voice in the back of my head is so loud it's like he's standing beside me, laughing and shouting about how of course I don't have friends. I'd have to pay people to pretend to like me, and we didn't have money for that. I was too weird to have actual friends, so of course she wasn't my friend.

Stupid, Quinn.

"Let's go," Meyer demands before turning to the third guy. "Rory, call in cleanup. I want you with us."

"On it," the guy, Rory apparently, responds like a good

little soldier and taps on his phone before putting it to his ear.

The two of them start moving forward while I stay rooted to the spot, Hunter watching me closely.

Meyer turns back, almost glaring at me. "Can you walk or do you need to be carried?"

"I don't want to go with you," I respond, jutting my chin out while mentally cursing myself for the sass that is likely going to get me dead. He might be friends with Tommy, and he might have been helping keep me safe from Trent, but everything is different now.

Now I know the truth of who he is.

What *they* are.

Is Tommy like this too? He mentioned murder so casually, but I guess I hadn't really considered that he meant it… not really. Not like this.

Being faced with the truth is much harder than just being told something.

"Carry her," Meyer says to Hunter before turning and walking away, Rory keeping pace with him.

"Please don't make me do this, Angel," Hunter pleads with me, and I feel the fight leave my body. Fighting isn't going to get me anywhere, except maybe bleeding out on the floor like the other guy.

SIXTEEN

MEYER

Why the fuck is she here? This was not how I wanted this to go, but now my hands are tied. Murderous rage runs through my veins like lava. Not at her, but at the now-dead guy on the ground back there, and a little at Yen for bringing her here.

And at Luca for not fucking telling me they were here.

Everyone but her deserves my rage. She… she has suffered enough rage for a lifetime and I refuse to be just another person that does that to her when she doesn't deserve this ire.

"Clean up is on the way," Rory says, and I respond with a nod because if I open my mouth right now… well, I'm going to turn into my father and I refuse to ever become him. I vowed that a long time ago and I'm not about to fuck it up now.

I pull my phone from my pocket, hitting the screen before bringing it to my ear. The line rings twice before it connects. "Sir?"

"O'Connor, we're ready. Bring the car out back." My bark is vicious, laced with the poison that is my anger.

"Yes, Boss." The line disconnects swiftly and I let out a breath.

I glance over my shoulder as I reach the door, finding her standing back where I left her, quietly arguing with Hunter.

He has his own shit to work out with her but now isn't the time. "Hunter!"

My shout echoes through the large space and regret tickles the back of my brain when she flinches.

"Sorry, Angel." His words are low as he steps toward her and her squeak of surprise as he lifts her over his shoulder with ease is almost enough to make me smile. I always used to think I'd want a woman who knew her place, but I'm beginning to think the fire that lives in Quinn is everything I've been missing.

I've always liked to hunt my prey and it's always much more fun when they make it a challenge. I get the feeling Quinn is going to be the best challenge I've ever faced.

She doesn't know it yet, but we have already claimed her. Tonight just cements it.

Tommy might try to fight me on it, but the old man

knows when to push and when to not, and if he tries to push this… well, he'll learn quickly that I'm not fucking around.

"Put me down, you great lumbering oaf!" she shouts, beating Hunter's back with her closed fists, but he doesn't break stride. He's suffered worse than that.

Much worse.

We all have.

The smile that plays on his face tells me all I need to know. He's enjoying this as much as I am. My phone buzzes in my hand, drawing my attention from her.

O'Connor:
Outside

"Let's go," I say to Rory, who draws his gun and opens the door first. I still don't like that he does that, but the stupid hierarchy that comes with the games we play means that he feels the need to go first and make sure the area is clear of any threats.

Regardless of the fact that losing him would be as crushing to the empire we've built as if we lost me or Hunter.

Not that he sees it like that.

Never has.

Ever since my father gave him shelter from the streets,

gave him a purpose, and brought him into the family, his mind was set. He's always seen himself as expendable and broken, the blunt instrument crafted to break through the hardest of problems.

My father might not have been the best kind of dad in a traditional sense, but he made me the man I am today and I can't be angry about that. Even if I know I'd never treat my kid the way he did me and my siblings. Mom did her best to make up for how cold he could be, and for the other two, I know she did better. But I was the oldest… my father claimed me the moment he found out I had a dick and inflicted himself upon me in ways he didn't bother to with the other two. I'm sure they feel their own way about that, but I can honestly say that they got the better end of the deal.

We're all a little broken, but Rory means far more to me than he'll ever know. They're both like brothers to me.

I smile again as Hunter reaches us, our little captive still causing problems on his shoulder. She's curvy, but compared to Hunter, she's tiny, so she's hardly an issue. Yet, I can't help myself from running a hand down her lower spine and over the curve of her ass. She freezes and my smile widens just a little. "Keep struggling and you'll see just what we're capable of, Kitten. Put those claws away for now. We mean you no harm, but if you keep fighting, I will do what is necessary to stop you."

I practically feel the fight leave her body. As much as I dislike the threats, especially considering what I know of her past, these are as much for her safety as ours. I don't know *who* is outside and if anyone sees her with us while Rory is doing a sweep and they see even an ounce of dissent between us, she becomes a target.

The world we live in is encased in shadow and no one ever claimed it was safe, but I refuse to put her in more danger than absolutely necessary. If that means hog-tying her and stuffing her mouth, then I'll do it. Even if she hates me for it.

"Clear," Rory calls to us from outside.

"Are you going to walk?" I ask her. She responds with a sigh of submission that runs straight to my cock. The thought of her submitting to me does things it shouldn't, at least not right now. I get the feeling her submitting to me how I want her to is going to take some time.

Thankfully, I am a patient man.

Well, mostly.

Sometimes.

I nod at Hunter, who puts her on her feet, and she looks up at me, her stature one of acceptance, but the glint in her eye and the tilt of her chin as she looks at me is sheer defiance and I fucking love it.

"Good girl, Kitten. Let's go."

We head out to the car, with Quinn sandwiched

between Hunter and me, and O'Connor opens the back door, nodding to me as we approach. Rory rounds the car to the front passenger seat as I slide in the back. Quinn follows me in with Hunter behind her.

She looks around the car curiously, then looks over at Hunter. When O'Connor climbs in the driver's seat, heat spreads across her chest and up her throat. "You asshole," she hisses in Hunter's direction and I press my lips together to stop from smiling.

Oh, yeah. He's definitely got some work to do there.

"Oh, come on, Angel. It's not that bad."

"If I didn't think it'd get me killed, I'd punch you in the freaking throat, followed by a swift kick to your dick."

I wince as she bites back at him, that fire and anger in such contrast to what I've read, seen, and heard of her. It just makes me want her more, knowing that she's going to fight belonging to us…

Oh. I can't wait to win *that* fight.

Rory chuckles in the front seat as O'Connor pulls away from the warehouse at the back of Light Up, and I keep my eyes out the window, watching her reflection in the darkened glass. She stays silent for the rest of the drive, keeping her gaze forward as she glares out at the city.

Her eyes widen when we reach the house and, for a moment, I see it through her eyes. I grew up here, behind these walls and the giant gate manned with armed guards.

The huge, stonewash house lit up by spotlights and the imposing, shining water fountain that forms the center of the circular driveway by the main door to the house—also manned by armed guards.

I can't help but wonder if she's taken aback by the property or the men, but either way, I can tell she feels uneasy from how she starts to squirm in her seat. Placing a hand on her thigh, I lean in close, her hair tickling my nose as I murmur in her ear. "You have nothing to be afraid of here, Kitten. A small country's army couldn't get past the men and walls here."

She turns to me, blinking. "That might be true, but who is going to keep me safe from you?"

Even hours later, her words play on repeat in my head.

"Who is going to keep me safe from you?"

No one has ever asked me that. Those who fear me know they're not safe from me, and those who are under my protection know me well enough to know that the only reason you're not safe with me is if you betray me. And that's on the person betraying me, not me.

I will always do what is necessary to protect my people and what is mine.

And she is mine. Whether she knows it or not.

I remind myself as I turn over in my bed again that she does not know me or how any of this works, that her words shouldn't have been like a blade through my ribs. That she does not understand or know me.

Once she uttered her words, I climbed from the car and left Hunter to get her situated. I came to my office and dealt with everything else that happened yesterday, plus the barrage of new bullshit that had landed in my lap since, as well as tearing Yen and Luca a new one for no heads up. I finally crawled to my bed as the sun started to rise and the birds began to sing an hour ago.

Yet sleep still evades me and my mind has the way she looked at me on replay.

Like I was the big bad wolf in her story.

Frustration ripples through me.

I'm the one who has been keeping her safe, protecting her, working around the fucking clock to ensure her dickhead ex wasn't coming for her, and she has the nerve to look at me like I'm the bad guy?

I never claimed to be a good guy, but in *her* story? I'm definitely not the villain.

Fuck this shit.

I throw off the sheets and storm across to the window, pushing open the curtains and letting the sunlight stream over my body. The heat feels good on my skin and when the gardener working on the roses beneath the window pops up, seeing me and startling before smiling, it makes me glad I at least have boxers on.

My phone starts to buzz on my bedside table and I scrub a hand down my face.

I need coffee.

Ignoring my phone, I pull on a pair of jeans and shrug on a button-down, leaving it undone as I roll the sleeves up, letting out a deep breath before I undress again and grab my shorts. I want more of the sunlight on my skin and decide that this morning is going to need some laps in the pool. To wake me up and burn off this bullshit energy roaring inside of me.

Maybe bringing her here was a bad idea, but after last night, there wasn't another option. I need to make sure she understands what happens and doesn't call the police. Tommy might have said she's wary of the entire justice system, and authority in general, but that was before she saw us shoot a man between his eyes.

Not that he didn't deserve it.

He betrayed us, was helping the competition round up drunk girls from my clubs and selling them to traffickers.

My morals might run gray, but I draw the line at selling people.

Drugs and guns, they might not exactly obey the letter of the law, but people will do to themselves what they will. Selling a person against their will? That is a huge fucking no.

Even if I have technically kidnapped Quinn for the moment, that's different.

I get the feeling that, when it comes to her, everything will be different.

Grabbing my phone and pocketing it without looking at the ridiculous number of notifications, I pad down the hall, my feet slapping against the cold tile helping to focus my mind, until I hear voices coming from the kitchen.

"That is devil's food and you won't catch me putting it anywhere near my mouth."

I smirk at Quinn's obvious defiance and wonder if she's taunting Hunter or Carlos, my poor chef.

"Devil's food?" Carlos asks, and the bewilderment in his voice makes me pause before entering the room. I lean against the wall, the sun streaming through the windows opposite me helping to bring up my mood as my curiosity is piqued at their conversation.

"Cucumber," she responds, and I swear I can see her scrunching up her face in my mind's eye. It makes me smile. "It's gross, and disgusting, and just no. Cucumber does not belong on my breakfast."

"But it's part of my family pico recipe. You can't even taste it!" Carlos counters. His confusion and exasperation just feed my amusement.

"I don't care if it's laced with gold, it's not going on

my plate."

"Dios mio, woman! Rechazo el pico de gallo en su burrito. Qué tipo de monsturo a traido en mi cocina?!"

I laugh at his cursing and finally enter the room, heading straight for the espresso machine. "Buenos días, Carlos. Ella no es un monsturo, pero si muerde. Te consejo que no le pongas pico de gallo en su plato."

I feel her eyes on me as I set up the machine, already feeling the caffeine hit my senses as it starts to pour. Turning to face her, I spot the battle going on behind her eyes. She hops from one foot to the other, almost subtly, as her hands clench together in front of her, but her face tells me she wants to say something that probably isn't all that nice.

"What do you wish to say, Kitten?" I ask, a smirk on my face, and the fire lights in her eyes again. Oh, yes. Having her here is going to be fun.

"Firstly," she starts, that hesitation falling from her as she juts out her chin. "My name is Quinn. Secondly, you don't get to talk about me in a language I don't understand. It's rude."

"Well, Carina, I would never want to be rude to you, especially as you are a guest in my house. But I speak many languages, Spanish and Italian are just two of them. However, as a courtesy to my guest, I will be sure to speak English if you would prefer." I can't keep the teasing from my words, but I'm not sure it lands as intended when she rolls her eyes at me.

"Ha, guest. More like kidnap victim." Her eyes widen after the words fall from her mouth, like she can't believe she just said that, but I laugh and some of the terror leaves her face as she relaxes a little.

Just that small show of terror makes me angry, and I make a vow to do whatever it takes to show her she is safe here.

Carlos just continues to cook like he can't hear the bickering. His family has worked for mine for a long time, so I'm sure it's a learned skill, but I see the small smile on his face.

"You are not a victim of mine, Carina. If you were, you wouldn't be here, free in my kitchen, torturing poor Carlos. Also, Tommy knows you are here and he hasn't come riding in like some white knight. He told you to trust me, yes?" I pause, but she doesn't utter a word. "You are here right now for your safety and ours. What you witnessed last night needs to be explained so that no rash actions are taken."

She watches me in silence as she processes my words, and I watch the fight leave her once more. "Fine. But I'm still not eating the cucumber."

"You do not have to eat the cucumber," I respond softly, trying not to sound as condescending as I know I can sometimes be.

"Te estas hacienda suave, jefe," Carlos murmurs and I chuckle.

"Sometimes we have to bend to win in the long run."

Carlos plates up the breakfast burrito and hands the plate over to Quinn, who silently moves to the table by the patio doors. I can't blame her. I like eating there too, the sun shining in, looking out over the gardens my mother meticulously looks after.

Shit. Mother.

I grab my espresso, taking a sip and enjoying the dark roast as it fully wakes my senses.

"Usual de siempre?" Carlos asks and I nod.

"I'm going to go find Mother, then I'll eat. Are the others up yet?"

He nods in response. "Si, Rory comioy ya se due. Hunter esta acostado pero creo que espera a tu monstruo." He glances over at Quinn and shakes his head again. "Le dejo saber que estas aqui."

"Thank you, Carlos. Give me a half hour and I'll be back to eat."

He nods as he grabs his phone, I assume to speak to Hunter, but rather than lingering, I go off in search of a problem I hadn't taken into account when bringing Quinn here.

My mother.

SEVENTEEN

QUINN

This might be the most surreal moment of my life. I can't decide if I should feel terrified and try to escape, or if I should feel safe in the fact that there's no way Trent is going to get me inside this fortress.

Though, I'm not currently sure that Trent is my biggest worry.

Trent has never actually killed someone. At least, not as far as I know.

But then, Meyer and the guys… they've never made any attempts to hurt me, not physically, anyway. Even last night, they could have just 'dealt with me' rather than bring me here. And while I might not have exactly been a willing participant in being brought here, I'm hardly locked in a basement.

It's at this point, I laugh out loud and Carlos looks

at me like I'm crazy. Maybe I am. I've basically been kidnapped, but here I am, doing a little happy dance while I eat breakfast made by my captor's chef, worrying not about the men I saw kill someone last night, but worrying about the man who doesn't know where I am and feeling strangely safe all at the same time.

Yep, I might have officially lost it.

If I ever had it at all.

They haven't even taken my phone. I could have called the police. Not that I would, the justice system is about as reliable as a chocolate teapot, which I unfortunately know first hand and have witnessed as a spectator time and time again. But I guess that is part of why I feel kind of safe here. Tommy knows these people. Meyer said Tommy knows I'm here and I don't know what it is about him, but I believe him. He doesn't have a reason to lie to me, I guess. I could just check in with Tommy if I didn't believe him…

I close my eyes and tilt my face up, letting the heat of the sun soak into my skin. I don't remember the last time I felt this conflicted, but I am definitely blaming the tequila for most of last night.

Tequila might be my friend, but I think we need a break.

"Would you like anything else?" Carlos asks me, his English heavily accented as Hunter walks in the room.

Now *that* asshat has some explaining to do. Not that

I really let him speak much once we were back here last night, but I feel more betrayed by him and Yen than I do by Meyer. Meyer never pretended to be something or someone he wasn't.

Those two though… they broke my trust. They lied to me, even if they were lies of omission. Usually, I'd believe actions over words these days, but their actions lined up with their words. I guess they're both just good at lying.

I push that sting down, especially the one from Yen, and look back at Carlos. "No, I'm good, thank you. Do you think I'm allowed outside?"

Carlos looks over to Hunter, who hasn't taken his eyes off me since he walked in the room.

"Jefe?" Carlos raises a questioning eyebrow and I still have no freaking idea what he's saying.

Hunter folds his arms across his chest and leans back, resting against the counter. He's so tall his ass is basically on the freaking counter. "You're allowed anywhere you want after we talk. You might as well eat more, we both know you don't eat enough normally."

I quirk a brow at him, leaning back in my chair to face him properly. "And how would you know that?"

"Oh, I don't think you're ready for that answer yet, Angel. Now, what do you want to eat? Egg, bacon, and cheese bagel with pico?"

That reminds me, I need to check on Tina.

"Yeah, that's just creepy." I fold my arms, mirroring his position, but he smirks at me like he finds me amusing. I mean, it's not like I'm intimidating and I wouldn't expect him to think of me that way, but him smiling just pisses me off.

"Oh, Angel, you have no idea. Now, do you want the bagel or not?"

I nod, refusing to answer verbally. I'm still really hungry and, despite the cucumber in the pico, Carlos is a really good cook. The burrito was to die for and Hunter is right about one thing... I definitely haven't eaten much lately. Bonsai for dinner last night was the first real meal I've had in ages.

"Rosca para ella y un omelet para mi, mi amigo. Por favor."

What is with the Spanish in this house? Are they all multilingual? I can't help my curiosity about them. Everything I know about them is such a contradiction and yet... they seem just like normal people. I mean, I've barely spoken to or seen Rory, so I can't speak for him, but the small amount of time I've spent with Meyer, he just seems like a typical businessman who has his life together, and Hunter? Well, he seems like a total fuck boy, but that isn't exactly a rarity these days.

Hunter moves to the coffee machine and pours two mugs before coming to sit at the table with me. He slides me a mug, pushing the sugar pot on the table toward me, leaving the milk alone.

How much, exactly, does this guy know about me?

I shake it off, knowing he already alluded to the fact that he's not going to tell me anything about that, and put some sugar in my coffee before taking a sip.

Goddamn. Does everything here have to be next-level good? Even the bed I slept on was amazing. I thought the bed at home was a cloud, but if that was a cloud, the one here was like… marshmallow. I even woke up to fresh underwear, a pair of jeans, and a tank folded up outside the door of the room they put me in and, weirdly, it all fit perfectly.

Probably another thing that won't be explained, but I'm still grateful for the fresh clothing. The thought of wearing the alcohol-soaked skirt and top I went out in last night sends a gross shiver down my spine.

"So…" Hunter starts before trailing off. "I should probably explain some stuff, huh?"

I shrug and take another sip of my coffee. "For all I know, everything you tell me now will be just another lie, so talk if you want to. I'm here until you unleash me so I can go outside in the sunshine. Unless I can just go home?"

"Yeah, that's not an option." I roll my eyes at his response. Of course it isn't. Why would I be able to just forget last night and continue on with life like normal?

Well, my version of normal, at least. "So, first, I *do* live in the apartment building. Was our meeting by chance? At first, yes. Of course, I knew who you were, even if I didn't say anything because it would've been awkward and weird."

"More awkward and weird than this?" I ask, eyebrows raised, and he laughs.

"Touché. Anyway, I will apologize for not telling you who I was, or that I knew you, but I'm not going to apologize for anything else. You were put in the apartment to keep you safe and being down the hall from me meant that if every other failsafe in place didn't work for whatever reason, I'd be there."

"Oh," is all that falls from my lips. What else can I say, really?

"Yeah, *oh*. Plus, if I remember correctly, I asked your name that night and you were the one who said, and I quote, *does it matter*?" He laughs softly as Carlos lays a plate in front of us, mine with my bagel, his with an omelet. I guess that's what they were saying to each other.

Heat rises up my chest as his words register. "I forgot about that."

"I bet you did," he counters before taking a bite of his food. It's not fair that he's this hot even when he's eating. I'm supposed to be mad here but all I can think about is that thing he did with his tongue in the elevator as he licks his fork. "So now that's done, can we get back to you not being pissed at me?"

"I don't know," I respond with a shrug before taking a bite of my bagel. God damn, that's good too. "I guess that depends on what happens next."

"That's fair. What do you want to happen next?" he asks, tilting his head as he studies me.

"I already said that I'd like to go home and you said that wasn't an option."

"Other than going home?"

I let out a sigh and shrug again. "I have no idea. I don't understand why I'm here. I'm not going to the police. Since you guys know my situation, you must know that much already. I don't have anywhere to run and I like the life I've been building here. It actually feels like something close to normal, or at least, what I imagine normal looks like."

"Okay."

He doesn't say anything else, just continues to eat his breakfast, so I do the same, frustrated that I have no more answers than I did when we started this stupid conversation. When I finish my bagel, I thank Carlos before turning back to Hunter. "Can I be unleashed now?"

He smirks at me, his gaze running down my body. "Oh, I'm not the one who will leash you, Angel. That's way more Rory's thing." He winks at me and heat rises up my chest again, but I roll my eyes despite it. "But you can head outside now if you want. Just know that trying to escape is futile. We basically have a small army here, you'll be monitored at all times."

"Of course I will." I sigh but stand anyway. I'm not about to miss out on exploring this place just because I can't escape. I figured as much from what I saw and heard last night.

I push open the patio doors, stepping out into the heat of the morning. The birds are singing as my nostrils fill with the scent of the flowers that line the walkway. They run in both directions from where I'm standing and seem to stretch the entire length of the house.

The sound of water draws my attention and my feet take me in the direction of the noise.

I've always been curious and I knew it would probably get me in trouble one day, but since I'm basically in the deepest trouble I've been in, it can't get much worse, right?

When I find the source of the noise, I pause. I don't know what I expected to find, but it wasn't Rory doing laps in a pool.

For a moment, I freeze, watching the powerful man tear through the water like it's nothing. The ink of his skin shines as the sunlight glints off the water. Realizing I'm now the one being a creeper, I turn to leave when I hear him speak.

"You don't have to go. I'm nearly done." His voice is low and gravelly, something I didn't notice last night. Turning back to him, I meet his bright blue gaze and feel stuck. Everything about him screams run the hell away, but something about him calls to me.

"Oh I wasn't… I'm just looking around. Working out the confines of my gilded cage."

Where is all of this snark and sass coming from? 'Cause every time it falls from my lips, I feel shock and a little pride in actually standing up for myself.

He watches me closely, like a hunter stalking its prey. "This is no cage. I've been in cages. Trust me, you'd know if you were truly trapped."

A shiver runs down my spine as he speaks, not once breaking eye contact.

"But if you'd like, I can show you around. I have some free time this morning." His offer shocks me more than my sass does.

"Oh, erm, I don't want to be a bother."

Andddd there goes my people-pleasing babble. She's back.

"You would never be a bother, Quinn. Not to me." I blink at him, unsure what to say to that. "Sit. I won't be long, and then I'll show you around."

My feet move before I really take note of what's happening and I find myself sitting on one of the lounge chairs that line the pool while he continues to swim.

I thought my life was weird before, but today is just full of surprises.

He wasn't lying. He does about fifteen more laps before he pushes himself up onto the side of the pool by my feet. It takes all of my willpower not to ogle him in his swim shorts. His very obviously powerful body is a work of art, both in muscle and ink. The huge phoenix on his back has me so mesmerized that I startle when he clears his throat.

"So what have you seen so far?" he asks as he grabs the towel from beneath the chair I'm sitting on. I hadn't even noticed it there.

"Erm, the room I was escorted to last night, the kitchen, and then a bit of the yard as I walked from the patio to the pool."

The corners of his lips turn up and it transforms his entire face, softening his features. It only lasts a second and I get the feeling that he isn't one to smile often.

"Okay. Well, follow me. I'll get dressed then I can show you around and show you where you shouldn't be going if you don't want to end up with a gun in your face by accident. Have you met Angela yet?"

"Who is Angela?" I ask, blinking at him.

The corners of his lips tilt up for a moment again. "Meyer's mom. She lives here too, along with his little brother and sister."

"I'm sorry, what?"

"You didn't think that this huge house was just for the three of us, did you?" he asks, the amusement apparent in his teasing tone.

"Honestly, I hadn't thought that much about it. Meyer's entire family lives here? Why on earth would he bring a captive to the house where his family lives?" Confusion runs through me. Maybe he's not as normal as I thought, because none of that makes sense to me.

"That would be a question for the boss man himself. I don't have an answer for you." Except the way his eyes light up, I get the feeling he's also not telling me everything. "Come on, let's go. Obviously, you found the pool. If you keep heading in this direction you'll find the tennis court, basketball court, and outdoor gym."

He points off in the distance and I try not to let my jaw hit the floor. "Just past that is what looks like a bunker. Do not go in there. That's where our guys live, and in there… well, there are different rules." He pauses, looking directly at me, like he's trying to make sure that I heed his warning, so I nod, keeping my mouth shut and refusing to admit I'm curious about what different rules there are.

He motions to the wall of glass that shows a long hall

with multiple doors off of it as we start walking back the way I came. "This side of the house is where the three of us stay. Meyer's office is on this side too, and it's where he'll meet with associates. Do not go down there without one of us with you."

I don't know what it is about him, but I take his warnings seriously. Whereas with Hunter, it always feels like a taunt or a challenge. With Rory, I feel like he's being honest with me and doesn't want me to get hurt.

None of which makes sense, but I've always said my mind is a special and weird place to be.

We reach the door at the end of the hall and he opens it, motioning for me to enter in front of him. I follow him down to one of the doors in silence, just the sound of our footsteps on the cold tile filling the space between us.

When he opens another door, motioning me inside, I realize this must be his room.

Except this room is almost the square footage of my entire apartment, which is no small feat. There is a spiral staircase on the far right of the room and, as I look around, I conclude he must sleep up there because down here is just a huge living space.

"I'll be two minutes. Make yourself comfortable."

"You really don't have to rush—"

"Quinn, stop," he says, cutting me off, and I clamp my jaw shut. "I don't mean to stop you from speaking, but you don't have to people-please with me. I offered to show you around and I'm going to. You are not a bother, I'm not rushing or changing my routine for any reason other than I chose to, okay?"

I blink at him, my mind stuttering at his words. It should creep me out that they all seem to know me so well, but I just nod, letting him lead me to one of the huge leather sofas, and sit on it before he heads up the stairs.

Yeah, this morning is definitely surreal.

Pinching my forearm, I let out a hiss. Nope, definitely not asleep.

The curious part of me wants to look around, check out his stuff, try to work him out, but the smart side of my brain keeps my ass firmly on the sofa. Probably not worth angering the very large, potentially very scary guy who is undoubtedly not afraid of getting his hands dirty.

He quickly appears again, a pair of jeans and a black T-shirt in place of the swim shorts he was in before. Even the gun holster on his shoulders is freaking hot, which it definitely shouldn't be, especially with a gun on each side of his waist.

I'm supposed to be running from violence, so tell me why that sight is so hot? Could it be because I know he doesn't mean me any harm? My therapist would probably say I find comfort in it because he could probably protect me from the monsters that chase me, but I don't want to think too hard about that right now.

"You good to keep exploring?" he asks as he strides toward me and grabs his phone, watch, and a ring that he slides onto his thumb from the table on the other side of the sofa.

I nod, standing. "I'm good as long as you are."

His eyes darken as he watches me, and the corners of his lips tilt up once more. "Oh, I'm sure I'll be holding you to that."

EIGHTEEN

It's been two days since my tour of the grounds with Rory was interrupted by business and I haven't dared to venture further than what he showed me. I've desperately wanted to take advantage of the pool, but despite clothes magically appearing in the room I've been put in, there are no swimsuits.

I really need to figure out how to get them to let me go back to my life. While being here is a bit like a vacation, that's also just me looking at being a captive through rose-tinted glasses. Honestly, I'm not sure how I haven't freaked out more, but I guess I'm more broken than I thought before.

They've told me, repeatedly, that trying to leave is a pointless exercise, but I also haven't seen any of them for the last two days, so I'm going a little stir crazy.

Not that I haven't noticed my new shadow who refuses to speak. I've been calling him Bruno—because, obviously, we don't talk about Bruno—and trying not to be intimidated by the giant mountain of a man, armed to the eyeballs, who hasn't let me out of his sight.

I have yet to see him eat or sleep, so maybe he's a robot? That might explain why he doesn't speak.

See?

I'm going stir crazy.

I really need to get out of here and back to my life.

Even if I am a little convinced that the reason I haven't fought too hard to 'escape' is because Meyer, Rory, and Hunter fascinate me like a moth drawn to a flame—I'm also convinced if I get too close, I'm definitely going to get burned—but also because I know Trent can't get me here. Even if he knew where I was, I doubt he'd ever have the resources to get to me.

And that is exactly what I meant when I called this place a gilded cage when I was speaking to Rory. It's still a cage, I cannot leave, but it has definite upsides to staying in it.

Yep, officially losing my mind.

I've spent the time alone playing out conversations in my head. What Yen might say as to why she lied to me, assuming she was even truly my friend. Friends do not lie to each other the way she lied to me.

A conversation with Meyer about letting me go, about how I might barter for my freedom. I've yet to work out a conversation sequence that ends with me getting my way though. I'm just hoping it's a conversation I can have that doesn't get me locked in a room. They obviously trust me a little, despite the guard, because I have my phone. I could've called anyone—though, who would I really call? Tommy is friends with Meyer. Yen? I have no idea where her loyalties lie, but probably with Meyer since they saved her the way they did and she probably already knows where I am anyway.

I don't have anyone else to call. Obviously, I'm not calling the police. I get the feeling that would be futile anyway. I've read enough books to know that the morally gray boss guy usually has at least a few police on the payroll to ensure things run smoothly. It's probably different in real life, but it's not like I can just outright ask Meyer what sort of morally gray boss he is and what that means for me.

Or can I?

God, I really need to find someone to talk to.

Turning quickly, I find Bruno five steps behind me. Grinning at him, I flutter my lashes, hoping I can get the mountainous robot man to finally speak. "Bruno?"

He looks at me like I'm crazy, but doesn't answer. "Can we leave the compound so I can actually, ya know, talk to other humans? Maybe go back to my apartment? I was being monitored there before, can't I just go back to that?"

He blinks at me, still not saying a word.

"Do you speak?" I ask, my frustration growing, and he still says nothing. Though, amusement flickers in his eyes for a moment.

I growl out a cry of frustration, throwing my hands in the air. "I need to do something besides wander the halls of this monstrous house. Pleaseeeeeeee."

Feeling like a petulant child, I place my hands on my hips, almost tempted to stomp my foot to see if it will get me anywhere.

"Are we a little bored, Angel?"

I turn to find Hunter striding toward us, a bemused smirk on his face. Yeah, he is *not* a person I wanted to speak to yet. He might've explained some things, but that doesn't mean I've forgiven him for lying to me the way he did.

Even if me not learning his name was also my fault… I get to be mad, dammit.

"What do you want, Hunter?"

"Meyer wants to see you. He and Rory are finishing up a call, so I volunteered to come find you." His eyes dance with glee, like he can see that he's pushing my buttons and getting off on it.

Probably is.

Asshole.

"I don't want to speak to you," I respond, folding my arms across my chest. "Bruno is great company though." I turn to look at the man in question and discover my guard has disappeared without a freaking sound.

So maybe he's a robotic mountain ninja?

"Well, you don't have to speak to me, sweetness, you just have to come with me. Otherwise, I'll have to send Rory to get you."

I quirk a brow at him and blow out a breath. "Is that supposed to be a threat? Rory is lovely."

"The thought of Rory coming after a person rather than me is enough to make most grown men piss their pants," he responds with a laugh.

I shrug, accepting defeat. "He's not so scary."

"I'll be sure to let him know you said that." His smile is wide, like he's taking great joy in the fact that I don't find Rory terrifying. But *Rory* hasn't done anything to me for me to be afraid of him.

None of them have, really, but I'm not ready to face that truth yet.

Meyer was the one I saw shoot someone, but he's shown no signs of aggression toward me. Hunter lied to me, sure, but again, no signs of aggression. Really, it's only knowing the potential of what they're capable of, along with the many men with guns on the perimeter of the property, that has kept me from trying to escape.

"Are you going to come willingly or do I need to carry you again? Personally, I think it would be quite fun to replay that. Having you pound on my back like that in front of everyone made me hard." He winks as I scoff at him.

"Note to self… don't let the barbarian carry you."

"We both know how much you like it when I'm hard. I can still feel the cut of your nails on my skin and hear your whimpers from that night, Angel. We'll be recreating those memories real soon."

"Over my dead body," I bark back, despite my body coming alight at the reminder of that night.

Two years I managed to go without sex and I was fine. But being around him… apparently, I become a wanton hussy because, despite feeling the way I do toward him, I respond to even the slightest of connotations.

Not that I'm going to let *him* know that I'm wet or that my nipples pebbled at the thought of just how he pulled those whimpers from me.

Absolutely not.

"Lead the way, jailer number two," I sass and he laughs again.

"Oh, after you, Angel," he says, motioning toward the house.

"I don't know where we're going," I respond, rolling my eyes.

He grins at me again. "I know Rory showed you around. We're heading to Meyer's office. Now let me be at least a hint of a gentleman. After you."

Rolling my eyes again, I sashay past him, feeling his eyes on me. "You just want to stare at my ass.

"Guilty as charged. And oh, what an ass it is."

His words make my hips sway just a little more as I saunter off toward Meyer's office because, as much as he infuriates me, the thought of someone like him being brought to his knees by someone like me...

It's a little intoxicating.

I knock once on the door when I reach Meyer's office, but Hunter is behind me almost instantly, leaning around me to grab the handle and open the door. He puts his finger to his lips before placing a hand on the small of my back and leading me into the room.

Meyer is sitting at his desk, leaning forward on his elbows, his chin resting on steepled fingers when I hear another voice and realize he's on the phone.

"This isn't done, Marino. You took it too far."

"We merely responded to what you started. This is *your* mess and you couldn't handle the fallout. So I dealt with it and reaped the rewards of your fumbled opportunity. If you want to renegotiate, I suggest that you bring something more enticing to the table." He hits a button on the phone and the room goes silent. That's when I notice

Rory standing in the shadows in the far corner. The sun filters through the shuttered blinds, illuminating the room just enough to make him out.

"That seems to have gone as well as expected," Hunter says from behind me as he ushers me into a chair opposite Meyer's desk.

"You know the Demons always bite off more than they can handle, then throw their toys when we have to clean up their mess." He shrugs off his jacket and rolls up the sleeves of his shirt while watching me, and I squirm in my chair beneath his gaze.

The errant thought of bringing him to his knees flashes in my mind and heat creeps up my chest as wetness pools further between my legs.

So not the right time for this, Quinn. Get a grip on yourself.

Almost in direct defiance of my insides, I straighten my spine and meet Meyer's gaze. "I was summoned."

Hunter barks out a laugh as he drops into the chair beside me and Meyer even smirks a little.

"Yes, I suppose you were. Are you settling in okay?" he asks, like he didn't bring me here without giving me an option.

"I'd much rather go home and get on with my life," I tell him honestly. I figure, with the type of man he seems to be, which is much like Tommy, honesty is going to get me further than pandering to him like I had to do with Trent.

"That isn't an option. You'll be living here now."

"Excuse you?" The words fall from my mouth as I climb to my feet. "The hell I will. You already know I won't go to the police. I'm not going to say anything about what I saw because I'm not stupid. What other reason do you possibly have to keep me here against my will?"

"You're ours now." Meyer's words are blunt and to the point and I can't help the laugh that bubbles up my chest and spills from my lips.

"I am not some toy or possession you can claim ownership of."

Meyer smirks at me as he leans back in his chair. "No, you are far more than that, but what I said is still true. You belong to us now. You will remain here for your own safety, you will be cared for, catered to, and have everything you could possibly want."

"What I *want* is to get back to my life!" Exasperated, I start to pace, feeling their eyes on my every movement. "It might not have been much of a life, constantly looking over my shoulder, but I was free. Freedom isn't something I've had the most of in my life and you don't get to take that from me."

"Oh, Kitten, you're still free. Except here you're safe. Eddie will keep watch of you when one of us cannot be with you, but I'm working on making sure that's as little as possible."

"Who the hell is Eddie?" I explode, trying to take a deep breath to stop angry tears welling up.

"Bruno," Hunter chirps and Meyer looks at him, confused. "Don't ask," is all he says to his friend, who nods.

"No. I will not live this way. It is not living. I want to go back to work, to my apartment. Hell, I'll clear my debt to you and just leave totally."

Meyer barks out a laugh, leaning forward so his elbows rest on his desk once more, and his eyes narrow as he watches me closely. "Not an option. I will say it one more time. You. Are. Ours. There is no negotiation. You can be as free as you like within the confines of what keeps you safe."

I throw my hands in the air, a tear slipping down my cheek. "That isn't free. This is no different than the life I was running from. If this is my life, I might as well have never left."

Meyer slams a hand on the table, making me jump, and Rory moves to stand beside me as if to protect me. "Stand down, Rory. We both know I would never harm her." Rory doesn't move, and Meyer stands, moving around his desk and crossing the room to stand in front of me.

He cups my cheek, thumbing away the tears that fall. "I will never hurt you. None of us are anything like Trent and your life here will be nothing like it was then."

I shrug, not trusting my voice around the thickness in my throat.

Meyer sighs, dropping his hand from my cheek, but grabs my chin to lift my gaze to his. There is a firmness in his stare, one that makes me realize exactly why he is in charge and why they're obviously so successful at what they do, whatever that is. "But you will stay here and you will be safe. You will belong to us, and you will abide by the rules in place. You have been seen with us, which makes you a target, and I will not be responsible for harm coming to you."

I turn to Rory, who looks at me like he's torn between my tears and agreeing with Meyer. "And you told me this wasn't a cage."

Since I left the three of them in Meyer's office with my shadow back in place, I've been sitting by the pool watching the birds, jealous of their ability to fly off to wherever they want. Carlos brought lunch out to me, which I picked at. Not because the food wasn't as delicious as always, but because between the lump in my throat and the twisting of my stomach, I feared I'd either choke or be sick if I tried to eat much of it.

I did at least drink the lemon water he brought out to me. The day is a scorcher and, while I might feel helpless and angry, like I told the three of them earlier, I'm not stupid. Maybe stupid enough to have landed myself in this mess, but not stupid enough to get dehydrated.

Picking up my phone, I contemplate trying to call Tommy. Chances are, he's checked in with Meyer over the last few days so he knows where I am, and these people are his friends. He trusts them.

I'm also not sure, even with everything Tommy is capable of and has seen me through, that he could get me out of here. He came to these people because their resources were bigger and they could help keep me safe.

I just never contemplated it would be them I needed rescuing from. It's highly unlikely Tommy factored that in either and I can't fault him for that because it's not like any of this even sounds believable, let alone something you'd have a contingency for.

Telling me I am theirs. Like some sort of freaking caveman. I am a human, dammit. I don't belong to anyone but myself. Am I indebted to them? Yes, but debts can be cleared. Even ownership can be bought.

What if they sell me?

No, I shake that thought from my head, remembering what Yen said. They might be into some bad shit, but selling people goes against their morals.

Morals.

Ha!

They'll kill and kidnap people, but not sell them.

Now that's a moral compass my therapist would have a field day with, I'm sure.

"Doctor is here for the girl," I hear a male voice say. I turn to find someone talking to Bruno—whose name might be Eddie, but he will remain Bruno in my head at the very least because my brain won't accept any different.

Bruno nods at the man, who walks back into the house before looking over at me. "Come."

The one word makes me want to smile. "He speaks!" Somehow that one word feels like a win on a day when I feel like I've lost so much. Despite the fact that nothing has changed since this morning physically or mentally. Before my 'talk' with Meyer, I had clung to the hope of going back to my life. I lost that today and the losses have been swift and deep. So this win, regardless of how small, feels significant.

He doesn't speak again, just stares at me like I'm crazy.

"It's okay, you don't have to speak again, Bruno. Now that I know you *can* speak, I'm going to turn you into a chatterbox. Especially since you're basically my new shadow. You won't be able to resist." I focus on this as a plan, winning over my stoic shadow, because better to fixate on that than the loneliness and helplessness that has been swirling inside of me for the last hour or so. He doesn't so much as smile, but I let it go.

"Where to?" I ask, hoping for another word, but he points inside and I grin. "I'm getting close. You'll speak again, just you watch."

I don't know *why* he doesn't speak, but I intend to find out. If only I had a friend in this freaking fortress to help me figure it out. As angry as I am at Yen right now, a part of me wishes she was here. She'd get Bruno to talk. Hell, she'd probably figure out a way to persuade Meyer to let me go home. She knows them better than I do, knows which buttons to push. I'm here fumbling in the dark and falling at each hurdle.

Following the direction he pointed in, I head into the kitchen and hear voices in the entry hall just off it. Looking over at Bruno, he nods, so I walk toward the voices and find Meyer with a man who I am assuming from the medical bag in his hand is the doctor the other guy mentioned.

Meyer smiles upon seeing me and I quirk a brow at him. Am I supposed to pretend to be happy to see him? To be here? At least with Trent I knew my place, knew the role I had to play. Here I'm clueless. "Here she is. Quinn, this is Robert, our family doctor. He's just going to check you over and make sure everything is okay with you. I understand you haven't seen a doctor for several years."

Of course he knows that. Ugh. I'm really starting to

despise how much these men seem to know about me when I know almost nothing about them.

Biting down on the rude retort that threatens, I take a deep breath and turn to the doctor. "Lovely to meet you, I'm sure. It has been quite a while since I had a check up, but I feel perfectly fine."

The doctor smiles at me warmly, his dark eyes like melted chocolate. "Oh, I'm sure you do, but it can never hurt to check. So many things can lie undetected in the body and better to be sure than run any risks, yes?"

Awesome. Another frustratingly correct male in my life. Just freaking great.

"Of course," I respond, clenching my hands to fists behind my back. I run my gaze over the doctor, noting the gun on his hip.

Does anyone walk around here unarmed or is it just me?

It occurs to me that I still haven't seen or heard anything of Meyer's family, even though Rory told me they live here. I wonder if they're here at the moment. If they're prisoners like I am or if they actually live their lives the way they want.

Not that that matters right now, but it's a nice momentary distraction from the thought of going with this doctor.

"Shall we?" Meyer asks, and Robert nods, heading down the hall in a direction I haven't been before. Where the kitchen runs to the right of the entrance hall, and Meyer's family lives in the wing to the left, the doctor heads toward the back of the house.

To be fair, I hadn't realized there was anything that way and I haven't been up to the second level from the staircase in here, beyond the first door on the right, which is my room. Maybe I should explore some more.

"Quinn." I look up at Meyer, wondering if he's going to say anything further, but he doesn't. Feeling defeated once more, I take off down the hall, following the doctor, who stops at a door almost at the end of the tiled walkway.

Following him into the room, he moves back to the door once I'm inside. "I think we'll be okay just the two of us," he says to Meyer, and the angry, sad girl inside of me does a fist pump at someone telling Meyer no—even if it's not directly.

Without waiting for a response, the doctor closes the door and turns to smile at me. "Better. So, why don't you take a seat, Quinn. We'll go through your history and then I'll do my assessment, take some blood to run some tests, and anything else I think might be needed once I know some more about you."

At his words, I begin to take in the room and realize it looks just like a room you'd find at the hospital. There are machines galore, an examination bed, and just… who the fuck even has this inside of their house, and why the hell do they even need it?

"Quinn?" The doctor calls my name again, pulling my focus back to him as my heart starts to race in my chest.

"Sorry, I, erm," I pause, not really knowing how to explain the epic amount of overwhelm flooding my system right now after the events of the last few days. I have no idea how much he knows, how much he'll run and tell Meyer if I do say anything, and once again, the overwhelming helplessness fills me, making the panic swell.

Dropping into a crouch, I clutch my knees, dropping my head forward, trying to suck in air.

"You are safe in here, Quinn," the doctor says and the urge to laugh bubbles up but my panic overrides it.

If only he knew the truth.

I don't think I'm truly safe anywhere anymore.

"Deep breaths, I'll get you some oxygen to help," he murmurs, and it registers enough that I nod, but not enough to do anything to the debilitating panic gripping my body. I can't move, can't really think beyond breathing, can't *do* anything.

His hand rubs up and down my back before he loops something over my face and I acknowledge in the recesses of my brain that it's the oxygen he mentioned when he tucks it into my nose. Crouching beside me, he continues to rub my back until breathing feels a little easier and my body starts to relax.

"Does that happen often?" he asks when I finally manage to untangle myself and sit on the floor properly. He stays on the floor with me, not looking at me with pity but with concern.

"Not so much anymore," I tell him once I've taken enough breaths that I think I can actually speak. I hesitate for a moment because I don't know him. He's a stranger to me.

"You don't have to talk to me, but whatever you say, stays between us. Doctor, patient confidentiality."

I still feel a little uneasy, but Meyer brought him here, so he obviously trusts him. I guess that means I can too? "When I first ran, they happened a lot. I'm fairly certain panic is the only thing that kept me moving the first few weeks until I found Tommy." I pause, wondering if he knows who that is, but he smiles in recognition and nods for me to continue. "God knows I didn't eat or sleep much back then. After Tommy, they still happened, mostly when my ex would send his flowers and taunts, but even then, they stopped after a while. Today has just been a day. Sorry."

"You don't need to apologize to me, Quinn. I understand you've been through a lot. Panic attacks are common in people who have lived through what you have. It's totally understandable that a lot of change might overwhelm you like that."

I bark out a dry laugh. "Yeah, something like that."

He looks at me like he understands, which makes me realize he knows exactly what's going on with me. Which means he's in Meyer's inner circle. Which also means he's absolutely no help to me. Not beyond making sure I'm not dying anyway. No, he's here to make sure I'm a healthy captive.

Just freaking stellar.

"Can you stand?" he asks gently, and I take a minute to assess my body, finally nodding when I know I can get up without falling flat on my face.

He stands first, offering me a hand and I shakily take it, letting him help me to my feet. He walks me over to the bed and I hop up onto it, my legs swinging off the side like a kid on a chair too big for them.

"So, let's start at the beginning, shall we?" he says softly, smiling at me with those kind eyes of his, watching me closely.

"Beginning?" I ask, a little confused.

He nods, taking a seat and pulling a laptop from his bag, opening it and tapping away on the keyboard for a moment before bringing his attention back to me. "Any history of major illnesses in your family?"

"Not that I know of," I tell him, shaking my head. "Don't you have this information in the files I'm sure Meyer has on me?"

He smiles again, this one a little less warm. "I have some, but I like to ask my own questions."

I nod, not wanting to piss him off too, and go through answering all his questions—from what vaccinations I had when I was young, to illnesses I've had, to the many, many traumas sustained from both my father and Trent. It's weird to actually speak about it all like it happened to someone else. I guess I have trauma to thank for the dissociation here and, for once, I'm grateful that I can't feel it.

His face gives away nothing the entire time I speak, and once I finish listing off the many injuries, he nods. "I'd like to take you in for some scans, full body ones, to ensure there are no breaks that haven't healed properly and nothing else going on internally considering the extensive history. I can't see anything like that in previous admissions."

"Trent didn't really allow for much," I tell him quietly, looking down at my hands as I pick at the skin by my thumbs. I haven't done that in years, not since I found the courage to leave Trent, but reliving everything, I feel small. Weak. Useless. Trapped. Helpless.

All those things I thought I had escaped.

"I see," is all he says, but there's something in his voice that makes me look up at him. His jaw tics where it's clenched, but I can't tell if he's angry at me or not, so I stay quiet. "Let's draw some blood and then I'll move on to my assessments. Is there any chance you're pregnant?"

I bark out a laugh and shake my head. "Not at all. I'm on birth control."

"Any unprotected sex, even with being on birth control?"

I open my mouth to say no, then curse myself internally. "Yes, but that was a while ago, and I've had my period like normal since."

He nods, tapping away on his laptop. "Okay. I'll still run the test since I'm drawing blood, but I don't see it being a major risk if you've had your period. What birth control are you on?"

"I have the implant," I say to him, tapping on my arm. "Though, I think it's due to be changed soon."

"May I suggest a change to the shot? I'll be seeing you fairly regularly anyway, so appointments won't be a problem, but I've known a whole host of women who have had issues with the implant and I'd rather you not have to experience that."

"Issues?"

"A ninety-day period was one of the ones I was told about," he says, wincing.

"Oh, hell no," I say with a shudder. "Absolutely not. Swap me over. As long as I don't have crotch goblins, I don't care."

He chuckles at my obvious horror, or maybe at my phrasing, but I'm too horrified to care. That sounds like literal hell on earth.

"Okay, we'll do that for you today too. Let's get this started, shall we?"

He draws my blood, removes my implant, gives me the shot in my ass, which stung more than I thought it would, along with a host of other shots. One of which went into my back and hurt like hell. He did reel off a ton of wordy bullshit in doctor talk about what he was doing, but most of it went over my head.

"I'll speak to Meyer about getting you to the hospital for a scan, but otherwise, I think you're good to go. Once I have the results from your bloodwork, I'll let you know if we find anything, but from my observations, you seem in good health."

I jump down from the bed, and nod. "I did say as much."

"And as I said, better safe than sorry."

Feeling awkward, I head to the door, unlocking it before turning back to him. "Well, thanks I guess. I'll see you soon."

"You will. And remember, no unprotected sex for at least seven days while the shot settles in."

I bark out a laugh, "Yeah, no danger there," I tell him before opening the door, finding the hall empty. My heart dances in my chest at the momentary opportunity for freedom.

I practically skip down the hall, leaving the doctor alone, and head to the room I've been allocated. This might still be a cage, but right now, no one knows where I am and that little piece of freedom is one I'm going to cling to with all I have.

NINETEEN

HUNTER

"You sure this was the best way to do this?" I ask Meyer again, who stares at me like I'm a defiant child. "I'm not saying I have a better way that comes to mind, but still. She's already had a pretty shitty day."

"She's having a shitty day because she's being stubborn," he responds before finishing his espresso. "If she wasn't so defiant—"

"Then we probably wouldn't want her," Rory interrupts, and I smile.

"You're not wrong."

Meyer scrubs a hand down his face and lets out an exasperated sigh. "You're right, we probably wouldn't. The fact that she's a fighter is part of her charm. But does she have to fight me so hard? I'm just trying to do what's best for her."

I lean forward, feeling the frustration coming from him in waves. "She's probably heard that a lot too. Seeing her cry nearly broke me, man. I'm not saying I want her to leave, especially when she doesn't have any idea of the risks that sit with her now that she's been seen with us, seen at the house, but we could've been softer about it."

"Maybe," Meyer says, relenting a little.

"And since Rob is implanting the tracker in her, maybe we can give her the illusion of freedom for now." I'm not usually the guy with the plan, I'm just the guy who charms people into going along with Meyer's plans, but maybe, just this once, I can use his own weapons against him, for Quinn. I'm sure he'll get over it if he realizes the manipulation.

His reaction if he does, I'm sure, is going to be far less of a meltdown than if Quinn ever finds out she now has a tracker in her spine. Now *that* is going to be an argument for the record books, but I'd rather argue with her and have fun making up after than have something happen to her and us not know where she is because we didn't put the tracker in her.

He tilts his head, as if contemplating my idea. "It's not the worst idea. We can dip her toe out in the world, and if she doesn't try to run, we can maybe look at a little more freedom. But she doesn't leave the property without one of us with her."

"I'm sure she'd agree to that if it means she gets to go out."

"I still don't want her back in the club though." I roll my eyes at him but cover it by scratching at the bridge of my nose. I might be a possessive asshole sometimes, but Meyer makes me look easy breezy.

Rory stays suspiciously quiet about all of it, but he's always been the stoic one of the three of us. He tends to speak only when he thinks his words will carry weight. Like earlier. I know he likes to think of himself as more of the psychopathic brawn of the operation rather than the brains, but he doesn't give himself enough credit.

"I'm sure we can work on that with her, but she's going to want some sort of illusion of independence," I counter. "Her working at our club, with our people, is probably one of the safest ways to do that."

"I hate it when you make sense," he grumbles. "Maybe, but not yet. I need to make sure that this thing with the Demons is taken care of. Plus, the Knights keep sticking their nose in our business and I want that shut down before we do anything."

"The Knights?" I ask, taken aback. They've always kept out of our way and we've done the same with them. The billionaires play in a different league than us. Even if we hustle the same products in the same overall area, we've never had issues before. "You think they'll be a problem?"

"Not if I can help it. Do we have an update on the shipments getting back here?" he asks, turning to Rory.

"Everything's going to plan. The four trucks have split off in different directions, but the trackers are in place and the drivers have been in touch, as have the guys following them. For now, it's all quiet. No kickback from the Ghosts yet."

The Ghosts being the ones the Demons tried to rip off and failed. Thankfully, my guy in the Demons let me know what was happening and we were there to swoop in and save the day while reaping the rewards of their fuck up.

Two trucks of guns, one of dope, and the other... well, that truck we'll be dealing with when it arrives. We had an agreement with the Ghosts and Demons, and that truck was full of underage girls from Europe. Part of our agreement is that those we deal with don't trade in skin.

They broke that agreement and there will be hell to pay for it.

Once we get the girls somewhere safe.

Which reminds me, I need to check in with Yen. She usually helps us settle the girls because she knows what they've lived through in a way few others can comprehend. She's also been up my ass about Quinn, so I need to deal with that too, but right now, I need to refocus on what the fuck Meyer is saying.

"—make sure it's handled, and that Greyson knows we know."

"Consider it done," Rory responds. "As for Quinn, she asked to go to her apartment. I could take her there tomorrow to collect her things. It might make her feel more at home here and gain us some favor with her."

"I think you're likely the only one she's not pissed at," I say, laughing. "Did you know she told me she doesn't think you're scary? Like, at all?"

He almost looks impressed, but the look drops from his face quickly and he shrugs. "She doesn't know any better."

Meyer's phone rings, and I swear I hear him curse under his breath. "Hello?" he says as he lifts the phone to his ear. "What do you mean she won't get in the car? For fuck's sake, I'm on my way."

He hangs up and stands, pinching the bridge of his nose. "Mother won't get in the car with O'Connor. Apparently, she's having a fit because I told her I would collect her and Shae from the airport. So I guess I'm going to go and deal with that."

I press my lips together to stop from laughing. Big bad mafia boss being brought to heel by his mother. I mean, most Italian families work that way, but it's still super funny to watch and never gets old. Watching Meyer crumble to his mother's iron fist has always been an amusement of mine. Maybe because my mother wasn't worth a damn, and because his places her family above all else, but I've always had a soft spot for her.

"I have to go and deal with Elise," Rory pipes up, and they both swing their gazes to me.

"Oh no, how terrible for me. I guess I'll stay here and keep an eye on Quinn." I put my hands up in mock surrender while I pull a face like my day is about to be so much worse than theirs.

"Fuck you," Meyer says, flipping me the finger as he grabs his car keys. "Take her to the apartment tomorrow, Eric will be here, so it'll be good to get her away from the house."

Rory nods, the corners of his lips tilting up momentarily. "Sure thing."

They both head out, leaving me to go and track down Quinn. Oh, yeah… my day is the worst.

After spotting Quinn gazing out of her bedroom window at the pool, I pulled a few different swimsuits from the lockers we keep here for guests and had Marta, the housekeeper, take them up to her room.

I stay in the pool house, TV playing low, paying exactly no attention to it as I wait for her to emerge and, oh man, is it worth every agonizing moment of patience when she finally walks outside.

She picked the dark green one piece with cut outs on her stomach, only just covering what *needs* to be covered and, fuck me, I already know I'm a goner. The black slip she has covering her shoulders drifts to the ground once she stops and she glances at the pool as if she's trying to decide whether to take a dip or not.

Every part of me wants to go out there and swim with her, but I'm also very aware that I'm probably the last person she wants to see right now. She might have talked everything out with me about sleeping with her without her knowing who I was, but I can tell she hasn't actually forgiven me for it yet. Despite the fact that she went toe to toe with Meyer earlier, I get the feeling that she'd still prefer to see him over me right now.

It stings a little, but I shoulder it, knowing that she'll come around eventually. The connection we had, the chemistry, it's hard to replicate or ignore and I know— hope—that once she realizes just what I'm willing to give up for her, to do for her, she'll forgive me.

Until then, I'm going to watch her like a creeper.

This is usually Rory's bag. I'd rather be upfront and center than hiding in the shadows, but for her, I'll do what I need to.

She walks toward the pool, pulling her highlighted hair into a messy bun on top of her head before dipping a toe in the water. The smile on her face lights her up and I take pride in the fact that I did that. Even while she's furious with me, I made her smile. Not that she knows it was me, but I'm going to take the win where I can.

I know I could go over there, go all caveman on her, and I know that she'd bend to my will if I press the right buttons, but enough has been taken from her in her life. I don't want to take anything else from her if I can help it. But I absolutely will if it's in her best interest.

Like keeping her here.

She might not know exactly *why* it's safer, but it's not on me to explain it to her. Meyer made that decision and I fell in line, mostly because I agree it's probably not the greatest idea to tell her everything yet. But I do know that it will keep her safe, so I'll stick to it.

She slowly swims a few laps before climbing from the pool and lying down on the lounger where she let her slip fall to the ground earlier. Part of me wants to take her a drink, try to talk to her while she's in a good mood, but I also don't want to invade her peace.

God damn being this conflicted.

I'm not the guy who sits back when he wants something. I'm the guy that storms ahead and takes it. And the thought of taking her right there on that sun lounger, where anyone could see us? Yeah, I'm rock fucking solid.

It's part of why I stopped the elevator when I did. I

know there are cameras in there. Anyone could've been watching, and being watched... watching... totally my thing. Knowing that people can see she's mine, that they can't have her the way I can. Hell fucking yes.

Change the thought pattern, Hunter.

It's fucking difficult because just look at her. She's all freaking curves and soft skin. Knowing how she reacts to my touch, the sounds she makes as she comes...

Fucking exquisite.

A glint catches my eye and I notice one of Rory's guys in the distance watching her. The glint shines again when I realize his hand is in his fucking pants.

I don't fucking think so.

Without a second thought, a red haze clouds my vision and I storm from the pool house in his direction. I don't even give him a second to speak or pull his hand from his dick before I slam my fist into his jaw.

Rage like I've never known takes over me. The thought of him watching her like that...

No. That's my thing, no one else gets to do that to her without her knowing. Fuck that.

I slam my fist into his stomach as he tries to stand, causing him to double over. Grabbing his hair, I slam a knee into his face, his cry as his nose explodes is like a song to my soul.

"What the fuck!" he screams, but I don't stop. I push

him to the ground and stomp on his dick.

"She does not belong to you!" I growl at him before kicking his side, watching with too much delight as he curls into a fetal position.

"I'm sorry," he cries out and I hear more voices. Guys from the staff house appear, stopping before they reach us when they realize it's me out here.

"She is off-fucking-limits, under all circumstances. Same rules as Shae, do you understand?" I run my gaze across all of them, nods and murmurs of agreement calling back to me. "If I catch any of you so much as glancing at her again, I'll cut your dick off and feed it to you. Make sure everyone is aware."

My rage isn't even close to sated, but I've had eyes off her for too long already so I turn and head back to the pool house, finding Eddie standing guard nearby. Apparently, he was watching too, but Eddie is different. One, Quinn has the wrong equipment to excite him, and two, he's as loyal to Meyer as Rory and me. He wouldn't dream of touching her.

The others, however... I'll let Rory deal with them if anyone else thinks they can cross that line again. He'll make me look like a pussycat.

I grab ice from the freezer in the pool house and put it in a bucket, shoving my fist in so the bruising doesn't appear too bad, if at all, then take my post back up to watch her. Apparently, she didn't notice anything because she's lying exactly where I left her, eyes closed, enjoying the sun on her skin.

Voices in the distance alert me to the fact that Meyer is home, and moments later, I realize that another type of hell is likely about to break loose as Shae, Meyer's little sister, steps outside and spots Quinn.

That is not a friendship any of us are ready for, but the smile on Shae's face tells me that we better buckle up, ready or not.

TWENTY

QUINN

Glancing over in the direction of all the noise, I don't see a thing, but I've seen and heard enough fights to know that someone's getting into something. Lying back on the lounger, I try to ignore it. Whatever it is, it has nothing to do with me and I'm not about to stick my nose into someone else's fight. I've fought and lost enough today already.

I can still feel eyes on me, but I spot Bruno out of the corner of my eye. Should've known. Of course I couldn't do something as simple as lie by the pool without a chaperone.

Meyer might have said he was trying to keep me safe, but I call BS. I was supposedly safe before, when I was at the apartment and working the bar, so I don't get what is so different now if they supposedly trust me the way they say they do.

I shake my head, trying to push the angry thoughts from my mind. I said this afternoon was going to be relaxing when the housekeeper—who, it turns out, is my secret clothing delivery person—Marta, appeared at my door with swimsuits that still had tags on them. After trying on a few, I settled on the green one piece that is going to give me more than a few hilarious tan lines, but it's not like anyone is going to see me naked anytime soon.

Pushing out a deep breath, I reposition myself to soak up the beautiful warm rays of sun that are beating down on me. I don't remember the last time I actually relaxed like this... or if I ever actually have. Despite my anger at Meyer, at least in this moment I don't have to worry about Trent, or anything, really, so the opportunity to actually relax is one I want to grab with both hands.

So tell me why my stupid brain will not stay quiet, opting instead to repeat the conversation from earlier on a freaking loop.

The commotion dies down and I try to take another deep breath. Who would have thought relaxing and being zen would be so freaking hard? Everyone on TV always makes it look so easy, like they find peace almost instantly. Yet, here I am, having been out here for like, an hour, still unable to truly rest.

I even tried swimming a few laps, which I haven't done

since college, in the hope that the physical exertion might help quiet my mind.

More fool me.

All it did was make my shoulders ache. Apparently, I'm more out of shape than I realized. At least while I'm trapped here, I can try to get in better shape. Rory said there was a gym and there's a pool. What else do I need?

Look at me, trying to find the silver lining to my gilded cage.

I let out a small, dry laugh, shaking my head at my own twisted sense of humor—thank you, trauma.

"So, who are you?"

I open my eyes, blinking against the tears that fill them at the brightness of the day, and find a beautiful, sun-kissed, dark-haired girl staring down at me. She moves to the lounger beside me, sitting and crossing her legs beneath her as she watches me.

"Erm, I'm Quinn. Who are you?"

She nods her head as her eyes widen in recognition. "Ah, you're the new bird in our pretty cage. Nice to meet you, I'm Shae."

I laugh as I sit up and she quirks a brow at me. "What's so funny?"

"I've been calling this place my gilded cage for days." She grins at my response. It's a wicked grin that screams trouble, which is reflected in the glint of her eyes, and I think I might love her already.

"Oh, I see. Yeah I'm going to like you. Are you enjoying the pretty cage so far?"

I roll my eyes and let out a sigh. "Not particularly. The cavemen in charge aren't exactly the best of hosts."

"Yeah, my brother isn't the best with people, neither is Rory, but I'm surprised that Hunter hasn't been the hostess with the mostest." She looks at me like I'm a fun new jigsaw puzzle for her to work out and it hits me that this is Meyer's little sister that Rory told me about.

"Hunter… well, he can go sit on a ten inch dildo."

Shae bursts out laughing, clutching her stomach as she does. "Yep, definitely going to like you, but what the hell did he do to get on your bad side? You look so… cute and innocent. I can't imagine you disliking much of anyone."

"Looks can be deceiving in the deadliest of ways," I mumble, looking down at my hands, thinking of Trent, before looking back up at her. "He's just a fuck boy and well, liars aren't really my bag."

"He lied?" she asks, looking shocked. "That's pretty out of character for him. Color me intrigued. As for looks being deceiving, I understand that more than I'd like."

She tugs on the sleeves of her jacket and bunches the cuffs around her hands. Looking at her, I realize if I paid attention, I would have noticed she was Meyer's sister straight away. She looks just like him, just more feminine.

From the dark hair, to the amber eyes. Her jaw is far more dainty, but still strong and her lithe frame is obviously powerful. She carries herself like someone who is more than capable and she knows it.

I wonder what it must feel like to live that way. To know that you don't have to fear much of anyone because you can handle yourself in any situation.

"So what landed you in our pretty cage, Quinn?" she asks, leaning back on her lounger. I do the same and Carlos appears with a pitcher of what looks like lemonade and two glasses, placing them on the table between us before disappearing without a word.

"I don't know that I can tell you that," I say to her, almost apologetically.

"Business then. Understood. I'm surprised you're here though. Usually, business matters aren't brought to the house. Unless it's some important meeting or a show of power. You really are an intrigue."

I shrug, feeling her gaze creep over me. "I'm no one special, just someone your brother is helping who stumbled somewhere I shouldn't have. I'm hoping I'll be going home soon."

It's her turn to laugh and she draws my gaze. "Oh, Quinn, if you think that then you don't know my brother at all. And looking at you, I'm thinking he's never going to let you go."

I shake my head and roll my eyes. "Maybe this time, mister big boss man isn't going to get what he wants."

"Yeah, I knew I was going to like you," Shae responds with a grin. "If I wasn't convinced you're firmly Team Dick, I'd think of more creative ways to encourage you to stay."

She wags her brows, pulling another laugh from me. "You are beautiful, but yeah, tits just don't do it for me."

"You ever tried?"

I shake my head, smiling wider than I remember doing in a long time. "No, no I haven't."

"Then maybe you just haven't discovered your love for tits." She winks at me playfully. "But for now, I think maybe I'll just save you from the testosterone in this house so you don't feel quite so trapped all the time. It's amazing what having a friend in this world can do for the soul." For a minute, her mask slips and I see the lonely girl beneath it. The sadness there calls to the darkness inside of me, like finding like, and I reach out to take her hand.

"I think a good friend might be exactly what I need."

After spending most of yesterday with Shae and laughing more than I have in about a week, discovering this place has a movie theater, complete with popcorn machine, cotton candy machine, and a ton of other stuff that made the little girl in my head squeal with joy, and spending the night watching cheesy rom coms, booing at the leading men, I'm feeling a little lighter than I have since the night I stumbled upon Meyer shooting some guy in the head.

I still don't know why that happened, but I don't see me asking anytime soon, either. I'm not sure I'd get an answer even if I did.

But now I'm sitting in the kitchen with Carlos, who is humming and dancing along to music that plays softly while he cooks me eggs Florentine and I feel… almost peaceful.

Don't get me wrong, I still want to go back to my life, even with the prospect of Trent finding me, because my freedom is worth more to me than almost anything, but a night of laughter with Shae was exactly what I needed.

"Good, you're up already," Rory says as he slides into the chair beside me. I startle, because I didn't see or hear him enter the room. It's still astonishing to me that a guy of his size can move in the shadows the way he does.

Heh, another mountainous ninja.

"I am," I say, stating the obvious, but deliver it with a smile since Rory is probably the only one of the three men effectively holding me hostage that hasn't been an ass to me yet. Hell, if anything, he's been nice.

"We're heading back to your apartment this morning,"

he states, and my heart picks up its pace with joy.

"We are? Thank you so much! I thought Meyer said I had to stay here. This is amazing!"

"No, Quinn," he says, cutting off my excited ramblings. "We're going to go and get your things, maybe take some time out in the city to go shopping, get anything else you need, but then we'll be coming back here."

"Oh." The word is dull and lifeless as the wind leaves my sails at his words. "But I liked my apartment."

I'm really going to miss that tub.

"Is there something here that isn't fitting your needs?" he asks, all business, and for a moment I see what Hunter had implied about him, that part of him that makes men tremble at the knees.

"You mean other than my freedom being taken away?" I let out a sigh and shake my head. "No, the amenities in the house are just fine. My room is fine. The bathroom is fine. It's all just peachy."

"Quinn—" he starts, but I shake my head, cutting him off.

"No, Rory. I've made it clear what my wants are, but apparently they don't matter. So it's all just fine. Don't expect me to be happy about being held captive when I've spent the last two years running from my last captor. This might be a prettier package, but underneath the layers, it's no different."

He nods, like he's weighing my words and making a decision. "Fuck it, Meyer can be pissed at me, but I don't want you to feel like that in our home." He pauses, running a hand across his head then down his face. "Originally, we wanted you here because of what you saw. We had a good feeling we could trust you because of Tommy, but then you were seen with us. Here. Threats have been made because of assumptions of what that means you are to us. So while Meyer is being a caveman about how he's going about it, he's just trying to keep you safe."

"Oh." The single syllable falls from my lips as I try to process what he just said. I was seen with them and someone made threats. Why would anyone make threats about me? "Threats? But why?"

"Because it's rare that we'd travel together, with someone who no one has seen before, I guess? I don't claim to understand the idiots who think making threats against us is a good idea when we've proven, many times over, that it's really not." He pauses when Carlos brings over my breakfast and watches me intently until I take a bite. "But for now, no one will believe us if we say that you're not important to us, so you're here. Which, yes, will just fuel the rumor that you're important to us, but better to fuel it and keep you safe than leave you to the wolves."

And just like that, I feel like an asshole. Like a petty, insolent child who's been throwing her toys. "Why didn't

Meyer just tell me that?"

"Because he has control issues," the man in question states as he enters the room, striding toward the coffee machine.

"She deserved to know," Rory says unapologetically with a shrug.

Meyer turns to look at him, a silent conversation seeming to pass between them in the moments that their gazes meet. "Doesn't matter either way now. Have you told her the plans for the day?"

"Yes, he has," I input, not really enjoying being talked about like I'm not in the room. "Which is what led to his confession. Thank you both for allowing me to get my things."

I concede my part in the conversation and continue eating my breakfast, half listening to their discussion as they talk through Meyer's plans for the day. It doesn't make total sense to me, and at times he switches languages when talking to Carlos, so I stop even trying to keep up.

"I just need to grab some stuff from my room, then I'll be ready to go," Rory says to me before draining the mug of coffee Carlos put down in front of him earlier. It occurs to me that I don't think I've actually seen Rory eat. He's rarely even in the kitchen. But Meyer seems to be in here almost every time I'm in here, watching me like a hawk as I eat.

Weird thing to notice, but well, it's not like I have much else taking up my brain capacity right now.

"Yeah, I'm good to go whenever," I tell him with a small smile. I'm already fully dressed, having put on the denim cutoffs, white tank, plaid shirt, and flat white sandals I found laid out for me earlier. Still weird getting dressed this way, but after today, at least I'll have my own stuff.

Taking the small wins, all things considered.

"You look beautiful today," Meyer murmurs when Rory has left the room, and I blink at him, wondering if he actually said it or if I've lost my mind. He smirks at me and I realize he did actually speak.

"Erm, thank you?"

His smirk widens as he turns to face me. "You're welcome, Kitten."

"Is there a reason that none of you use my actual name?" I quirk a brow when he chuckles at me. Really, that's not quite right because I *think* Rory uses my name, but I can't remember a time when Hunter or Meyer actually called me Quinn.

You'd think after changing my name a dozen or so times while I've been running that I wouldn't really care, but there is something about the two of them using weirdly intimate nicknames that gets under my skin. They haven't earned the right to use nicknames. Well, maybe Hunter. He did earn a ton of points that night in the elevator, even if he's lost most of them since, but still.

Totally not the point.

"Maybe I just like seeing the fire in your eyes when I call you Kitten." Delight dances in his eyes as he teases me and I open my mouth to retort when Rory reenters the room.

"Oh, good," I say with a happy sigh. "Time to go."

"I'll see you later, Kitten," Meyer calls out as I walk away from him toward Rory, and I flip him the bird behind my back, which just seems to make him laugh harder than before.

"Everything okay?" Rory asks, looking at me with puzzlement as we leave the room.

"Oh, yeah. Just peachy," I tell him, trying to dial back my sass. "Just your friend being an ass."

That draws the first real smile I think I've seen from Rory, even though it disappears quickly. "Yeah, he has a tendency to do that. But if he's letting you see that side of him, it means he likes you. He isn't truly himself around most people. You've probably noticed."

I think over his words as he leads me out the front door, down the steps, and opens the door to a kitted-out Defender. "Up you get."

He puts his hands on my waist and practically lifts me into the car after I spend a few seconds working out just how I'm going to climb the frame of the giant machine.

I'm not small, but damn this thing is big.

The drive to the apartment doesn't take as long as I thought it would, though I guess that makes sense since Hunter was bouncing between the house and his apartment. We ride in silence except for the music playing in the background, which Rory turns up when he sees me mouthing along to *Thrive* by Cassadee Pope. It's sweet of him and I can't help but wonder if, like Meyer, I'm getting to see a side of Rory that not many people see.

I don't know *why* they'd give that to me. All things considered, I was just a job for them and now I'm a more complicated job. But if I take into consideration what Rory told me earlier, I've been a total brat and they've been almost overly-accommodating in making sure I stay alive.

An apology is probably in order, but I need to ruminate on what I'm going to say. I'm still mad at Hunter and I'm still mad that I'm in this situation because they dragged me back to the house with them in the first place, *but*…

Well, I don't know what comes after that yet, except for that gross feeling inside of me that tells me I should be way more thankful than I have been. Though, if they had just told me the truth from the beginning, we wouldn't be in this place of me feeling like I need to apologize.

Maybe I'll call Tommy. He usually has a way of helping me muddle through the jumble in my mind and coming to a logical conclusion that doesn't require me overthinking every single detail of every potential response for three weeks.

When Rory has the car in a space in the underground parking lot—which I didn't know existed... way to be observant there, Quinn—he leads me to an elevator that brings us up to the lobby.

"Good morning, Quinn!" Eric calls out happily. "And to you, Mr. Beeston."

Rory Beeston. Huh. Not something that goes with his supposedly scary man image, but then, who is named for their image?

You're squirreling, Quinn. Focus.

"Morning," I reply to Eric, following Rory as he exits one elevator and presses the button for the one that goes up to my apartment. It's then that I realize he has his own key to get into my apartment, which is good, because I didn't even think to grab my keys when we left the house. The elevator dings and we step inside, Rory nods to Eric as the doors start to close and, once again, the tension in here is stifling.

There is something about him that is larger than life and I haven't noticed it before. Maybe it's because we're alone, maybe it's because I'm in an enclosed space with him, or maybe it's the fact that he's the first man in my life that has been truly honest with me—outside of Tommy—and put my needs first that has me recognizing it now.

It's potent and intoxicating and calls to that feminine part of me that would really like for someone capable to just deal with my monsters for me. The independent part of me despises that side of me, but it doesn't make it any less prevalent and Rory would absolutely be the guy capable of slaying all my dragons.

The elevator dings again just before the door opens and I shake off the thought. Definitely not where my mind should be. Ever. Especially when I've slept with one of his best friends and have definitely had similar thoughts about his other best friend.

Maybe two years without sex made me a little crazed. Or maybe it's this whole situation I'm in. Whatever it is, it needs to stop.

"Let me make sure it's clear," Rory says as he opens the door to the apartment, placing his arm in front of me to stop me getting any closer.

The hairs on the back of my neck rise as a shiver runs down my spine. "I thought this building was secure…" I whisper.

He shrugs. "It's supposed to be, but I'm not willing to put you at risk for complacency."

I don't really know what to say to that so I nod and stay quiet, hanging back as he pulls a set of keys from his pocket.

Without a sound, he opens the door and disappears

inside. Holding my breath while I wait, I hear nothing but the rushing of my blood in my head. It feels like an age, but it can't be more than a minute before Rory reappears. "All clear."

Letting out a breath, relief floods my system. I really didn't need that level of panic today, but I guess it's a good reminder. I've definitely been... what was it he said? Oh, yes. *Complacent* while I've been at the house. I didn't even keep an eye on traffic as we drove here to make sure no one was following us, or check our surroundings before I got out of the car.

Anyone or anything could have been waiting for me.

Complacent and careless isn't something I can afford to be.

I follow him into the apartment and a wave of sadness washes over me. "I really did like it here," I tell him. "It's the first place in a long time that actually felt like home."

He watches me closely, not saying a word, so I suck it up and resolve to stop sulking. Being safe is key and being here might be safe, but it's not as safe as the house.

That is what I need to keep reminding myself.

"This shouldn't take long. I'd say help yourself to anything in the kitchen, but I'm a terrible host and the fridge is usually empty. I doubt Yen has been shopping while I've been gone, if she's even been here at all." I try to keep the bitterness from my tongue at the mention of the person I thought was my friend, but I know I fail when his brow scrunches up.

Without saying anything else, I head into my room, grab my suitcases from beneath the bed, and start to pack up my stuff.

As promised, it doesn't take me too long. I definitely have more than the backpack I arrived in the city with, as per Tommy's insistence, which is exactly why I bought suitcases all those months ago. Even so, with the trinkets, towels, and bedding—all of which I'm sure I won't even get a chance to need until I can leave the house, but who knows when that will be—I don't know if I have enough space.

"Will someone else take the apartment while I'm at the house?" I ask Rory when I finish packing and head back into the kitchen. "Or will I be able to come back here when the threat has passed?"

He scratches the back of his neck and I try to wait as patiently as I can. "I'm not sure on the logistics yet. We won't know how long the threat will stay in place, so better to bring everything and be safe rather than sorry."

I try not to let my sinking heart show on my face. I'd assumed as much but that doesn't make it any easier to hear.

Emptying the safe in the kitchen of my important documents from Tommy, I slide the folder into the lesser filled suitcase, along with the few trinkets from in here.

Moments later, the sound of a key turning in the lock sounds and Rory is in front of me in a blink, gun raised at the door.

"Woah, woah, woah, no guns needed." Yen's voice is frazzled and I hear her footsteps falter as Rory keeps his gun raised. I place a hand on his back and he relaxes, lowering the firearm. "What's going on?"

She can't see me yet and I'm thankful for the moment to gather myself before facing the person I thought was my friend. I take a breath and step around my protector, finding Yen closing the front door.

"Oh, Quinn! Thank God you're okay! Meyer wouldn't tell me anything about where you were. I've been worried sick."

"Worried? Really? So worried about me because I'm your friend? The one you lied to about who Hunter was? About why you were living here in my apartment? About why you even approached me in the first place?" The last two are just assumptions, but the way her face drops tells me enough to know that I'm right.

"Quinn, let me explain," she says, harriedly. "No, I didn't tell you who Hunter was, but I figured you knew, and if you didn't then there was a reason he didn't want you to know. And yes, I approached you because Hunter asked me to help keep an eye on you, but that was just the start. I offered to move in because you're my friend and I was worried about you. It just happened to suit the bosses' needs that I'd be here too. It wasn't an order, not like the other stuff. I am so sorry. I wanted to tell you, I just didn't know how and I was still following orders. I owe them all so much…"

She trails off and I shake my head, trying to process it all. "I won't say everything's okay and I won't say I forgive you, because right now I still don't, but I also doubt I have time to stand here and argue it out."

I look back at Rory, who nods, backing me up despite me knowing there's no time limit on this trip since he offered to take me shopping. I just don't have the energy to have this conversation right now with so much else still churning through my mind.

"But we'll talk when I'm allowed out of the house again."

"You're at the house?" she asks, eyes wide, and I look to Rory again. I probably shouldn't have said anything, but they apparently trust her far more than I do right now, so I wait for his input. He nods again before pulling his phone from his pocket and tapping away at the screen.

"Yeah, I'm at the house. I got a morning pass of freedom."

"Why are you at the house? What do you mean freedom? Is Trent here?"

Rory steps forward as I open my mouth to speak so I stop. "Hunter will check in with you later, but we need to go."

"Oh, um, okay. I guess. Will you be coming back here, Quinn?" she asks, taking in my bags.

I shrug and zip up the open one before wheeling them to the door where Rory takes one from me. "I don't know yet, but probably not."

"I'm sorry," she says quietly. "I'll pack up too and head back to my place."

"Good idea," Rory responds to her, and she bows her head, moving toward her room.

"I really am sorry, Quinn."

I turn to face her as Rory opens the door and, for a minute, I almost want to crumble. But crumbling never got me anywhere. "Yeah, I know. Me too."

TWENTY ONE

Unpacking was a pitifully quick task and Rory disappeared once we were home. I don't know if it's because he sensed my souring mood after running into Yen or if he actually just had something to do, but either way, I'm kind of glad for the alone time and a chance to process everything running through my mind.

When I was younger, I would read to escape the horrors of my world, to find distraction in a land far, far away. As I got older, that became something I was able to do less and less so I found solace in other things, but none of them feel like enough to get me out of my head right now.

I feel like I want to climb out of my skin and there isn't another way to describe it. I just feel so freaking uncomfortable and I want to just forget for a while. Except there's no escape here. There's nothing but quiet, even if I don't want to infect someone else with my mood and I'm half glad to be alone, that doesn't mean that I don't want to forget. Because processing means facing things and facing things can be terrifying.

I haven't wanted to hide from the thoughts in my head quite this badly for years, and I don't understand why I'm feeling so frazzled, so triggered, so entirely out of sorts, but I am. The urge to go running hits me and I don't even like to run.

Regardless, I dig through the drawers in my room for the workout clothes I just put away—a frivolous purchase on one of the many shopping trips with Yen that I agonized over for days after—and then head downstairs to find the gym that Rory mentioned.

Moving through the kitchen, I spot Marta and smile, hoping she can help me. "Marta," I call out with a wave. "Rory said there was a gym here. I don't suppose you could tell me where it is, could you?"

"Of course I can, sweetheart. You don't want the outside gym, though. That's for the workers and not that nice. Let me show you the fitness suite that the family uses." She smiles at me, patting my shoulder before walking out of the kitchen.

I hurry behind her, heading down the hall to where I had my examination with the doctor, except she heads right to the end of the hall and opens a door. "Down the stairs you'll find everything you could possibly want. Let me know if you need anything else."

"Thank you!" I call after her as she rushes away before looking down the stairs. The lights are already on down there and I don't want to interrupt anyone, but the bubbles beneath my skin reach fizzing level, making my decision for me.

I need to *do* something.

Skipping down the stairs quickly so as to try and tamper the anxiety without talking myself out of the decision to come down here, I make up my mind that whoever is here probably won't mind the intrusion.

At least I hope not.

When I reach the bottom, my jaw drops. Marta wasn't wrong when she called this a fitness suite. It's bigger than the gym Trent had me signed up for when we got together— he thought I could do with dropping a few pounds. That probably should've been my first red flag but, apparently, rose-tinted glasses meant I saw no red.

There are treadmills, ellipticals, bikes, rowers, and a whole host of weight racks, benches and stuff I don't even recognize.

Pulling myself together, I beeline for the closest treadmill, hit quick-start, and ramp up the speed to a fast walk to ease myself in. Music plays throughout the room and I look around, seeing no one despite the lights and music being on.

Maybe they're just always on.

I try to quiet the thoughts by increasing the speed. Once I'm at a run, focusing on the burning in my lungs and just how out of shape I am as sweat runs down my back, my thoughts are nothing but the fact that I really need to get in better shape.

So I push until the sweat stings my eyes, my legs burn as much as my lungs, and I know I'm going to regret this later. But right now? The sweet escape of pain is worth every moment of remorse I might face later.

Only when my legs feel like they're actually going to fail me, do I hit the stop button. Once the treadmill stops, I double over and suck in oxygen like my life depends on it—which it might.

"That position won't help you feel better."

I squeak, jumping upright at the voice, and find Meyer leaning against the wall to my right in nothing but a sleeveless muscle tee and sweats.

So much for being more aware of my surroundings.

"Breathe in long and slow, upright, and it'll feel better quicker," he explains, and I try to do what he says, following his breathing, trying not to think about just how fucking gross I am right now when he's standing there like some muscled, tattooed Adonis.

It does make me more glad for the workout jacket I

have on over the sports bra though. Because, while my ink would be on show, so would my scars, and if I can hide them, I will. I don't really care so much when people see, but people ask questions once they do and reliving it all... yeah, nope.

"Thank you," I say once I have found rhythm enough in breathing to form words again. "I'm sorry if I interrupted your workout, I just needed to get out of my head."

"You didn't interrupt anything," he responds with a small smile. "I was down here to get out of my head too. Except, I was racking up weights rather than running."

"Probably better for your lungs than my idea. Especially when I literally never work out."

He laughs, shaking his head. "Well, you can come down here to escape whenever you like. My home is your home, for as long as needed or wanted."

"Thank you," I whisper, mulling over the meaning of his words as he hands me a towel. I run it down my face, feeling almost instantly better.

"Is it anything you want to talk about? I've been told I'm a very good problem solver. And I know it might be hard to believe, but I'm also a pretty good listener if that's what you need."

I tilt my head as I observe him. He offers me his water bottle, which I take, thirstier than I'd realized, and sink almost half the bottle. "Maybe you should tell me why you were wanting to get out of *your* head. That's probably a better distraction for me than delving into my issues."

The words make me realize I need to rearrange my appointments with my therapist, or at least make them aware of them so Bruno can escort me since I doubt I'll be allowed to go alone. Considering I don't get to do anything alone right now, I'm pretty sure it's a safe bet.

"I'm fairly certain you don't want to hear about the things that keep me up at night," he responds as he takes his bottle back, leaning against the wall again.

"And why would you think that? I'm aware you all seem to know a *creepy* amount about me and my habits, but that doesn't mean you know what goes on inside my head."

He watches me closely, studying me almost, as if trying to work out if I'm messing with him or not.

"You're not wrong… but in my world, my problems tend to lean toward the things you were running from."

"So your problems are men who beat women to a pulp for fun and then gaslight them into believing it was their own fault?" I quirk a brow at him, watching as his fists clench and his jaw tics.

"No, but politics and the snakes that come with that, or violence and blood, which isn't something you should be entrenched in any more than you already have been." His voice is curt, the total opposite from the teasing tone he had just before, and I withdraw a little. I don't want to provoke him too much. He may not have hurt women before but I've learned the hard way that people are capable of many things they didn't think they'd ever do.

"Why don't we change the subject? Are you hungry?" he asks, surprising me. "I gave Carlos the night off because I felt like cooking."

"You cook?" I ask, shocked, though I don't know why. I don't really know him at all.

He chuckles softly. "I do. Cooking soothes me. My mother taught me how to cook, despite my traditional upbringing, she swore that my brother and I wouldn't be as useless as my father, that we wouldn't be a burden to the women she hopes we eventually make our wives."

"She sounds like a good mom."

He smiles wistfully. "She is, you'll probably run into her around here now that she's back from her trip, but her social calendar is more full than a Hollywood socialite', so maybe not."

I giggle at his description, the picture in my head is not at all how I imagine his mom actually looks, but his description is enough to picture a Ruby Wax-Paris Hilton crossover and I know I'm never going to scrub that image from my mind.

"Do you cook?" he asks as he touches a panel on the wall, turning off the music and dimming the lights.

"I try," I say with a shrug. "I've never been the best at it but I can get by."

"Okay. Well, go shower and meet me in the kitchen in half an hour?" he asks as he motions for me to go up the stairs in front of him.

I smile, surprised by the turn this day has taken. "That sounds like fun."

He waits at the bottom of the stairs till I reach the top before heading toward his room, I assume to grab a shower himself, so I head upstairs to my room, going straight into the ensuite and turning on the shower. I catch a glimpse of myself in the mirror and pull a face.

Beet red, hair slick yet still pointing in a dozen different directions despite my ponytail.

What a sight.

Ignoring that, I grab a quick shower, washing and conditioning my sweat-slicked hair, before rushing through drying my mop and getting dressed again.

Three minutes to spare.

That's what I get for doing my hair, I guess.

Barefoot, I skip down the stairs and find Meyer already in the kitchen, head in the refrigerator and the counter already covered in an abundance of food. "Are we cooking for an army?"

He pulls back from the fridge to look at me and I smile, hoping the teasing came across properly. When he smiles back, looking much lighter than he had before, I let out a quick sigh of relief.

"I don't know how to cook small," he tells me. "We've always had a full house, so I learned to cook for the masses. Now, if I try to cook and scale it back, it never tastes the same."

"Makes sense," I say as I pull a stool out from under the counter and slide onto it. "What are we cooking?"

"Nothing too fancy. I'm thinking chicken and broccoli Alfredo with a roasted garlic and mozzarella garlic bread, a side salad and, of course, wine." He looks at me, almost unsure, but my grin widens.

"Oh, nothing too fancy then," I tease. "Far better than the Cheetos or takeout I've *been* living on."

He rolls his eyes at the insinuation and I can't help but wonder how old he is. He has this air about him when we're away from here that makes me think he is way older than me, but now? He seems younger, more at ease, and I'm beginning to question even the little I thought I knew of him.

"Can you butterfly the chicken?" he asks, glancing over at me.

I nod. "I won't say I'm, like, the best at it, but I can. Why am I butterflying it for Alfredo?"

"Because it cooks better on a low heat and is more tender this way," he explains, passing me everything I need, and I get to work doing what he asked while he sets pasta to boil, chops broccoli, mushrooms, and starts to prep the sauce. He walks me through everything he's doing as he does it before taking the chicken from me and cooking it until it's browned and adding it to the simmering sauce.

Watching him cook is mesmerizing. Even as he chops the top off the garlic, places it in foil before smothering it in oil and salt, then placing it in the oven, it's hard to tear my gaze from him.

"Nearly done. Now, for the important part," he says, winking at me. "The wine."

"Ah, but of course, we cannot forget the wine."

He opens what I thought was a low cupboard but turns out to be a wine fridge and pulls a bottle of white from it. "A chardonnay will go perfectly with this," he murmurs as he opens the bottle then grabs two glasses, pouring a small amount before handing it to me.

I take a sip, letting the light, dry taste wash over my tongue. I'm not much of a wine girl, but I can appreciate a good bottle. "I like it."

"Good girl," he says with a glint in his eye before pouring me more as I squirm in my chair.

Flitting around the kitchen, he pulls a loaf of bread from God only knows where and cuts it in half before pulling the garlic from the oven. Once it's cooled enough, he squeezes the cloves into a bowl that sits in another full of ice and mixes the garlic with butter and herbs.

I lost track of exactly what he was saying somewhere around the time he rolled the sleeves of his shirt up. There is just something about strong forearms that is distracting as hell. They really shouldn't be. Especially not here, with him… yet, here we are.

He spreads the garlic butter on the bread and tops it with freshly sliced mozzarella before sliding it in the oven. "There, just a few more minutes."

Lifting his glass to mine before taking a sip of the wine, I feel like I've stepped into the twilight zone.

"So, other than cooking, what other special skills do you have?" I ask, and he quirks a brow at me. "Not like that, you fiend."

"Well a beautiful woman asks about my special skills, of course that's where my mind goes," he teases. "But I am extremely talented at mini golf."

"Mini golf?" I ask, taken aback, trying not to laugh.

"I've never been bested," he declares, and this time I can't stop the laugh.

"Yeah, but is it skill or people not wanting to beat you?"

He grips his chest with his hand and staggers back. "You wound me, fair maiden."

I cackle harder at his theatrics, which he only stops when the timer on the oven starts to beep.

"I hope you're hungry," he says as he starts to dish up

the food, carrying it over to the table.

"Thank you for this," I earnestly tell him. "I feel like I really just watched you work."

"You're welcome. Like I said, I like to cook. It soothes me. Now come, eat, before it gets cold."

He pulls a chair out for me, so I grab my wine, hop off the stool, and walk around to the table, where he pushes my chair in. "Such a gentleman."

"Only sometimes," he says, teasing.

He sits, looking at me expectantly, and I can't help but wonder what he's like when he's not a gentleman.

TWENTY TWO

Sitting at breakfast the next morning, I feel… out of sorts. Part of me feels lighter—whether that's because of my playful evening with Meyer, because I have my things here, or just because I know the truth of why I'm actually here now, I don't know—but the other part of me feels at odds with the sliver of peace in my soul.

There's nothing quite like being at war with yourself to start the day off right.

Carlos has music playing as he hums and dances while he cooks, but even he has left me to it this morning while I stare out at the early morning sky, nursing my mug of coffee. Shae popped by, placed her breakfast order, said good morning, and disappeared again. She obviously isn't a morning person, but she was also undoubtedly ordering food for more than just her. She said something about a dinner, but she was half asleep so I told her we'd catch up later.

"Have you decided what you'd like to eat?" Carlos asks, his heavily accented English pulling me from my musings.

"Could I get my egg, bacon, and cheese bagel?" I ask him while chastising myself for not going to see Tina when I was out with Rory yesterday.

Maybe I can get him to go out with me again today.

"Si," Carlos calls back, at least that much I know in Spanish. I get up and make another cup of coffee, hoping that the caffeine helps me put the pieces of my mind together enough so that I can try to enjoy feeling a little lighter rather than feeling guilty about it.

Carlos places the food in front of me once I'm sitting again and I try to eat it with as much enthusiasm as usual but, just like my coffee, it tastes almost bland because my brain will not shut up.

It's infuriating.

"Morning all," Meyer happily calls out as he strides into the room all suited up, looking every bit the apparent mafia boss he is. We talked some more about what his world actually consists of over dinner last night and, while I'm sure *he* wouldn't use the term mafia, that's the one my brain is clinging to.

He has wars with other 'families' in the city, as well

as treaties with others. The same for the local gangs, like the Ghosts and the Demons. I'd already heard about the Demons but, apparently, it was the Ghosts who issued the threat on my life.

So nice of them.

He runs counterfeit money for others through the clubs to clean it for them, and has a ton of other legitimate businesses that Hunter oversees, as well as dealing in drugs and guns. He didn't give me all the details, but an overview at least, which I think is another reason I'm conflicted.

Should I let myself feel at peace here when so much blood is the reason this place is safe?

I mean, it's not like I've done anything. Hell, I still hardly know them, but I'm reaping the benefits of what they do and I have been for months.

It's also made me question what else Tommy is involved in with them to have been able to afford moving me around so much the last few years without breaking a sweat while I fretted over every penny.

I never really asked him what he did, and the one time it came up in conversation, he told me I was better off not knowing. Which, if he's involved in this stuff, then yeah, probably. If I'd have found out about this two years ago when I met him, I'd likely have run from him too.

It's amazing how two years of running has blurred my moral lines. Though, that could also have a lot to do with realizing that the 'good' guys aren't always so good. I mean, Trent and Meyer are the perfect description of the 'good' guy and the 'bad' guy, but I know which one I feel safer with.

"Morning," I respond when he finally sits down beside me. "Busy day?"

He nods, taking a sip of his espresso. "Meetings. So many boring meetings. Though, I was thinking, if you would like, you could come with me today. I ran you through some of what we do last night, but the meetings I have today are on the more… legit side of what we do, so I don't see any harm in you gaining insight into that."

My eyes go wide as shock filters through me. "You want me to go with you?"

"I mean, it's selfish really. I'm sure you'll make the meetings far less dull, plus you have a fascinating way of viewing things, so I'd also like to pick your brain after and see what your opinions are."

His eyes glint with mischief and I can't tell if he's being serious or not. The two sides of him are so vastly different that the gulf between them is enough to get lost in.

"I mean, yeah, okay. That would be great. I'm never going to say no to being allowed out." I stick my tongue out at him so he knows I'm half teasing. It feels like we've had the discussion of my freedom and safety *way* too many times over the last two days.

"Oh, yes. You'll be shackled to me, but you'll be allowed out to play," he says, winking.

"I guess I should probably go get dressed. What sort of meetings are these?" I ask, looking down at my pj pants and hoodie.

He smirks, leaning back in his chair. "Oh, I don't know, I'm pretty sure you'd be welcome in what you're wearing."

I throw my napkin at him, laughing. "Don't be an ass."

"We're meeting with some business associates that run in political circles, does that help?" He watches me closely as I mentally run through the clothes I have upstairs. I doubt I have anything even remotely close to what I'd call appropriate for those meetings, especially considering his suit.

Although... a smile pulls at my lips as I remember some of the random things Yen had me buy.

"I think I can throw something together."

"Good, we'll be leaving in forty-five minutes," he says as Carlos places an omelet in front of him.

Jumping to my feet, I feel more energized than I thought possible today. "I can totally be ready by then."

He laughs as I dash from the room and all I hear behind me is, "She'll never be ready in time."

I climb into the passenger seat of Meyer's car, shocked that he's been driving us around all day, even if this Mercedes is beautiful and has more presence than a stately home. Not that I've said anything about it because, while I now have an understanding of what he does and I'm slowly getting to know him, I still don't know *that* much.

His eyes roam over my body when he climbs in beside me, pausing a moment at where my boobs are bound in this blouse before trailing down to my skirt, then my bare legs.

Turns out I had the perfect secretarial outfit in the form of a pencil skirt—albeit the thigh split probably isn't *that* professional—a white blouse with a thick black belt around my waist, and a longline black cardigan to pull it together. My only issue was the shoes and Marta helped with a pair of red-bottomed black heels that went perfectly, but I don't even want to think about why they had spare Louboutins, in my size, just lying around.

"The cogs in your brain are almost visible, Kitten. What's going on in that pretty mind of yours?"

I smile while staring out the window. One day he'll call me Quinn and, that day, I'll throw a freaking party.

"I was just thinking that today has been nice, hanging out with you, even with the boring politicians and their people. Learning different things about what you do, it's not something I've ever even considered knowing anything about. I would never have guessed that you were so close with the mayor, for starters, and it made me realize that I still don't know that much about you. About any of you. Which puts me at a disadvantage because, as I've mentioned before, you guys know a *creepy* amount about me, but also, you've all done so much for me. It feels odd that I know so little about you all."

He glances over at me before looking back at the road. Traffic is insane in the middle of the city, there is no way in hell you'd find me driving here willingly. "What would you like to know?"

"I don't know," I say with a shrug. "It's less of a twenty questions thing and more of just wanting to observe more I guess? Like, I've learned more about you in the last twenty-four hours than I have in the entire time I've been in the city, and that's not just because of what you do. I also learned that you prefer red wine to white, that you love to cook, you prefer a good vodka rather than bourbon. The small things. What makes you human."

Pausing, I glance out the window, the traffic coming to a standstill. "And that's still more than I know about the others. Rory is so quiet, so when he speaks, I know it matters, and he's said some things that make me think he's experienced things that make my life look like a trip to Six Flags. Hunter is… well, he seems like the more jovial, forthcoming one, but when I think about it, it's more surface level stuff that he gives out to people. He doesn't really give much of his true self. And even if I'm still kinda pissed at him, I can't stay mad forever."

"Yes, well, being pissed at Hunter is just a baseline we all tend to have on a daily basis. That is something you'll come to learn in time." It occurs to me then that he's talking as if I'm going to be with them for the foreseeable future, but he continues to talk, distracting me from my thoughts. "And while I understand *why* you're mad at him—"

Oh, God, the embarrassment. Of course he knows I slept with Hunter.

"—I also know my friend well enough to know that he wouldn't have hidden things from you unless one, it was my say so, or two, it was in your best interest. I know that doesn't make it less infuriating, but sometimes knowing the why helps. I'm also not saying you have to forgive him right now, but Hunter is one of the best people I know. If you're one of his people—and you're obviously someone he's chosen to be a part of that very small club—then he would take a bullet for you without a second thought."

"He's chosen that?" I murmur, quietly, but he hears and nods.

"We all have. We accepted Tommy's request to help you, learned about you, and that was it. But then we met you and now you're here, in my car, living in my house."

"I thought that was for my safety?"

"Oh, it is, Kitten. But I can't say that I'm not happy about how it's all working out."

"That doesn't make much sense to me," I respond, more than a little confused.

"I wouldn't expect it to. I'm not exactly saying this how I would've wanted to. Or when, but here we are." He sighs, the engine rumbling to life again as traffic starts flowing. "But let me ask you this. Would it be so awful if you became one of our people?"

"You mean, work for you? Not at the club?"

The corners of his lips tilt up as he glances over at me before focusing on the road again as we leave the chaos of the city, taking the entrance onto the interstate to head back to the house.

"No, Kitten. I mean, to be *ours*."

I blink at him, because what the what? "You already tried to tell me once I belonged to you. I didn't know what it meant then and I still don't know what you mean now."

He laughs, shaking his head again. "I have a better idea."

Not explaining any further, he continues to drive and I sit contemplating what he might mean. Because he can't mean what I think he means…

Because being theirs… All three of them? Is that a thing? The way he says it makes it sound like a thing, but it's so… not accepted by society. Like, it's not even a thing that's been on my radar. And what does he truly mean? Just being a fuck toy for them? Because, well, Hunter was outstanding and made my head spin and it's not like I haven't thought about him and Rory that way, but they're best friends.

Surely, that's messy?

It takes me a minute to realize Meyer has pulled off the interstate and we're going down a dirt road. Apparently, the Mercedes makes even the bumpiest of roads almost comfortable.

We reach the end of the road in what looks like a turning circle cut out of the woods beside us.

"Where are we?" I ask, glancing around. I know I should feel a little unhinged, but I don't. Weirdly, I trust Meyer. He's done everything possible to ensure my safety, I doubt he'd risk me now.

"No more questions, Kitten. Let me show you what I meant."

Without giving me a moment to respond, he climbs from the car and makes his way around to my side, opening my door. He offers me a hand, helping me to get out onto the uneven ground in these shoes, and closes the door with a thud.

I move to step away from the car, but he presses against me in a moment, arms caging me against the car so I can't move. The hard plains of him make my head spin as blood rushes through me.

"I don't understand."

His eyes sparkle with delight as he leans down, his lips barely a hair from mine. "How about I make you understand, Kitten?"

I blink at him, trying to process it, but then his lips are on mine, claiming them like a great prize, and yet again, I am his helpless captive.

But this time, I'm really not that angry about it.

Pressing my hands against his chest, I clutch the lapels of his jacket in my fingers as my toes curl from just his kiss. I can feel him *everywhere.*

The hardness of his body as he leans into me, the very prominent dick that presses against my stomach, his leg between mine, making my skirt rise.

"This is your last chance to tell me no, Kitten, because if we do this, I meant what I said earlier. I want you to be mine. Ours."

I still don't know exactly what that means, but he nips at my lips and a whimper falls from me.

"Use your words, Kitten."

"Yes," I say breathily, noting that I might regret the submission later, but right now, I want him. I've pictured it a dozen different times, but none of my fantasies were even close to how I feel just from his kiss, let alone anything else.

"Good girl." His breath is sharp, like he's trying to control himself. "Now, I want to play. Are you willing to play?"

"What is the game?" I ask, my words feeling like mountains to climb.

He grins before kissing me again. "I want you to run."

My heart stutters in my chest at his words. "Run?"

"Yes, Kitten. I want you to run like your life depends on it. I want you to fight me. Then, when I've earned it, I want you to surrender to me." His pupils dilate and his dick twitches against my stomach.

I've heard about primals, read about them plenty, but before Hunter, sex was a chore for me. Something taken from me. And while this is him taking from me, what with me being his prey, he's still asking my permission, which makes it a world away from anything Trent did. I also know that I can say no to him and he'll accept it.

"Do you want to play?" he asks, his gaze not leaving me.

My insides are on fire with anticipation and want, which is exactly how I find myself saying yes. I want this. I want *him*, however that looks. This is my power to reclaim and I know I'm safe with Meyer, even if he's pretending I'm not.

"I'll give you a one minute head start," he says breathily before kissing me until my head swims once more. When he pulls back, I can feel his heart racing in his chest beneath my hand. "Go."

The word is ragged, but I don't hesitate. Kicking off the heels, deciding that a potential splinter in my foot is better than a broken ankle, I take off running on the trail into the woods.

The seconds pass so quickly, despite me trying to keep track of them in my head while I run, looking for somewhere to hide, but there's just trees.

So many trees.

I hear a howl from behind me and my heart races even faster.

It's him.

He's coming.

In a matter of seconds, it's like I'm in a scene from *The Blair Witch Project* except I know exactly who's coming for me and, as much as I have this ingrained need to run, I kind of want him to catch me.

My vision is unfocused, everything in my peripheral blurry, colors blending into various shades of greens and browns as I run as quickly as my legs will carry me, the thrill of the chase flooding through me and making my heart race.

I didn't know this could be so much fun, but I am so here for it.

"Oh Kiiiiitten…" I skid to a stop, ripping the slit in my

skirt a little higher. It sucks, but it means I can run faster now. I pick up my pace again and my bare feet are assaulted by the tiny rocks and scattered branches along the trail, but my brain refuses to acknowledge the inevitable pain from running full force with no protection. Meyer is teasing me, calling out the ridiculous nickname he's chosen for me, though I'm kind of starting to love it. Not that I'll tell him that.

His voice is closer than it was when I heard the howl, which means outrunning him is likely impossible. So I try harder, even though I don't really want to get away.

My heart is beating right out of my chest, like the possibility of danger, of death, is real. I have to remind myself a couple of times that this is a game. A kink. This is not...

A cracking of a branch that is way too fucking close makes me jump, but I suppress the yelp and swallow down any other noise he could hear from his position. Looking right, then left, I do a complete three-sixty before heading toward a huge trunk lying diagonal from my position.

My heel lands at an awkward angle on a big branch, but I ignore the searing jolt of electric pain that races up my leg and to the pit of my stomach. When I reach the trunk, I slam my back against the bark and place my hand over my mouth to avoid making too much noise with my breathing.

The smell of damp wood and fresh flowers overpowers anything else, the sound of my trepidation beating in my ears cancels out all other signs that he could be closer than I thought.

Closing my eyes, I concentrate on every tiny sound around me. The scratching of a running squirrel, the sound of a bird's intermittent song, the snapping of a branch.

The trunk is big enough that it hides every part of me, or at least I think it does. To be sure, I slide down—catching my cardigan on the bark—and try my best to make myself as small as humanly possible.

My breathing slows down one tiny notch, but my heartbeat is still going double time, so much so that I'm afraid of passing out and not getting to experience Meyer in all his glory.

With both hands on my mouth, I turn my head to the right, but see nothing, then turn my head to the left and—

"Miss me, Kitten?" This time, I do scream and instead of laughing it off and saying something like "Hey! You win, let's fuck now." I push against his chest and bolt like a thief in the direction of the trail where I plan to... fuck if I know what I have planned. I'm in flight mode, my logical brain unable to convey to my literal instincts that I'm not, in fact, in danger.

So I run.

Even though I know it's a safe danger.

My brain is bouncing between the two, blending our game and reality, so I try to focus only on running.

Behind me, Meyer's laughter is ominous, but also hot as fuck. Is it possible to be turned on and scared out of my mind at the same time?

Yes, yes it is.

Except, it's exhilarating. Not at all like I thought it would be and it makes me want it more. To be able to flip my fear into something fun. Pleasurable.

Something new.

This time as I run, I'm not concerned with the sounds I'm making because I'm pretty sure by now that he has X-ray vision and he's also part vampire. How else was he able to see me *and* sneak up on me?

I find a shrub that's growing alongside two trees and, without thinking of what kind of animals or—God forbid—bugs are hanging out over there, I jump over the coarse leaves and crouch down with my arms over my head.

At this moment, I'm convinced that in a horror movie I'd be the first idiot to be slashed without having the time to scream. As I'm hiding, the pain from my bare feet begins to really make its presence known. Every inch of my feet are throbbing, some places with an acute pain that tells me they're open cuts.

It's fine. I'll be fine.

I already know he won't let me get really hurt and he'll

look after me when we're done, but for now, I revel in the pain because it means I'm winning.

I begin to wonder if I lost him. I can't hear anything. Then again, I didn't hear him earlier either. Except now I'm doubting his abilities. Like, maybe I really did ditch him. What happens if he doesn't find me?

Confident that he's somewhere in the wrong direction, I slowly rise, my head peeking out just enough for me to see my surroundings when the scent of spice and musk catches me off guard.

Snapping my head to the side, I scream into the woods as his hand slaps against my mouth and his eyes come level with mine, a lethal grin making him look deadly and sexy all at the same time.

My heart races from the shock but I'm also wet, my panties clinging to my flesh as he leans down closer and growls, "We need to stop meeting like this, Kitten." His eyes drop to my chest where my boobs are practically falling over the gap in my blouse. That gorgeous smile pops wide, his pearly whites flashing like an omen.

His words, however, kick me out of my stupor. With all the strength I possess, I push against his chest once more, but he's anticipated my move. His body rooted in place, he reaches down with his free hand and wraps his fingers around my throat, pulling me up so I'm standing again. He doesn't apply pressure with his hand, just his fingers on the sides lightly so my breathing isn't restricted. It kicks my heart rate up again, but when I can breathe easily, the edge of panic flows away, allowing me to give in to the heady feeling of being caught.

"Do you give up?" I can see it in his eyes, he doesn't want me to hand myself over to him. He even told me as much earlier so, like a good little kitten, I do as I'm told.

"Fuck you!" Thrashing and kicking and punching whatever flesh I can reach, I get a shiver of satisfaction at hearing him grunt a couple of times. My eyes are closed, like the horror movie character walking that I am, but I really don't care.

His hand falls away, my neck free from his hold, and I bolt in the opposite direction, convinced he'll let me go like he did last time.

Oh, how wrong I am.

Searing pain in the back of my head makes my entire body freeze. Pulling me back by my hair with one arm locked around my waist, Meyer throws me down on a bed of dead leaves. With some kind of vampire witchery, he twists me around so that he's lying on top of me with both of my wrists trapped in his hold.

My brain stutters, but then I see the way he looks at me and remind myself he isn't trying to hurt me. He seems to see my fear and gives me a second to take a few deep breaths.

I should give up. I should just give him my surrender, but I know he wants to earn it and I don't think he has yet.

Planting my feet, I push up, my hips bucking as much as possible. I catch him off guard for a split second, but it's just enough for his grip to loosen and for me to get enough room to throw him off me. Crawling backwards, I lock my jaw as my palm hits something sharp and a burning sensation brings tears to my eyes.

"Do you know how fucking sexy you look trying to run from me?" He stands, walking my way as I try to skitter away like a bug about to squished.

"I'll scream!"

"God, I hope so."

Holy shit, his voice is like chocolate-covered strawberries, smooth and rich with a tart undertone. I'm so wet, it's laughable. I wonder if those Blair Witch assholes got horny while running for their lives.

Probably not. They were sane.

Me? I'm the opposite. I want him to catch me but at the same time, I want this adrenaline to keep coursing through my veins. It's addictive when it comes like this. It's new and heady and I want to never feel it any other way ever again. I feel a little nuts to want this so much, given my past, but this doesn't feel crazy, and I think that's because of Meyer. He makes me feel safe, which makes this okay and not even close to something I shouldn't want.

When Meyer finally decides to pounce, I'm not entirely ready for him, but it doesn't matter. We scramble around the dirt and leaves, my back getting scratched, even through my clothes, but all I feel is wetness between my legs and an overwhelming need to be filled by him. I fight him as much as I can, groaning every time his hard-as-steel cock rubs against my stomach and his breath fills my ears.

It doesn't take him long to subdue me, pinning me down at the hips with one arm over my throat and one hand clutching both of my wrists above my head. I'd fight, but I'm exhausted. More than that, I want this. I want him inside me. I want him to make new memories when I feel like this.

"I surrender," I whisper, taking sick pleasure in the way his eyes light up and his entire body locks up like it's game time.

"Oh, Kitten, you're going to regret those words in all the best ways." When his mouth comes down on mine, we clash like two celestial forces, brought together by the forces of nature. His tongue is pushing inside my mouth, our lips gliding and sliding as he dominates the kiss like he does with everything else in his life. I may not know much, but this I do know.

My hips buck again, but this time it's to feel his cock press against me, to know what's coming. Still, his mouth doesn't pull away.

Even though I've given him my surrender, my body is still in fight mode, bucking and pulling on my wrists to rid myself of his hold on me. This only drives him harder, gets him more invested in our little primal game. He's kissing me with his entire body, chest to chest as his cock grinds into me through our clothes.

"Do you still surrender?" I grit my teeth at his question. Part of me wants to keep fighting, keep pushing him. I want the game to continue. I want the lack of control in a controlled environment. In any other context, this would be terrifying. The adrenaline rushing through my bloodstream, though, is like a high I've never experienced before.

"Yes."

"Good girl."

That tiny second of praise is all he needed for me to melt into his touch and relax my muscles just enough for him to slide the hand that was on my throat right between my legs.

I moan as his fingers graze the tender skin of my inner thighs. Leaning closer, he presses on my wrists as he brings his lips to mine, a whisper-touch as he speaks. "Your pussy is so hot it's practically burning my hand."

I should be embarrassed by his words, but instead, I thrust my hips up just enough for his finger to caress my panty-clad pussy.

I'm getting impatient, tired of lying here on this forest bed with whatever creatures trying to live their lives. I need him to do something.

Anything.

Like he can hear my frustration, he grunts across my lips and pushes two fingers up my pussy, panties and all. It's an odd feeling, like he's there but not there. His impatience must be as legendary as mine because the next thing I know, my panties are gone and his fingers are back inside me. Thick, talented fingers pumping in and out of me as I ride him without a single care in the world. I'm fucking his fingers and I'm not ashamed.

"Fuck this." Arching my back so he can get even deeper, I almost miss his words as he pulls his hand away from between my legs, hikes what's left of my skirt, and kneels at my core, my legs over his shoulders.

What follows is pure bliss. His mouth lands on my pussy, his tongue fucking it like he fucked my mouth. Domination is one thing, what he's doing is decimating me for any other man.

Hands on my ass, he presses against my flesh and pulls apart the globes as he devours me. Lips and teeth and tongue all working together, assaulting me in the best way.

I'm in the middle of the fucking woods as Meyer eats my pussy like a champion, a gold medalist at cunnilingus, and I'm the lucky girl who gets to experience it.

I'm fisting the ground beside me as he laps up my juices, my fingernails scratching the earth beneath me while he sucks on my pussy lips. It's fucking glorious. *He's* fucking glorious. This whole fucking scenario is perfection made only better when he sucks my clit into his mouth and my entire body lights up like the Fourth of July. My back arches toward the sky as a cry erupts from my lips. Still, Meyer keeps on sucking on my clit.

I can't breathe, my chest feels tight as he flicks my clit then returns his tongue to my cunt and drinks everything I have to give him.

I may feel like Jell-O right now, but I still feel empty. I need him inside me, I need to quench this hunger he's created in me.

"Dick. Inside. Now." Sentences are too difficult for me, so I'm using essential words to get my point across.

He gets it.

Pulling me up by my wrists, he bends enough to pick me up by my bare thighs and push me against the nearest tree. I inhale the deep forest scents that surround me as he brings his cum-covered mouth to mine and feeds me my orgasm. I taste myself, revel in the fact that my body made him this hard.

Making quick work of his button and zipper, my hazy mind barely has time to register the beauty that is his cock as it springs free and bobs against his stomach. It's long and thick and perfectly impatient with a bead of cum peeking out from the slit at the head.

I can't wait to—

"Oh, my God!" Banging my head against the bark, I forget about the pain as he dives into my pussy as far as he possibly can.

We both groan, our heads tilted toward the sky as we savor this moment. The first time his cock pushes against my walls, buried inside my pussy from head to root. It's the only time this will be his first and it's memorable.

"Goddamit, I knew you'd be fucking perfect."

I bite my bottom lip, my lids heavy with lust and my pussy squeezing his shaft, begging for him to move.

Pulling out just enough to tease me, he holds me with one hand as the other flies to my chin, his thumb pulling my mouth open by the bottom teeth.

Just as he pushes back inside me with a brutal thrust, he spits in my mouth then forces it closed.

"Swallow." I don't even think, I do as he says just as he pulls back out and slams inside me again. Over and over he grinds against my clit as his dick pummels my pussy like he owns me.

I don't complain. In fact, I want more. I want harder. So I do the only thing he'll understand.

I fight.

Thrashing away from him, I try to get down, hoping

he won't allow it. Hoping he'll understand exactly what I'm after.

When he puts enough space between to look me straight in the eye, I know without a single doubt that he understands perfectly.

His eyes have a devil's spark to them, his grin promises filthy gifts, and his words are a reminder that he's the master of this game and I'm just his willing pawn.

"Oh, Kitten… I thought you'd never ask."

This time, his fingers latch onto my pulse points at my throat as he rears his hips back and plunges inside me over and over again at a mind-blowing speed. He's not making love, far from it. He's fucking the sanity out of me. My back is scratching against the bark, my mouth open in a silent scream as he steals every one of my gasps when he buries himself to the hilt.

Each and every time.

I can barely breathe, somehow making this whole fucking experience even better, more dangerous.

Every time he bottoms out, he grinds his groin against my clit, creating fiery sparks up and down my nerve endings. I've never felt anything like it. It's insane and it's the best thing in the world.

"Time to say thank you, Kitten, by coming on my cock."

Holding me up only by my thighs, he thrusts in and

out, in and out, over and over again until I don't know if this is real or a dream I don't want to wake up from.

"Now, come right fucking now." I don't know how it's possible, but I obey. My body releases all the pent-up adrenaline in my bloodstream as my orgasm forces my body to shake between the tree and the hard lines of Meyer's body. I gasp against his tight hold on my throat, my mouth opening and closing as I yell out my pleasure without uttering a single sound.

When Meyer freezes, I know he's joining me. My eyes open and I'm met with his wild eyes and clenched jaw. Even though he's pinning me down, I push against his hold and lick his bottom lip.

It's like a switch is flipped on. Meyer's eyes lock onto me as his mouth slams against mine, kissing the breath right from between my lips. We're all tongues and teeth, fighting for control even though we both know who's had it this whole time.

It was me. At any time I could have stopped this, but there was no fucking way. I wanted this as much as I needed it.

As his cock pulses inside me, flooding me with his cum, I truly relax for the first time today. His body melts against mine, almost crushing me as he gets his breath back, but once he does, he stands, putting himself back together while I stay where I am.

I'm kind of over the bug thing in this moment because I am also a melty mess.

He smiles down at me, examining me before his brow furrows. "You're hurt."

"I am?" I murmur, and he curses under his breath before leaning down and picking me up. "You all seem to have a fascination with carrying me."

He chuckles softly as I nestle against his chest. He holds me steady as he walks us out of the woods, which turns out to be less than three minutes away.

Huh, guess I got more turned around than I thought in there.

"We care about you, Kitten, and if you think I'm letting you walk on those feet right now, you don't know me very well at all."

"I'd say I know you much better than I did this morning," I tease as he shifts my weight to open the car door before sliding me into the passenger seat and pulling the belt over my dirty, torn clothes. He chuckles as he pulls a twig from my hair.

"Yes, I guess you do. Now rest. I'll get Rob to meet us at the house to make sure you're actually okay."

"I don't need a doctor," I groan, but he just stares at me and I already know it's a losing battle. "Fine, fine, but I'm pretty sure he has better things to do than patch me up after sex."

"He does what he's told... unlike some people I know." He stands and closes the door, and I stick my tongue out at him as he rounds the car.

"I can think of better things to do with that tongue, Kitten," he teases once he's in his seat.

I wink at him, wanting to see just how far I can tease him. "Oh, so can I, but I guess I'll have to see your doctor instead."

His hands clench the steering wheel as the car roars to life. "Well, Kitten, I guess you better be good for the doctor, otherwise I'll just have to punish you after."

His words are so serious, but all I can do is giggle. "Oh yeah? *Such* a deterrent."

He glances over at me, his eyes dark, but a smile playing on his lips. "You have no idea."

TWENTY THREE

I won't say I've hidden the last two days, but I also can't say I've left my room much either. Not that my trip with Meyer wasn't fun... I mean, who hates orgasms? But I've been trying to work out what it is I actually agreed to and if it was a good idea.

Wanton me was ready to agree to sign over my soul, and it kind of feels like I did, but I can't decide if I regret it or not. Which is the weirdest dilemma to be in. Surely, regret should be potent enough that I would know if I regretted that decision, but...

Here I am, hiding in my room for the third day in a row, waiting for the clock to tick over to when I know Meyer usually leaves for the day.

I haven't seen Rory or Hunter for days and I almost feel bad that I haven't asked where they are, but I'm also learning that knowing everything isn't always a good thing.

Except, right now, I'd really like to know every tiny freaking detail of what I agreed to when I told Meyer I'd be 'theirs'.

Because I still don't know if he meant as a live-in fuck toy or if it's something else. I'm kicking myself a little for not asking more questions, but he seemed more interested in showing rather than telling the other day.

Maybe Hunter will have a better way with words. Do I really want to ask him? I'd ask Rory, but I already know that him and words are… yeah, he's definitely the strong, silent one of the three.

How is this even a problem right now? Compared to the problems of my past, this doesn't feel like it should be an issue and yet, here in the bubble they've created for me, all of my other problems seem null and void, so this is all I have to fixate on and agonize over.

A knock at the door has me groaning into my pillow. When the second one sounds, I know I'm going to have to answer. Kicking off the sheets, I pull up my hood so my bird's nest for hair is hidden before unlocking the door and opening it just enough for me to see Shae standing outside.

"Oh." I sigh before stepping back, letting the door open wider as I plod back to bed. "You okay?"

"Good morning to you too, Sunshine," she chirps as she strides in before closing the door. "What's got your thunderclouds all out and stormy?"

"I don't even really know," I tell her, frustrated at myself. Because I mean it, I shouldn't be in this rut. I knew what I was doing, I've been in *much* worse situations, but it's like my insides are having a temper tantrum and I have zero control over any of it. "I wish I could just wave a magic wand for, like, funk-be-gone."

"Did my brother do something?" she asks, coming to sit on the bed with me. I'm a little jealous of how lithe and graceful she is, but I push the thought away. I'm happy with my body, she just happens to look like a cross between a model and a dancer.

I think over her question for a minute then shake my head. "No, he didn't do or say anything. I had a great day, I was fine when I got home that night too, I just woke up feeling out of sorts the next morning and haven't been able to shake it."

She nods like she understands before crawling across the bed to sit beside me, pulling the covers up so we're both snuggled up to our chins. "This sounds like a case of the 'I don't wanna's' which is remedied with chocolate, movies, and bed. And tacos. Because they fix almost everything."

"That does sound kinda perfect," I say with a soft sigh. "But you don't have to wallow with me, you probably have stuff to do."

"Oh, stop," she says, looking at me like I'm being an

idiot. "Do I look like I have anywhere to go?"

She pulls down the sheet, revealing her leggings and hoodie before pulling them back in. "I get it, I'm trapped in the gilded cage too, remember? I might have a little more freedom than you do currently, but not much. Sometimes all the restrictions take their toll and you just need time to wallow."

"Why are you trapped?" I ask her cautiously, not really expecting an answer because she hardly knows me, but I can't help but ask. I've seen her pain hiding behind her smile, it feels like my pain, but everyone has their own shadows to claw their way out of. "You don't have to tell me, I'm just... well, nosey I guess."

She laughs, but it's dry and doesn't quite reach her eyes. "I was young and I made a stupid decision that put me in a seriously fucked-up situation. I was kidnapped, essentially. Held, tortured, raped, more... but let's not do an entire trauma dump today." She winks at me, trying to make light of what I'm sure was a horrific experience, and I'm not going to push. "Needless to say, once they got me back, I was locked down harder than before. I'm not entirely against it. I never want to experience that again, and this place, as cage-like as it is, is home. It's safe and, while I bitch about it, and sometimes even fight against it, I know the risks of breaking the rules."

"I'm sorry," I say quietly, regretting asking the question

a little. "I didn't mean to pry into something so awful."

"We're all a little broken," she says, smiling softly. "Now, today isn't about me, it's your wallow, so let's just push my dramatics back in their box and get back to it shall we?"

"As long as you're sure," I murmur, feeling guilty about wallowing when she seems to have far more reason than I do to wallow. She rolls her eyes at me before sticking her tongue out. "Okay, so if you're here, how do we get provisions? Do we need to get out of bed after all of the dramatics?" I ask, teasing, trying to match her mood. If she can be cheery with her dark and twisties, so can I.

Fake it till we make it.

She pulls her phone out of her pocket and waves it in her face. "Nope! You have your shadow, who is just down the hall, by the way, and I have mine, who is now standing guard with yours. Since there are two of them, one of them can be our snack bitch."

"That doesn't seem fair," I say uneasily.

"Fair, shmare. It's not fair that we're birds with clipped wings, but here we are. The least they can do is provide snacks." She taps away on her screen, grinning wide when it pings. "Tonio is on it. He's under strict orders to retrieve *all* the snacks."

I giggle softly. I'm not even really sure what that means, but Shae doesn't seem like the half-measures type.

"Now then, where's your remote?" she asks, and I just blink at her.

"Remote? I don't have a TV," I tell her starkly, and she barks out a laugh.

"You've seen this house, do you really think you don't have a TV? Someone save me," she continues to laugh as she launches herself over me and opens a compartment on the side of the bed I hadn't noticed.

In my defense, you can hardly see it, even though I now know it's there.

She grabs a remote, hits a button, and the end of the bed pops open, followed by a whirring, before a TV rises out of the end of the bed. "Well, shit."

I've literally been lying in the dark and quiet because I didn't think there was a TV in here.

Shae cackles again as she turns the TV on. She flicks through the films, setting up a playlist of what to watch, and just as she starts the first, there's a knock at the door.

"Come in!" she hollers, and a man, who I assume is Tonio, appears with four giant bags in his hands. "This is why you're my favorite, T."

She beams at him and he rolls his eyes. "Yeah, yeah, yeah. You mean I'm the only soft touch around here that will bend when you want them to."

"Maybe," she coos, fluttering her lashes at him playfully. He drops the bags on the bed, quickly glancing at me before turning back to her.

"Do you need anything else, your highness?" The deadpan look on his face alone is enough to make me laugh, but mixed with the question, I can't stop the cackle that bubbles up.

She looks at me before laughing too. "No, that's everything. For now anyway. I'm going to want tacos later."

"I'll let Carlos know," he says, before nodding and leaving the room.

Shae grabs the bags and upturns them onto the bed, chocolate and bags of popcorn and chips and God only knows what else spills out onto the covers. "Now this? This is how we wallow."

After my day with Shae, I'm feeling a bit more like myself. I still couldn't say what inspired my sad girl days, but I'm also trying not to focus on it and look forward.

Except I was informed by Meyer at breakfast this morning that tonight we're having a big family dinner, which is why I've been quietly freaking out. Not because there's a dinner, but because I still don't really know my place here and Meyer's mom is cooking apparently. His brother will be home this afternoon, Hunter and Rory will be home, and it will be *everyone.*

I'm trying not to feel like I'll be a circus act on display, but the thought of being the center of attention, even the slightest possibility of it, makes me want to run away. I've never been the girl who wants the spotlight. No, thank you, I'd much rather hide in a corner.

Family dinners are such a foreign concept to me. We never ate as a family when I was growing up. Hell, I've never even met any of my family outside of my parents because they removed themselves so far from the people they're related to that I just kind of grew up alone. I never missed it because I didn't know any better, and if the rest of my family were anything like my parents, I'm probably better off having never known them, anyway. But still...

It's making tonight seem like this *huge* deal when it probably isn't, but I cannot make the voices quiet to a level where I can look at it logically and not feel bubbles under my skin.

Maybe I should pretend to be sick?

I shake my head as I pace in my room. Totally won't fly. Even if the guys believed it, Shae would be in here dragging me from the room by my hair. We might not have spent a ton of time together, but I feel like I've known her my entire life.

Maybe it's because we're both trapped, or maybe it's because she told me a little about her own trauma.

Whatever it is, it's how I know she won't let me miss the stupid dinner.

So I just need to suck it up and deal, but right now I don't want to be an adult about it. I just want to squirrel away and hide. I'd much rather go back to work at the bar and face Harper than meet Meyer's mom.

My phone rings, jolting me from my minor meltdown, and I smile when I see Tommy's name on the screen.

"Hey!"

"Hey, Quinn girl. How's things going there? Haven't heard from you in a while, so wanted to check in."

I laugh softly and shake my head. "You mean Meyer hasn't kept you up to date on my movements?"

"Oh, no. He has. That's why I'm asking how you're doing. Honestly, I expected to hear from you already and I was starting to get a little worried." I frown at the concern in his voice. Did he expect me to call in the cavalry?

"I was going to call, but I didn't want to put you in a weird position. Plus, could you even get me out of here?"

He blows out a breath and I can hear him take a glug of his drink. "Probably not, but if you really want out, I can try."

I press my lips together and drop back onto the bed so I'm staring up at the ceiling. "Honestly, Tommy?" My voice is quiet. Not quite a whisper, but barely more. "I have no idea what I want."

"I'm sorry, Quinn girl. Maybe sending you to them wasn't the best idea, I just… I figured they would be more than equipped to keep you off Trent's radar, and if not, they'd have the power to deal with him if he did show. I never expected this."

"You don't have to apologize, Tommy," I try to reassure him. "I agreed to this plan and this is kind of my own fault for getting sloppy. If I hadn't been drinking, I wouldn't have stumbled through the wrong door and seen what I saw. Everything from there is just the consequences of my actions."

"What you saw?" he asks, and I bite my lip.

Shit.

"Erm, yeah. The reason Meyer brought me to the house in the first place."

He curses down the line, enough to make a sailor blush. "What happened, Quinn?"

I pause for a second, but decide that Tommy has never let me down. I can trust him. So I tell him everything that happened and everything that's gone on since I've been at the house, making sure to leave out the details of my sex life but include everything else. It feels a little like confession.

"Well shit, Quinn girl. This makes a little more sense now. You sure you're okay there?"

I nod, then realize he can't see me. This isn't FaceTime.

"I think so. They've done everything they can to ensure my safety. These threats seem legit and I don't think they'd lie to me about that. Would they?"

"No, I don't think they would. Do you want me to come there?"

I worry my lip, considering his question. Would it be nice to have him here? It would. Tommy is like my security blanket these days. But would it actually make a difference to anything? Probably not.

"It's okay. I can handle this, but thank you. If I need you, I promise I'll ask."

"As long as you're sure."

I smile. It's nice to know that someone cares. I haven't had much of that in my life. "I'm sure, Tommy. I'll figure out how to make this work for me."

"Oh, I have no doubt about that, Q girl. Have you met Angela yet?" Something about the way he says her name piques my curiosity.

"You know Angela?" I ask slyly.

"You could say that," is all he responds with. There is definitely a story there and, someday, I'm going to get it.

"No, I haven't met her yet. She told me she wants to do a big family dinner tonight because everyone is finally home at the same time, but I've been trying to figure out how to dodge it."

He bellows out a laugh. "Oh, sweet girl, there is not a

chance you'll get out of that dinner. You could be on your deathbed and she'd still drag you to her table to eat. But you'll be fine, Angie's bark is far worse than her bite."

"Don't think her bite is something I need to worry about," I murmur, and he laughs again.

"No, probably not. Not if Meyer's keeping you at the house. Angela might be his mom, but she respects that he's the head of the family. Always has. Any idea who else will be at the dinner?"

"Not a clue," I tell him honestly, shrugging. "Even if I had names, I have no idea who anyone is anyway."

"Well, give Angie my love and I wish you good luck. Not that you'll need it, of course."

"You're filling me with so much confidence here, Tommy."

He laughs again and I groan as I pull myself up from the bed to sit with my legs tucked underneath me. "You'll be fine, Q girl. I've gotta go, but check in with this old man a little more often, okay?"

"Sure thing, old man," I tease.

"Be safe, Quinn."

"You too," I murmur before the line disconnects.

Talking to Tommy has made me feel a little better, and really, I probably should've just called him at the start of my sad girl days. Talking to him usually helps me clear my head—at least it has the last few years.

A knock at the door sounds, drawing my attention, so I hop across the room and open the door a crack, finding Hunter standing there.

"You're back."

"Miss me, Angel?" he asks as I open the door fully.

I let out a scoff. "You wish."

"Oh, you have no idea," he says, his eyes darkening as he leans down toward me. "But right now, I'm here to be your chaperone."

"Chaperone?" I ask, confused.

"Yes, Angel," he says with a smirk. "Angela has summoned us all."

TWENTY FOUR

After running around like a headless chicken trying to put on clothes worthy of the shirt and dress pants Hunter had on for the dinner, deciding nothing was good enough and pulling a floaty forest green dress from my closet that I definitely don't remember buying then pairing it with some black flats, I take a deep breath. I already ran the straightener through my hair and put a coat of mascara on my lashes.

"Is this okay?" I ask Hunter again as we leave my room and he chuckles, shaking his head.

"For God knows how many times, it's perfect, Angel. You look beautiful."

The way he looks at me as he offers me the crook of his arm when we reach the top of the stairs makes me doubt him, but it's a little too late now. I already spent longer than I should have getting dressed.

Laughter sounds from the kitchen, so I offer Hunter my arm, because he seems to be refusing to move without it, and we descend the stairs together. "Deep breaths. Meyer invited a few extra people to help you feel less on display," he whispers as we get halfway down the stairs and relief relaxes my shoulders a little.

Thank God for that.

"Who else is here?" I ask quietly as we reach the bottom of the stairs.

He grins down at me, but less in that aloof, arrogant way that he has, and more of a warm, trying-to-make-me-feel-better kind of way. "You're about to find out."

We walk into the kitchen, which is buzzing with people, my stomach flip-flopping as we go. The thought of Trent infiltrating this crowd pops into my mind, but I try to shake it off. There's no way that he'd manage that.

Right?

"Finally!" Shae calls out as she approaches before wrapping her arms around me. "Thought you'd convinced him to run away with you."

"Didn't even think of that. Dammit!" I mutter, and she laughs as she pulls back.

"Well, good," she says, her smile making her seem lighter than I've seen her in all the time I've been here. "Now, let me steal the pretty girl, Hunter. I'm far more people-y than you are."

"We both know that's a lie," Hunter says with a chuckle. "Just don't get her drunk before she meets your mom. Meyer will kill us both."

"Noted," she says with a nod before linking her arm through my free one and dragging me along with her into the throng of people.

She drags me over to someone who is very obviously her brother. He's a younger version of Meyer, but I couldn't say if he was older or younger than Shae just from looking.

"Teo!" she cries when we reach him, letting me go and flinging herself at him. "How goes it, little brother?"

Well, that answers that.

"By less than a year, Shae," he says, rolling his eyes. "You doing okay?"

His gaze roams over her protectively before he turns to me. "Who is this?"

"Quinn," I say with a smile, but the corners of his lips turn down.

"I wasn't asking you," he snarks at me. "Your latest toy, Shae?"

"Not quite," I hear from behind me. Meyer moves beside me, his hand on the small of my back. "You should know better than to be rude to my guests, Mateo."

Mateo's eyes go wide at his older brother, fear flickering through them before his gaze bounces back to me. "Sorry, bad habits."

"Don't worry about it," I tell him, shrugging as Meyer moves his hand from my back to my waist, tucking me into his side.

"Do you have a drink?" Meyer asks me, causing me to look up, realizing he's so close at this angle that I have to shake my head to tell him no because I'm trying not to think about the last time we were this close. "Then let's fix that and introduce you to some friends, shall we?"

"Sure," I say quietly, smiling up at him quickly.

"I'll catch up with you later, Mateo." Meyer's brother nods at him and Shae mouths a 'sorry' to me, but I shake my head to let her know it's fine.

"Don't be too hard on him," I say to Meyer as he leads me across the room to where he has a bar set up. "He was just being protective of Shae, I'm sure."

"Doesn't matter," he responds. "Red, white? Something else?"

"Matador?" I ask and he nods, pouring the drink, much to my surprise. Not many people know the drink. Handing me the glass, he pours himself two fingers of vodka before turning to face the room.

"You ready?"

"Not even a little," I tell him honestly. "Where is your mom?"

I glance around the kitchen and realize I can't see

anyone cooking.

"She's in the catering kitchen. She prefers to cook in there so I set the bar up in here instead."

"There's a freaking catering kitchen here?" I ask, and he chuckles at me as I shake my head.

"You'll learn this place through and through soon enough. Now come on, let's mingle." He pulls me toward where Rory and Hunter are standing with two other guys who look about my age. "Gents," Meyer says as we arrive. "This is Quinn. Quinn, this is Denton and Reed."

"Nice to meet you," I say tightly before taking a sip of my drink.

"You too," Denton says, his southern drawl thick and his smile friendly.

"You work for Meyer?" Reed asks, his gaze bouncing to Meyer's hand on my waist before coming back to meet mine.

"Not exactly," I tell him, because well, I kind of *do* work for him at the club, but I don't think I'm going back there and I have no idea how to actually describe my place here.

Like, at all.

"A lady of mystery, my favorite." Denton's words are accompanied by a cheeky smile, and Hunter clips him on the back of the head.

"You might be a lawyer, but I'll still bury you, dickhead."

Denton laughs, rubbing the back of his head. "Just

trying to put the lady at ease. She seems a little nervous."

Hunter and Rory both turn to look at me, but I realize that Meyer and Reed are still locked in a battle of wills and eye contact.

"I'm fine," I say, lightly, moving just enough that I can run my hand discreetly down Meyer's spine. He relaxes under my touch. While I don't understand it, I also don't want to be the reason he has a problem with his friend—which is the only conclusion I can come to right now since the only words Reed spoke were to me.

"More drinks," Hunter announces, noticing what I have. "Reed, come help me carry them."

He grips the younger man's shoulder tightly, drawing his attention from Meyer. "Yeah, sure."

Rory's phone rings and he glances at Meyer before leaving the room to take the call. I watch him leave and smirk as the crowd parts for him, even when people don't see him coming.

Apparently, he has a presence with everyone whether they realize it or not.

"Everything okay?" Denton asks Meyer. "I know he's pretty new, but you can trust him."

"Uh-huh," Meyer responds before swallowing the contents of his glass in one. "How are you finding the Golden State?"

"It's nice," Denton says with a shrug. "Can't say I

don't miss home though."

"Where are you from?" I ask, then realize how rude that might've sounded. I should know better than to speak without being spoken to.

It takes me a minute to realize he's speaking to me and I totally zoned out as fear flooded me.

"Are you okay?" Denton asks. "You've gone awfully pale, miss."

Meyer steps back and looks down at me, concern obvious from the slant of his brow. "What's wrong?"

"Sorry, I just… flashback moment," I try to explain, looking down at my hands as I wring them out. "Trent… I wasn't supposed to ask questions or speak to his friends and I just, I spoke and then… fear response. I'm okay though."

"Who is Trent?" Denton asks, his confused gaze bouncing between the two of us, but Meyer grips my chin and lifts my gaze to his.

"You never have to be afraid like that here, Quinn." He holds my gaze and I can hardly breathe from the intensity of it.

"What did I miss?" Hunter asks as he and Reed appear again, breaking the moment with Meyer, who releases me but tucks me back into his side.

"Nothing major," Meyer says just as a commotion on the other side of the room starts. Voices get louder, followed by a cheer, and Meyer rolls his eyes.

"Good to see the cousins are having a fun time," Rory snarks as he returns, his gaze bouncing to me and Meyer's arm around me before tipping up to Meyer. "You got a minute?"

"Sure," Meyer responds, removing his hold from me and following Rory from the room.

I wonder what that's about.

"I'm from Texas," Denton says, moving a step closer to me. "Just a small town there you've likely never heard of."

Thankful that he doesn't ask more questions about my freak out, I smile at him. "So how the hell did you end up here?"

"Law school," he responds before taking a sip of the drink that Reed hands to him. "I met Hunter via Teo at a party. Teo was complaining about how I was kicking his ass in every single class and they hired me before I even passed the bar. Might not have been every lawyer's dream job, but working with and for people you can consider family? That is priceless."

"And now he spends all his time managing the lawyers on our team, pulling out his hair because he's a young buck that's too smart for his own good."

"I'm twenty-eight," Denton responds, laughing. "Not sure I'd consider that a young buck."

"Younger than me," Reed mutters, the alcohol seeming to embolden his tongue as the bitterness runs from it.

"Same age as me," I say with a shrug, "and I sure as hell am not an established lawyer running a team."

"Yeah, well, he's five years younger than me. You guys should respect your elders." Hunter laughs at his own joke. "Meyer would agree though, I guess, since he and Rory are only a few months older than me. Obviously, they'd agree."

Huh. How had it not even struck me to find out how old they are? I guess my mind has been on more important things, but knowing that Meyer is like, mid-thirties and this is his life... I can't imagine the pressure, the weight that he carries. I've barely been able to manage the weight of running, let alone being responsible for all that he is.

"Yeah, yeah, old man," Denton teases back, their back-and-forth making them seem like the family Denton declared them to be. I keep quiet, just observing the three of them, how Reed becomes more and more withdrawn the closer Denton and Hunter get as the liquor flows.

Thankfully—or not, I haven't quite decided yet—someone I don't recognize, which isn't that shocking at this point, announces that dinner is ready.

Hunter ushers me along with him, his hand taking the place of where Meyer's was before. Reed notices, his brows flying up as he notices the touch, but he doesn't say anything, though his disgust is all over his face.

I tuck that nugget of information away for just in case. The last thing I want tonight is drama—at least, drama because of me. I'll happily sit by with popcorn and watch everyone else's drama.

People start to filter from the kitchen out to the entrance hall and across into a room I haven't been in before— shocker—that has the longest freaking dining table I've ever seen. It looks like something off the History Channel that kings would have had in their castles.

"Ready?" Hunter asks as we stand at the threshold.

Moments later, Meyer and Rory appear behind us. Hunter to my right, Meyer behind me, and Rory to my left. There is something intoxicating about being this close to the three of them. For a moment, I nearly ask Meyer right then what he meant about being theirs, but then Shae and Mateo appear in front of us with a woman who is very obviously Angela.

The siblings must get their hair and coloring from their dad, but the eyes, the smile, the way they carry themselves? That comes from the woman before me, who is watching me closely.

"My beautiful family," she sighs, cupping Hunter's cheek. I hate the way I feel like such an outsider in this moment, like I'm intruding. I move to step to the side, so I'm not in front of Meyer, but his hand appears on my shoulder, like he knew I was about to bolt. "I am so glad we could get everyone together to celebrate."

"Mother," Meyer starts, Shae and Mateo sniggering behind their mom. "This is Quinn. Quinn, my mother, Angela."

"It's lovely to meet you." My words come out far more timid than I'd like, but I feel like I want to crawl out of my skin, yet again, so I shouldn't be surprised. For the billionth time in my life, I wish I was normal, that being around a ton of people didn't make me feel… different. Didn't make me feel so uncomfortable that I want to climb under the table and hide.

"I'm sure the pleasure will be mine," Angela says, her gaze roaming over me, judging me, though for what I don't know. Her face gives nothing away.

She turns to Rory, smiling at him. "My beautiful, quiet boy. Come, all of you, sit, I did not slave away all day for the food to go cold. Quinn, you come sit next to me."

Without another word, she turns and moves to sit at the head of the table, very obviously enjoying her matriarch status.

"Come on," Meyer murmurs while my heart pounds in my chest. Sitting next to his mom was not the plan. I was going to hide in the crowd, next to Shae, while she filled me in on the who's who of the dinner.

Shit.

"Do not look so afraid, Kitten. She'll feed on it. Show those claws we both know you have and she will respect you more for it." I look back at Meyer, who is a hair's width from me as we move in sync, and he looks at me, smiling like he's trying to reaffirm his words.

"He's right," Rory tags on. "Mama Marino will eat you alive if you don't hold your ground."

Somehow, despite Meyer saying basically the same thing, Rory's words carry more weight. Probably because I know he only speaks when he knows his words have meaning. I might not know much about him, but I do know that. He looks at me with a light teasing in his eyes, but under it, I see my own want for him reflected back at me.

Need flits through me in response, but I shove it down. Now is *not* the time, but it's good to know he feels the pull too. I was beginning to think he wasn't part of the 'belong to them' deal that Meyer mentioned, or that he just wasn't interested. I guess he might just be a little more reserved than the other two, but I'm going to tuck away that little nugget for later. If he's not ready, I'm not going to push him. Time is something I'm sure we have plenty of.

"Don't be absurd," Mateo mutters. "Mama is a pussy cat."

"Only because you're the baby," Shae teases him. "Come on, Teo."

Taking his hand, she drags him to the opposite side

of the table, sitting in two of the spare seats next to their mom, and Hunter follows, taking the seat between Shae and Reed.

"Here you go," Meyer says quietly as he pulls out the chair next to Angela. I take a seat as he pushes the chair under, before taking a seat next to me. Only once he is sitting does Rory scope out the room and take his own seat.

"None of that tonight, little lion," Angela says, looking at Rory. "We are family here. There is no threat."

Rory nods at her, but doesn't become any less rigid.

Angela turns her gaze to me and I clasp my hands together on my lap, repeating the words Rory and Meyer said to me before. I can do this, have a backbone. I've stood up to three of the supposedly most terrifying people in the room plenty of times, so why is she so intimidating to me?

My mother was a meek woman who sold me out to save herself far too often, so it's not like I'm used to larger-than-life women, but maybe that's exactly it.

The only woman I've met with a presence like Angela's is Harper. Yen on a smaller scale, and Shae, but Shae isn't as fierce. Meyer obviously surrounds himself with strong women and I can't help but wonder if that's the case, why he'd want me around.

"So, Quinn, how is it that you now seem to be living in our home?" Angela asks as servers come around, filling water glasses and wine glasses for everyone.

Taking a breath to steady myself, I straighten my shoulders, trying to be the sassy version of myself that the guys have brought out of me occasionally. *Fake it till you make it, Quinn.*

"Well, you see," I start, tilting my head and painting a smile on my face. "Your son kidnapped me then declared I couldn't go back to my apartment, so he had dear Rory here take me to pack up my stuff and officially move me into the room I'm essentially being held captive in."

Her face doesn't move the entire time I speak or for several beats after. Those closest to us stay silent, despite the noise further down the table, as if holding their breath, waiting on her response.

"Certainly seems like something he'd do," she says before taking a sip of her wine and turning her focus to Meyer. "So, you kidnapped her? Are you going to keep her hostage? Kill her? Marry her? I need some grandbabies. After all, I won't be young forever and neither will you."

"Mother," Meyer groans, while his siblings laugh opposite us. "Seriously? That's where your head went when she told you I kidnapped her?"

Angela shrugs at him, smiling before taking another sip. "Well, you Marino boys have a way with the women you covet. Your father wasn't any different, nor his brothers, father, or grandfathers before them. You take what you want and deal with the fallout later. It's only fair of me to make assumptions. Plus, I did ask if you were going to kill her first."

Hunter bursts out laughing on the other side of Meyer, and Shae joins in. "Mama Marino, please, never ever change."

"I haven't changed a day of my life, I'm not about to start now."

The conversation is interrupted by servers starting to bring out food, and I let out a sigh of relief when Angela turns her attention to Shae and Mateo.

"Sorry about that," Meyer murmurs. He almost seems embarrassed. *Almost.*

"It's fine," I whisper back. "She's... definitely one of a kind."

"She's something, that's for sure," he says, running a hand through his dark mop of hair. "Just remember to eat at least two rounds, she'll get offended otherwise."

"Noted, small plates but multiples."

He shakes his head, keeping his voice low. "Not small, she'll see your game. Don't tell me you can't eat because I've seen you, and those curves... yeah, I definitely want them to stay. Eat, enjoy, just eat a lot."

I laugh at him, shaking my head at how ridiculous he's being, but it occurs to me that maybe he's not being that silly. Angela glances at the two of us, smirking when she sees how close we're speaking, and I realize she really meant it when she mentioned him marrying me.

My breath hitches in my chest. Is that what he meant when he asked me to be theirs?

It can't be. Right?

Right?

TWENTY FIVE

By the time the meal is over, I'm a few drinks deep, as is everyone else, and I feel a lot more relaxed. Could be the alcohol, could be that Meyer hasn't left my side, could be that Angela turned her focus on the cousin down the table, Angelo, who is two years older than Meyer and isn't married yet.

Apparently, she wants tiny humans running around and isn't all *that* bothered where they come from.

A thought occurs to me, so I lean into Meyer. "Where are your aunts and uncles if your cousins are here? Is this all of your cousins?"

"Feeling a little curious, are we, Kitten?" The smirk on his face as he props his arm on the back of my chair when he leans back is as infuriating as it is hot.

So I shrug, because I've noticed that his eye twitches

every time I do it, which means he probably isn't a fan of that, but he's the one who told me to have a spine and claws. That's exactly who I've tried to be all night. The version of myself I might've been if I hadn't grown up the way I had, or maybe even if I'd escaped them but never fallen prey to Trent's trap.

Regardless, being this version of myself is empowering and the whole fake-it-till-you-make-it thing feels really appealing right now.

"Tonia and Jess's parents are on a cruise right now with Bobby and Becky's parents," he says, pointing to people further down the table.

I am so never remembering all these names.

"Teysha, Lauren, Kevin, Buck, and Jesse are all siblings. Their dad died a few years ago, and their mom... well, she and mine don't always see eye to eye. They're probably in a spat right now." He takes a sip of his drink, naming off more cousins, telling me which part of the world their parents are in or why there is another family feud going on with the older generation. It's all pretty amusing.

"So you're basically saying your family is huge."

He grins, nodding. "Yes. Some people here are family, but not by blood, which is why their parents aren't here, but this is just a small handful of people that mom actually likes."

I snort a laugh then clasp my hand over my face. "God,

that hasn't happened in years."

"It's cute," he teases, booping my nose like a loon. "Why the laugh anyway?"

"Well, I'm here and your mom does *not* like me."

He turns to face me, becoming serious for a minute. "She doesn't know you yet. She'll come to love you, you'll see."

Pausing for a moment, his gaze locks with mine before he takes my hand and brings it to his lips. "It's impossible not to."

"Let's get this party started, shall we?" Shae is so loud as she drops onto my lap that I almost wince, but then I laugh as she loops her arms around her brother's neck. "Pretty please come and dance with me, Mey. Teo is being a spoilsport."

Glancing around, I realize that Mateo isn't in the room. I mean, this is his home, so if he's had enough, it's not like it's weird that he disappeared. I don't know him, so I don't know if him being a little bratty or introverted is out of character.

There is definitely something about him that I can't quite put my finger on, though. Laughing to myself, I shake my head. My judgment in people obviously isn't sound. Not if you look at my track record. So maybe I'll just shut down that little voice.

"Fine, fine," Meyer concedes and Shae jumps to her

feet, clapping her hands. It's amusing to me that she's only a few months younger than I am, yet, Meyer treats her like a little kid.

They all do.

"You next, Hunter!" she says, pointing at the blond who is now sitting across the table with Rory. "Then you, Lion Man."

As they walk away from the table, I look over at the two, then decide to scoot over to the other side with them. "Why Lion Man?" I ask as I drop into the seat next to Rory.

"Because *ROAR-y,*" Hunter says, making cat-like swipes with his hand with the widest grin I think I've seen on him. Rory rolls his eyes while I giggle.

"Oh, yeah. I guess that makes sense."

"It's stupid, but Mama Marino has called me Little Lion since I came to the house. It just kind of stuck."

"I don't think it's stupid. You seem fiercely loyal, a lionheart of sorts." He blinks at me, then just shrugs.

"Maybe."

"Would you like to dance, Angel?" Hunter asks. While I *am* still a little mad at him, I'm tired of being angry and carrying the weight that comes with it. I also can't remember the last time I danced with a guy...

"Sure." I climb to my feet, a little unsteady, but Rory grips my waist from where he's sitting. I place my hands on his arms before leaning forward and kissing his cheek.

"Thank you."

Before he can respond, Hunter whirls me away toward where everyone is dancing. The music is a mashup of old school songs, stuff from before our time, and newer hits. I have no idea who put the music on or even where it's playing from, but it's loud enough to be dance worthy, but not so loud that I can't hear Hunter speak.

We dance like idiots for a few songs, making faces at each other. I can't help but cackle loudly when he jumps around and wiggles his ass at me. He's a total loon, but this is so much fun that I'm glad I decided to stop being mad at him.

Being mad is exhausting.

The music slows and Hunter steps closer to me, looping his arms around my waist, so I clasp my hands behind his neck and sway with him.

"I could do this forever," he murmurs as he rests his cheek on the side of my face. "Just like this."

I rest my head on his chest, not saying a word. Because what do I even say to that? Really, I need to talk to him, to Meyer, to all of them at once I guess, and work out exactly what it is they want from me because this not knowing my place thing is enough to drive a girl insane.

Letting out a sigh, I pull back and open my mouth, but as I go to speak, three gunshots crack through the air.

The music cuts out and the room turns into chaos until

a voice shouts above the madness.

"STOP!" I look around and find Rory standing on the table.

"Teo, take everyone to the safe room," Meyer demands as Rory jumps off the table.

"Go with them," Hunter says to me, but my hands are shaking and I feel frozen. "You will be safe, just go with them. It will be safer for you there. It might be nothing, but if it is something. No one will get through the defenses but, just in case, go with them."

Everyone is already leaving the room, just Shae is trailing behind, waiting for me. She looks as afraid as I feel and my brain kicks up the memory of what she told me happened to her. That's enough to get my ass moving since she has far more reason to be afraid than I do, and if she can manage, so the hell can I.

"Be careful," I say to the three of them. Each of them nod and I head over to Shae. Once we're walking, I glance back, seeing just their backs as they go to deal with whatever is going on. A little voice in my head chimes in that I might not see them again and it hits me.

I *want* to see them again. I *want* to be theirs, whatever that means.

Despite the shock that filters through me as more gunshots crack through the air and Shae starts to run, dragging me along behind her. I *need* them to survive.

The house shakes and Shae lets out a scream. Gunfire sounds closer and she freezes.

"Come on, Shae," I urge her, trying not to panic. I have no idea where the panic room is. I can't see anyone else now and I'm a little worried that, despite hauling ass, we're going in circles.

The house is big, but it can't be *this* big.

Or am I really just so lost because of the adrenaline in my system?

My hands tremble as I grasp Shae's shoulders and shake her, but it's like she can't see or hear me.

Shit.

What the fuck do I do?

I glance around the hall, wishing I knew this place better, and drag Shae through the closest door to us. It's just a small guest bedroom, so definitely not as safe as a panic room, but it's got to be better than being out in the hall.

"Shae," I murmur softly as she slides down the wall, clutching her head, eyes scrunched closed.

She chants the words, "Not again" over and over.

"Shae, please."

Silence echoes around us and it's somehow louder than when there was gunfire.

She scratches at her arms, hard enough to draw blood, and panic fills me. I don't know what to do.

I look frantically around the room, spotting the dresser. Moving as quickly but quietly as I can, I tear through the drawers and finally find some towels. She's stopped clawing at herself now, but she's back to pulling at her hair.

Grabbing the towels, I move back over to her, trying to clean up the blood on her arms, then try to pull her hands from her hair, but it's no use.

It's almost like she's lost inside her head and the rest of the world doesn't exist.

Voices call out down the hall, but with the door shut, I can't hear what they're saying. Uncertain, I debate risking opening the door to see who is out there. Hunter said no one would make it inside the walls, let alone the house.

But what if he was wrong?

The voices grow louder but I still can't make out what they're saying, though I can hear doors opening and closing.

My heart picks up its pace. What if they're not on our side?

Shit, shit, shit.

"Shae," I whisper-shout, but nothing. I open the door next to where she slid down, revealing a small closet. It takes all my strength but I manage to get her to move into the closet.

The handle on the main door to the room twists and I slam the closet door shut, holding my breath as I turn to face the door.

"And who is this?" The bald man standing in the entrance to the room smiles at me, his yellow and blackening teeth on display enough that my stomach twists.

Fake it till you make it, Quinn.

Jutting out my jaw and straightening my shoulders, I lock my gaze with his. "No one you want to mess with."

His grin somehow widens. "Oh, breaking you will be fun." He reaches behind him and my breath catches as I suddenly find myself staring down the barrel of a gun. I freeze, unable to look away from the weapon in my face.

He steps toward me, reaching out with his free hand, palming my boob over the thin fabric of my dress, and I want to scream, to cry, but the gun holds me captive.

Yet again, I'm at the mercy of a man and helpless.

Rage strikes through me and I want to knock his hand away from me, gun be damned, but I can't make myself move.

Humiliation and shame run through me as his hand runs lower, pulling my skirt up to cup me. "Oh, yeah. You'll be fun to break."

Gunshots sound in the distance again, seeming to distract him enough to stop touching me. Like he forgot the reason he was here in the first place.

"Out," he says, motioning with his head to the door, keeping the gun firmly on me. "Now."

My knees shake as I try to follow his demand, focusing on not glancing at the closet in the hope that he doesn't find Shae.

I step out of the room and movement to the right catches my eye. Hunter stands there, a finger to his lips, so I stare forward again. "Keep moving!" the man shouts from behind me, pressing the gun in between my shoulder blades. I jump, squeaking at the hard pressure on my back and take another step as he pushes forward.

He clears the doorway and the gun disappears from my back.

"Stupid move, asshole," Hunter says and I turn around, finding him standing with a gun pressed against the guy's temple. "Betraying us was fucking idiotic."

The guy opens his mouth to speak, but seems to think twice when he spots the three other bodies in the hall that are currently lying in pools of blood.

Meyer and Rory round the top of the hall at that moment, Rory spattered in blood, Meyer with his sleeves rolled up, both disheveled yet entirely unfazed.

"Are you okay, Kitten?" Meyer asks when he reaches me, and I nod automatically.

Oh, yeah. I'm all rainbows and sunshine.

"He hurt you?" Rory asks, glancing at me before turning his stare on the guy who had me at gunpoint.

I open my mouth to speak but shame slices through

me and words escape me. So instead, I nod and look at the ground.

"Motherfucker had a gun pressed into her back when I found them," Hunter spits, drawing my attention back to them, and Rory's face turns stormy.

"Did he touch you?" Rory asks me, not taking his eyes from me. I stay still but he must see the humiliation on my face because he clenches his fists. "Oh, he's mine."

"Shae," I utter to Meyer, trying to change the focus of this whole situation. His brow furrows like he doesn't understand what I'm saying. "She's... she's not in a great way. She's in the closet."

"You got this?" Hunter asks Rory, who nods. "I'll get Shae."

Meyer nods, relief that I don't quite understand flitting across his face. "Thank you."

Rory takes the guy and leads him down the hall in the opposite direction they came from as Hunter enters the room I just left, leaving me standing with Meyer.

"Come on, Kitten. Let's go get the others." He tucks my hair behind my ear before roaming his eyes over me, as if to make sure I'm really okay. "Then, I'll explain all of this."

"Okay," I say quietly, the adrenaline seeping from my system, leaving me exhausted and confused. None of this makes sense to me, but then, I don't understand this world yet.

Though, I get the feeling I'm soon going to know more than I ever wanted. I guess I should've been careful what I wished for.

Once we let everyone out of the panic room, Meyer ended up dealing with all of his family, calming his mom, and sending them all home. He kept me stuck to his side the entire time, keeping a hand on me, grounding me, and somehow, despite everything, I still felt safe.

He finished dealing with everyone about an hour ago and we've been in his office since. He's been on the phone doing a whole lot of shouting while I've been sitting on the floor near the fireplace that he lit for me, staring at the flames.

I should be a mess right now. Terrified. Wanting to run. Freaking out.

But somehow, I'm not.

The problem is, I can't work out if I'm just numb and that all of that is still to come, or if I'm just… okay.

I can't imagine being okay, I just stared down the barrel of a gun. Hell, I can't even remember what the guy that put the gun in my face looked like, but I can very clearly see it pointing at me. Feel it digging in between my shoulder blades. And yet… I'm calm.

Color me shocked.

Shae hasn't been far from my mind the entire time we've been down here. I know Hunter said he'd get her, but I don't know how he would've pulled her from the mental state that she was in. She told me some of her shadows, a trauma bonding of sorts, but she obviously barely scratched the surface when we were talking because that reaction... I still don't know how to process that either.

Meyer quiets, drawing my attention from the flames to look up at him where he's leaning against the sill of the window. He's rubbing his temples and looks like the weight of the world is sitting on his shoulders right now. He hasn't explained anything yet, but he's been a little busy and I don't know that I'm in a place to really properly take in anything he might tell me.

"What's running through your mind, Kitten?"

I tilt my head as he watches me. He pushes to stand, as if he's going to come toward me, but is interrupted by a knock at the door.

It opens and Rory's head appears through the gap. Once he sees we're in here, he steps in, Hunter following moments later.

"It's handled," Rory says to Meyer, who nods, pinching the bridge of his nose again.

"What did you learn?"

Rory glances at me before answering Meyer's

question. "He came to us loyal but turned a few weeks ago. Something to do with his brother that I'm not quite sure I'd normally believe, but I made sure it was truth."

He pauses and I turn my gaze back to the fire. I'm not sure I want to know exactly how he ensured he got the truth, but also, I can't help but question why knowing he must have gone to extremes doesn't bother me like it should.

I don't like violence but... right now, I want him to have done all he could to find out what happened. More because of Shae than what happened to me. This is a place she should've been safe. Even if she made snide remarks about it being her cage, I could tell that she didn't hate it. Or at least, she didn't dislike the idea of being trapped here where no one could reach her as much as I did.

But these people took that from her, even if just for a moment.

It can't have been more than twenty minutes between the first gunshots and Hunter finding us, but it felt like hours. For Shae... I can't even imagine.

I tune back into their conversation, having missed a good chunk while lost in my thoughts.

"—there were three others. One got away, but he won't be lost for long. The others were already dead when I found them. Lucky assholes."

Meyer nods. "I've been on the phone the entire time

you've been gone. Dario swears he didn't know a goddamn thing, but I don't trust that asshole. His people wouldn't act without him."

"They might," Rory grumbled. "There's been a lot of whispers going on over there. Cole has been keeping me updated, the loyalties are shifting and Dario isn't winning the votes the way he once did. Cole had no idea tonight was happening, which makes me think this was Giovanni."

Meyers brow rises, a flicker of disbelief in his eyes. "Dario's little brother is making a power play?"

"Rumor has it he has some powerful friends outside the club that want to see him sitting upon the metaphorical throne."

None of this makes any sense to me, but I stay quiet. Meyer said he would explain everything and I trust him to not lie to me. I mean, why would he at this point? I'm here, listening to all of this. They know I'm not going to the police, they know I'm not running—not that I could even if I wanted to—so I keep my mouth shut, my focus half on them as I try to warm up from the fire beside me.

"Fucking hell," Meyer hisses. "What a mess." He pauses for a moment before turning to Hunter. "How is Shae?"

"She's not great," Hunter says, frowning. "She still hasn't come back to herself, none of the usual tips or tricks are working. I don't know what triggered her exactly, but all things considered, it could have been anything. Your mom is with her now, but I think she's going to need to go back."

"Back?" I ask quietly, interrupting.

I turn myself so the fire is behind me, facing the three of them.

"How much has Shae told you?" Hunter asks me as he drops onto the chair by Meyer's desk.

"Not much," I admit. "Enough that I know she was taken, that it was bad, and she has that darkness inside of her, but not enough that I was prepared for tonight."

Hunter glances at Meyer, then Rory, who takes the other empty seat, before looking back at me. "Shae was taken while she was traveling, her attempt at finding herself while getting to see the world. She had a guard with her, but Shae used to despise her protection detail, didn't see the point. So she slipped them one night and ended up being taken by traffickers."

He pauses, like he's waiting to see if I have anything to say, but I keep quiet, waiting to hear the rest.

"She was fed drugs until she couldn't fight back anymore, until she'd beg for more and did whatever they wanted just to get a hit. Be that for escape or just for the drug, I don't know. By the time we found her... well, it took us too long."

"Is that when you found Yen?" I ask, curious at the

similarities in the story.

Hunter nods. "It was. We got nearly fifty girls out that night, a few guys too, but it was barely a dent in the operation."

I nod, my heart hurting for Shae and Yen—despite my current feelings toward her, I'm not a heartless bitch—and what they must have experienced.

"When we got her back, we put her in rehab to get clean, but realized pretty quickly that she needed more. So she spent some time in a facility to help her get to a place where she could be herself again, whatever that looked like. It took her a long time to get over the fact that she wasn't going to be the person she was before. But what you experienced tonight? That was how we found her, several times, between rehab and the facility."

"So you're sending her back?" I ask, looking over to Meyer.

He lets out a sigh before answering me. "I'll do whatever she needs. She hasn't had an episode in years." His fists clench on the desk in front of him and it occurs to me that he feels responsible for what happened to her. Both then and now, despite the fact that the first thing likely had nothing to do with him.

Heavy lies the crown.

"If she needs to go back, then she'll go. If she can pull herself out then, when she does, I'll ask her what she wants.

But it might be for the best." He pauses again for a beat, and the way his eyes darken makes my heart beat furiously in my chest. "Because after tonight, it's inevitable. We've teetered on the precipice of peace for too long and tonight shattered that. She needs to be prepared and so do you."

"What does that mean? Am I going somewhere now too?" I ask, confused.

He shakes his head, his gaze never leaving mine.

"Not if you don't want to, but things will be changing. I can't let this go unanswered. You come for my family and you'll regret even the whisper of a thought. I need to know you can handle being here, Quinn, that you meant what you said to me in the car, about being ours, because this is the one and only out you get. War is coming and it's going to be bloody."

My mouth goes dry, wondering how I went from my biggest worry being Trent finding me, to being caught up in whatever this is going to be. And still, I find myself nodding, unsure if I'm going to regret my impulsive decision or if it will be the best one I've ever made.

At this point, Trent doesn't even feel like a blip on my radar. At the start of this day I didn't think that that was a possibility, let alone my reality. Not even in my wildest dreams. But my heart rate evens out, my breaths are steady, and my mind feels stronger than I think I've ever felt.

"I meant what I said," I tell them, locking eyes with

each of them before turning back to Meyer. "I'm not going anywhere, war or not. I might not have wanted to be here to begin with, but I'm here, and even if I hadn't meant what I said before, they came for Shae. Whoever it was that Rory just took away violated me in a way I swore no one ever would again. I'm tired of running from my demons. Just tell me what to do because, this time, I'm in the fight."

TWENTY SIX

THREE MONTHS LATER

Things are too quiet. Have been for months. Considering Meyer said war was coming, nothing seems to have happened.

Shae has been gone since the morning after the attack, Angela along with her, leaving me here in a giant freaking sausage fest of a compound.

I mean, sure, I've spent a ton of time with Meyer, Hunter, and Rory, but not how I thought I would. Meyer asked me that night in his office if I meant it about being theirs and I agreed to that and all that came with it. But, despite my hours with them, working out, eating, learning how to fight, learning who the players in the games they play are so if I see them when I'm not on the compound, I know to be alert, not one of them has attempted to touch me again.

Should I be focused on that?

Absolutely not.

Am I?

Well duh, a girl has needs, and after my last two experiences of sex, my eyes have been opened and playing by myself just isn't scratching the itch the same way it once did.

Before them, I'd almost come to believe that good sex was a lie made up by Hollywood and authors. I knew that Trent raping me was obviously not what was supposed to happen, but even before he showed me who he really was, sex with him wasn't great. I still mostly faked it.

Same with the guys I'd been with before him. Not that there were many, and of the ones there were, a few were just one night stands and I assumed drunken fumblings with college boys were just a learning experience we all go through. But it was all still very… mediocre.

Now I know different.

I also know it wasn't a fluke with Hunter, because my time with Meyer… Holy. Freaking. Shit. I swear I get hot under the collar just thinking about it. Not only because he showed me how much fun the chase could be, but because he made me want it. Made me enjoy the thrill of the chase and completely freed me from another of the bindings Trent still had on me.

The two of them showed me sides of myself I hadn't

realized existed, sides of me I might have always been if it wasn't for my parents or Trent. As angry as that could make me, I refuse to be bitter about it, because I know now, and I'm clinging to that.

This frustration is close to boiling point and I've come close to just walking around the house naked to see if it makes a difference, but I'm not sure poor Bruno would survive it. They might not have touched me, but I've seen the looks, heard about what Hunter did all those months ago when I was by the pool—he just shrugged it off like it was nothing, of course—but I *know*.

What I don't know, is why they've avoided touching me lately.

I keep trying to tell myself their focus is elsewhere, on the war that is supposedly coming, that there are stresses they shoulder that I still don't know about because, despite them letting me in, I'm all too aware that I still don't really have a clue about what they do or what is going on. But I meant it when I said I was in. I want to be included. I want to help. I want to be of use.

Trent hasn't even really crossed my mind since that night, when I realized that he was firmly a part of my past and that this life had far bigger dangers than him. Tommy has been keeping an eye on him still, checking in on me every week or so—and I am *certain* I heard Angela's voice once when we were on the phone. Not that he's confirmed or denied it, the sneaky so-and-so—but it's almost like Trent's given up on finding me. Tommy told me that he'd tried, had done searches, stalked social media sites, checked in with people from my past that I might once have tried to reach out to. He even tried to speak to my old landlord. But no one knew anything, and he's had no luck with his searches.

I can't tell if I'm relieved that he's quit or if I'm worried he'll try harder again at some point but, according to Tommy, Trent got himself in a bit of hot water, beating a suspect, that temper of his rearing its ugly head. That alone tells me he's unraveling, which should scare me, but like I say, there are much bigger dangers in my near future than Trent.

Like the possibility of another attack here.

Like the chance of being attacked on the very few occasions I've been allowed to leave.

Not that Bruno has left my side. I almost feel bad for him, having to trail me. The only time he's not guarding me is when I sleep, and I only know that because I found Shae's old guard standing outside my door one morning at four a.m. because I couldn't sleep and decided to go work out in the gym instead.

Considering Meyer's declaration of war, the last few months have been almost, dare I say it, boring.

Not that I'm trying to jinx anything, but nothing's

happened. At least not that I've been told. Being on the outside is more than a little frustrating, considering Meyer said that night he'd fill me in, but since then, I've been told just enough to make it clear that the danger is real, but nowhere near what someone who was truly one of their people would know.

I'm making assumptions, of course, but still... how do you declare war and then have three months of nothing?

Unless it hasn't been nothing and they just haven't told me.

Good God, I'm losing my mind going around in circles like this.

Hitting the stop button on the treadmill, I slow my pace until the tread stops, and try to catch my breath, all while trying to ignore the sheer amount of sweat on my body. My fitness has come leaps and bounds the last few months, mostly because it's all I've had to do.

The loneliness creeps in sometimes, but I've tried to keep myself distracted the best I can since me going back to work was an absolute no and Shae isn't here. So I'm not going stir crazy yet, having Carlos teach me how to cook—and learning some very basic Spanish—has been a hilarious way to keep busy, and I can now make like five things that are more than passable to eat.

Once I've showered, I head downstairs, wandering the big empty house for the umpteenth time. I've managed to discover most of the secrets this place has to hide at this point, but there are some locked doors I haven't gotten past, including where Angela, Mateo, and Shae live. I'm not about to enter their space without permission, and Mateo avoids me pretty permanently anyway.

I might just be losing my mind. I can't work out any harder today, otherwise, my body will rebel tomorrow—learned that the hard way early on—and Carlos isn't around to do any cooking today, he has the day off, so I'm bored.

And whiny.

And oh, God do I hate whiny.

I can't even sit still enough to read and distract myself that way, there's a restlessness that's like a buzzing under my skin. I just need to *do* something.

"Quinn?" I turn at the sound of the voice, finding Rory coming through the front door. He watches me closely, as if studying me.

"Everything okay?" I ask, surprised he's home in the middle of the day.

"Quiet day," he responds. "Figured I'd come keep you company."

Oh, thank God.

"Oh," is all I say out loud. "Thanks. What did you want to do?"

He moves a few more steps toward me until I have to tip my head back to maintain eye contact with him. "How has your training been going?"

I shrug, because I kinda suck, but I'm getting there. "Antonio hasn't quit yet."

He chuckles softly, shaking his head. "How about I go through some training with you? Antonio is great, but he's a little soft hearted sometimes."

"You think you'll have better luck teaching me?"

He quirks a brow at me and leans in so close I can feel his breath on my skin. "Oh, Baby Girl, I know I will."

My heart picks up in my chest, slamming against my ribs. My body is going to hate me since I already pushed too hard this morning, but I'm curious what it is he thinks he can teach me that makes him better suited for it.

"Go get changed and meet me back down here. Ten minutes, Quinn. Don't keep me waiting."

Holy mother of everything. My body is trembling with exertion and not in the fun way I've been used to more recently. Breath leaves my body and Rory manages to flip me onto my back for the umpteenth time since we started training a few hours ago.

"Focus, Quinn!" he demands as he pins me to the ground, hand at my throat, his face so close to mine that I can see the sweat on his brow. I tap his arm and he releases me.

Rubbing at it as I sit up, he frowns. "Sorry, I shouldn't have done that."

"It's fine," I tell him softly. "Just flashbacks, ya know? But if someone does attack me, they're not going to care about flashbacks, they're going to use it against me. Better that it be you that I get used to it with than be caught off guard by one of them."

He nods as he sits down beside me. "I understand that."

We sit in silence for a few minutes until my throat doesn't feel like it's going to close anymore and I watch him as he looks out into the distance. "Do you like what you do for Meyer?"

I bite my lip once the question is out, wondering if I should be asking something like that. Not that I'm entirely sure *what* it is that he does, but I know he seems to be the guy that does the... what do they call it on TV? Oh, right. The wet work.

Even the name is a little gross.

It makes sense that Hunter would say everyone is terrified of him if he has this reputation for being the guy that'll make you talk at whatever cost, I just... I can't see that version of him. Maybe I'm naïve, but he seems too... I don't know. Like, there's light inside of him, but it's just bogged down. Maybe it is. Maybe he does enjoy what he does.

"Sorry, that was probably too personal."

He laughs at me, shaking his head. "Considering what I know about you, not too personal." I shrug when he pauses, running a hand down his face. "I'm good at what I do. I've always had a… penchant for pain and blood. Knowing just what to do to cause the right amount of damage to get what I want. Their pain is like a balm to my own."

I keep my face as blank as I can because it makes a bit of sense, but I can't help but wonder if that's why Trent hurt me. If hurting me eased his pain.

"What?" he asks, watching me closely again. I blink at him, wondering what he means. "What's going through your head? I can see your mind working."

So I tell him the thought I had, and his eyes darken. "No. Trent isn't the same monster that I am. He hurt you to make himself feel more like a man. To control and manipulate you. He hurt you because he liked making you feel small, because that made him feel big. I am nothing like him."

"I didn't mean that you were… it just kind of popped into my head. Sorry, I—"

"Don't apologize, Quinn. Not to me. Ever. I am a monster, that much is true, but I would never hurt you."

I scoot toward him and place my hand on his arm. "I don't think you'd hurt me, Rory. That's not what I meant at all. You've been nothing but good to me. You don't have to be out here trying to help me. Hell, you guys didn't need to help me at all. You could've killed me that night. I'm sure plenty of others would have. Instead, you brought me here, protected me, made me one of your own. You might think you're a monster, but I don't think you are. I think you do what is necessary to keep those you love safe. No matter the cost."

"Oh, I am definitely a monster, Baby Girl. Don't doubt that." His eyes are fierce as they lock with mine. "But you're right, I'm a monster that protects the people important to me."

He pauses a beat and the corners of his lips turn up, but then his eyes flicker with doubt and the smile disappears.

"What? What just happened?" I ask.

"I had a thought, a more... fun way to help you get over some of your issues with Trent, but then I thought twice. My idea of fun could just hurt you more."

I squeeze his hand again and shake my head. "I don't think you'd hurt me. What is your... brand of fun?"

He presses his lips together, like he's deciding whether or not to tell me. I get it, this seems personal, but if he has a more fun way than me getting my ass handed to me to help me overcome some of my triggers thanks to Trent, then I should be able to decide if it's something I want to do.

"I am not a gentle man, not by any stretch of the imagination. I like the fight, the challenge, and then the submission. The thrill that comes with it all."

He stops, as if giving me a chance to stop him from continuing. "So, a little like Meyer?"

"A little," he says with a smirk. "But not exactly. Meyer is what we'd call a primal. He loves the chase, the animalistic side of fucking and possessing you, then treating you like a princess. Mine is a little more brutal than that."

"Oh," I say, pausing while I try to process it all. "But you wouldn't actually hurt me?"

"Never," he says vehemently. "You'd agree beforehand, hence the consensual part of CNC. Safe words are a real thing, Baby Girl. There's a lot more to it than just pure brutality."

My brain runs on overload, because this *should* all sound horrific to me. Should make me want to run away screaming... but it doesn't. I might have been fairly sheltered with some stuff, but I can use the internet. I know what CNC is, and I know I should probably be horrified by it. If it was anyone else, maybe I would, but I want to see that side of him, because hilariously, despite everything, I do feel utterly and completely safe with him.

"And if I wanted to... play? Then what?"

His eyes flash, the heat in them scorching my skin. "Then we'd play. After we lay out the rules. But... and don't take this as me saying you're not capable of making decisions for yourself, maybe we could ease you into my sort of fun."

"What does that mean?"

He moves toward me, pushing forward until I have to lie back, him hovering above me. "Would you rather me show you than tell you, Baby Girl?"

My mouth goes dry as I'm caged beneath his arms, the power rolling from him in waves is enough to make me dizzy. I always said he wasn't scary, but right now? I can see why people fear him But rather than it scaring me, I want to see every single part of him.

"Yes."

Just the one single word falls from my lips, and in a blink he has me up, over his shoulder, and we're striding toward the house. Not one person says a goddamn thing as he hauls me across the short distance, and when he finally puts me down on my feet, I'm in his room. "Upstairs."

I look over my shoulder at him, wondering if I should shower before we do this, but before I can ask, he barks out an order. "Upstairs, Quinn. Do not make me tell you again."

A shiver runs down my spine, but the good kind. A trickle of a memory of Trent saying something similar tries to push into my mind but I shove it away. Rory is not Trent. I asked for this and I know if I tell him to stop, he will.

He might be a monster, but he's not a monster to me.

And that's the difference.

He growls from behind me and I move my feet, heading toward the spiral staircase in the corner of the room. "Undress and lie face down on the bed."

I nod, registering the order as I make my way up the stairs, glancing back at him, feeling his gaze locked on me with every movement. He's standing still, almost vibrating as he watches me. "Now, Quinn."

I pick up my pace and enter the upper level. Pausing when I step into the room, I blink at the dark, vast space. A huge bed takes up the wall to the right, the far wall is made of glass, and to the left, there are dressers lining the room and a TV mounted opposite the bed.

Simple, yet masculine and entirely Rory.

I start to undress, my hands trembling with anticipation. I'm not sure what to expect and I know that's why my hands are shaking, but it's a good shake. Taking a deep breath, I remind myself that Rory wouldn't hurt me and work through each muscle group, relaxing myself before I pad naked to the bed and lie face down in the middle like he asked.

Time feels like it lasts an eternity as the anticipation builds inside of me while I lie here, wetness pooling between my legs at the possibility of what's to come.

Footsteps on the stairs make my heart pound faster in my chest and my pussy clenches at the thought of him.

"Such a good girl," he purrs. I turn my head to the side and find him in nothing more than boxers, staring at me.

The man is a work of art. He is raw, tethered power, and the thought that I get to play with that is terrifying in the best kind of way.

I stay quiet as he walks across the room, my curiosity piqued when I hear drawers opening and closing.

"Safe word?" he asks and I blurt out the first thing that pops into my head.

"Jellybean."

My cheeks heat but he doesn't laugh. "Jellybean is good. Anything you want to strike off-limits now before I start?"

I think for a minute, then shake my head. I want to experience him for everything he is. He already said he would start me off easy, so I trust that.

"Give me your words, Quinn."

"Nothing is off-limits right now." I bite my lip, wondering if I'll regret that, but deep down, I already know I won't.

"Okay. Just remember your safe word, okay?"

"Okay," I murmur.

"Now close your eyes." His voice is like silk over my skin, low and gravelly, yet smooth somehow. I do as I'm told, clenching in need.

His fingers trail up the back of my ankle, up my leg,

before dipping between my thighs, another growl escaping him. "So wet already."

I say nothing, handing over complete control, but tap into my senses so I can take in every little movement and sound he makes. Every touch is amplified by the fact that my eyes flutter closed and I have to anticipate his every movement. When his touch finally lands, my heart skips a beat.

His finger plunges inside me until his knuckles bump against my pussy before he immediately pulls out and slides the now-wet digit around my asshole. Shock flits through me, but I go with it, allowing my body to react to him without overthinking it, my ass rising off the bed as though following his retreating finger.

He doesn't stop there. His finger continues its trip up my body, gliding along my spine one way before retracing its way right back to my ass. This time, he follows the opposite leg until he reaches my ankle. When he touches the arch of my foot, I jump, the tickling sensation getting the best of me.

"Your skin is flawless. I'd love to imprint myself on you so I can see myself on you always."

I gasp, air getting trapped in my lungs by the visual. I can't believe the idea of him leaving marks on me actually turns me on—especially after everything—but being with him, with them, makes all of that start to feel like a whole lifetime ago. I push away the thought and bring myself back to this moment.

With him.

Reteaching my body that not all of this has to be linked to bad.

Pushing two fingers inside me, he chuckles. It's dark yet full of promises I oh-so-desperately want him to keep.

"My good girl likes the idea of a little pain with her pleasure?" It sounds more like a statement than a question and a little shot of apprehension flits through me, but I keep my lips sealed.

I want this. To experience the line between pain and pleasure that he's offering. I want to play his game and rewrite the rules of my memory at the same time while I feel safe in having the control as I explore this side of my desires.

Without warning, the sting of skin on skin on my ass cheek makes me yelp. I fight the urge to open my eyes, obeying his request and finding it makes every sensation heightened. The sting is there, but it's laced with pleasure and promises rather than the pain I've experienced before.

Behind me, I hear a drawer open then close. The distinct sound of his footsteps making their way closer to me kickstarts my heart to beating double time. He's obviously got something in his hands, something he would keep in the dresser, but the possibilities are endless and the wait is torture.

He's doing it on purpose. I know it. Like he's trying to tease the patience out of me one vague clue at a time. Goosebumps rise on my skin as something light and soft retraces the path his fingers took only moments ago. Up my leg, between my thighs, against my pussy—as I'm getting wetter by the second—teasing the crack of my ass before running along my spine.

It could be a feather or maybe soft ribbon, I don't have a clue, but it's making my entire body react, from the shivers down my spine to the heat between my thighs.

Whatever it is, he circles it around one wrist then the other before he rests them at the small of my back. It's soft and thin, pressing against my skin. Next, he takes my ankles and brings them up to my ass, again with the material wrapping around my flesh.

My body reacts on instinct as he ties my wrists to my ankles, my thighs spreading wide open like a present to this man.

"Beautiful." I notice the roughness of his voice, the way it hitches just a fraction, like the sight of me all tied up is getting to him. It's that that pushes away the glimmer of panic that threatened a second ago. The sound of his voice, the power it lends me… it's intoxicating because nothing gets to him, he seems too impenetrable. And yet… I can hear it.

He's back at the dresser, now. I can hear him moving things around before he pushes the drawer shut again. When he returns, he lifts my blindfold, and I find him standing at my head as he crouches down to my level.

"Open your eyes, look at me." I tilt my head to the side and do as he asks, my vision needing a moment to adjust to the dim light. "I'm going to blindfold you and from this moment on, I need your trust. Are you good with this? I know this is a lot all at once, and I don't want to push you too far, too quick."

Heat licks at my insides in anticipation. Not just at what's happening, but at his words and the fact that, even in this moment, my wellbeing is still forefront to him. I never thought that this would be so hot, so freeing, but it is, so I nod.

"Words, Baby Girl." His low voice is raspy, like he's restraining himself and it's taking everything to keep him in place.

I lick my lips and nod again. "You have my trust, Rory. Implicitly."

The words are barely out of my mouth before he's over me, taking just a few seconds for him to wrap the blindfold around my head and make sure it's nice and tight.

I'm at his mercy and, if I'm being honest with myself, I'm completely okay with it. I'm a little shocked by it, but also, not at all at the same time. I meant what I said, I trust him, and I know he won't hurt me.

Pushing two fingers inside me, he rubs gentle circles over my clit with his thumb. He's too gentle, too tender, and it's at odds with the way I'm exposed to him, yet it makes me pliant and almost makes me forget I'm at his mercy.

My hips begin to push against the mattress, seeking out more of his touch, wanting him to fuck me into oblivion. That's when he stops everything. His fingers and thumb are gone and I'm left empty and wanting, a lusty mess on this bed without the possibility of touching myself either. The only relief I can get in this position comes from him and I can't feel him, dammit. Frustration curls in my stomach, my need growing with each moment he's not touching me.

"Miss me already?" His voice drops an octave and his words would be sweet, almost loving even, in any other setting. But here, he's playing with me. It's like he wants to keep me on the cusp of arousal until I lose my mind.

I'm pretty sure it won't take long.

The distinct sound of a bottle cap opening catches my attention, the pop of the top and the squirt reminding me of hand cream or lotion.

It's only when his fingers graze between my ass cheeks that I guess the bottle was lube. In this position, he doesn't have much access to my ass but he somehow manages it anyway, rubbing up and down my crack without quite rubbing over a part of me that, until now, has remained untouched.

He pushes one finger, then two, inside my pussy, scissoring and preparing me for, what? I'm really not sure.

"You're so wet, I could use your cum as lube." He sounds like he's in awe and that kind of praise does something to me. The fact that my body's reaction pleases him burns a red hot need inside me.

Behind me, the mattress gives way to his weight and I imagine him kneeling between my legs, worshiping me. It's a ridiculous thought but it's there all the same. His moans of approval tell me he's enjoying the view and that's all I need to know to feel safe.

From the tightness in my pussy, I'm guessing he's pushed in a third finger. I shimmy, trying to get more comfortable but all it earns me is a spanking to my ass.

"Behave."

The burn on my ass cheek travels up my spine and right back down to my pussy. Who would've thought that would be so hot? Cause it sure as hell wasn't me.

"Hmm, looks like you're a fan of spankings. Good to know." The teasing tone of his voice jars me, like I'm playing with multiple versions of Rory, a different one each time he speaks.

All too soon, I'm empty again, his fingers trailing up my ass and spine, dragging my cum over my skin. He stops for a moment before something hot and wet traces the trail right back to my pussy moments before I feel his tongue there, licking and sucking until I'm a writhing mess on the bed.

"You're a delicious little thing, aren't you?" Sounds of his mouth licking at his fingers invade my senses and the visual behind the blindfold is doing crazy things to me. Why does a man sucking on his cum-coated fingers sound so hot?

He's back again, pushing in and out, getting me all worked up by fucking me with his fingers, stimulating every one of my nerve endings then stopping it all right when my body begins to let loose.

It's sweet agony.

Rory grabs onto the ropes that tie my wrists to my ankles and drags me to another part of the bed before releasing my ankles and flipping me over onto my back. Blood flow rushes to my extremities, my feet and toes going numb before the prickling begins.

I forget all about that as I cry out into the room when his mouth begins kissing my pussy with long, languid strokes of his tongue before flicking at my clit. My hips seek him out, rocking up as I leverage myself on the bed, pushing up on my feet to get more of his mouth on me.

He allows it once. The next time I squirm, he stops everything. I whimper at the loss of his talented mouth, but in the next second, his face is close enough that I can smell myself on his breath.

"You want to come, beautiful?" There's a sharp edge to his voice, like the serrated side of a knife, when he speaks.

"Yes."

"Then I suggest you relax or the only thing you'll be doing is wishing you had." A groan of frustration threatens, but I swallow it. I clamp down my teeth and concentrate on staying still, letting him give me the pleasure I so desperately want right now.

"Good girl."

Before returning to my soaking wet pussy, he slides his hand under my head, wraps his fingers around my ponytail and lifts my face just a few inches off the mattress.

My taste on his lips is like an aphrodisiac that's been injected into my veins. I become crazed with it, kissing him back like my life will end if he steps away. Our tongues circle each other, our lips slipping and sliding as he deepens our kiss, searching me out as much as I do him. It's when his teeth clamp down on my bottom lip that I know I have to be good if I want him to continue.

And God, I really do.

This time, I gasp when his mouth returns to my pussy. There's no teasing, no hesitation, nothing but pure want. Just a tongue deep inside of me with two, strong, hands clasping my thighs and spreading them apart enough for his upper body to fit. I do everything I possibly can to keep my thighs from squeezing him because I need him to continue. I need him to lick every inch of me until I can get the release he's pushing me toward.

With my eyes blindfolded, I'm reduced to only my mental images. Rory on his knees, his large shoulders taking up all the space, the cords of muscles along his arms straining as he holds my thighs apart, his mouth… oh, his talented mouth… fucking my pussy as he takes everything he wants from me.

Everything I willingly give him.

I gasp again as he rolls my clit between his teeth, light scrapes that feel like a thousand tiny bolts of lightning attacking my nervous system. It's glorious, I can't deny that.

Biting my bottom lip, I taste blood from the pressure of my own teeth on my skin, the only way for me to keep from moving or screaming or, God forbid, give him an order like, "Goddammit make me come!"

That would be bad, right?

"You're soaked, beautiful, like little waves lapping at the shores of your cunt." Then he slams two fingers inside me as his tongue flicks my clit over and over again without mercy.

I'm going to die. Die from the need of coming and he's my willing and unrepenting executioner.

"Give it to me, now. Come on my face." His words are like the mechanism that releases the imprisoned waters of a dam. I take in a deep breath and let everything out. I shake and cry and scream his name like a prayer and curse. I buck up, my clit rubbing against some part of his mouth or face or I don't fucking know.

All I know is that the overwhelming feeling that courses through my body is consuming. A lot to take in and too much to control. I come and I come and I come so hard that I think I actually lose consciousness for a minute.

I can't fucking tell since I'm blindfolded, so it's just as dark as before, except now my legs are folded up and over my stomach with one of his hands, I'm guessing, holding me down. As he plays with my pussy, Rory scoops up my cum and uses it to lube up my ass. Around and around he goes, applying more and more pressure as he does.

"This little hole is going to let me in, isn't it?"

"Yes." I don't second guess myself, or what he's planning, because I want this.

God yes, please, just take me.

I don't say any of that because I'm too busy enjoying the feel of his digit just as it breaches my ring of muscle and teases my rim just enough to make me cry out when he steps away.

Who knew that would feel so good, dammit?

I'm so glad I didn't say anything because, when he

comes back, his lube-covered finger slides into my hole with ease. I whimper, the breach giving me a sense of fullness.

He adds a second, I know this because the burn is more potent, he's stretching me, teasing me just enough to make sure I can take more.

I suck in a breath, preparing myself...

This is hot as fuck but, am I really going to take his cock?

TWENTY SEVEN

RORY

She's going to take my cock and she's going to beg for more.

Lying here on my bed, all trussed up and blindfolded, she looks like a fucking dream. Mostly, she looks like a very wet dream with her pussy open wide and her juices coating her flesh. Every time I push into her ass with my fingers, she gets wetter, her juices trickling down to where my fingers fuck her pretty little hole.

"How are you feeling?" I need to remember that this is all new to her, that my special brand of lust is different from anything she may have experienced before. Mostly, I need to know she's present and that she's okay. That she knows she still has power here.

"Full." I hold back the need to chuckle because she's nowhere near full... yet.

Pushing my fingers deeper into her ass, I close my eyes and bask in the sounds she's making. The mewling like a cat in heat seems fitting since her pussy is hot as fuck.

But before any of that, I want her mouth around me, I want to watch her swallow my cock all the fucking way down.

Grabbing her by the ankles, I turn her around before walking to the side of the bed. I pull her to the edge until her head hangs off and her hair is draped all the way to the floor.

"Show me your tongue." My order comes out even and controlled and she doesn't even hesitate, opening her mouth and sticking her tongue out like she's presenting me with a gift.

"So pretty."

Standing behind her, I push my boxers down and kick them off to the side before taking my dick in my hand and stroking it slowly as I watch her try to anticipate my moves. It doesn't take her long to realize I'm about to shove my cock inside her mouth and see just how far I can go before she chokes.

It's such a beautiful sight, a seductive sound.

Pushing the head of my cock down onto her lips, I coat around her mouth with my precum like I'm carefully applying lipstick. She darts out her tongue, giving me tentative licks, and I allow it only because the hot feel of her is making me crazy.

"Do you like the taste of me? Of my cum?" She hums her approval, kissing the slit and using the tip of her tongue to tease me.

I put an end to that shit because there's a difference between taking a chance and topping from the bottom. I don't allow the latter.

"Such a good girl. Let's see how much you can take. You're going to take it, aren't you, Quinn?"

Pausing, she nods again, her eyes wide, and my cock twitches at the sight of her. "Pat my thigh if you need to tap out." Moving fast enough that she's startled, but slow enough that she could stop me if she wanted, I straddle the top of her chest and push my dick past her lips. Holding both sides of her face steady, I begin to fuck her mouth in shallow thrusts without shame. I wonder how far I can go before she gags on me. Will she tap out and make me stop? Will she use her safe word?

I push my dick further down, inch after torturous inch disappearing inside her mouth as I try to take it past her gag reflex.

She's about to cough and I've only got three quarters of my cock in her.

"Breathe through your nose. In and out. Concentrate on your breathing and relax your throat." It takes her a minute to adjust, to consciously think about what I'm asking her to do, and my patience is saintly to say the least because what I really want to do is plunge inside and live there.

I see and feel the moment she gets it. Her features loosen and her breathing evens. With her mouth in a perfect *O*, she allows me passage and I don't hesitate. I slowly push past her gag reflex and don't stop until my entire dick is inside her, down her throat.

Every time I bottom out, I can see my dick stretching it, the bulge moving in time with my thrusts. I start out slow, watching her, making sure she's comfortable with the rhythm.

As her eyes begin to water, I wonder if she's enjoying it as much as I am. Releasing one side of her face, I reach down her chest and pinch her nipple, causing her to instantly buck and close her mouth around my dick.

Fuck me, that's so good.

I do it again but, this time, she anticipates my move and keeps her throat nice and open, her mouth a perfect round vessel.

"That's my good girl."

Thrusting in and out, I bring my hand back to her head, wiping her tears as they fall across her temples from behind the blindfold.

Fuck this, I need to see her eyes.

Pulling out for just a moment, I flip her over and rip the satin fabric off. Sitting her up, then pushing her to her knees, I seek out her eyes to get lost in them as she tries to focus, her pupils adjusting to the difference in light. It may not be very bright in my room, but it's a fuck load more light than she was seeing behind the blindfold.

"Look at me when I fuck you."

She doesn't hesitate, her eyes searching me out from her position. We stare at each other while I push my dick back in her mouth and teach her to swallow cock like a champ and, fuck me, she's a natural.

It's not going to take me long to come if I keep looking at her like this. It's too fucking hard to contain myself when I've got her staring at me like I own her world.

Goddammit, I could spend my life buried inside her and it wouldn't bother me one bit.

But I don't want to end it like this. I want her to feel the warm jet of my cum when I release inside her.

Carefully pulling myself out, I keep her jaw steady, making sure she doesn't get hurt in the process. Not to mention her teeth on my dick, that's never a good outcome.

"Time to see how well prepped you are."

Bending to her level, I graze my lips across her mouth and plunge my tongue inside her welcoming mouth, kissing her long enough to taste myself on her tongue.

It's a heady feeling, the mixture of us.

With a little regret, I break away and stand to my full height, lift her back to where she was positioned before making my way to the other side of the bed where her pussy and ass eagerly await me.

My cock hurts with the need to fuck her. To pummel her. I need to let loose and her pussy is the perfect place to start.

Grabbing her ankles once more, I pull her to me until she's lying completely across the bed before I reach up and untie her wrists. I'm guessing she's going to be sore, having stayed in that position for so long, but it's par for the course.

Quinn rubs her wrists but her attention is solely on me, on what I'm about to do. Her gaze runs down the length of my body, appreciation clear in her eyes and it turns me on even more knowing she likes what she sees.

"Spread wide."

Again, she obeys and that too makes me hotter than a summer day in Louisiana.

I kneel on the bed, right between her thighs, and grab her hips. As I align my dick to her entrance, I dart my gaze up to her awaiting one and, without looking away, I slam inside her from tip to root without so much as a moment's hesitation.

We both groan at the feel, the hot, velvety glove that surrounds my dick is like a little piece of heaven just for me.

Rearing back, I push in and out, in and out, a rhythm

so steady it becomes a tempo of pure lust. Our skin slaps every time I hit rock bottom, our cum mixing the hornier we get, and when I reach up and pinch her nipple again, I swear I can feel her walls contracting around my cock. It takes everything in me not to come right then and there.

I'm consumed with her, completely taken by the perfection that is her cunt, but I'm not done. I promised her things without even saying them and I intend to honor those promises.

With one hand leveraging her by the hip, I use my other hand to detonate her clit with a gentle flick of my finger.

"Come on my cock, Quinn. Now."

It's a glorious thing, Quinn coming. As she screams out her release, I'm mesmerized by the arch of her back and the strain of her slender neck. With her chest heaving up and down, I lose my rhythm a little, too busy watching her, completely entranced by her.

Tiny gasps continue as she begins to come down from the intensity of the orgasm and it's all I can do not to bust my nut right away.

Pulling out completely, I gather her come with my finger and bring it to my mouth, sucking on my digit like it's my favorite ice-cream flavor.

"So fucking good."

Using two fingers, I scoop up more and bring it to her asshole, pushing my fingers inside and reminding her that she's already been prepped.

Little by little, I stretch her muscles and once I'm certain she's ready for me, I align the head of my cock with her entrance and push. My eyes are solely on her, watching her reaction. Judging if I can continue or if she'll use her safe word.

I push a little more, then a little more still.

Her face is tight, which is normal, but she's not in any unreasonable pain and I can't wait for her to feel complete pleasure.

Little by little, my entire dick disappears inside her hole and I'm pretty sure I'm about to pass out from the pleasure.

Rearing back my hips, I push right back inside her, fucking her ass with abandon. In and out, I make her moan then scream my name. Quinn's hands grab the comforter, her fingers fisting the material as she searches out for more. She needs more.

I'm not in the business of leaving my girl wanting.

As I'm losing my mind fucking her perfect, tight little hole, I rub even circles around her clit and hold myself back, waiting for her to come with me.

I don't know how I do it, it's a fucking miracle I didn't come in her mouth, but somehow, I do.

Quinn gasps, I pinch her clit, and the rest happens in a whirl of roars and screams and bucking bodies. We come together, me in her ass, her on my fingers as the room spins and my mind is utterly blown.

It's only when we've both calmed down that I realize she didn't have permission for that last orgasm.

I must be getting soft.

I've spent the last three days wrapped up in Quinn while Meyer and Hunter have been dealing with the politics of what we do. The shit I keep myself far the fuck away from. Give me blood over vocal venom any day.

I pour her a cup of coffee while Carlos whips up a smoothie for me before heading back to my room, where I find her still tangled in my sheets. Her creamy skin against the dark blue of my sheets is such a stark contrast, even with all of the ink that covers her body.

Though, if she thinks I missed the scars beneath the ink, she has another thing coming. I haven't asked yet because I know how hard it can be to talk about my own scars and I daresay some of hers are far more traumatic than some of mine. I grew up in depravity and shadows, and while she's hinted at how her life wasn't exactly top tier before Trent, and the fact that I can see some of her trauma in how she carries herself and reacts to certain things, I'm not sure just how far I can push her yet.

I sit on the chair in the corner of the room, watching her while she sleeps peacefully for a change. Every night so far has been plagued with nightmares and I get the feeling that they haunt her whether she's in my bed or not.

Just another reason I'd like to pay her ex a visit and show him just what a monster really looks like. But Tommy said she didn't want that... so I've stopped myself, fighting the compulsion. Though I can't help but wonder *why* she doesn't want that. Revenge is best served cold... preferably by a sharp blade, but there are many ways to skin a cat.

Maybe I'll ask her when she wakes. There has to be something that she wants. I feel like we've taken a lot from her lately, and the threat level has evened out, which is exactly what Meyer and Hunter have been dealing with. Assuming all goes well, we should be able to give her some freedom back. If that's what she wants.

I can't imagine she doesn't. She's been good about being locked up in her gilded cage, as she calls it, but I can see that she's slowly going stir crazy, like a lion in a cage at the zoo. All she's done the last few months since the attack is work out, train, eat, sleep, and repeat.

Admittedly, the three of us haven't been around much, which we all feel pretty shitty about, but trying to get everything back on even playing fields hasn't been the easiest. I can't count on both hands and feet the number of bodies I had to drop to get the attention needed to get this meeting of the heads of clubs and families together to renegotiate peace.

I'm fine with war, but I have something to lose now and I'm not willing to have that happen.

In a very short time, she's become everything, and despite that fact, I've tried to keep my distance while she's adjusted to being here. Being one of us, being ours and everything that might mean. It's been Hell.

It's part of why I caved so hard when I found her the other day. Resisting her has been one of the biggest challenges of my life and for someone who prides themselves on their ability to wait, that's saying something.

She calls to me like some sort of siren, her song just for me.

Well not because I know she isn't just mine, but when we're here, like this, I can pretend that she is. Thankfully, jealousy isn't something that has ever come between my brothers and me, and I don't see her being a cause of it either. We've always been good at sharing. Money, homes, women…

Though no woman has ever been anything like Quinn… or had the three of us this enraptured.

Still, I don't see it being a problem. We made an agreement and none of us would have entered into something we didn't think we could stick to.

A groan from the bed draws my attention from my thoughts and I smile as she stretches out, her hand hitting the sheets where I had been when she fell asleep, and the little noise of dissatisfaction that comes from her.

"Coffee, Jellybean?"

She rolls over to face me, a coy smile on her lips. Using her safe word as a nickname might not be the best idea I've ever had, but it's ours. Our own little secret and private joke.

"You treat me so good," she says with a happy sigh as she sits up in bed, doing her grabby hands at me. Her hair is a mess, she's wrapped up in nothing but my sheets, and it might be the most beautiful she's ever looked.

When I tell her as much, heat streaks across her chest and cheeks. The feeling that comes with knowing I affect her so much just makes me want to tease her and toy with her all day every day, so I can know the stain on her skin is because of me.

Part of me wants to brand her, paint myself on her skin, but considering her past, I'm not about to force her to do anything... strongly encourage, maybe, but I'm discovering that even I have my limits. Monster or not.

Well, when it comes to her anyway. Everyone else can get fucked. If they don't follow orders, they tend to end up dead anyway, but that's an entirely different thing.

I move to her, coffee in hand, gifted by the smile that

reaches her eyes when her hands wrap around the still-steaming mug of coffee, sweetened exactly how she likes it. I'm a details guy, what can I say?

"Have you been up long?" she asks, her voice still half full of sleep before she yawns. She's so freaking cute in the morning, it hurts.

God, who even am I right now? Freaking cute.

"A few hours. I worked out, did the rounds, then figured I'd bring you coffee. I didn't think you'd sleep much longer, considering it's almost noon."

Her eyes go wide, mouth dropping into an *O*... so adorable.

This needs to stop, even in my head goddammit. I do not use the words cute or adorable. Freaking siren song, that's what it has to be.

"It's nearly lunch time?" she asks, blinking at me. "I never sleep this late."

"I guess you needed to rest," I respond, the egotistical smile I can feel on my face isn't even enough to dampen my mood. Knowing I've given her an intense few days is a badge of honor as far as I'm concerned. Hell, she's barely left my bed.

Which is exactly how I like it.

If only she didn't covet her freedom so much...

I'm not one to clip the wings of birds and I don't intend to start now.

"Any news on when everyone's going to be home?" The way she says home gives me a warm, foreign feeling in my chest.

Needs to stop.

"Meyer and Hunter should be back today."

She nods and, for once, I can't read her. Not that I'm worried, I know her well enough by now to know that she'll talk when she's ready. I wonder if she's figured me out yet...

"Is Shae coming home soon?" Her voice is small as she asks, and just like that, it's like she flickers to the sad, lost little girl I can only imagine she used to be. The image leaves my mind the second after it appears, replaced by the woman who is slowly stealing my entire focus.

"Her doctors are reporting good progress. And by that, I mean she's driving them nuts with her demands to come home." She laughs at my response, and I feel a little lighter. "I'm going to speak to Meyer today," I tell her as she sips her coffee. Her brows rise in question, but she doesn't interrupt me. "About you getting some of your freedom back. I know these last few months have been hard on you, but you've done everything we've asked. As long as the last few days have gone well, I don't see why we can't, but I need to speak to Meyer to see how they went first, so please don't get your hopes up too high, Jellybean."

She puts down her mug on the bedside table and

launches herself at me, wrapping her arms and legs around me.

Won't find me complaining.

"Thank you, thank you, thank you!" She sounds so excited that I should be happy, but all it tells me is just how lonely she must have been lately to be this excited just at the prospect of freedom. I didn't even tell her what that might look like, which just reinforces how lonely she must have been.

Fuck me, I hate that. That we did that to her. By choice or not, to keep her safe or not. We're not supposed to be the reason for her sadness.

"Anything for you," I say, kissing her forehead. "Now, what do you want to do today?"

"Honestly?" she asks, bashfully. "I've been enjoying our days in bed…"

She trails off and I can't stop the smile that tips up the edges of my lips. I move so that my hands cup her ass cheeks and lift her until she's firmly seated in my lap. Her ankles cross behind my back and I smile as I feel her fingers interlock behind my neck. "Oh, Jellybean. I'm sure that I can make that happen for you, as long as you promise to be good."

"Oh, I swear it," she responds with a wicked grin on her face.

I tighten my grip on her, enjoying the sound that comes

from her probably a little too much. "Good, because I have every intention of making you keep that promise."

TWENTY EIGHT

QUINN

Four days in bed has been amazing... well, technically three and a half, but still. It's been great, but the prospect of getting some freedom has me climbing the metaphorical walls of my mind. I've tried to do everything that's been asked of me the last few months, all while trying to not complain because I'm aware that there has been a *lot* going on and I'm far from top priority.

But the idea that I might be able to get some sense of my life back has me as excited as a kid at Christmas who's been told it's going to last a whole week, followed by a week of toy shopping and chocolate.

I might be a little more excited than even that, but my point stands.

Freedom.

Before this, after everything with my parents and

Trent, I worked so freaking hard to get my freedom. It's like the precious pearl of my existence that was always kept from me, locked up in some cage, with a guardian so fierce protecting the key, it was hopeless to wish it could be mine.

But I got it and I coveted it like the precious gem that it is to me.

And then, that night at Light Up happened, and it was taken from me once again. I know I fought at first, but when I found out that my life was in danger—again—I caved, the way I did when Trent stole it from me. Maybe not quite to the same extent—Meyer, Hunter, and Rory are nothing like him—but I laid down and let it happen. I stopped fighting, even though a small part of me hated myself for it, I knew it was for the greater good.

So I did what was asked of me, and I didn't fight. I played my role because everyone had important shit going on, even if I didn't know what that important stuff was. Because part of my role meant asking no questions and just going along with it. It's a role I know well, I was trained for it from birth, and I slipped back into that Stepford daughter, people pleasing, have-no-needs bodysuit so well that I almost hadn't noticed how suffocating it was.

Almost.

Have I been losing my mind a little? Well, yes, there's nothing like tasting the finest of things and it being taken from you, but I can adapt in a hurricane. It's how I've survived my entire life to this point, really.

But now, with a light at the end of the tunnel, I want to run full speed ahead and see if I can catch it with both hands. Patience is a virtue I usually embody, but after my talk with Rory earlier, I'm chomping at the bit to get to Meyer. I know he said to give him a chance to speak to Meyer, find out what the lay of the land is, but it's so close I can almost taste it and I'm ravenous.

I've been pacing in my room ever since Rory dropped me off here with the sweetest of kisses, telling me that Meyer was back and he'd come find me when he had information. I showered, tried watching TV, Hell, I even tried getting myself off, but nothing has been enough to get that spark of hope away from the front and center of my mind.

I check the time on my phone again, trying to grasp the sliver of patience I have left. It's nearly eight, I know that means we're eating soon, so they have to be almost done… right? Surely they have to be done soon.

Please, God let them be done soon.

I scroll past the many messages I have from Yen, Belle, and the others that I haven't responded to and a pang of guilt twists inside of me, but I blow out a deep breath and try to release it. At first I didn't respond because I was angry at Yen. Then because I didn't know what to say. And then because I didn't know what I *could* say. And now it's been so long that responding just feels awkward and weird.

Shooting off a message to Shae, despite the fact that I know she doesn't have her phone and hasn't responded once in the time she's been away, I let out a sigh. It's just been my way of trying to not lose my mind completely and letting her know that once she's allowed her phone back, I missed her dearly and if she tries to leave me again, I might cuff myself to her.

Especially if the boys are off playing mafia. No one around here has ever used that word, but my very creative and vivid imagination has been able to summon no other word for the way they operate.

They kill people, deal in drugs, guns, and God only knows what else. I know they have legitimate businesses as covers as well but they also have a small army living on this compound of a property and everyone is armed to the eyeballs. They have a panic room that fits one hundred people for God's sake.

I don't know that there *is* another term for what they are.

If there is, my brain can't conjure it. Let's put it down to one too many head injuries maybe.

I laugh out loud at myself, the sound almost maniacal.

Screw this, I cannot stay in this room one second longer. Pocketing my phone, I leave the room, Bruno my ever present shadow as I bounce down the stairs like I'm full of pep and joy.

I am not, in fact, full of pep and joy, more anticipation and a readiness to fight Meyer if that's what it takes. We're at the point of threats be damned. If I don't leave the walls of this property, I might need to go and join Shae for a stint, because cabin fever is *real*.

When I reach the bottom, Bruno is there a second later, his silent ninja ways still intact after all these months. He still barely talks to me, unless, of course, I talk at him incessantly, then I think he just loses his shit and tells me anything to make the talking stop.

Poor guy. I should probably be nicer to him, but I don't know *how* to be nice to him because he won't freaking talk to me.

"You know," I start at him, and he instantly rolls his eyes. "If you'd just talk to me, I'm sure we'd be great friends, Bruno. I'm a good friend. I think. Or at least, I could be. But I don't know what you like to do, or eat, or anything, so you just follow me around in my boredom. Imagine if I knew what you liked... we could watch a movie you'd enjoy from time to time or something. Or eat your favorite foods. Listen to a podcast that you like while I work out."

His eyes crinkle at the edges as he tries not to smile and I fist pump the air. "I'm going to break you, Bruno. You'll talk to me one day, you'll see. Mark my words, oh silent one. One day is coming!"

"Are you torturing poor Eddie again, Angel?" I turn and find Hunter smiling wide at me, leaning against the door frame to the kitchen.

"No. I don't do the torturing. I leave that to Rory and the rest of you. I was merely stating my case for friendship to make his life easier."

Hunter chuckles, shaking his head, and I can't help but grin as I shrug at him. "His job is to keep you safe when we're not around, Angel. Talking or watching his favorite movie isn't going to help with that. It would be a distraction."

"But the poor guy is a silent, mountainous ninja! He's with me almost all the time, surely he gets to have a little fun. Like, just a smidge?" I pinch my fingers together in the air, the smallest amount of light passing between the pad of my thumb and forefinger as I attempt to make my point.

"He has plenty of fun, don't you worry." Hunter takes his gaze from me, to the big guy behind me. "You're done for the week, go spend some time with Joey and the kids. We'll all be home for the weekend, so she'll be covered."

"You sure?" Bruno asks him and I gasp, pushing my forefinger into his chest.

Who the hell is Joey?

"Dammit, why will you speak to him and not me!" I huff, totally sounding like a toddler.

Maybe I was wrong before, I think I did lose my damn mind already.

He looks down at me and, for a minute, I think he's going to speak, but then I feel hands on my waist and I'm lifted into the air. "Leave Eddie alone, Angel. Anyway, I have a feeling you want to come with me."

"I do?" I ask, just accepting the fact that I'm being carried around again. These three manhandle me like it's a sport and sometimes accepting the princess treatment is easier than fighting it. Who am I to decide I'm not a princess every now and then? God knows I've played Cinderella often enough, sometimes it's nice to be the princess rather than the downtrodden.

Plus, I already know fighting him is futile. Rory officially zapped me of most of my energy the last few days. All I have left is this nervous, excited anxiousness that's keeping me going.

"Yes, you do." He doesn't say another word. Instead, he just carries me through the kitchen to the hall leading to where him and the others live. It doesn't take long before he's knocking on the door to Meyer's office.

It occurs to me that I still haven't seen his or Meyer's room. Like, I'm nosy, but not stupid. Intruding on their personal space just isn't something I'm going to do, but I'd be lying if I said I wasn't curious. A murmur sounds and I assume Hunter understands what it is because he opens the door before we enter the room. He pushes it shut once we're inside and puts me back on my feet.

Meyer and Rory are facing us, sitting on one of the sofas opposite the fireplace—which definitely weren't in here the last time I was—with the one opposite them empty. The whole room is different.

When the hell did Meyer have time to redecorate? And how the hell did I miss it?

I glance back at Hunter, who smirks at my confusion. He places a hand on my lower back and leads me to the open, empty sofa closest to us. Taking a seat in the corner, I fold my legs beneath me and get comfortable, pulling on the sleeves on my hoodie so the cuffs cover my hands, despite the fact that it's so warm in here.

Comfort outweighs temperature sometimes and this is definitely one of them.

All of my bravado and anxious energy washes away now that I'm sitting before them, trepidation filling every extremity as exhaustion crashes over me. I glance at Rory, hoping to get a hint of how the conversation went but, like normal, I get nothing from him. He's like a freaking statue sometimes and reading him is next to impossible.

"So," Meyer starts, leaning forward, his elbows on his knees as he locks his gaze with mine. "Rory has petitioned for you to gain some freedoms back and with how the last few days have gone, I think we can agree to some new rules."

"Thank y—" I interrupt, but pause when I see the look on his face.

"But there will still be restrictions and stipulations. This won't be like before. You mean too much to me, to us, to risk you."

I press my lips together, trying to think over the words that want to rush from my lips before I say something rash.

"You agreed to be ours," he continues. "But we never fully discussed what that means and for that, I'm sorry. Things have been busier around here than usual, but that is no excuse for us not making you a priority and being attentive to your needs and wellbeing."

He pauses again, like he's waiting for me to speak, but I'm not really sure what it is I'm supposed to say here. So I say exactly that and the corners of his mouth tip up.

"That's understandable. So let's clear some things up, shall we?"

The smirk doesn't leave his face and there's a matching one on Hunter. Rory is stoic as ever, but even he seems a little less tense than he was when I entered the room. He nods at me once, almost as silent as Bruno, but I take the move as encouragement.

"Okay, so what's first? Freedom, rules, or explanations?"

My gaze bounces between the three of them, not sure who is going to answer, but I can't say I'm surprised when it's Meyer. It's usually him as the mouthpiece for the three of them.

I guess that's to be expected, considering their typical hierarchy, even though Meyer swears up and down that he considers the other two to be on equal standing with him. Though I already know they both disagree with that particular statement. It's a strange dynamic, but I guess it's worked for them long enough that nothing is likely to change it.

"Let's start with explanations." I glance back over to Meyer and nod without interrupting him. "You have a small idea of what we do, but over the coming weeks, you will spend time with each of us, learning the different aspects of what that entails. That is, if you still want to."

He pauses and I nod again, resolving to keep my mouth shut until he finishes so I don't lead us off on some merry tangent that I often have a habit of doing. It's probably the explanation for why I haven't learned as much as I could have yet.

"This will seal your place with us, Kitten. Once you're in, there is no getting out." His words are so final that it steals my breath for a moment, but he continues like he's trying not to notice the edge of panic. Not that I'm changing my mind now. I've never been one for half measures. "That also means you belong to the three of us. Entirely. You will be ours. In public, at home, together, apart, it does not matter. You will belong to us equally. You will be treated as such by all who work for us and those we do business with. It means more change for you and more potential risk, but I'm confident we can keep you safe, even with the new higher status that comes with us making it known what you mean to us."

So he did mean what I thought he did all those months ago.

"I am aware we have been neglecting you a bit lately, but that stops now. A peace has been brokered and agreed to, which means our focus, while divided, will be more on you and your needs."

"My needs?" I ask, a little confused. *I have needs?*

"Yes, Kitten," he says with a soft chuckle. "Your needs. And I don't just mean safety and orgasms. Though we'll do our best with that too."

Hunter laughs beside me as I squirm in my seat, Meyer's eyes burning into my skin as heat creeps up my neck. So casual with the talk of orgasms...

I guess this is just a part of my new status quo, but that's probably going to be harder to adjust to than the lack of freedom has been.

"Okay," I say quietly, mulling over everything he's said.

"You will move to the empty room in this corridor. However, most nights will be spent with one of us. The room is more so you have some private space rather than an actual bedroom."

"Erm, do I get any say in that?" I sass, quirking my brow. I mean, I'm all for playing musical bedrooms, but it would be nice to at least feel like I got some input.

"No." The three of them say the word in chorus, like it's rehearsed, but I know from Hunter's laugh that it's not.

Well I guess that's that and I'm trying real hard right now not to be triggered.

"Any other non-negotiable rules about this particular agreement?" I ask, folding my arms over my chest to try and disguise the pick up in my breathing and heart rate all while hoping my voice didn't shake. *They are not Trent, Quinn. That isn't what they meant. They are* NOT *Trent.*

"You are free to sleep in your own room, Quinn," Rory interjects. "No one will force you into bed." He stares at me like he's seeing into my soul while reading my mind.

"No, that isn't what I meant," Meyer states, running a hand down his face. "For all my skill with words, when it comes to you, Quinn, I seem to find myself a bumbling fool too often. No one will force you into bed. We're just greedy when it comes to you and want you close." He softens his face, tilting his body toward me. "What I'm trying to say, and failing miserably, is that we would just prefer it if you were with one of us, but no choices like that will ever be taken from you."

I blink back the tears in my eyes, refusing to let them fall. How Rory knew what was running through my mind is beyond me, but he always seems to know what I'm thinking.

"There is a gala fundraiser in two weeks time, we would like you to come with us. It will be our first major outing since the new peace deal and a good opportunity to show you off to the people in our world."

"Gala?" I ask, bug eyed. I don't do freaking galas. I trip over my own feet on a good day! Galas sound like what the other half of humanity does. The rich people who have nothing better to do than spend money. Like, the stuff you see on TV, and that is not my life.

"Yes, Kitten. Gala. The meeting you came to with me? Devin Saunders. He wants to run for office, so everyone who is anyone, the good, the bad, the dirty, and the white knights will be in attendance, all to see if he is the player they're backing and putting money toward."

"That sounds insane," I mutter. "This part of society makes no sense to me."

"Me either," Rory adds from where he's sitting. "But appearances are as important as power these days, and we must show a united front."

I blink at him, wondering if that's the most he's ever

said when the four of us are together like this.

"Exactly that," Meyer agrees. "So one day this week we will take you shopping for a gown. We'll call it a test run for being out in public together. Get you used to how people are around us, and also, we get to spoil you so I call it a win-win."

"Shopping?" I groan. "I hate shopping."

All three of them laugh at me then.

"Oh, we've heard," Hunter says, chuckling. "But I'm sure we can think of a few ways to make it less… tortuous for you."

"Why does that sound like torture is exactly what you have in mind?" I mutter.

"Moving on, shall we?" Meyer says, drawing focus again, and I let him because shopping is gross. I don't want to, but I'm also fairly certain that going out in public with all three of them is going to be a whole event, so best that I get used to it in a low key setting before this stupid gala.

God I hope Shae is home before the gala. Maybe she can come too. Share some of the chaos.

"Yes, let's," I say when I realize he's waiting on me to respond.

"Freedoms and the rules that come with it."

I sit up a little straighter, trying not to get over excited.

"Obviously, you will continue to live here. The apartment will be there as a safety option for you since almost no one knew you were there, but this will be where you stay unless there is a danger directly related to you being here." Meyer says it in such a way that even if I wanted to argue, I couldn't. Thankfully, I gave up on the idea of going back there a while ago.

"Okay," I say, nodding. I can't tell if he's shocked by the ease of my acceptance, but he moves on swiftly anyway.

"Obviously you will still have Eddie watching you, but if and when you choose to leave the compound—which must be run past one of us first—there will be a team that goes with you if one of us cannot. Tonio is being moved to the center with Shae since she has more freedom there now, so Teo will be on rotation for your protection, as will a few others Rory has handpicked. You will be introduced to them all tomorrow so that you know who should be with you. If there is anyone who ever says they work with us who hasn't been shown to you, do not trust them."

"Understood," is all I say, though the thought of having Matteo around doesn't exactly fill me with joy. He was very open about his dislike for me when we met originally. Be that him looking out for his brother, or what, but he obviously wasn't a fan of mine. I wonder how well he took the news that he'd be guarding me. But I keep my mouth shut because he's Meyer's little brother and is obviously close with all of them. Who am I to say anything? I just hope he's not around too much. "Do I get to go back to work?"

My question, albeit sounding hopeful, isn't something I think I'll win. Which is confirmed when Meyer shakes his head. "It's not safe enough. And that's about the clients and the staff as well as you. If someone were to come for you there, we don't have enough people to keep you safe and avoid people around you getting hurt."

My heart sinks a little. I hadn't thought of that. I'd hate to be responsible for someone else getting hurt. It's why I secluded myself when I thought Trent had found me all those months ago. Even though he's only come for me in person twice over the last two years, I know it's a risk I take when I'm around others. I don't think I could live with myself if someone got hurt because of me.

"I understand," I tell them, trying not to sound as disappointed as I feel.

"However," Meyer continues, drawing my attention back to him. He gives me a small, sad smile, telling me without words that he hates disappointing me. "You will be able to move freely otherwise. You can go where you like as long as two guards are with you, or one of us."

I take a deep breath, letting it sink in.

Just like that, I'm free again. Kind of. There are definitely still compromises, but all things considered, it could be worse. Hell, they could've just told me no. What would I do? Try to fight the army of guards to try and escape?

This way, at least I'm not a prisoner. Not that I'm sure I ever was, but these last few months have definitely been a trip. Wrapping my mind around everything that's happened since I got to the city isn't the easiest. Which reminds me. "Can I start seeing my therapist again?"

Meyer smiles at me, and nods. "Yes, we vetted her before, she's good. We'll work out a schedule so you can get back on track with her. I never intended for it to stop for this long—"

"But life happened," I finish for him. "I get it, I just… working with her helped, and while working out has been helping in other ways, using the tools she started to teach me, I know I'm far from healed."

"No one ever fully heals," Hunter tells me, squeezing my thigh. "We're all works in progress, but it's how we deal with what we're dealt that is important."

"Thank you," I whisper, to all of them and none of them directly. Tears slip down my face as emotion swarms me. I knew that losing my freedom was hard, that just accepting this new normal tore something from me, but I understood. I slipped on the skin of old me and went with it.

Now I get to press it off and try to continue finding myself again. The thought is liberating and, before I know it, I'm back in Hunter's lap, sobbing into his shoulder. He stays silent, just letting me cry it out.

No one says a word until the tears subside and I've managed to gather myself. "Sorry," I say, embarrassed. "Not entirely sure where that came from."

"Crying is good for the soul, remember." I look over at Rory and he smiles, parroting words at me that he told me a while ago. It's enough to make me smile and I feel a little like myself again. "Now then, how about we eat?"

"Yes," I say, my stomach growling at the mention of food. It makes a thought pop into my head and I smile wider. "And then... then we can plan tomorrow!"

Even as I climb into the G-Wagon, I still can't quite believe that I won. Well, kind of. Rory is still with me, and I'm not going back to work, but I'm leaving the house and going into the city. It didn't take much to convince Rory to go out for breakfast so I could see Tina, though Carlos looked at me like I'd kicked his puppy by suggesting that we not eat his food.

Rory hits the start button, the engine roaring to life beneath us, and my excitement is almost childlike—I'm aware that there's a problem there, that my willingness to slip into basically being a prisoner again, followed by such joy at being let out, but I'm going to leave that particular problem for my therapist once I start seeing her again. Right now, I'm just going to enjoy my morning.

We pull out of the gates and start down the quiet single lane drive that leads from the house. Rory leans over, hitting a button on the screen on the console and somehow, my Liked playlist is already connected to his car. I quirk a brow at him in question but he doesn't acknowledge it. Instead, he takes my hand, linking his fingers with mine, before resting our hands on the gear shift stick.

There's something possessive yet protective about his movement that makes me feel almost giddy.

I can honestly say I've never had a guy in my life like Rory.

Like any of them.

I haven't even thought about Trent in my excitement of heading outside. Probably because I'm certain Rory wouldn't let him get to me, even if he tried. But Tommy said it's almost like Trent's given up. He did a deep dive, got no answers, got angry, then got busy.

Oh how terrible for me. So sad.

I giggle quietly at myself and Rory glances over at me. I blow him a kiss and the corners of his lips tip up. This happiness is a weird kind of joy that feels kind of like I'm high. Not that I'd know what being high feels like, but I imagine it's a little like this...

At least, that's how TV shows it to be.

"You ready to see your friend?" he asks when we enter the outskirts of the city and the traffic increases.

"I wouldn't call her a friend," I explain to him, chewing at my bottom lip. "She's more… a kindred spirit. I saw so much of myself in her and it broke me a little. Knowing where she is in her journey, too scared to leave because what if the alternative is no better, ya know?"

He glances over at me again and nods, though I'm fairly sure he doesn't actually know, but I'm sure most people can empathize even if they don't. Not that I'd wish true understanding of this particular thing on anyone. Not even my worst enemy.

It doesn't take him long to get us into the city and to where Tina's truck is parked.

"Do not get out of the car yet," Rory demands before climbing out. I feel a little silly waiting on him to open my door. I'm perfectly capable, but I know he's on high alert since it's my first time out of the compound in a while and he feels like he's completely responsible for me. He doesn't need to be, but I know telling him that is futile.

He opens my door and offers me a hand, which I take, and he helps me down from the huge truck.

"Mmmmm coffee," I sigh when I step out of the car, breathing in the heady scent that seems to override all of the others that should be present.

Though that could just be my utter dependence upon

the beautiful caffeinated little beans.

Rory takes my hand before I get a chance to bounce over to the truck.

Maybe I need to tone down this joy just a little. I really do feel like a toddler who's just discovered freedom in walking.

I squeeze his hand, nestling into his side before we start walking, and just that small movement seems to relax him a little. Not that that stops him from scanning the entire space around us or allows him to drop his alert level even a smidge. Not that I'm going to hold it against him, because if I wasn't with him, my hypervigilance would be sky high.

I haven't felt this relaxed out in public in... well, at least since I left Trent. But before that too, because if I'd been out and done something he deemed embarrassing to him, I'd have been punished for it.

I push that thought from my mind as Rory kisses the top of my head before leading me toward the food truck. We get in line, which is crazy long today, and I lean up against him in silence while we wait. I hear Tina before I see her, but she doesn't sound quite as cheery as I remember.

When I see her, my heart sinks, and her lack of pep hits me.

I feel Rory tense when he sees her and I don't blame him.

Her lip is split, her eye is purple, there's a cut across

the bridge of her nose, and her left arm is in a brace.

Oh, Tina.

Anger bubbles up inside of me as my sadness starts to dissipate. What the actual fuck happened to her to mean that she ended up like that and is *still working?* I'm not one to curse often, but seriously, *what the fuck?*

"Are you okay?" Rory murmurs to me, wrapping his arms around me from behind and resting his chin on my shoulder. There's something comforting in being held like this and it's almost enough to push the anger down.

Almost.

"Not even close," I respond, my jaw clenched as I make fists then relax my fingers as I try to work through the extreme change of emotion. I don't remember the last time I felt this much rage. "This shouldn't be a life people are inflicted with. It's cruel, sadistic, and just fucking wrong."

He presses his lips together and buries his face in the crook of my neck. "Bad timing, but you cursing is kind of hot."

I roll my eyes at him and feel his shoulders shake as he chuckles at me. It's only a moment of relief though before he grows serious again. "You want me to handle it?"

I glance back at him and realize he's deadly serious. He really is unlike anyone I've ever met. I mean, Meyer and Hunter would likely offer the same thing, but I already know that Rory would deal with it in a way that would end with his flesh painted in the blood of whoever hurt me. That he'd ensure with his last breath that my wish had been granted. The others would handle it, but likely in a much less... feral way.

"Let me speak to her first," I say quietly, knowing from experience that it's not that easy, because even with the threat removed, the scars are still there. Plus, I didn't want Tommy or them to 'handle' Trent because I wasn't sure I could handle the stain on my soul... though, maybe that's just because it's for me. The idea of 'handling' Tina's situation is real appealing right now.

He nods once, squeezing my waist as he does and I lean back to kiss his cheek. Because I also know that even if he really wanted to go and deal with it, if I said no, he'd respect that.

The three of them might have issues with control, but I also know they'll respect any boundaries I put into place and respect me enough to take me at my word. They might be cavemen, but they're cavemen with *some* restraint. Though I'm sure there's plenty I don't know about them that would likely nix the idea of their restraint, but for now, I'm sticking with that opinion.

When we finally reach the front of the line, I've just about gotten my rage under control. Mostly thanks to the hold Rory's kept me in this entire time. Something about the pressure is making my insides squidgy, which is great, and I definitely shouldn't talk to Tina anywhere close to as angry as I feel, but goddamn him for having that sort of power over me already. Sometimes it's too easy to forget that I've only really known them for a few months.

"Hi—" Tina starts, some of her pep back in her greeting, but she stops when she sees me. Rory releases me and steps aside to give us some space. Her lip quivers a little and she blinks quickly as if trying not to cry. "Quinn."

Her voice breaks as she says my name, a tear slipping down her face. Without thinking, I dart away from Rory, moving around the truck, and dive inside to wrap her in a hug.

"Truck's taking a break," Rory bellows outside, his tone allowing zero arguments, at least none I hear as Tina breaks down in my arms.

"It's okay," I whisper to her, stroking her hair as she sobs into my shoulder. The front of the truck closes with a bang and she jumps. "It's okay, it's just Rory giving us some privacy."

She blinks at me before her shoulders start to shake again.

We end up sitting on the floor, this poor, broken, beautiful bird crying in my arms while Rory stands at the door, guarding the space for us so she can break in a safe place.

"I'm so sorry," she says through hiccups once the sobs

start to subside and she rubs at her puffy eyes and tear stained cheeks.

"You have nothing to apologize for," I tell her softly, with a small smile. "Do you want to tell me what happened?"

Her bottom lip starts to quiver again and she looks so young that every protective instinct I have roars to life. "He just... I made him angry. I tripped when I was bringing him his dinner and it spilled down him and burned him."

She hangs her head and that fiery anger inside of me turns my stomach, a metallic taste in my mouth as I try to calm myself. "You tripping isn't your fault, Tina. And even if it was, this is not a reasonable reaction to you spilling food, even if it did burn him a little. Fairly certain he wasn't eating dinner naked and didn't end up with third degree burns on his dick. And even *then*, this is still not justified."

"I know."

Her voice is so small as she pulls herself into a ball that my heart breaks for her. Mostly because I've been exactly where she is. Knowing that it's not right, but still feeling responsible for it all. Like it was my fault, because it must be, right?

"Do you want help?" The question is hesitant, not because I don't want to help her, but because I know I offered her help before and she turned me down. I also know how hard and how terrifying it is to accept help, let alone ask for it. Especially if you're not at a place of readiness to actually leave. Some people never get there and, as much as it breaks my heart, I have to accept that Tina might be one of those people.

"I don't even know where to start or what help looks like."

I glance over at Rory and he just nods at me, which means nothing, really. I have no idea what he means, I'm just hoping it means that he'll back me up with whatever is about to fall out of my mouth.

"You can start by moving out and filing a restraining order, or you can go as far as getting a new identity and getting the hell out of here."

She lets out a tiny, desperate bark of a laugh. "I can't do any of that. I have nothing. No family, no friends, nowhere to go."

Her despair eats at my insides and I wonder how no one saw in me everything I can see on her face right now.

How the hell did no one in our town see what he was doing to me? Is it really that easy to not pay attention to the world around you?

I reach forward and take her hand, squeezing it gently. "You have me and I can help with everything." Tilting my head toward Rory, I give her a smile. "You might have noticed the Hulk over there. He'll come with us to your place while we get your stuff and I happen to know an empty apartment that needs some love right now too."

The shadow of a smirk that breezes over Rory's face isn't lost on me. I know Meyer said that place would be a safe house for me, but Tina needs it more than I do right now. Besides, it's huge. Even if I need it as a safe space, I can share it with her if it comes to that.

"But he knows where I work. I need this job. It's the only thing that's mine. It doesn't pay much, but I'm not qualified for most things."

Glancing at Rory to see if he's going to tell me to stop, my heart tugs a little when he nods again, like he knows exactly what I'm about to do, almost encouraging me.

Looking back at her, I try to give her a reassuring smile. "How are you at bartending?"

TWENTY NINE

After spending all of yesterday with Rory helping Tina get packed and moving her into my old apartment, with the promise of sorting out a job for her at HellScape ASAP, we spent the evening explaining it all to a very amused Hunter and Meyer.

As per my suspicion, Meyer wasn't exactly delighted that I put her in my old apartment, but he also accepted my decision to help someone in need. He said he'd speak to Harper and get her job at HellScape set up and ready for her when she was healed. He also sent someone to watch the apartment, take her to the hospital to get checked, and be around if she wants to go back to the food truck until she can work at the bar, all so she can still be safe. I trust that whoever they sent to her will protect her the way they would me. Sure, Tina isn't exactly like, my person, but everyone needs help sometimes. While I can't help directly, Rory basically gave me permission to use what they have given me access to for her.

Was it me possibly overstepping? Yes. But Meyer has told me almost too many times that what is theirs is mine, and to use it however I want to. Even if he was a little grumpy that my safe house is in use, he still respected my decisions and accepted that this was what I wanted to do without arguing about it.

I definitely sat on my shaking hands the entire drive back to the house after getting Tina settled, because that historic fear response in me reared its ugly head and I was terrified the entire way back that I was about to be in a world of trouble. Obviously it wasn't, and I clearly need to keep working on that particular response, but it worked out in the end, so I'm just trying to focus on the win.

Especially when I'm currently wedged between Meyer and Hunter in the back of a black sedan with Rory up front and O'Connor driving because I'm being dragged shopping.

Shopping.

Gross.

Even having become a little more relaxed about it, what with Tommy's insistence and Yen's penchant for shopping… those times somehow felt different. I already know that Meyer is looking forward to this trip almost *too* much. He basically growled at me that if I even thought about looking at a price tag, he'd just buy the entire store. I still haven't worked out if I felt more sick over the thought of him doing it, or the fact that he *could* do it.

Like, I know he has money, that much is very obvious, but *that* sort of money is a whole different ball game.

So now my normal dislike for shopping feels somehow heightened. Especially because we're shopping for the godforsaken gala I'm being dragged to with them. Which means this isn't just shopping, it's high scale, boutique, couture, gown shopping with all the frills that come with that, and it's not something I've ever experienced in my life. I'm going to be a fish out of water and fully floundering.

So much fun.

Give me a pair of jeans and sneakers with a red solo cup party any day. I know I can be a bit of a chameleon and fit into most surroundings—proved that much to myself while pretending to be different people as I bounced across the country running from Trent—this isn't exactly a crowd I've had experience blending with.

"You're fidgeting, Kitten," Meyer murmurs in my ear before taking my hand and placing it on his thigh, topping it with his own. "Is everything okay?"

I chew on my bottom lip and contemplate telling him I'm fine, but I already know he's too observant to believe me. Staring down at my hands as I twist them in my lap,

I try to find the right words to explain it without sounding like a brat. "Just a little apprehensive about shopping. I'm not the biggest fan in general and it feels like there's a lot of pressure on this trip because of the gala and stuff."

Hunter stays quiet beside us but there's no way he isn't listening to our conversation, no matter how muted. Rory and O'Connor can probably hear it too and I don't exactly love that either, but I signed up to be theirs and this is part of that, I guess. I just need to suck it up.

Meyer shifts in his seat so he's almost completely turned in my direction before pressing a finger under my chin and tilting my face up so I can't not face him. "If you really, truly, do not wish to come with us, I will not force you. That means the gala *and* this shopping trip, Kitten. I can't say that I don't want to have you on my arm, knowing that every single man in the room will want you and can't have you because you belong to me. To us. But I will also never make you do something that makes you as uncomfortable as you appear right now."

My stomach twists because I feel so conflicted. Not going to this gala feels like a step back. Not with them, but with me. I've come so far, grown so much, that something like this shouldn't feel this intimidating. Especially with them at my side. But at the same time, I feel… less than. Like every other person in that room is going to see me as an imposter. Because why would someone as broken as me ever be with them?

Even saying it in my head sounds wrong because I know the truth, but I'd be lying if I said Trent didn't take a sledge hammer to my self worth and sometimes it's really hard to get that voice out of my head.

Today is, apparently, one of those days.

"Is there anything you're not telling me?" Meyer asks, releasing my jaw. His eyes never leave mine.

Sometimes it's a little scary how all three of them just *see* me. I always thought I had a good poker face. Hell, I survived on it for two years, so either it's gotten worse or they just see me in a way no one but maybe Tommy ever has before.

Hunter moves his hand to my thigh, resting it there in a quiet show of support. Very unlike him, but he's been a little withdrawn lately. Maybe I'm missing something with him. I tuck that little nugget away for later and bring my focus back to now, his quiet support—which I accept without hesitation—and to Meyer's question.

Deciding to be honest, I blow out a breath while I try to find the confidence to explain all of the thoughts running through my head. In the end, it falls from my mouth like a rambling stream of consciousness that barely makes sense to me, but he listens intently, nodding in all the right places as I word vomit the swirling vortex of my mind all over him.

He lets me finish, the look on his face growing darker with every word of rambled, broken confidence falling from my lips. His jaw tics as he clenches it, but he still doesn't say anything and my stomach twists at his silence.

"I'm not angry at you," he says, obviously reading me again. "I am infuriated that you've been made to feel that way and it makes me want to break many, many things, including Trent's face, but none of my anger is directed at you, Kitten. You are worth more than any of the bullshit you've been told. You deserve everything, more than that, and any one of the people at the gala would be lucky to know you, even just for a minute."

The car pulls to a stop and I glance out the front window, realizing we're on a street on the wealthy side of the city. A quieter area where Main Street is lined with small boutiques where one square of material probably costs more than I've made in the last two years of working. I try to push that thought away and let Meyer's words filter in. Not that it's that easy, but I cling to them like a security blanket to make me feel better.

This should be fun, a girl shopping with her three... boyfriends? I guess? Yeah, that's weird. Not thinking on that one too hard, but still. The point is valid. This is supposed to be fun, I should be thinking about ways to tease them from the dressing room, ways to playfully push their buttons with outrageous requests. That's what this scenario is supposed to look like right? At least that's how it looks like in my books and the movies I've seen.

The three of them climb from the car and Hunter ducks back in, offering me his hand. "Your spree awaits, m'lady."

His ridiculous words combined with his cheesy grin are enough to pull me from my head and make me laugh.

"Are you supposed to be my white knight?" I ask, giggling as I take his hand and climb from the car.

"Oh I wouldn't go that far. I'm definitely more of a dark knight aesthetic, don't you think?" He strikes a pose, making me laugh again, and it's like the chokehold on my heart loosens a bit and I can breathe easy. I just need to get out of my head and actually enjoy life, overthinking it all is getting me nowhere.

Meyer is on the phone and Rory is talking to O'Connor, so I turn my focus back to Hunter for direction.

"Definitely the dark knight," I agree as he offers me the crook of his arm. "Where to first, kind sir?"

"I mean, personally, I think we should start at the bottom."

I blink at him, trying to work out what he means when he starts to wag his brows at me. "Lingerie, obviously."

Laughing again, I shake my head. "Of course that's where you want to start. Fairly certain I should get the dress first so I can make sure that the underwear isn't showing with the cut of it."

He scratches at his chin, overly playing up his thinking. "By Jove, you might just be right. Dress first it is!"

"Who knew you had a secret fantasy to be English," I joke and he winks at me.

He steps closer, pressing against me so I have to look up at him as his blond locks fall into his eyes. "Oh, I have plenty of fantasies you don't know about yet, but you're going to learn."

My pulse races and I open my mouth to respond, but Rory appears, followed by Meyer moments later.

"Are we ready?" Rory asks as he finishes tapping on his phone before sliding it into his pocket. Hunter takes half a step back, like he's giving me room to breathe again, but looks down to me as if it's actually my choice what we do next.

Yet another reason I know the three of them are nothing like Trent. Power is willingly shared here and power or control aren't things I had even a glimpse of in my old life. I glance at the three of them, feeling lighter than I have all day, my heart swelling at the new life I'm starting to carve out for myself with them at my side and nod. "Let's do this."

We're in the fifth boutique of the day. Meyer has cleared

it of all people and basically booked out the entire store, making the poor store assistant lock the doors so that no one else could get in—just like he's done at every place we've been to so far today. Somehow, at this point, my embarrassment about it has just evaporated. It was weird and gross the first few times, but I've just kind of accepted that this is who he is.

Plus, despite me not yet finding a dress I like that is suitable for the gala, he's managed to spend enough money in each place that no one has quibbled over the loss of other customers while we've been shopping.

I'm currently refusing to even think about how much money he's spent today because I don't want to be weird and he obviously isn't bothered by it, which is mind-blowing to me, but I guess if I'd grown up with all of this, it wouldn't seem so strange to me.

Maybe, anyway.

The young store assistant finishes serving the only people who were in the boutique then locks the door once they're gone.

Meyer is still talking to the older woman, who I'm assuming is the manager, and she is falling all over him.

Because of course she is.

While he's busy with her, Rory is out back doing God only knows what and Hunter is sitting on a sofa, sipping a glass of champagne, because that's how rich people shop, apparently.

So weird.

While they're all doing their thing, I head to the rack that has what looks like the sort of thing suitable for a gala. However, what today has taught me is that finding something for the gala that doesn't make me feel like a pod person isn't the easiest thing in the world.

I flick through a few and there is just so much… poof. I'm sure it looks amazing on some people, but when Hunter insisted I try one of the typical princess-style dresses earlier, it just made me look like a kid playing make believe. It also just didn't suit my body shape at all. My hips are way too curvy for that dress. I looked like I'd ballooned and just no. I'm going to be self conscious enough without worrying about the dress I'm wearing.

"Did you find anything?" The young girl asks hesitantly.

I smile at her, hoping she doesn't think I'm some sort of tyrant—I'll leave that to Meyer. "Not yet," I admit. "This isn't exactly my typical style, so I have no idea what I'm after."

"I get that," she says quietly, glancing over to where Meyer is still being fawned over by the manager. Her hand on his chest sends a spike of jealousy through me, but I try to push it down because we're just here for a dress. "This isn't my style either. Why don't you tell me your style and I can see what we have in the back?"

See, why can't other store assistants be like this? Though, she doesn't really seem like the other people I've talked to today. She might be the first person that hasn't just dismissed my presence, despite the fact that we're shopping for me.

"I'm more of a muted tones or black, jeans, Converse, and band tee kind of girl. I don't think I've ever worn a gown before today. Hell, I barely wear dresses."

She laughs softly and nods. "I feel that. Okay, you keep browsing, I'll go see what else we have. When Melinda is finished embarrassing herself, have her show you to the fitting room and I'll bring options straight to you."

I glance over at Meyer and the woman who is apparently Melinda, and roll my eyes. She is practically tripping over herself to fawn over him. One part of me wants to laugh it off and the other wants to go over there and stake a claim… but I'm not sure I have the right to do that.

"I'll do that, thank you," I pause and glance at her name badge. "Thank you, Katy."

"No problem, see you in a few! Good luck."

I take a deep breath and keep flicking through the rack, the laugh coming from Melinda grating on me like nails on a chalkboard. Meyer isn't that funny, she really needs to tone it down.

Grabbing a few different black dresses, a navy one, and an emerald green one, I saunter across the store, planting myself between Meyer and the woman drooling over him. I catch Hunter smirking from the corner of my eye, leaning forward to watch me like fireworks are about to go off. I'm not a bitch and I'm not going to cause a scene, but jeez lady.

"Can you show me the fitting room?"

She glances down at me like I'm a petulant child and sighs before looking back at Meyer. After being dismissed all day, and her still laying hands on Meyer, I've had enough.

"Lady, take your hands off of him and show me the goddamn fitting room. He's here for me. All three of them are. If you can't be a professional instead of throwing yourself at your customers, you should probably see someone about impulse control."

She blinks at me and I quirk a brow, not backing down. Not sure where the backbone I have in use currently has come from, but her audacity is just making my ass itch. It's rude and unnecessary. Am I being rude back? Yes, yes I am, but we've been in here like twenty minutes and she's spent the entire time laying hands on Meyer and drooling like a bitch in heat. It's gross and disrespectful, especially when I came in with him.

Meyer presses his lips together and steps up beside me, resting an arm around my waist, tucking me into him, a silent show of support while she opens and closes her mouth, like her brain hasn't quite caught up to the situation.

"I believe my girl asked you to show her to a fitting room," Meyer says firmly and she finally closes her mouth, letting out a squeak before turning on her heel and walking to the back of the store.

"Please, follow me," she says when she realizes we're not behind her.

Hunter bursts out laughing from his perch on the sofa and claps his hands together. "I think I like you jealous and feisty, Angel."

I roll my eyes at him and start to follow the woman to the fitting room.

"Make sure to come show us everything," Meyer murmurs in my ear before moving to go and sit with Hunter. Rory enters the room from the back of the store as I'm moving toward where Melinda is very impatiently waiting for me. She huffs as I reach her, so I look her dead in the eye and raise an eyebrow, almost baiting her to say something.

"Did I miss something?" Rory asks, watching the interaction between us.

Hunter just laughs again from behind me. "Dude, you have no idea."

"I'll be out in a minute," I say to him and he nods, looking a little confused before moving over to where Meyer and Hunter are sitting.

Melinda unlocks a door at the back of the store and glares at me as she opens it. "Here you go, just call me if you need anything."

I give her a saccharine smile before heading into the room. "Thank you so much."

Closing the door behind me, I feel a little gross at my behavior toward her. I usually commend myself on being kind and polite to everyone, but goddamn she is awful. I flick the latch on the door and hang the dresses I have on the hooks in here, glancing at myself in the wall of mirrors.

Hunter would love it in here.

The thought alone has a blush creeping across my cheeks, but it's not like he hasn't told me how much he'd love to watch me get myself off, or fuck me in front of a mirror... or record it so he could watch it later. Last one definitely isn't happening, but this room would be the equivalent of Disneyland to him.

I shake my head to expel the thought and glance back over the dresses. None of them scream *the one* at me, but maybe they'll look different once I try them on.

It doesn't take me more than a minute to undress, folding my jeans, T-shirt, and jacket on the chair in the corner next to where my Cons are tucked away—can't say I'm not at least neat, I guess. I stare at the dresses again, deciding to play it safe and start with the black ones.

Let's face it, black is my color. It goes with everything

and on these dresses, its effortless class.

I slide on the first, a one shoulder with a full sleeve, bandage-style dress with a mermaid skirt, and balk at my reflection. Not that I have any dislike for my body—beyond my scars, which are absolutely hidden in this dress—but part of my phoenix is on show over my shoulder and it just feels like my ink ruins the aesthetic of the dress.

Don't get me wrong, I love my ink, but it's not exactly the upper-class thing to wear as an accessory. At least, I don't think so.

"How's it going in there?" Rory's voice filters through the door, so I tottle over toward it—another reason this dress is a no, I can barely move above the knee—and unlock it, sticking my head out the opening.

"So far, it's bad. But fingers crossed."

He pushes the door and I step back, letting him see me. He's seen me in much, much less, yet I feel more vulnerable with him seeing me in this than when he had me tied up. "You look beautiful, but you also look uncomfortable."

"I feel it," I admit to him. "On to the next."

"Okay, let us see though. These two are driving me insane already wondering what you're wearing in here."

I giggle a little, shaking my head but not the least bit surprised. "I will, even if I look ridiculous."

"You could wear a garbage bag and not look ridiculous. You'd still look beautiful, so don't sweat it. Just please don't leave me with their constant stream of thoughts tumbling out of their mouths."

I press my lips together, trying not to laugh too hard at him. "I can do that."

"Good girl," he murmurs, pressing his thumb against my bottom lip, tugging at it as he drags it down. "Hurry up and show us the next one."

He turns and walks away, leaving me more than a little flustered. I close and lock the door, pulling off the mermaid monstrosity and put on the next black option. A strapless A-line that has boning in the bodice. It's very simple, no frills, and it's probably my favorite of the day, but it's still not… it doesn't feel like a *wow* moment.

Regardless, I do as asked and head out to where the guys are waiting.

"Goddamn. Remind me why I'm waiting out here instead of being locked in that room with you?" Hunter groans, biting down on his fist. "It's like a second skin."

"You do look stunning," Rory adds, his gaze raking me up and down.

Meyer leans forward, his elbows on his knees, and just stares at me. "You have me mesmerized, Kitten. Do you like it?"

"I think it's the best one of the day," I answer, trying to feel confident in the answer.

"That isn't what I asked," he says, watching me closely.

"Do you like it?"

"Yes, but I don't love it," I tell him honestly.

"I do, does my vote count? Though, I'd love it more on the floor." I laugh at Hunter's outburst, shaking my head.

"Wait!" I hear called from behind me and find the young girl from before. "I found it! It was hidden away, but I knew I'd seen it, and with your coloring, it's perfect!" She holds up a black garment bag, a wide smile on her face.

"I guess I'm going to try on another dress," I say with a smile, glancing back at the guys before following the girl back to the fitting room.

She wanders into the room, so I follow behind her as she hangs up the dress. "Honestly, I was half worried it was sold, but it was a commission piece that the owner decided she didn't want, so it's been back there for ages. You look about the same size as her, so I'm hoping it fits because, honestly, I remember crying on the inside so hard when she didn't take it. I am not a gown girl, but goddamn…"

She trails off and I can't help but laugh a little. "Well, now you've built it up, I'm almost excited."

"Let's hope I didn't build it up too much!" she murmurs, before unzipping the bag.

The forest green color pokes through the zipper and I already feel like I'm going to love it. I can't even say why, just something about the color feels peaceful. When it's unzipped, she pulls back the bag so the dress is fully on display.

"Don't judge it till it's on. I know it doesn't look like much on the hanger, but just… let's get it on you so you can see it properly."

"Okay," I say with a nod, trying to work out if I even like it beyond the color, but I'm willing to wait until it's on for final judgment since it's not like any of the other dresses are *the one*. I slip out of the black one, trying not to be too conscious of her being in here as she unhooks part of the dress at the shoulders then fiddles with the buttons and zipper on the back.

She doesn't even notice that I'm just in my underwear, but I guess this is her job and she does this all day. Holding the dress open, she helps me step into it, lifting the material until it's high enough for me to slip my arms into the full sleeves.

The zipper goes up with ease and she reclips the material at my shoulder before letting it billow to the floor, and I stand, speechless, staring at my reflection.

The dress is a nude mesh-like material that makes it almost look like I'm naked, but forest green gems make beautiful patterns up the arms and bodice to cover what would need covering if I *was* naked. The pattern extends down to the skirt, filling the space, a thigh high split up one side, and extends down both arms. The material at my shoulders melts down behind me, a cape of forest green that extends to the floor.

It is… like nothing I could have even tried to dream up, yet…

"It's perfect," I whisper.

"It fits like it was made for you!" The girl exclaims while I stand, stunned silent, still just staring at my reflection.

She opens the door and I follow her out, trying not to fall too in love with this dress because… I don't know why, but falling in love with a dress feels weird.

It is beyond stunning though.

I round the corner to where the guys are sitting and their conversation just stops.

"Holy fuckkkkkk," Hunter groans, leaning back on the sofa and moving to stare at the ceiling.

"Yes," is all Rory says, his eyes not leaving me.

"For the first time in longer than I remember, I am truly speechless," Meyer utters. "We'll take it," he says over my shoulder to where I'm assuming the girl, Katy, is standing.

"Really?" she asks, and I look back to see the wonder on her face.

"Yes," Meyer responds before looking at me. "Even if you don't want it for the gala, that dress shouldn't be on anyone but you."

"I… I don't even know what to say." I pause, trying to

gather my thoughts. A dress shouldn't affect me this much, but I feel… powerful, at peace, comfortable, confident, all the things I've always wanted, and it seems mind boggling to me that a piece of clothing could make me feel that way.

"You look… there aren't words in existence to explain just how breathtaking you look, Quinn." The sound of my name on Meyer's lips is enough to make my brain short-circuit. He never uses my name. Except that once. But it's how I know he's being serious.

"I… thank you." I run my hands down the dress, feeling tears fill my eyes. I quickly blink them away, desperately trying to work out the myriad of emotions running riot inside of me right now.

Hunter is the first one to stand and wrap me in his arms. "I don't know what's going on in that pretty mind of yours, but this is the life you deserve, Angel. Anything that came before this was a fucked up, obscure road to get to where you belong. Here, with us. I don't know if you're just overwhelmed, but no matter what else happens, you need to believe me right now when I tell you that you belong here. You deserve all of the good things, even something as simple as a pretty dress that you look almost otherworldly in. I know you're plagued by the voices of other people telling you that it's not true, but let mine filter in there too and be louder than them."

"Thank you," I murmur again as I lean into him, letting

his warm, clean scent wash over me and help me find a moment to center myself. "I want this one for the gala. I can be in that room in this dress."

"Then this is the dress."

I stay wrapped in his arms for a moment before I realize that everyone is probably watching my mini melt down and embarrassment twists my stomach. "I should probably go take it off and stop making a scene."

"You're not making a scene, and as much as I'd love to peel this from you, I'm going to let this nice young lady help you out of it while Meyer deals with the old bat that runs this place."

"I don't like her," I whisper and he chuckles.

"Oh, I know. We got that loud and clear, Angel, don't you worry. Now go get changed so we can go home and I can reaffirm just how much I'd like to peel this off you."

"You're a sex pest," I tease and he leans back, grinning down at me.

"Only for you, Angel. Only ever for you."

THIRTY

The gala is tomorrow and I am a mess. A straight up, anxiety-ridden, hot mess. Despite the fact that I've barely even thought about it since our day shopping because, between the three of them, they've kept me so busy and distracted with decorating plans for the room they're moving me into today, training—including how to shoot with Rory, which has been freaking hilarious because apparently I'm a natural and that's hot—and just general busy-body stuff.

I kinda love them for it because today is the first time I have downtime and all I can think about is tomorrow, which has me *spiraling*. Meyer already told me he has someone coming to the house to help with my hair and everything—which I'm grateful for because my roots are officially a mess and there is no way I can go to the gala with this much grow-out. *God, that's so superficial and I kind of hate that the thought is even in my head, but also, gala*—but that doesn't mean I'm not worrying.

The dress is hanging in my new closet, in its garment bag, along with a pair of forest-green heels we found online that are accented with gold and match the dress perfectly. I'm not usually a fall over myself about a pair of shoes kind of girl, but even I can appreciate that the lace beauties are exquisite and will go so well with the dress, it's almost obscene. Funnier that it was actually Hunter who found them, but I guess I'm learning more about them all every day.

I'm still outrageously aware that there is so much I don't know about them, that there's likely some things I'll probably never know. I also feel like over the last two weeks we've grown so much closer and I finally feel like they're my boyfriends. Still such a weird thought. It feels so high school to call them boyfriends, but I don't have another word for it. The fact that I have three of them... well, I'm wrapping my head around it, but only in the manner of how it'll be perceived outside these walls, because here, no one even blinks about my relationship with each of them.

A knock at the door pulls me from my manic thought patterns and I smile when Meyer steps into the room, phone in hand. "I have a surprise for you, Kitten."

"A surprise?" I ask, feeling beyond spoiled because

he's so good to me and I'm still half waiting for the other shoe to drop.

He holds up his phone and I let out a squeal when I see Shae's face on a video call. I dive across the bed and he meets me in the middle of the room to hand me his phone. "Bring it back to me when you're done." He kisses my forehead, says goodbye to Shae, and leaves the room, closing the door behind him.

I drop back onto the bed, grinning like an idiot at the screen, then promptly burst into tears. Shae laughs, tears running down her face too. "Wow, I thought *I* was a mess," she jokes through her tears and I half-laugh, half-sob in response.

I hadn't realized until this exact moment just how lonely I've felt since she went away. I spent most of my life not having close female friends, so I didn't miss it. I'm still not fully over the whole Yen lying to me thing, so I haven't seen her, but I connected with Shae so instantly and we were so comfortable around each other, like two kindred souls. When she went away, I obviously supported it because it was what she needed and I just kind of tucked that emotion away when I slipped into my Stepford body suit. It seemed easier for everyone if my emotions about things went in a box that I wrapped with chains and threw into the lake of despair in the pits of my mind.

But seeing her now, it's impossible to ignore how

lonely I've felt, despite the fact that seeing her face brings me so much freaking joy.

"I miss you so bad," she says and I hiccup, wiping at my face like a loon.

"I miss you too. How are you feeling?"

She grins at me, tears drying on her cheeks. "Like I'm ready to climb the walls to break out of this place. I appreciate Meyer for making sure I got the help I needed because I thought I was way past having to come back to places like this, but I am *sooooo* ready to be home."

"Are they letting you come home soon?" I ask, trying not to get my hopes up too much. Sure I've been spending a ton of time with the guys, and it's been awesome, but what I discovered in the small time I had with Shae is that there's nothing quite like finding your friend soulmate, that person who just gets you. The person who understands what you're feeling even when you can't put it into words for most people to fathom. The person whose shadows and demons align with yours in a way that means you don't have to explain the reasons you might overreact with one thing that seems like nothing, but then not blink when something that would break most people happens, because that's just how your brain works.

"One week. Just one week and then I'm free!"

"Yes! I love this for us. For you, but for us. How are you allowed on this call right now? I've been texting you for months."

"Oh, I'm not on my phone. That's in a locker with all of my other stuff that isn't clothes that I arrived with. I'm only allowed calls like this with Mom and Meyer, and even then, they're super restricted. I promise I wasn't ignoring you, I would neverrrrrr."

I grin at the horror on her face. "It's fine, I know you wouldn't. Plus, it's not like you haven't been dealing with a heap of stuff, my overthinking brain was just curious."

"Oh, I get that, entirely. Now come on, spill, tell me everything that's happened since I left… unless it includes my brother's dick, cause gross. And no, that doesn't extend to the other two, cause they're like my brothers and it's still weird, but it's different." She pulls a face, sticking out her tongue, and I laugh again, a weight I hadn't even realized I'd been carrying lifting from me.

We talk for what feels like hours and just seconds all at the same time before the nurse tells her she needs to get off the call.

"I want so many pictures of you all dressed up. I bet you look freaking hot in the dress. It sounds beautiful."

"I can do pictures," I promise, trying not to let my disappointment that she has to go show on my face. "And just one more week and we can catch up for reals."

"Hell yeah we can. Tell those boys to enjoy the next week, cause once I'm home, I'm stealing you for a bit."

She winks at me, making me giggle again. "I better go before Nurse Ratched comes back and sees me still on here. Love you guys."

"Love you too, see you soon! Be good so they still let you out!"

"Oh, I'm always good," she says with a wink, then waves and the screen goes gray for a second before going back to Meyer's home screen.

I deflate a little because I miss her, but decide to suck it up because a week is nothing and it's not like I don't have enough going on before then between the gala and training that I'm sure it'll go quick enough.

Shuffling off the bed and out of the room, I head down to Meyer's office to give him his phone back. I knock on the door, waiting a second before opening it, and smile when I find him typing away on his computer.

"All good?" he asks when he looks up and sees it's me.

"Beyond good," I tell him with a smile as I cross the room and hand him his phone back. "We can go get her from the airport when she's back, right?"

He grins at me and nods. "Yes, if that's what you want. I'm not sure I could say no to you about anything at this point." He reaches out and grabs me by the waist, pulling me onto his lap. I curl into him, leaning my head against his chest.

"Oh, I don't know about that," I tease. "Fairly certain

you could manage it."

He tilts his head, his smile softening. "You're right, I could. I probably wouldn't enjoy it that much though."

"Maybe," I joke, sticking my tongue out at him.

"Is it terrible that your sass just makes me want to fuck it out of you?" His question is a low rumble as he presses his mouth against my cheek and a shudder runs down my spine.

"Maybe, but maybe I'll run away from you and see how you feel then."

His hold on my waist tightens and I clench up with anticipation, ready to push him to the point of no return. "Such a tease."

"Only a tease if I don't mean it," I murmur, wriggling in his lap just enough to make him suck in a breath. "Loosen your hold and you'll see if I'm a tease or not."

He nips at my shoulder before loosening his hold and I pause for a second before darting out of his lap and across the room to the door.

He leans forward, eyes dark as he watches me like the prey he wants me to be and my pulse races with excitement. The low growl that comes from him spurs me on just enough to push him a little more, knowing just how much fun the reward will be. I twist the handle, making sure I can run before he's out of his chair, then wink at him. "Ready or not, bet you can't catch me."

I've spent all day being waxed, tweezed, hair dyed, cut, styled, having my makeup done, and being poured into the dress and shoes. We're currently in a limo outside of some huge, yet stunning, historic building, waiting for our turn to leave the car and enter the gala. My stomach has been flipping for the last five minutes, despite the good spirits the guys are in and the general relaxed vibe in the car.

What's worse is I can't put my finger on why I feel so off, other than a feeling of impending doom. Thank you, my beautiful, catastrophizing brain, for making a fun night feel like the literal end of the world. I'm fairly certain I've managed to smother most of the outward signs of how I'm feeling because the guys are still acting normal, which I'm thankful for because I vowed to wrangle this feeling into a box before I step out of the car. I refuse to be the reason their good mood is cut short or our night is ruined. While I already know they wouldn't blame me for it, I'd beat myself up about it then probably feel even worse *because* they were so nice about it.

I stare out of the window, taking a few deep breaths to settle myself, and when we reach the red carpet that leads up the steps, someone approaches the door. Before they so much as touch the handle, I'm tugged back toward Meyer and Rory slides down the seat on the side of the limo so he's the one by the door as it opens. "Safety first, Kitten."

Leaning back into him, I roll my eyes. "Fairly certain the guy opening the door isn't going to try to run away with me."

"I don't think you've seen yourself in this dress. Especially with your hair pinned back like this. Trust me, we nearly skipped tonight entirely." His murmur in my ear sends a shudder down my spine.

"Come on handsy, time to go," Hunter teases as he follows Rory out of the car. He waits, offering me a hand, which I'm grateful for because, despite practicing walking in these heels the last few days to try and wear them in, I still don't exactly feel like an elegant and graceful being in them.

Meyer exits behind me, putting a hand around my waist, while Hunter keeps his hold on my hand and Rory stands in front like he's guarding me. Camera flashes go off as the guys lead me up the stairs. The moment is beyond surreal. I don't understand the media being here, but I guess Meyer did say this was a political fundraiser, so it probably makes sense.

Except if they took pictures of me and actually caught my face, despite Rory being in front of me, Trent could find me. Panic rips through me, for what feels like the first time in forever and I stumble. Meyer and Hunter keep me upright but I can't stop my legs from shaking.

We get inside and they immediately pull me to the side.

"You're okay, Quinn," Rory says softly, stroking my cheek while Meyer wraps his arms around me from behind and Hunter keeps his hold on my hand. "Your picture won't make it off any cameras if they managed to get you. We already have things in place. He won't find you. Even if he did, we would deal with it before he got to you. Tommy is watching him and will keep us updated."

My heart is pounding against my ribs and, while his words seem logical to my brain, my heart doesn't seem to want to absorb it right this second. I take a few more breaths while they surround me and the panic starts to ease.

"I'm sorry," I murmur, looking at the ground when I can finally speak.

"You don't need to be sorry, Angel," Hunter says firmly. "He messed with you and it's going to take more than a few months of therapy to get over that."

"But Rory is right," Meyer murmurs in my ear. "Even if he found you, we'd deal with it. You don't have to be afraid. Not anymore. We won't let anyone hurt you."

I take in a deep breath and hold it for the count of three before releasing it, repeating it a few times before finally getting myself under control again, even if I do still feel a little shaky. "Thank you, and I know you say I don't have to be sorry, but I still am. This is supposed to be a fun night and I freaked out and ruined it before we even made it in the door."

"You didn't ruin anything, Kitten. We should have warned you about the media. I'm sorry," Meyer says as he squeezes my waist. "Trust me, having you pressed up against me really isn't a hardship."

Hunter laughs and Rory shakes his head while I roll my eyes. "I don't even know what to say to that."

"Do you want to go home?" he asks, and I know if I say yes, we'll all pile back in the car and they won't say another word about the night, or ever make me feel bad about not staying, but I didn't spend all day getting plucked within an inch of my life to go home at the first hurdle. Especially when they're so sure that I'm safe here.

"No," I respond resolutely. "You said Tommy is watching him and I trust that. Tommy would tell me if anything was wrong and I trust you guys to protect me."

I push away the little niggle that it's been a hot minute since I heard from Tommy, but I'm sure the three of them would know if anything was wrong.

Right?

Absolutely right. Breathe, Quinn, we got all dressed up, let's go and try and enjoy the night.

"Let's go do the party thing. Plus you said the food would be good and I'm starving."

Hunter grins at me, shaking his head. "Of course it's

the food that keeps you here."

"Hey, good food shouldn't go to waste," I tease, quickly sticking my tongue out at him as Meyer releases me and comes to my side before putting his arm around my waist once more.

"Come on then, Kitten. Let's go show these rich assholes just how good you look and let them wish they were us for a night."

I roll my eyes at him, but say nothing because I know he'd just argue back with me. Instead, I straighten my shoulders and lift my head up high. This crowd might not think I fit here, but I fit with these three, wherever they go, and that is the only knowledge I need to get me through whatever the rest of this night holds.

So far, this night has been so much more fun than I thought it would be. I've danced, laughed, and enjoyed the company of my guys. I mean, I've also been bored to tears by some of the conversations that I've been privy to, but I'm taking the good with the bad, especially since the good has outweighed it.

Meyer got dragged away by the politician of the night a few minutes ago when the dinner dishes were taken away, and Rory went to try and save him not long after, leaving me with Hunter, who has been coming up with fake stories for the socialites here tonight. To say it's been amusing would be a hideous understatement. I've laughed so hard that I've almost cried.

The food has been divine too. My dessert is currently staring up at me and I'm wondering just how much of it I can eat without bursting out of this dress.

"One day, you're going to look at my dick the way you're looking at that brownie," Hunter murmurs and a laugh falls from me so loud that the rest of the table looks at me. I'm kind of over the judgment of the people here tonight and part of me wishes Shae was here because watching her run circles around these people would've been great, but also, I wouldn't want her to be lulled to sleep by some of the dreary conversation.

"Play your cards right," I say back to him quietly. "And maybe I'll look at your dick like that before I choke on it. Maybe even before we leave here tonight."

His eyes go wide, his spoon halfway to his mouth, frozen, almost in disbelief. "You start making promises like that, Angel, and I'll tear you away from this table quicker than you can say boo."

"Boo," I tease, before taking a bite of my brownie. I moan as the bitterness of the dark chocolate mixes with the tart raspberry puree. Goddamn, that's good.

"Moan like that again and you won't be finishing the

dessert," Hunter promises, his hand running up the slit of my dress, his fingers caressing the skin at the apex of my thighs.

Two can play at that game.

I use my other hand to take another mouthful of the brownie, moaning as I rub his dick through his pants. He jerks up in his chair and I smirk at him when his eyes narrow at me. "Oh, Angel, you have no idea just how badly you're playing with fire."

"I'm pretty sure I do," I tease back. "Maybe I just like the idea of getting burned."

His eyes practically glow as he stares over at me, his entire body leaning in toward me. I can feel the excitement and anticipation rolling from him. "You want to play, Angel?"

"I don't know what you mean," I say innocently, fluttering my lashes at him. "Games aren't really my bag."

"Oh, I'm fairly sure I know just how to get you to join the team sport, Angel. In fact, I bet I can get you to scream as loud in here as I did that night in the elevator, even though you tried real hard not to."

My cheeks flame and his smirk back at me tells me just how much he's enjoying my reaction to him.

"Never," I prod. "I don't think you even really made me come that hard that night. It was the tequila making me fuzzy. Probably couldn't make me scream here if you tried." Baiting him like this is more fun than I thought it would be, even if it does still feel a little foreign. Especially in a place like this.

"Oh, really?" He asks, leaning in so close that I can feel his breath on my skin. "Want to test your theory, Angel? Because I am more than willing to rise to that particular challenge."

"And how exactly do you suggest we give you that opportunity?" I ask, licking my lips slowly, his eyes following the movement avidly. "Plus, wasn't I the one that was supposed to be devouring you like I'm devouring my dessert?" I take another bite, moaning again. Partly for effect, partly because it's just that good.

"Oh, Angel... I'll let you devour me good and right, don't you worry. I wouldn't dream of denying you. Now how about you head to the bathroom, the one just as we came in, and wait for me. I won't be long."

I stare at him wide eyed for a minute, wondering if he's serious, but when he holds my gaze, I know he is. A wave of apprehension rushes through me, but I push it back. Playing with him is way more fun than giving in to fear. Fear has taken enough from me, I'm not going to let it keep winning.

Taking the last bite of my brownie, I dab at my mouth with my napkin like a goddamn lady, then stand and walk away from the table without a word. Thrill rushes through me at the prospect of the game we're playing because this is what life is supposed to be about. Fun, exciting, risk taking.

I can feel his eyes on me as I head toward the entrance of the room and spot the bathroom to the left, right next to where the three of them huddled with me when we arrived.

At least this will be a much more fun memory of the night.

I duck into the bathroom and step in front of the mirror, straightening out my hair, laughing at the obvious excitement on my face. In a moment of madness, I lean forward and peel off my panties, because why not make it a little more fun.

My breath hitches with excitement when the door opens and I stand up straight, glancing in the mirror, ready to see my blond haired Adonis.

Except what I see turns my blood to ice and I'm frozen in place, despite everything inside of me screaming at me to run.

Trent steps forward, the gun in his hand pressed against my back, and I want to vomit when he leans forward and sniffs my hair. That's when I notice the blood spatter on his white shirt. He's dressed in a tux, except his tie is loosened around his neck, and there's a tear in the shoulder of his jacket.

This can't be happening.

Tommy was supposed to be watching him.

How is he here?

Icy fear trickles down my spine and every part of me that's been training to fight him freezes. I can fight, I can't run, it's like everything shuts down and I can't even scream.

He runs his nose up my cheek and I gag, swallowing the vomit that rises. He takes the panties from my fingers and presses them against his face as he pushes the gun harder into my back. Glancing at the panties in his hand, his sadistic grin widens. "Oh, Sweetheart, I knew you'd be missing me, but I didn't think it would be this much. It took a lot to get to you, but I made a few new friends who helped. Even if it took spilling a little blood, we both know that wasn't going to keep me from you after all this time." My heart stutters, because I don't know who he's talking about.

Tommy?

Hunter?

He should be here by now.

Why isn't he here?

He moves slightly and pain splinters through my head. It takes a second to register the sight in the mirror, the gun above my head where he hit me with it. My vision starts to falter and I feel my legs go weak. I try to grip the counter, to stay conscious, to buy time for someone, anyone, to find me. Just *something.*

But then I see the syringe in his hand, and in a blink, a stinging pain explodes in my neck as he plunges it into my flesh. "I imagine after slutting it around like you've been doing, you have a whole host of new things to show me. Now, you sleep. I'll get out of here before one of your little thugs decides to come and find you. By the time you wake up, we'll be home. You belong to me, Quinn. You should know better, but I'm going to make sure you can never leave me again."

SIGN UP FOR MY NEWSLETTER TO HEAR ABOUT UPCOMING RELEASES

ABOUT THE AUTHOR

Lily is a writer, dreamer, fur mom and serial killer, crime documentary addict.

She loves to write dark, reverse harem romance and characters who will shatter your heart. Characters who enjoy stomping on the pieces and then laugh before putting you back together again. And she definitely doesn't enjoy readers tears. Nope. Not even a little.

Visit her website at http://www.lilywildhart.com to sign up for the newsletter or find her on social media through the links below.

ALSO BY LILY WILDHART

THE KNIGHTS OF ECHOES COVE

(Dark, Bully, High School Reverse Harem Romance)

Tormented Royal

Lost Royal

Caged Royal

Forever Royal

THE SAINTS OF SERENTIY FALLS

(Dark, Bully, Step Brother, College, Reverse Harem Romance)

A Burn so Deep

A Revenge So Sweet

A Taste of Forever

THE SECRETS WE KEEP

(Dark, Mafia, Reverse Harem Romance, Duet)

The Secrets We Keep

The Truths We Seek